T0356274

FIREWEED

FIREWEED

A Novel

LAUREN HADDAD

ASTRA HOUSE
NEW YORK

For information about permission to reproduce selections from this book,
please contact permissions@astrapublishinghouse.com.

This is a work of fiction. Names, characters, places, and incidents are products of the
author's imagination or are used fictitiously. Any resemblance to actual events, locales,
or persons, living or dead, is entirely coincidental.

Astra House
A Division of Astra Publishing House
astrapublishinghouse.com
Printed in the United States of America

Library of Congress Cataloging-in-Publication Data

Names: Haddad, Lauren, author.
Title: Fireweed : a novel / Lauren Haddad.
Description: First edition. | New York : Astra House, 2025. | Summary: "Fireweed
is a subversion of the missing woman plot that follows a white housewife's
misguided investigation into the disappearance of her Indigenous neighbor"—
Provided by publisher.
Identifiers: LCCN 2024036237 (print) | LCCN 2024036238 (ebook) |
ISBN 9781662602900 (hardcover) | ISBN 9781662602894 (epub)
Subjects: LCGFT: Detective and mystery fiction. | Novels.
Classification: LCC PS3608.A2645 F57 2025 (print) | LCC PS3608.A2645
(ebook) | DDC 813/.6—dc23/eng/20240909
LC record available at https://lccn.loc.gov/2024036237
LC ebook record available at https://lccn.loc.gov/2024036238

First edition
10 9 8 7 6 5 4 3 2 1

Design by Alissa Theodor
The text is set in WarnockPro Regular.
The titles are set in Antina Bold.

To my grandma Stella

An old *Frenchman* ... could not sufficiently praise its property of healing wounds. The leaves of the plant must be crushed and then laid on the wound.

Peter Kalm, Travels into North America, 1753

Of rank and unpleasant scent, [it] is the first plant that appears when the ground has been freed from timbers by fire: if a piece of land lies untilled the first summer after its being chopped, the following spring shows you a smothering crop of this vile weed.

Catharine Parr Traill, The Backwoods of Canada, 1836

CONTENTS

FIREWEED

Prologue 2001

I remember the day Beth went missing clear as a stream.

I can see that morning and all that was budded—already burgeoning, all that would soon flare bright as the fireweed in high definition. Can see myself as if watching someone else. Stepping out into the backyard, limbs deer-tail white, laundry bin at hip. Topknot bobbing in the crosshairs. Blissfully, stupidly, stubbornly unaware. I can see her, too, though I couldn't back then. Wouldn't, until she was already slipping away.

The kitchen radio was on, "Drops of Jupiter" again, and I was humming along even as the sound waned, lifting up and shaking out T-shirt, pillowcase, bra in milky swatches—Dove bar, pork fat, baking soda, snow—and pinning them against the wind.

There wasn't much washing those days. With no kids and Sam up at the coal mines in Murray River, it came in spurts. Two weeks on, one week off, though I guess the inverse was true for me, the loads he'd bring home enough to offset any mornings not spent folding boxers. I'd toss those in the dryer, but when I was on my own, I liked the line. Nothing to get your whites whiter.

The grass would shine, frost-blanched as if it'd been dredged in flour, up until the end of June, usually, but that morning was different. Unfettered green. Summer was here, weeks early, an olive branch. Compensation for a particularly merciless winter. I kicked off my yard shoes and planted my bare feet on the ground—cool and stiff enough to remedy my haste. "Blink and you'll miss it," Nana liked to say, tut-tutting her head. Summer in Northern BC. I shoved my shoes back on.

"Morning."

I jumped. I hadn't noticed she was there. Rachelle, my backyard neighbor, perched cross-legged in the lawn chair that faced my clothesline head-on, unspooling feathery plastic from a fresh pack of du Mauriers, her soot-black hair raked back. She flicked at her lighter, the golden band still cuffed around her ring finger blinding.

A wire fence bisected our scant plots, but it sagged low, barely grazing my belly button, and we each had a plain view of the other. There was our side: evenly mowed, row after row of delicate new green, Canadian flag proudly waving in the breeze. And there was hers. The neighborhood dump. More battered appliances than a pawnshop, red clover and dandelion outstripping the grass. It was better before, when Al was alive. Or at least more accepted. At least Al was white.

"Morning" was what I said, Nana's voice surfacing again. "Uncivilized is what," she'd recite, jaw clenched. "There's a reason they call them savages."

It was simple bad luck, the only Indian in the neighborhood, and there she was, butted right up against us. Our eyes didn't meet. They never did. I stared at the washing, clearing my throat. It'd been clogged with the smoke from her cheap cigarette.

I finished the pinning as quick as I could and turned back toward the house. I'd been planning on doing some weeding that morning, but it could wait. I had to run to the store anyway. Sam was due home that afternoon, and the fridge had been all but cleaned out—nothing but a few packs of bacon in the freezer, some spare Tyson nuggets that'd been fossilized.

I opened the door to my LeSabre. *E.* I restarted the engine, but the needle didn't budge. I'd replaced the ignition coil earlier that week, and with money tight enough, I guess I'd been hoping the car might run on sheer grit. Being broke germinates all sorts of magical thinking. There was a jerry can somewhere, but the garage was Sam's domain, and by the time I'd have found it, he'd have been pulling in. Quicker just to catch a ride. The Safeway wasn't far.

I had enough cash to buy steak, Sam's favorite, and there was a sale on Yukon Golds, so I found myself cradling one of those big, netted sacks as I waddled back toward the highway. I was standing at the counter pouring cream into a pot of steaming, drained potatoes when I heard Sam's truck pull in.

"Howdy," he called, opening the door.

"Hi," I shouted through the veil, still mashing fast as I could manage.

"Man alive, I'm wiped."

I couldn't see him from the kitchen, but I could picture him well enough, parked in the chair beside the front door, tugging his heels from his work boots, the laces already undone, fat tongues flopping over like two burnt slices of bread. He drove like that when he was close to home. *Less heavy lifting, hey?* He'd wink, a boot collapsing to the floor. Tapping a bladder, splashing water on his face. Tucking in his undershirt. Sam was a man of routine.

"But look at you. Standing over a pot of some good-smelling something, too." He lumbered over, pecking my cheek.

"And it's just about ready." I scraped the last of the potatoes into a bowl, spoon singing as it rounded the bends of the pot. "Sorry, hun, took me a little longer at the store."

"No worries, baby. Been driving five hours. Another few minutes won't hurt." He swung open the fridge and pulled out a can of Labatt. His solid frame had been padded with a few extra pounds, and I noticed there were two identical holes in the toes of his socks.

"What's that you said about the store? I thought your Buick broke down."

"It did." I cranked open a can of peas, emptying them into a saucepot. "I got it fixed, but I didn't have much for gas." I turned to face him, but he'd left for the den, was no doubt already cranking the lever on his recliner. On cue, I heard the game switch on. "I got a ride," I hollered.

"A ride?" he hollered back. "With one of the girls?"

I pried the steak from the pan and slid it onto a plate, its juices splattering red across the trim of my halter. "Just over on 16." I turned on the tap, working a drop of dish soap into the stain. I'd throw it in the wash later with the rest of his load, I remember thinking, when the announcer was cut off midsentence.

"What do you mean 'on 16'?"

At the time, I'd misinterpreted Sam's tone. I figured his team was in the toilet, his back was acting up again, that he was just altogether flat-out beat. I lifted his plate and started toward him. How could I have ever guessed?

"With a driver. Like I always do when I'm low on cash." I nudged his arm, teasing, setting his plate on the end table beside him. "Sure you've only been gone two weeks?"

His head was bowed, one hand working his brow like there was something—coking coal, sawdust, bitumen, blood—he was trying to wipe clean. He jerked away from me. Was no misinterpreting that.

"Not funny, Jenny." Any warmth in his voice had been doused. He yanked his Canucks hat on, tugging at the brim, the top half of his face, the familiar bend in the bridge of his nose, his eyes—precise, perfect blue—shrouded. "We're not that hard up. Haven't watched the news today, huh?" I shook my head.

"A girl went missing on 16 a few days ago, right around here. Hitching, like you." He turned back toward me, his gaze on the carpet. "Beth Tremblay. They've been searching for her all day, but they haven't found nothing yet."

It felt like the breath had been wrung out of me. Prince George was ticketed as the capital of the North, but it still had the feel of a small town. Nothing like that had ever happened before. We'd all done it in a pinch. When you needed a lift, you stuck out your thumb. Or, at least, you used to.

I felt exposed, skimpy ties roped around my neck. I hadn't even had the good sense that morning to zip on a sweatshirt. The game clicked back on, skates slashing at ice.

"Sorry," I squeaked, words slippery as some table-warmed butter. It was all I could manage to say.

It was the top story on every station, the manhunt already underway.

They showed pictures of her, Beth, her strawberry blonde hair haloed at the top of her head. Standing sideways on a cracking drive-way, thumbs looped around the straps of a red hiking pack. Squatting in front of a lake under the kind of pale light where it's impossible to tell whether the day's beginning or ending, freckled arms tangled around a sister or friend.

The picture that's still out there, the details that have been lodged between the folds of our minds, the one they used on all the flyers, the news updates, the billboard. A school portrait where her likeness, from the crown of her head to the middle of where her heart lay beating, was suspended in atmosphere, like a bug encased in amber, like if you'd hacked open an amethyst—purple eddying endlessly behind. Like if she was already lost.

Like if she was already someplace else, waiting to be found.

The store of silver hoops inching up her left ear. The smear of raspberry gloss on her lips, the same shade as her fuzzy sweater. The blue of her eyes, murky seawater, unreflecting, looking directly into the camera, directly at all of us, at no one.

I didn't know her. No one in town did. She was from Ontario, but by now I've forgotten where. She was working as a tree planter that summer, was trying to reach Smithers for a music festival on some days off. The police were notified when she didn't show up for planting that morning. No history of mental illnesses, no psychiatric prescriptions. When we lost her, she was twenty-four, one year older than Anne-Marie and Missy, the same age as I was then.

The first billboard went up the next day, her name printed in blocky red. *MISSING: 25,000 DOLLAR REWARD.*

That billboard's still up, ten years later, over by the Roll-A-Dome at the intersection between 16 and 97, unchanged except that her forehead, the bottom lobe of her right ear, her left upper lip, have been stripped off in tatters.

The billboard's still up, but no one ever got that reward. She's still gone.

And she's not the only one.

PART I

Beth

one

I was pouring my first cup of coffee the next morning when I got a call from Missy. There'd been talk about meeting that day, but I hadn't been counting on it.

"Can we come over?" she asked in her signature rasp. "Kayden had a stomach bug all week. If I don't get out of this house, I swear I'm going to burn this place down."

"Sure thing," I said, brightening.

Sam had left early for Mackenzie to help at his parents' farm, and I had the house to myself again, nothing on my list but dinner. I was eager to welcome in some other voices, ones that weren't emitted from the radio or the TV or the inside of my own head.

I called Anne-Marie to invite her, too, dug out some old toys Sam's sister-in-law had given us for when we'd need them—*wink, wink*—and put some cans of pop in the fridge. I used to keep a stock of them chilling, but all that had changed that spring with Missy's second and Annie on round two—or, technically, two and three. We hardly saw one another twice a month, let alone in one week like before. Plans were made, flimsy as nylons, and just as easily snagged. Not that I blamed them. The girls never seemed to have enough time, while I, on the other hand, was flooded, could feel the hours sloshing at my feet.

"Pretty soon you'll be wishing you had more time," Sam liked to say, curling an arm around my belly. "Any day now." He'd been saying the same thing for the past five years. I couldn't tell if he even still believed it. "Once we start our family."

Mama and papa and baby makes three. I didn't have much experience with that number. I put on another pot of coffee and layered some slices of whole wheat bread with mayo and mustard and ham.

We were sitting at the porch table, kids playing in the yard, Missy's baby slung around her shoulder, Anne-Marie gnawing at a thumbnail glittered pink, when talk turned to the subject of the summer, what every conversation seemed to circle back to, the recipient of all of our collective thoughts and prayers. Beth.

In just twenty-four hours, we'd learned so much about her, all of the ordinary facets of her life enlarged under our meaty lens. She was a Sagittarius. Her parents were happily married. An animal lover, she'd take her dogs camping. She'd graduated from the University of British Columbia at the top of her class. In just twenty-four hours, Beth was no longer a stranger. She'd almost begun to feel like a friend.

"It's crazy, hey?" Anne-Marie was solemn, her round face crowned with wisps of flaxen baby hair. She'd never lost the weight from her last pregnancy, and her chin had begun to soften into her neck, rendering her even sweeter, milder, than before. No edge, all motherly cushion. "They say it happened right around here. She was last seen at the Esso, the one by the motel."

"Bon Voyage?" Missy was digging in her purse with one lean arm, her freckled breasts squeezing against each other, distorting the rhinestoned letters embellished across them. BEBE.

I glanced down. Hers were grapefruits. Mine were limes. She was my oldest friend, but I could still feel self-conscious around her. *The perfect woman*, everyone in high school—the girls included—had come to a consensus. A ten.

"Ironic, ain't it?" She pulled out a cigarette. I reached for the baby.

"Give her here if you're going to smoke."

"Take her." Missy shrugged Brielle into my arms, pausing before flicking her lighter. "You know, Jim told me this has been happening for years."

Years? I fidgeted in my seat, fanning the smoke from my face. Anne-Marie used to smoke, too, before the pregnancies, but she was so discreet that until you saw the tawny butt in your ashtray, it'd slip your mind she even had a habit. Discreet wasn't exactly Missy's style.

"Indian women," she continued. "Working the highway. Like the ones around Fort George Park. Occupational hazard, I guess."

Anne-Marie and I nodded. There were always stories. You play with fire. Missy took another drag.

"But it's never happened to someone like Beth. Educated, good family, and all that." She clucked her tongue, repeating the question everybody was asking. "If it could happen to her, who's next?"

My face turned red. I thought of how mindless I'd been, on autopilot, smiling as I strapped myself in. Chuck eye, milk, Cheerios, bologna. I never would have even seen it coming; my final thoughts predominated by Oscar Mayer, Dairyland.

"Are they really sure it happened there?" I still didn't want to believe it, that it could all change so radically from one morning to the next. "We used to hitch all the time, remember?"

"That was over a decade ago, Jenny." Missy stamped her cigarette against the silver face of her can. "We were kids, for fuck's sake. Stupid."

"It's just, you're talking like she's already dead." I looked to Anne-Marie for backup, but her head was turned, her teeth at a pinky nail. "We still don't know what happened to her. She could've gone for a hike, could be camped out somewhere, with no way of hearing the news." There had to be another explanation. "We don't even know if she went missing on the highway." The more I spoke, the more convincing it sounded. These things didn't happen. Not to girls like Beth. "She could've gotten a ride to another town." Like me. "Maybe there's been some sort of mistake."

"'Mistake'?" Missy repeated, jaw slack. "She was last seen getting into a stranger's vehicle." She enunciated the last two words as if they were a reprimand. "Even if she is 'camping'"—her fingers wagged—"out in the bush or out on the highway, what difference does it make? Gone is gone."

I went quiet. I knew she was right. Everything had changed, but not overnight. *You're still a kid until you have a kid*, Missy's favorite way to sum up my shortcomings. Another way they were both paces ahead.

There was a prolonged lull. Kayden pinned Tanner, Anne-Marie's boy, over by the lodgepole pine.

"Kay!" Missy sat upright, holding a hand over her brow like a visor. "I hope you're playing nice!" She slumped back in her chair, bringing half a sandwich to her lips.

"Pugh." She spit out her bite. "I swear, Jenny, I don't know how you eat this shit bread."

"It's better for you," Anne-Marie said softly. "I'll eat what you don't finish." Missy thrust over her plate.

"I heard something else," Anne-Marie continued. "What some people call 16." Her hands were resting on her globe of a belly. Six months looked closer to full term with two swimming in there. When she told me, I'd had to strong-arm a smile. She and Missy were so fertile, it was almost offensive. "The Highway of Tears. Ever hear of that?"

"Because of one disappearance?" Brielle was starting to fuss, so I stood to bounce, patting her back and pressing my lips against her downy head.

"Haven't you been listening, dummy?" Missy poked at my side with an acrylic nail. "It's like what Jim was saying. Apparently, there've been more." She was back in her bag, groping for another cigarette.

"Speaking of Indians." Her eyes darted up and over, across the mowed grass of my yard. Rachelle was out, standing on her porch, sipping right from the round lip of a big bottle of Ocean Spray.

"For fuck's sake." Missy shook her head. "I bet she don't even have a clean glass."

Rachelle's back door was open, and from what we could see, her house was a pit, the mess spewing over, reined in only by the mesh of the chain-link fence.

Lawn chairs in various stages of disrepair, a broken washer, an old bed frame hacked into pieces with what must have been a very dull axe. A deflated kiddie pool; a woven mat of rotting leaves suspended in snow-melt; one stray hot-pink flip-flop; one yellow rain boot; no fewer than three coolers, all missing their lids, receptacles for more leaves, more brackish, blackened water.

A baby swing attached to nothing, ropes snaking through the torn grass. Strewn throughout the chaos were more toys than you could count on six sets of hands, popping up as easily as some milkweed seeds scattered.

The cherry on top of the whole shit sundae: a rusting red truck with cinder blocks in place of tires, like a compost pile of aluminum and steel. *Eyesore* was too tolerant. It was an *outrage*.

She was striking a match when her daughter bounded toward her. The girl was small, but she must have been about five already, had been a *baby* baby—a third appendage bolted to Rachelle, no more than three months, by my estimation—when Sam and I had moved in.

She had another girl, too, a one-year-old who fanned a lot of heated talk. Al hadn't lived to see the birth, the moment his second child emerged into the world, considerably darker than her mother.

Rachelle removed the cigarette from her lips and shook out the flame, stretching her arms toward the girl.

We were warned about them when we first visited the house, the reason our place had been on the market so long. Al was a long-hauler who'd met Rachelle in Vancouver on his route. Pushing sixty, he must have been at least twice her age, though, truth be told, she wasn't easy to pin down. Without her daughters in tow, she could've passed for eighteen.

People said she was a hooker, had to be, but the way Al told it, she was tending bar, and he was drinking. It was a good neighborhood, and it made people mad when he brought her back to it. Then, when he died of a heart attack while working the oil sands in McMurray, Rachelle stayed put. That made people madder.

She paced her yard, her girl's gangly legs tethered to her waist, close enough so we could make out the cross clasped around her neck, gold, probably plated. Her body swaying, her mouth pressed over the girl's ear. She must have been singing, but all we could hear were low hums.

The girl dropped from her arms and picked up a warped Hula-Hoop, swinging it wildly overhead. Rachelle turned, her profile toward us, her eyes on the procession of near identical houses spanning either direction. She was beautiful, no two ways around it, her features smooth, seamless, as if she'd been carved out of soap. More reason to hate her.

"I just feel sorry for that girl," Missy said, swiping a wand of pus-pink gloss across her puckered mouth. *Desire*, the bottom sticker read.

"Who?" I asked, my eyes still on Rachelle. The Highway of Tears, the phrase a barbed lure.

"Beth," Missy groaned. "Jenny Bean, sometimes you are something else."

The potato harvester was on the blink, Sam had called to say just as I'd been buttering the green beans. He needed to give them at least one more day, was easier to just spend the night. He knew I'd understand. Being the son of a farmer meant Sam's time off was more often than not time on in Mackenzie. I'd gotten used to it, being alone. I made myself a plate of reheated steak and switched on the news, forking the beans directly from the pot.

"A popular young woman working as a tree planter for the summer plans to surprise a friend at a music festival but never arrives. *Crimestoppers* needs your help to find twenty-four-year-old Beth Tremblay.

"She was last seen at an Esso station located at 4888 Highway 16. At about 8:45 a.m., a witness saw a woman matching Beth's description walk toward a greenish-yellow car similar to this one."

A side view of a hatchback with a clouded paint job appeared.

"It's important to note that no one actually saw her get into the vehicle. The driver is described as a white male between twenty and forty years old, wearing a white T-shirt. When she went missing, Beth was carrying a red backpack from Mountain Equipment Co-op. Here's a photo of Beth wearing that pack."

The cracking driveway, the strawberry blonde bun.

"Do you know what happened to Beth Tremblay?" The camera zoomed in on the reporter's face. "If you have any information that can solve this case, call the police. Or if you wish to remain anonymous, call *Crimestoppers* at 1-800-555-0155."

"'1-800-555-0155,'" I repeated, finding a pen and jotting it down.

No one saw her get into the vehicle, but someone had seen her walking toward it. How had that happened? Were they suddenly distracted? Had they turned their head just a second too soon?

Maybe there really was more to the story. Maybe my theory hadn't been so off.

Maybe Beth had kept walking—past the car, past the highway altogether, right into the bush, densely studded with pines. Maybe she wasn't really missing. Maybe she was hiding. From something, or someone. I lifted the crocheted blanket from the couch and wrapped it around my shoulders, an acid-colored stole. Nights were still cool, and while I'd been watching the news, it had begun to rain. My garden needed it. It'd been an unseasonably dry spring, and people were already starting to fret about the dust, the wildfires that were sure to come.

I flipped on the electric kettle and stood at the kitchen sink, peering toward my window at the woman reflected back to me, my sole company for the night.

The possibilities were endless. I sipped at my tea. But what would a girl like Beth be hiding from? Her father was a heart surgeon. Her mother wore pearls. Beth's nose looked like it'd been plucked off a Disney princess. Girls like her didn't just go missing. Something must have happened. Something bad.

I switched off the light, and the woman vanished, absorbed into the wet dark.

Back then, I was working at the soap store at the Pine Centre Mall, ringing up bottles of shower gel and body lotion that smelled like cut grass and turning fruit, those spuming orbs of chalk that'd stain your tub water pink, but that winter, they'd whittled my schedule down to two half shifts per week.

I used to dread opening the store on Mondays, but that morning, I was missing it. Showering early, picking up a double-double at the Timmy's on my drive there—the tone it set, somewhere to be.

Instead I was back in my kitchen, the only action the drip of the coffee maker, the sizzle of two frying eggs. I launched the bread from the toaster, screwed open a jar of runny raspberry jam. A first attempt with Anne-Marie from the past summer. Or maybe it was the *past* past summer. Her first pregnancy. *You're next*, she'd have winked, the maxim both she and Missy had long since abandoned.

The phone rang, jolting me back. It was Mom needing a favor and, naturally, needing it right away. Even before my schedule had changed,

Mom always assumed I wasn't up to much. I tucked the receiver under my chin as I continued scrubbing the dried yolk from my plate.

"Shelly's got some drama again. I need to go to the salon and cover for her. Problem is, I got Ray's kids. And you know what their mom's like." I didn't, but Mom never missed the opportunity to inform me. "Probably still sleeping off last night. You wouldn't mind coming and watching them, would you?"

Ray was the latest pony in Mom's carousel of men, and the youngest by far. Only four years shy of being in my graduating class. André, the first ex I can remember, had had fourteen years on her. After him, she drew a line—no men past thirty-five, no matter how far from that number she climbed. Not that the younger ones treated her any better.

"Sure," I agreed. I always agreed. Besides, I liked Ray's kids. Wasn't their fault from whose loins they'd sprung.

I huffed up the three flights of stairs to Mom's apartment and stepped onto the doormat, the tops of my Keds obscuring the letters imprinted across its coarse fibers: *WELC HO.* I rang the bell.

"It's open," Mom shouted, the scene spreading out before me like a road map. Before I even opened the door, I knew exactly where she'd be: planted on the couch, feet rotating in circles atop the polished coffee table, cigarette smoldering in hand. TV blaring. Kyle parked beside her, glued to the screen, his baby sister, Dawn, on the carpet below, pacifier caulking her mouth.

I turned the knob. Sure enough, there was Mom, mantled in smoke, Kyle to her left, his tiny hand darting in and out of a family-sized bag of cheese puffs. They were watching the news, the same *Crimestoppers* segment I'd seen the night before. The floor in front of them was empty.

"Ray's mom have Dawn today?" I walked past them, scoping the kitchen. Spotless as usual: din of the dishwasher, metallic particles of Windex in the air. No Dawn.

"Hello to you, too," Mom said, pressing mute. "She's out on the balcony, playing. I was just about to check on her." She crushed her cigarette into an ashtray and slid her feet from the coffee table to the carpet.

Her fingernails and toenails were glossy, painted her signature shade: poison-apple red.

"Can you believe what happened to this Beth girl?" She'd turned the audio back on. She wasn't budging.

"Hi, Jenny." Kyle grinned, his lips dusted orange.

"Hey, buddy." I patted him on his shoulder before reaching for the balcony door.

There on the Astroturf was Dawn, gnawing on the foot of a blue-eyed baby doll—oblivious to the beating sun. No hat, no shirt. Only a diaper.

"Yen!" She looked up at me, thrusting the doll into the air.

"Hi, sweetie," I said, scooping her into my arms.

Her diaper felt like it'd been filled with wet soil. I sniffed. Barnyard. She must have been sitting in it for a while. I carried her into the washroom and rinsed her under the tub's faucet, popping open the bottle of after-sun gel.

With Dawn's sunburn soothed and diaper changed, I shuttled her into the room she shared with Kyle when they stayed there. My old bedroom, the walls still sponge-painted that same awful pink. Pepto-Bismol, calamine. The color of feeling itchy, unwell. I remembered how I used to lie awake in bed, watching as faces and mountains and snakes pieced themselves together from splotch to splotch. I pulled a dress over her head and set her down in her crib, whose mattress, I noticed, was missing its sheet.

"Be right back." I took a deep breath, exhaling my exasperation. Her little face was bright as a lesion.

"Mom," I said, standing directly behind where she sat.

"What's it now, Jen?" She didn't bother to turn her head.

"Can I talk to you?"

Despite my anger, my tone remained neutral, as if asking her to pass the relish. I'd become adept at concealment, a survival tactic to keep all from bursting to flame. Mom could be so explosive. I'd learned, over the years, not to be the one to strike the match.

I glanced over at Kyle. "In your bedroom."

She craned her neck. "Honey, no. I've got about five more minutes until I have to get ready. I just want to finish my program before I'm on my feet all day, is that too much to ask?"

"Whatever you got to say, just say it here." She tapped Kyle's foot. "You. Go check on your sister." He heaved himself off the couch, bag crinkling underarm, following her command.

"I don't need another lecture." She'd turned away again, clawing her freshly dyed hair into a knot at the base of her neck. It was blinding, blonder than ever. Platinum. Ray had a thing for Pamela. I'd never seen her natural color (she was in the salon too often for that), but her sister's, my aunt Erin, was the exact shade as mine. *Mouse fur*, Mom called it. As if, underneath all that peroxide, hers wasn't.

"I know you're tired, Mom, but if you're going to watch Ray's kids, you've got to actually watch them."

"She was fine." She waved a hand. "You're so goddamn dramatic."

"She wasn't fine." Dawn was a toddler, an innocent. I wanted to bop that stupid bun right off Mom's head. "She's eighteen months ..."

"Two, practically." Mom whipped around her head. "You got a knack for exaggeration, honey. Always have. Don't know how Sam does it." She clicked off the TV. "Now where the hell did I put those keys?"

She stood, starting to pace, starting to play her best-loved game, accountability trapped under a cup, cups shuffled around and around. What was it we were talking about again? Her keys? Sam? Me?

"So she can look after herself?" I was starting to lose it. "Change her own diaper?" It hadn't taken long. "You left her out there alone in the hot sun without even a shirt on. She's a baby, Mom. She needs care." With those last three words, Mom went rigid, her eyes yoking to mine. They'd gone dark.

"You know what, Jenny, you're right. I'm a god-awful mother. I fucked up with you, and now I'm fucking up with them, too.

"You should call Ray," she was starting to shout, the vein on her forehead pulsing. "Ask him what the fuck he's thinking leaving them with me. Better yet, call the state. Lock me up and throw away the key. Since I'm such a good-for-nothing, piece-of-shit monster." Spit flung from behind her bared teeth, her face mangled as a wrung-out mop.

Kyle's head appeared from behind the doorframe.

"I didn't say that," I said, quietly, backing down. There was no winning. Only pain. Every time, I'd tell myself I'd never let it get this far.

"You're not a monster." This was how it always ended, me left to douse what'd been ignited. Saying the words she was waiting to hear. "I'm sorry."

On cue, her face went slack.

"Look, Jen, I'm sick, you know that. My stomach hurts, I can't eat anything. Everything hurts. "Walk with me here, I have to get ready for work." She gestured, and I trailed after her toward her bedroom, as if she'd knotted a rope around my waist when I wasn't looking. "I'm trying, I really am. Believe me, I'm trying."

She peeled off all her clothes, including her underwear, standing stark naked in front of her dresser mirror and me. She was far worse off than I'd remembered, or maybe it was just the effect of seeing her nude, which must have been her intent. I could've blown, and she would've been knocked right back. I averted my eyes, taking a seat among the half dozen decorative pillows piled on her bed.

"I know it's hard with Sam gone so often," she said, stepping into a thong and yanking up a tube dress.

"I know you've been trying for, what, years already. Since the wedding." She counted on her fingers. "Five, Christ. I can't imagine. You happened just like that." Her fingers snapped. I winced. It was one of her preferred subjects. My idiot body. I folded my arms around a pillow, braided tassels bristling against my chin.

"If I could help you, I would, but I can't, Jenny. I can't. I can barely keep it together myself."

"You do look thin." I bit at my lip. *Thin* was an understatement. You could've fit a bowling ball in that thigh gap.

"I know," she said, uncapping a tube of lipstick. "Most of my clothes just slip right off me. I'm sick, I told you. I might not be around for long. So just give your poor mom a break for once, okay?"

"Have you been to the doctor?" I heard myself, on autopilot, asking. We'd been having this exact conversation for as long as I could remember.

"I'm too scared, Jenny. Sometimes it's better not to know. I just want to enjoy the summer and whatever time I have left.

"Shit." She glanced at the alarm clock on her nightstand. "I am late, late, late." Her tone light, peppy, even. She grinned, shrugging off the weight of what she'd just said.

Mom might've been sick. She was only forty-two, but she'd been smoking since she was twelve, taking only a nine-month hiatus, if that. The truth was that she was hungry, rarely eating anything that could be rightly called a meal, subsisting on the two-liter bottles of Diet Pepsi or Coke, depending on that week's sales, instead. A toasted slice of Wonder Bread. A Jell-O pudding. A sodden container of supermarket mashed potatoes. Half of a pink pickled egg.

Her weight didn't fluctuate so much as wither. Mom would go from thin to pencil-thin to next to nothing: an outline, a wisp, so slight you'd think she might disappear altogether. Another way women vanish.

I worried about her, had been since I was old enough to remember. She knew that, knew she could win every argument by simply lifting a finger and pointing to her pain.

"Look, sweetie, I got to run," Mom said, taking one last look in the mirror. "We'll catch up later." She started toward the door. "Ray left a twenty on the counter for lunch. You staying here, or . . . ?"

"I told you, I've got errands at home."

It wasn't an outright lie. There was dinner to fix, but that wouldn't take long, and the weeding in the garden could've waited until the next day, or the day after, or the day after that. The truth was that even though I'd spent my first eighteen years there, Mom's place gave me hives. As soon as I stepped in, I itched for an out.

"Ray's off before me, so he'll pick them up." She fished her keys from her purse. "Thanks a million." They jingled as she waved. So they hadn't been lost after all.

I heard the front door slam shut. I unlatched my arms from around the pillow and positioned it back with the others. It'd been pummeled, collapsing in on itself, like some dough that'd been punched down.

I stood to leave the bedroom but found myself stopping in front of her dresser instead, my hand around the knob of the top drawer. I couldn't remember the last time I'd opened it. I glanced at my reflection in the dresser mirror, the big brown eyes I'd only seen on one other person. I tugged.

There it was, where it'd always been, facedown under the pantyhose, safeguarded in its rickety metal frame. I'd memorized that picture—the only one I'd ever seen of him—its details as familiar as the birthmark across my left wrist.

He was lifting Mom up, her white heels kicking at air, the patchy grass of Nana's yard willed into a threshold. One arm aloft, her puffed sleeve blotting out the better half of his face, bundle of bleached roses fixed above them like a Christmas star.

The tar-black hair that tumbled past his ribs. The one bushy eyebrow, the one big brown eye. Two meaty hands that looked like they knew the inside of a carburetor. A fat band of gold blinking in the light. The start or end of a grin.

That was it, all I had of him, my father. Less than half a man. He'd vanished when I was only two. I didn't even know his name.

"We're better off without him." Mom refused to talk about him. *That was a mistake, end of story,* she'd say when I'd badger her. *That* meaning him, *that* meaning her marriage, *that,* it'd follow, meaning me. At some point, I learned to stop asking.

My interest waned. It piqued again, at twelve, when I first found that photo, but it ebbed just as quickly. No one ever brought him up, not Nana, not Aunt Erin—not even by accident. It was like he'd died, except people still talked about the dead, reminisced on who they'd been: handsome, impish, sure-footed, dim. What they'd done for work. Whether their thumb had been green or their backside Velcroed to a barstool. It was more like he never was.

I set the photo back down, closing the drawer. I didn't miss him, not really—it was what I often told myself. I'd never even known the man. The few tattered details I clung to pathetic in most light, flimsy as that one photograph.

Still, it was startling, how easily someone could slip out of your life. And in.

two

I plied the kids with a half sleeve of Oreos, opting for the scenic route. Riding along one river, then veering along the next. The Fraser River ran right behind Mom's apartment, and its confluence with the Nechako was a mere traffic light away. The two rivers merging for a moment into one, the watery arm in which our city was cradled.

It would've been quicker to turn the opposite way, but I never missed a chance to take River Road, even if it meant burning through some extra gas. I veered again, following the river's bends, the silver loupe that was hooked around my rearview mirror spinning, spritzing my arms with blinking crescents.

We used to walk for hours there, along the rivers, my aunt Erin and I, back when we spent every weekend together. The loupe was from her, the key, she'd call it, to all of the micro-universes—the mosses and mushrooms and spring ephemerals—waiting for us to unlock them.

Erin was the one who taught me words like *confluence* and *loupe*, how to tell the difference between a black spruce and a white one, to start tomatoes from seed. Every birthday, she'd take me camping, Erin identifying every wildflower along the trail. On cloudless nights, we'd haul her telescope out up onto the hill behind her student-housing complex. No one knew the night sky better. I was thirteen when she left.

She was at the end of her master's when she met Michael, a visiting professor in the Environmental Studies department. PG didn't have a PhD program. It was just a happy coincidence that Michael was moving back down to Vancouver as well.

"I'm flying you out to visit, soon as winter break," she'd promised, wiping my cheeks before cupping my face in her hands. That was in August. In January, a package arrived, four pucks of granular chocolate tied together with string. *Greetings from Tulum*, the post-card read.

Michael liked to travel during breaks, she'd explained on our answering machine. Things were so hectic. She was TAing that summer semester, but maybe next year. *Next, next.*

It wouldn't be long before I was graduating, she'd written on the back of another postcard. I should apply. I'd love it there—the thrum of the city, campus life. We could picnic at Wreck Beach. Weekend on the Sunshine Coast. Depending on what I majored in, I might end up calling her *Prof.*

Instead, we drifted, the calls dwindling, her visits petering out until they stopped altogether. The last time I'd seen her was at my wedding. Six years ago, then. She was smiling in the photos, but there was something else at play. Sadness, maybe. Disappointment. I'd gotten married the summer after graduation. Just like Mom had.

Michael was the keynote speaker at a conference in San Diego. They had to leave before dinner. "Don't take it too hard." It had been Mom's attempt to console me. "She's changed, Mrs. Professor." Erin was the first in the family to go to college, and the reaction veered from pride to resentment when she had the nerve to go again—and again. "Your aunt's always had a stick up her ass."

I felt a kick at my back.

"More cookies!" Kyle demanded, his voice calling me back.

"Almost home," I said, switching on my blinker, the light from the loupe marking me again.

It was Erin who'd bought me my first box of Kotex, who took me to Winners when she noticed my shoes running small. It was Erin in her Volvo when I missed the bus, Erin at her desk, dusting off her calculator after a failed algebra quiz.

Come visit! she'd urge at the bottom of every postcard. *You're welcome anytime.* In all the years since she'd moved, she'd never forgotten a birthday or holiday, the packages arriving exactly on time—even as our phone calls became nonexistent.

Mom had it wrong. Erin hadn't changed. She was just busy, in a new phase of life. Mom had always been jealous. Erin had always been like a second mother. Or maybe even more like a first.

———

Dawn drifted to sleep on the drive over. The groan of the garage, the wresting out from the car seat, even Kyle's desperate pleas to watch *Cops* didn't rouse her. She was out. Must have been all that sun. I lowered the blinds, fencing her in on our bed with some pillows, leaving the door ajar.

Kyle was at the TV, flicking through the channels, pausing on *Jenny Jones*. The theme was mothers and daughters who teamed up to play men, and one mom was slithering across the stage in a dress (though *loincloth* wouldn't have been an inaccurate description) that appeared to be made of pink sandwich wrap. The audience jeered, and she turned, baring her blurred-out ass.

"Let's watch something later." I clicked off the tube and handed Kyle an apple. "It's so sunny out."

I opened the porch door, a lawn chair under one arm and a mug of cold, milky coffee in the other hand. Kyle darted by, clutching Sam's old soccer ball.

"I'm the king of the world!" He chucked the ball into the grass and attempted a cartwheel, legs flailing up and knocking my mug onto my chest. I set the lawn chair under the shade of the pine, wringing out the bottom of my drenched shirt.

"Be back in a minute." I trotted back to the house in search of a change of clothes and a refill.

Dawn's breathing quickened before sinking back into its plodding rhythm as I eased into my room. Her face was angelic, her bare arms outstretched and still banded with the last of her baby fat. I stroked back her hair, catching a glimpse of myself in our mirror-paneled closet doors, my heart-shaped face serene, damn near motherly in the room's hushed light. I smiled. Was this what it'd be like?

Then, in an instant, we were submerged. Dawn must have heard the howl first. She burst out crying, jolted awake, expression wounded as if she'd been slapped.

"Help!" Kyle's desperate pleas came next. "Jenny! Quick! Come help!" I scooped up a screaming Dawn and scrambled out into the yard as fast as my legs could manage.

"Kyle!" I panted. I couldn't see him anywhere.

"I'm over here!" he answered. I turned around and around again. The soccer ball had been launched into the branches of the lodgepole pine, but otherwise the yard was empty.

"Here!" A grubby hand jutted from behind the spruce. Rachelle's side. I shifted Dawn to a hip and placed a hand on the fence's top rail. "Fuck," the word involuntary. It was scalding. I used Dawn's hat as a makeshift glove, hoisting myself up and over and shaking out my scorched palm.

"Kyle!" I shouted.

"Over here," he replied. "I'm stuck."

I'd barely been gone for more than a minute, and there he was across the fence, perched on top of the pickup's tarnished roof, the front of his shorts darkened. I heard her before I saw her, crumpled into a heap on what was left of the grass, Rachelle's oldest, sobbing—her hands glistening red, cradling her knee, the skin stripped bare. The truck's door was swung open, the polyester innards of the leather driver's seat exposed by one diagonal gash. She must have slipped while climbing, scraped her knee on her way down.

"Hi," I said, kneeling beside her, Dawn wriggling out from my arms. "You okay?"

The girl's brown eyes were wet, snot glommed across her cheeks like sap. My hand moved instinctively toward her, and I started patting her back.

"Can you tell me what happened?"

Before the girl could speak, I felt someone shove past me, partition of long, black hair. Rachelle's baby was bolstered over her shoulder, dark face glaring up at me before breaking out into a wail. As soon as Dawn heard the baby's cries, she started crying, too. When I reached out to comfort her, she batted me back, screaming until she was rasping. Was *this* what it'd be like?

"Hi, baby, Momma's here." Rachelle wrapped her free arm around the girl's neck.

"She okay?" Kyle had gotten on his hands and knees to steady himself.

"Shhh," Rachelle cooed into the girl's ear, ignoring him. "Let's get you on inside and fix up that boo-boo."

"Rachelle." I started toward her, but I don't think she heard me. So focused she was on tending to her daughter's wounds. "I . . ."

"Don't." She turned toward me, eyes darting to mine. "I should've been watching her. Even if it is my yard." My face went hot. "I was fixing a bottle for this one."

Her baby's chubby fingers grabbed at her denim shirt, its collar embroidered with a snaking red thread. She brushed the hair from her face, revealing a pink scar that spanned the length of her forearm. I realized I'd never seen her up close before. For the first time since we had moved in across from her, she became real, pulsing veins and staggered breath. The effect was startling.

"I should've been out here." I avoided her eyes. "I just went in for a minute. I can't believe he hopped the fence. And your truck." I shook my head. Not like it wasn't a hazard to begin with—but mounting it, that must have been Kyle's bright idea.

I wanted to say that, to say more, to show her how bad I felt that her girl had gotten hurt. If it had been anyone else, I would've. But I couldn't. The way she was looking at me, as if she knew everything people said. Everything I'd said. I just wanted to get out of there.

"Anyone gonna help me?" Kyle interrupted.

"Coming." I started toward the truck. I stepped onto the seat and propped my elbows on the roof. The leather was slick. I could see how easy it'd be to slip. "Grab on." Kyle yoked his arms to my neck.

Before stepping down, I noticed something beyond the truck, out of view from my yard. A garden or, at least, what used to be one, before the yellow dock and tansy and enough foxtail barley to choke a small dog had taken over.

Indians don't garden. It was common knowledge. Why they starved every winter before we came. They were hunters and gatherers—primitive, simple. At least, that's what Nana always said.

It'd probably been Al's, had gone to seed around the same time he did. Still, it was strange to discover, after all those years, what could be hidden in plain sight.

"My hero!" Kyle rammed into my legs, squeezing his arms around them and bashing his head into my rear end.

"Okay." I unlatched his hands, picking Dawn back up. "That your smart idea?"

He shrugged, kicking at a dirt-caked Pepsi bottle. "You know trespassing's a felony?" He shrugged again. "You're lucky she only scraped her knee. You owe that girl an apology."

I looked up to find her, but the girl and Rachelle and the baby had gone, leaving us standing, strangers, in the yard across from mine.

Ray was supposed to come around half past six, but seven thirty came and went, and there was still no sign of him. Northwood Pulp wasn't more than ten minutes from my house, the dank so concentrated that on humid days, you could taste it. They used sulfur to soften scrap wood into the pulp that would eventually become paper, and you could smell a pulp mill before you even began to approach it. PG was home to three of them.

The smell of money, we'd all joke, shrugging off the implications behind the stench. Like boiled cabbage, hard-boiled eggs. Familiar things, harmless. Like hot pools of spring water. Farts. When the research came out, the toxic particles with the unpronounceable names, why we lived five to seven years less than everyone else in our province, what else could we do but shrug it off? The mills weren't just an industry—they were central heat and pork in the frying pan.

Wedged below the citizens' weather section, taken downtown and at the jail, *Air Quality Readings: Good 0–25, Fair 25–50, Poor 51–100, Very Poor 100+.*

It's not money they're smelling, what Erin would retort, voice muffled beneath the bandana she'd knot around the back of her head on *Poor* days. "It's HS_2."

Erin was the one who taught me how to pronounce them. Methyl mercaptan, dimethyl sulfide, the particles from hydrogen sulfide, what was stitched across our air. The poison that was, increasingly, everywhere. Our soil, our drinking water, the breast milk of our mothers. Erin's other favorite comeback. *Good is a pretty wide net.*

I checked the clock. It was almost eight. Ray wasn't the type to work overtime. Didn't take a detective to figure out where he'd gone instead.

The kids were better off with me driving. I shepherded them into the garage.

We were all strapped in, gear in reverse, Kyle punching through the foil dot on his juice box when Ray pulled up, blocking me in.

"Hey," he shouted, craning his head out of his window. "Stop that car!" Mock-authoritatively, his voice tinged with glee. Ray was a big fan of *Cops*.

He stumbled out of his truck, pausing for a moment and smoothing back his hair. I stayed in my car, the doors locked. He tapped on the window.

"What's a matter, Jen, can't say hi to your uncle Ray?" He flashed his teeth, a wanton smile. He knew I hated that. When they first got together, it'd been *Big Brother*. After *Uncle*, what was left but *Daddy*? I cringed, cranking my window down.

"I'm driving the kids home," I said, forcing a smile. I didn't want another argument.

"Dad!" Kyle stopped slurping, lowering the crushed carton from his mouth.

Dawn's ears perked up in the backseat, repeating after Kyle, "Dada!"

"Hey, buddy!" Ray reached through the window and draped his arm over me, kneading his knuckles into the top of Kyle's head. The loose ends of his bun poked at my neck, and I could smell the hardbar on his breath, the stench of tobacco seeping from the creases in that stupid purple leather jacket.

Oxblood, he'd call it, popping its collar. *For men with balls as big as an ox.* He'd grab a handful of himself. Ray was vulgar like that around the kids, in front of me. Especially in front of me. I felt his arm brush against my breast. I hiked up my knee, jabbing him in his gut.

"Sorry," I muttered. An accident.

"What do you mean driving 'em home?" His arm retracted. "I'm here now. I'll take them." He could hardly hold himself up straight, silver rings clacking against the wing mirror for balance.

"It's no problem," I insisted. He was soused, that was certain. I placed my hands back on the wheel. "It's on my way. I got to stop at Winners anyway."

"Shopping? At eight o'clock at night?" He hoisted his jeans up by his belt. "Didn't you hear? There's a murderer out there." He leaned in close to me again. Ray's body was lean, but he still hadn't lost the baby fat from his face. Sometimes it almost looked angelic—rosebud of a mouth, apple-rounded cheeks—when it wasn't disfigured with drink. "Wouldn't want you to be the next Beth."

Even then, within days of her disappearance, she'd become a joke to some people. Some men.

"It's on my way," I repeated. "No trouble at all." But it was too late. His mood had soured. He was hoisting up his jeans again, his face clenched tighter than a fist. I should've just let him hang all over me—giggle, seem flattered. It's how Missy handled men. Ray's eyes drifted down to my tits, and I felt my stomach churn. But I was no Missy. I crossed my arms over my chest.

"Kyle," he commanded, eyes looking past me. "Get your sister and get your ass in the car. End of discussion. Finito."

He turned, staggering back to his Chevy. Kyle unbuckled his seat belt and started to open the door.

"No." I locked us in. Kyle looked up at me, lost. "We're just going to wait here a while, okay?" This was my property, the kids still in my care. Men like Ray didn't always get to win.

"I think," Kyle said, sucking in his top lip, "we better just go with Dad."

I glanced in my rearview mirror. Ray was back in his driver's seat, his fist on the horn, banging, like it was one of those padded mallets at the regional fair.

"Jenny?" Kyle clasped his hands over his ears. Ray had changed tactics, was leaning his whole elbow against the wheel. Dawn was starting to howl.

"Jenny?" I felt his little hand reach over. It was shaking. I put the car in park and unlocked the doors. Even if I was the one to take him there, home for him was Ray. *Finito. End of story.* There was no winning, I reminded myself.

As soon as the kids were packed in, Ray gunned on the gas, tires shrieking, one hand raised out of his window, a victory flag. He was the type of man to peel out from his grandma's. The thought floated up: Was my dad like that?

It was a game I knew well, one I'd started playing early. As a child, I would watch Mom scrub the stains from her shirt. Blood was a bitch to get out. If my dad were there, things would have looked different. If my dad were there . . .

A horn honked, Ray's motor thrumming, bringing me back to where I stood in my driveway.

"Asshole," I muttered, fanning the pipe dream and the stench of burnt rubber away.

I was greeted by the blink of the answering machine, a message from Sam. He wouldn't be back tonight either. Just as well, I thought, removing the ground beef from its bowl of cold water and stashing it in the fridge. I'd had enough company for the day anyway. I put a Hot Pocket in the microwave, breaking it open, the cheese blistering, marinara sauce bleeding down my hand.

I turned on the shower as hot as I could stand, scouring off my interaction with Ray with *Farm Apple*. By the time I stepped out, the room was milky with steam, the mirror above the sink fully effaced. I collapsed onto the ribbed cushions of our couch, nubby towel turbaned around my wet head.

I'd put on *Home Alone* for Kyle earlier, but I couldn't remember where I'd stashed the remote. Too tired to even turn on the lamp, I just sat there for a while in the particle dark—my eyes gradually adjusting, able to discern floor lamp from CD rack from big dead box.

A light appeared out of nowhere, a match scratched in a cellar. I looked out the back window. Rachelle was standing in the bright of her kitchen, untwisting a package of sliced bread.

Our houses were mirror images of each other, the same paint-by-numbers architecture that made up the majority of our subdivision, the living room opening into the kitchen, windows cast toward the backyard. I'd never noticed how easily you could see in. When Al was there, the blinds were almost always drawn. Or maybe ours had been. In any case, both were strung up now.

I scooted closer to the window, to the other end of the couch. She was at her counter, arranging two pieces of toast on a plate, the tops slick with peanut butter or honey or jam. She vanished. The light flicked off. Another set flicked on. She reappeared in her living room and switched on the TV, her feet on her coffee table—the end of her day. I wanted to see what she was watching, so I went into my kitchen, sidling up to the window to get a better view. Her head turned toward me. *Shit.* I dropped to my knees. She couldn't have seen me—my house was pitch-dark. Was there a word for it? In line at the Safeway, stopped at a traffic light. The inner awareness that you're being watched. *Paranoia,* Sam would've said. *Being female.* Missy would've rolled her eyes. Rachelle had turned, but no one was there. The thud in the basement, the creak overhead, the rustling in the bush out back. *It was nothing,* she'd reasoned with herself, pivoting back toward the screen. Just the house settling, a fox that'd gotten into the trash. What André had said after Mom, certain she was being followed, had sprinted across the mall's parking lot back to her car. *Women and the stories they tell.*

Most times when I picture her, it's there in that lamp-lit shelter, the only element of change the shifting light from her wood-paneled TV. Safe. I wonder if she appreciated it then.

But how could she have?

You can't see the trapline until it's too late, your neck already noosed in its snare.

three

I began to notice her more and more.

   Not in an obsessive way. Our lots were practically on top of each other, the windows wide and bare. It would've taken effort not to see her—pouring her coffee, watching her programs, untangling her elder daughter's hair.

Sam had spent more time in Mackenzie than PG that week, and before I knew it, he was gone again, the house as lifeless as a tomb. Any action would've been welcome. Never mind that it was coming from *that* side.

Rachelle was home a lot. So was I. Every morning when I stepped into my kitchen, she was already there in hers. Setting out orange juice, milk, and Shreddies as I put on the day's first pot. Two eggs sunny-side up for me, with an Eggo or a piece of buttered toast on the side. Whatever her daughters didn't finish for her. She had her first smoke right after breakfast, out on the porch, where we'd lift our hands and avert our eyes. I'd wrap up watering and put on the day's second pot.

Every day around eleven, she'd pick up the red rotary phone that was nailed in near her fridge and balance its receiver in the crook of her neck. Some days, she'd hang it up almost immediately. On others, she'd stay like that for close to an hour.

Around two, she'd disappear—the basement, the washroom, the girls' bedroom or hers, the parts of her house that were screened off from mine. Putting the baby down, I imagined, sorting through the washing, shampooing her hair. Around three, it was always combed wet. It'd dry on her porch, her favorite lawn chair, the girls lost in her labyrinthine yard.

She'd vanish again shortly after dinnertime, the windows lifeless until eight or nine p.m. She ate in front of the TV. Always toast. Always a game show. *Jeopardy! Wheel of Fortune. Who Wants to Be a Millionaire?* Lights out was always before ten.

It was familiar, her life, cloistered, hermetic—TV providing the only adult companionship. No other voices except hers, her girls'. As if when Al had left this world, he'd trapped her inside that one, like a bug in a jar, the lid muscled tight. I hadn't seen a single visitor yet.

Friday, on the drive to work, I couldn't shake the sense that I was missing out. *Today's the day someone stops by,* I'd convinced myself. One of Al's relatives, a playdate for the girls, a sister with the same long, dark hair. Beth's real father, jacked-up and swarthy, bouquet of roses secreted behind his back.

It was as gripping as anything on the tube, the view into a neighboring world—watching someone else's days pass. I knew how it sounded, but it wasn't like I was casing the place or waiting for her to get undressed. I was just lonesome, curious to see what would happen next.

I was standing there, bunching cellophane with a fist, knotting ribbon around a set of mini shower gels for the young mom with her elbows leaned against her stroller when the thought first occurred to me. *Maybe I should just go over there.*

We both didn't have a lot going on. It was senseless, really, us poking around the house all day, roped off from each other on account of Rachelle being, well, what she couldn't help.

Besides, Rachelle wasn't like them. She woke early, had dinner on the table at the same time every night. She drank Ocean Spray, not Molson. I'd never seen her smoke in front of her girls. Her yard was disgraceful, was no excusing that, but maybe it wasn't completely her fault. The truck, for instance, that had to have been Al's. Inherited, like the rest.

I'd clipped a recipe for oven-fried drumsticks in the paper and had planned to make a batch to last the weekend. I didn't mind cooking when Sam was home, but switching on the oven when he was gone was too depressing, lambent light cast upon my solitary figure like an underscore. In his first years at the mine, I'd lived off bowls of Honeycomb, PB&Js, frozen nuggets, Kraft dinners, but I was trying to eat better, fix the faulty parts that kept me from carrying. Erin had obsessed over upping progesterone. Leafy greens were supposed to help. I tossed a brick of frozen spinach into my cart.

I stood in line behind a grandma, her yellow hair in rollers, about thirtysome cans of creamed corn in her cart. She was thumbing through a wrinkled wad of coupons with a pair of trembling hands. Looked like it might be a while.

Someone had left a copy of the *Prince George Citizen* on top of the tabloid rack. I picked it up. Beth, in the amethyst enclave of her school portrait, beamed at me from the front page. *Beth, We Love You, We Miss You* was printed above her like a tiara. I started scanning through.

What happened to Beth Tremblay? Star student. Heart of gold. Mom says, "We know she's still out there." Pastor says she was truly "a lily among the thorns."

It was coming on two weeks. They had to have found something. I skimmed to the bottom. *Still no sign.*

Rachelle's lights were out by the time I got home, and I felt my heart plunge as if I'd just missed a close friend or the latest episode of *Cold Squad.*

I'd been talking myself out of going over there the whole ride home. It'd been half a decade since we had first moved in. What, was I going to ring her doorbell with a Tupperware of chicken? Play like I hadn't been turning my head all those years, like everyone else? It's not like we had much in common besides our schedules or lack thereof. What would we have even talked about?

My heart plunged, and I realized that the neighboring light had been more than a novelty. It was a stopper in the way of so many drafts. The girls, and their babies, and their babies on the way, Sam's imprint on the other half of our king-sized bed. My idiot body, my idle hands.

Some days it'd felt like I'd been the one measuring formula, wiping sticky mouths, braiding hair. As if I were the mother of two perfect daughters. As if I weren't alone, or defective, at all.

I switched on the kitchen light, faced with the same tired reflection. I was slicing an onion, and I nearly chopped off my finger when I saw another light flick on, but it was just the neighbor to our left, an old woman, recently widowed, alone now, in her two-bedroom home. She'd never had any kids, her body a lemon—like mine. The days too long to pass up company. I'd go over there the next day. Drumsticks in hand.

Turns out, no poultry was necessary.

I was squatting over a patch of strawberries in my garden, yanking pigweed out by its fatty fuchsia roots, when Rachelle's shadow bled into mine.

"Jenny, right?" she said, her baby at her hip, pitch-dark hair coiled at the top of her head.

"Hey, yes. Hi." I stayed crouching, my neck craning upward. I couldn't seem to remember how to stand. I composed myself, lifting to my feet. I'd just been rehearsing what I would say when I knocked on her front door.

"I was hoping you could give me some gardening advice. I'd like to get mine going this year."

Gardening advice. I brushed the soil from my hands. Never in a zillion years would I have thought to open with that.

"If it's not already too late." She shrugged, her baby tugging at a loose strand of her hair.

"It's not too late." I thought of Erin and the calendar she had nailed to the inside of her kitchen cupboard. Everything was seeded before June. We were in July. "I mean, it is late, but there's a few things you could try. Maybe radishes." They weren't fussy.

"Radishes." She nodded, hiking the baby higher. "Figure it's good. For the girls." She paused, waiting for something.

"For sure." She was nervous. So was I. "I'd love to help." I smiled.

"Great," she said, her mouth a straight line.

I realized then that I hadn't ever seen it, her smile. It wasn't that she was dour, but she always seemed focused—wary, even. Had I been looking, I might've noticed the signs.

"You could come for some coffee and have a look. I put Beth down at two." *Beth.* I glanced at the fluff of dark hair. Rachelle had to have been following the news.

"Two works," I said, still grinning.

Rachelle's eyes focused past me. She paused, face inscrutable, before nodding and turning back toward her house, leaving me with the berries and the spinach and the onion tops, my shadow singular again.

I went back to my weeding. It was impeccable, her timing, I remember thinking, clumps of plantain in fist. Wasn't but a few minutes after I'd stepped out into my garden that she was there, in front of me, doing just what I'd been building up the courage to do. Was it possible I wasn't the only one looking for some company? Was it possible I wasn't the only one who'd noticed the new view?

My blood was pumping, the sun somehow brighter than before. I couldn't explain it. In the five years I'd lived there, I'd never given her much thought, the polite good-morning wave a reflex as unconscious as a sneeze.

Admittedly, when we first moved in, I'd bristled at the sight of her. It wasn't personal. Like everything else in her yard—the truck, the washer, the sky-high nettles—she just didn't belong. With time, I learned, like all the other neighbors, to mentally will her away. And now, there I was, flooded with the anticipation of stepping into the very house that, for all those years, I'd been actively squinting past.

I couldn't explain it.

Rachelle was beautiful, there was that, but so was Missy, sateen sash she'd been coroneted in at prom still nailed above her fireplace. They were quickening to be around, beautiful women, the ones men strained their necks to see. As if just being within range of their orbit, your worth was doubled, as if you, too, were hungered for, a jackpot—or, at least, a consolation prize. That wasn't it.

It was something else, something bigger. Like Rachelle had been placed under my loupe—the details completely different from what I'd expected to find.

I'd never known anyone like her. There were a few of them in every class, but by ninth grade, they'd all dropped out, and it's not like we ever really mingled.

I thought of the twins, two girls my age who hadn't made it past fifth grade. I couldn't remember their actual names. No one besides the teachers ever used them. By the time I was nine, I knew every slur, including the worst one. What Mom had said when we first moved in: "House is cute and all, but it's a shame about the squaw." Maybe it was only that, the taboo of it all. No one had ever had to educate me. It was a rule so self-evident, it was innate—felt, as palpable as the dank. You stayed on your side, and they stayed on theirs. And if you had the misfortune to live across from one of them, well, you simply lowered your shades and turned your head.

And yet there I was, blinds strung up. I'd never realized before, how easy it would be to just hop right over it. The fence.

Pinewood Drive ran parallel to our street, Spruceview Way. Pine and spruce, timber trees—those names (and their namesakes) were everywhere. The city's official signature was capped with a snowflake, but if you asked me, it should've been a two-by-four.

In addition to the three pulp, there were eight sawmills in town, the most, by far, in any province. A point of pride, we named everything—our schools, the mall, the hockey team, even the feedstore—after our ability to fell and process trees. Spruce, mostly. And pine.

We'd cut them down and process them and replant them. Cut down, process, replant. It was a cycle, a loop, an infinity symbol, with no beginning and no end.

Every summer, you'd see them, the crews of young Canadians stabbing at the soil, dropping sapling after sapling into rows as straight as the highway line. Reforestation programs. College grads from places like Toronto and Ottawa, taking a year off to see the North, to do good. Like Beth.

No one in Prince George ever did the planting. We were the ones doing the cutting down. Clearfelling, all evidence of any reforestation erased. Like plowing a field, or shaving a head.

We were the ones doing the processing. Feeding log under circular, headrig, band saw. Turning tree to lumber, forest to object: credenza, entertainment center. Two-bedroom home.

Like all the ones I was walking past. The drab vinyl siding, the sizzling blacktop, red flag after red Canadian flag. Our streets no different, really, except in name.

One, two, three, four, I counted down to where our house would've been. I stood, mouth agape. This couldn't be it.

The front belonged to a different person entirely. The lawn was just that, a lawn. Green. Not a single object yielded to the charge of the rain, the sun, the snow, the garbage man. Instead, there were trees: a cluster of birches; a trim, little spruce; a mountain ash, healthy and sprawling, in cottony flower. The grass even looked mowed. The rose-bush watered. A pot of hot-pink petunias dangled in self-orbit above the doorbell.

I pushed it in, but it didn't make a sound. I knocked. Crickets. I glanced at the front windows, but they were sealed off, the passive beige of the blinds. Could I have miscounted? I stepped back to recalculate when the door cracked open.

"Girls are asleep." Rachelle appeared, whispering. "Come on in." She waved a hand. Her bare feet padding down the hall. A no-shoes house, I noted, slipping off my Keds and leaving them by the mountainous pile near the door.

A pair of men's work boots stood upright in the corner, recently waxed, laces knotted in neat bows. I recognized them. Al's—ready and waiting—as if he were expected home soon.

It was uncanny, stepping into her living room. The interiors of our houses were nearly identical, from the ceiling lamps to the doorknobs, right down to the same unfortunate emerald-green carpeting. Like they'd been not built but cloned. The mess in there, the likeness, made it all the more jarring—what was possible, how far you could plummet.

It was worse than it'd appeared through the window, the carpet engulfed, a toy explosion, the screen on the TV a smudged patchwork of tiny hands. Dirty drinking glasses and dinner plates sprouted from every available surface, the couch housing what looked like at least two weeks' worth of washing. The smell cloyingly sweet, like yeasted bread.

A plate encrusted with pasta sauce sat on the arm of a recliner, an XXL work shirt draped over its back. Al again. His chair looked un-touched, the sauce hardened, like mastic. Was that the last meal he'd had before his heart gave out?

Beside the recliner, a dingy, mesh-back hat—a trucker's hat—hung on a lampshade. Lifelessly crumpled on a peeling leather ottoman, another work shirt. It'd been over a year, but from the looks of it, you'd have thought she'd lost him yesterday. Al was everywhere.

"This way." Rachelle cleared her throat, scooping up the plate. I blushed. She must have caught me gawking. Of course that wasn't his plate. She probably wore his old shirts like I did Sam's. I was embellishing, trying to weave with a few stray threads. Could I even be sure that those were really Al's boots? I thought of her baby, skin dark as molasses. Another story forming in my head.

Rachelle went into the kitchen, and I followed behind. She flicked off the coffee maker, dumping the plate into the sink.

"Coffee's ready." She opened the fridge. "What do you take? Creamer? Milk?"

"Milk's fine," I said, standing at the threshold. Seeing her kitchen table—the box of Shreddies, the cereal bowls, the crusts of some jam-tinged toast—my face burned again. I'd known exactly what would be on that table before I even saw it. Could she tell?

I took a seat, her back toward me as she rinsed out a mug. I tried to stay subtle, but there was so much to see. All that was too small to make out from my window, all that made her kitchen hers—more threads.

Snowy, horned, barn, striped. The first thing I noticed was that owls were everywhere. Splashed across her dishcloths, patterned on her oven mitts, costumed in a chef's hat on the front of a ruffled apron. Dotting the windowsill, perched atop her microwave, interspersed on a ledge over the sink among those pasty Precious Moments figurines. The wall clock had a beak and two brown wings, its eyes lemon yellow and peering. Either she loved them or someone thought she did, every gift she received owl-themed.

Tacked to her fridge, owl magnets: support for the dozens of photos plastered beneath them. Picking apples at an orchard, stringing tinsel on a tree, blowing out candles on a sheet cake, a party hat topping the older girl's head. The two girls in a bathtub, bundled up in the snow, the wan blue of a hospital gown, a plum-faced baby taking her first breath.

A school portrait of a serious little girl in a starched white shirt, her black hair scissored into a bowl. Its hues dated, the haze of the past. It must have been Rachelle when she was small.

"Sit." She handed me a mug. "Sugar?" She set a bowl on the table, plopping two cubes into her coffee and stirring.

Sitting across from each other like that, our mouths malfunctioned. Neither one of us knew what to say.

I glanced back at the fridge, as if that'd be any help. There was only one photo of Rachelle and Al together, and I kept returning to it. It was a close-up, their heads fused, a wisp of white lace, what must have been her wedding dress. They were smiling, but there was something off. How radiant Rachelle looked, like a starlet, Al's face chapped and bloated beside. Total mismatch, Al toadlike in comparison, more an uncle, or a gym teacher, or—it didn't *not* occur to me—a john. There was a post-card next to it, a faded field of sunflowers. I was reminded of our conversation earlier.

"How long have you had the garden?" I asked.

"It was here when Al moved in." Rachelle sipped at her coffee. "I always wanted to get it going. My mom had a big garden back home. Everything she touched just thrived."

Indians don't garden was what I was thinking.

"In Vancouver?" was what I said instead. Sometimes I wished I could scour the contents of my own head.

"Chilliwack." Rachelle fished another cube from the bowl. She hadn't broken out into a smile or anything, but when she talked of home, her face relaxed. There was even the start of a grin. "You know it?"

"No," I said, chewing a nail. "I've never even been to Vancouver."

As soon as I said it, I regretted it. There were stories she'd heard about people like me, no doubt. White trash who never left PG. That was the thing you could forget about talk. It went both ways.

"My aunt lives there," I justified. "I've been meaning to go."

"Hm." Rachelle stirred her mug. The conversation lulled.

There was a tiny muted TV on the counter behind her, the commercial for PG Auto Sales that was always on. A barrel-chested man wad-dling down a row of used trucks, candy-colored flags flapping above his bald head.

Beth's face appeared next, her static smile, those unblinking eyes. That morning, they'd announced that there'd been an anonymous tip to look for her remains behind the airport. They hadn't found anything yet.

"I still can't believe what happened on 16," I said. "It's so crazy, hey? That it could happen so close to home."

Rachelle was quiet, her spoon still clinking.

"The Highway of Tears." I tried to gauge her reaction, but her expression was flat. If that phrase meant anything to her, she didn't let on. "Have you been following the story?"

She shrugged. "Much as anyone," she said absently, digging in her back pocket for her smokes. "You mind?" I shook my head.

"I just hope they find her," I said. Rachelle reached over the table, lifting open the window with a palm. "I mean, you know, alive." She stayed silent.

The mood had veered. That look, the wary one, was back. Maybe it was the name *Beth*—it hit too close to home. Maybe she was thinking about her baby girl.

"I'm sure they will. They have to." I tried to backpedal, away from the despair. She'd turned her head away from me to aim the smoke out the window, the long black partition of hair.

"Women go missing every day," she was muttering from underneath it. "Ain't news." She looked back up, exhaling, her eyes elsewhere again.

Or maybe she was thinking about someone else.

I glanced back at the photo of her and Al, remembering what the girls had said. *Indians, working the highway.* Those women weren't anonymous to everyone. Maybe that phrase had meant something after all.

"Refill?" Rachelle eyed my mug.

"Sure," I replied needlessly. She'd already scooped it up.

She was topping me off between handless puffs when Beth started to cry.

"Just a sec." She plucked the cigarette from her mouth and crushed it against the underside of the counter, scrubbing her hands before dashing from the kitchen.

I did what I would've done at any friend's house. Leaf through an opened Bargain Finder, sip my coffee, not so much catalogue as glance innocently around. I chewed on a thumbnail, turning behind me.

Rachelle still wasn't back. I stood, feet carrying me to the fridge. I could always say I was looking for the creamer, I remember thinking, my hands reaching over to that photo and slipping it out from under the owl.

Rachelle really was a beauty. It was hard to believe that she'd willingly chosen Al. I flipped it over. *1991*, the timestamp read. She must have been barely legal when they'd tied the knot. Youth might explain it; we all made mistakes. Maybe Al had made promises. Maybe he was a means of escape.

I looked at the school portrait, Rachelle's witless round face. Had she had any idea what was in store for her? I checked the timestamp. *1967.* Impossible—I checked again. I was born in '77. The girl in that portrait was at least fix or six. Rachelle couldn't have been more than a couple years older than me, let alone fifteen.

But if it wasn't Rachelle, who was it? Her mother? Rachelle's backstory began to stitch itself, Singer-fast, together. Her mother only a teenager, her father absent, Rachelle placed in the state's hands—it was common enough, some might even say textbook, formulaic as an episode of *CSI*. After a childhood in foster care, even a jalopy like Al would've looked like a dream ride.

I heard something, a voice, and I panicked, placing the photo back. Rachelle was singing, her tone starbright. I crept out into the hallway. The door to the girls' room had been left open wide.

Her back was toward me, her baby in her arms, a moon revolving around its planet. The song didn't have any lyrics—it was more like a string of yips and yowls. Was that their language? I'd only heard it in Westerns, the whooping war cries.

If the other rooms were unkempt, the girls' was plain hazardous, emerald green snowed over with the trappings of girlhood: ratty stuffed animals, rogue markers and crayons, the books made from paperboard, all the toys made from plastic. Laundry seeded like catkins throughout. I spotted at least three tiaras and two crumpled A&W bags. A pair of broken angel wings glittered from the closet door handle, a scuffed-up baby doll, mouth plugged with a pacifier, cradled below in Al's old Canfor hat.

Two eyes darted up. The older girl was sitting upright on her bed clutching a stuffed dog to her chest. *The hell are you?* her expression demanded.

Standing there in the doorway, I felt like I was back at my window, edging toward an intimacy that wasn't mine. My ears burned. The girl had a point.

"Rachelle," I whispered. She didn't hear me, so I stepped inside, tiptoeing around the rubble. I tapped her.

"Sorry," she mouthed, still swaying. "With one, it's okay, but with two . . ." The older girl kept her eyes hot upon me, little head following my every move. As soon as Rachelle had stopped singing, Beth's face had turned red, and she erupted again. If Rachelle's voice was stardust, Beth's was lava.

"Shh, shh." She patted her. "I might be here awhile," she mouthed again before starting to hum, resting her head against the top of Beth's.

"No worries," I said, backing out and stumbling over a topless Barbie. "I'll just rinse my mug. I can let myself out."

"Leave it," she whispered between hums. "Maid'll be here tomorrow." She winked, eyes crinkling. My face mirrored hers. It was the first time I'd seen it, I realized. Her smile. It was even prettier than the photograph.

I left Rachelle's house with the feeling that I'd just gotten away with something, jaunty, electric—CD in coat pocket, Snickers bar under sleeve, heart drumming as I turned the bend.

As I was sitting with her beside her opened kitchen window, my empty house had been recast. As if it weren't mine. As if I weren't me. As if, for the hour, I'd tried on a new self.

The girls would never believe it. Missy always called me the boring one. Reliable old Jenny, always exactly where you expected her to be, guileless, in her stonewashed jeans and Keds. But not that day. Not by far.

My house came back into view, pointer finger to my bubble. The widow next door was out front, watering her dahlias. She waved. I waved back. Could she have seen me there? I quickened my pace. Our conversations had only ever been about how much she loathed Rachelle. *You stayed on your side, and they stayed on theirs.* It wasn't as innocuous as a little teenage shoplifting. I could never tell the girls, I realized, or anyone for that matter.

Anne-Marie might've understood, but she was hopeless when it came to keeping secrets, especially around Missy, who was like a hound, able to sniff anyone out. Wouldn't be long before Sam caught wind. He'd never managed to get past the bristling. The shock of seeing it, her blight of a yard, it was a lot to swallow after two weeks on. He was working his tail off so we could live across from *that*?

I wouldn't have to lie, exactly. All the runs to Safeway, the plates of grilled cheese, the hours-long blocks of *Cold Squad*. I didn't tell Sam everything I did while he was gone. I'd just have to be smart. The next time, I'd wear a hat. Nana's old saucer-framed sunglasses. What Sam didn't know wouldn't hurt him.

Besides, it was only coffee. It wasn't like I was really doing anything wrong, I reasoned. Unsure of whom I was trying to convince, anyhow.

four

The days passed unremarkably, with Rachelle returning to her usual rhythm and me to mine, fenced back into our adjacent, lonesome lives. Idle talk across the yard would inch further some mornings only to shrink back the next, with no mention of my coming by again.

It took the entire week for me to realize that she was waiting. She'd opened the door. It was on me to step inside. By then, Sam was already back. Our next cup would have to be postponed awhile.

"You miss me?" Sam asked, nestling my face between his calloused hands. The furrows across his forehead and in between his brows were deepening, and for a moment, I could see twenty years ahead: a face as treaded as a tire.

Every year at the mine shaved off two down home. We all knew the risks. It was meant to be temporary, but *temporary* always turned into *just one more year.* The mills only ever offered the same lowly position— general utility, grunt work with nothing pay. The money at the mines was too good to give up.

"Of course, baby. Always." He pushed his face into mine, tongue worming into my mouth. "Not now," I whispered, moving away. We'd just done it last night.

"You're still taking your temperature, right?"

"Every morning." I wasn't supposed to ovulate until the following week, but it was no use explaining that to Sam. When he was home, we tried every night, fertility chart be damned. *There's a reason they call it a miracle,* he'd say. *We just have to keep trying.*

Personally, I never saw what all the fuss was about. The way men talked, their desperation for it, as if it were essential, like clean water, bread. How it was always alluded to in movies, on TV. A whole lot of fanfare for the same sensation you could get from tearing down a rutted road.

At least Sam was gentle.

Maybe you're doing it wrong, Missy would tease, arching a penciled-on eyebrow. She'd been with more boys than there were in our graduating class, rumor being that she lost her virginity in sixth grade.

Sam was the only man I'd even been with. My first real kiss. First real everything. Well, technically.

The other thing, at that bush party in ninth grade—it didn't count. It couldn't. I barely remembered it.

"Okay." Sam pecked my forehead, easing onto his back. He'd never been pushy, not even on prom night. We'd waited until we were married.

"Was thinking about making a change," he said, sitting up. "Was talking to Jim, he said he might have some work in town."

"Missy's Jim?" I couldn't conceal my apprehension.

That big house on Toombs Drive, all those vacations to Disneyland, a corresponding Harley for each day of the week: all on the salary of a heavy-duty mechanic.

Yeah, right.

A year back, my suspicions were confirmed. Jim had gotten a bid at the mill where Ray worked. One night, after babysitting, I'd overheard Ray recounting the scandal. How he'd charged Canfor double, maybe triple, for the repair. How, a week later, during a rebuild of a different machine, they realized someone had stolen just about all the parts that weren't glued down.

"And that ain't even the best part." Ray had taken a swig from his beer, pausing to light the cigarette that was perched between Mom's lips. "Couple months later, and guess who's contracted out again?"

"Must got some magic hands," Mom had said, wedging her head into the crook of Ray's neck.

"More like a magic bag of cocaine that he's passing out to execs. Must have some dirt on someone pretty high up." Ray had shaken his head, less in disapproval than in awe. "I wonder who he's really working for."

Talk was often like that—slippery, far-off. That drugs were being moved through town wasn't surprising. PG was the nexus of the North. But the channels, they were so well buried, you'd hardly suspect there was anything underfoot at all.

Jim was my only connection to that world, and a distant one at that. He and Missy had met the summer after graduation, at the fair. Eleven years older, casting shadows in black, banded wads of bills weighing his pockets as if he were setting off to the Fraser to drown. Neither one of us had ever seen that kind of cash before. He'd shelled out near a hundred to win Missy a prize. A grimacing dolphin tall as I was in clogs that Missy wedged under my arm as I lagged behind them, plush sullied by the sodden ground.

"I could test it out," Sam was saying. "Could always find something else."

I nodded. We both knew it wasn't like that. Imagining an easy out with men like Jim was about as wishful as thinking he might offer unemployment benefits.

Ray had told another story that night, what had happened to his buddy Willy, a millwright at Canfor-Plateau in Vanderhoof, after his accident. He'd been fixing a chain when a bin dropped, crushing his shoulder and the length of his right arm. It should have killed him, but he'd dove between the chains just in time. Hydraulic failure, no one's fault. He was lucky, they'd said.

That was before the doctor's orders, any employer's worst nightmare: twelve whole weeks of paid leave. He was welcomed back to work with a mop placed in hand.

His job had gone up for bid while he was gone. It was plain bad luck, they'd said.

Willy started working as a runner because he was flat broke. No one knew about the pain meds, the same ones he'd been given post-op, until after his death.

"Remember that robbery on Old Summer Lake Road? The guy in the wheelchair?" A paraplegic who'd been found the next morning bear-maced and gagged with a tennis ball, extension cord binding his hands.

"That was Willy," Ray had said, the reason more men didn't change professions. "You can't say no to those guys."

Willy tried, apparently, and was found three weeks later. Near a cabbage field, in the front seat of a rusted pickup missing both license plates. The frosted tips of his hair stiff with actual frost.

It wasn't Sam's fault. His sense of duty could be blinding. It was what had always set him apart.

While he might've sat at their lunch tables and laughed at their antics, he wasn't like the other boys in our high school, the ones who grew rowdier—worse with each year. Sam spent every weekend in the seat of a rototiller. *A real man*, Nana had congratulated me. Sam had been born to provide.

We were nineteen when we signed our mortgage—the number so huge, it seemed more like a concept than a check we'd have to post each month. There were the payments on Sam's truck, the credit card debt. At the rate we were going, we'd be paying off the house long after we were dead.

"I could pick up more shifts," I bargained. "Or find something else. I heard Denny's is hiring."

"I'd just test it out," he repeated, not seeming to hear me. None of his brothers' wives worked one job, let alone two. "It'd be temporary." Like the mine.

"I can't be gone so much." He stood, face hacked apart, the slid-open mirror doors. "Once we start our family."

Mama and papa and baby makes three. One might've been a nothing number, but sometimes two was even less.

"It'll be good," he said, nodding his head, pulling on his T-shirt, zipping up his jeans. I knew that tone. That was the end of the conversation, if you could even call it that. He rapped on the wall before opening the door. "Put the coffee on, will ya, baby?"

"Sure thing," I said, still in my nightshirt, the pit in my stomach more like a canyon.

Sam sat on the back porch, mesh furled out in front of him, wielding a pair of cutting pliers. A fist-sized hole had appeared in our washroom window screen mysteriously, and it seemed to be growing, as if some animal were out there, fattening up on wire.

"Refill?"

He nodded, eyes still on the pliers.

It wasn't even ten, and he'd already blasted through his list: the lawn mowed, my washer fluid filled, the washroom sink snaked and draining beautifully again. His hair had lightened as it did every summer, his forearms substantial, strong enough to launch a snow tire. Sometimes, when I allowed myself, I could feel appreciative. Horny, even. But then the lights would turn off. In the dark, there was no avoiding it. What we were trying at—we were failing. I was. When I'd gone to the washroom earlier that morning, I'd been greeted with hexed red.

Our mugs clinked as I parked myself beside him. I'd blown out the elbow of one of my favorite sweaters. Green, with those little shell buttons, a hand-me-down from Anne-Marie I'd already mended twice. I was threading my darning needle when I heard Rachelle's door swing open, the *tap-tap-tap* of the carton in her hand.

"Morning." She waved.

"Morning," I echoed back. Sam nodded, still clipping. I bowed my head again.

"Jenny," she called out, my finger slipping. I'd poked myself with my needle, blood smudging onto my sweater. She was starting toward the fence.

"Fuck," I mumbled, finger in mouth. I hadn't mentioned it—I hadn't thought I needed to. She must have known her standing. I tried to give her a signal, pursing my lips and subtly teetering my head, but she remained oblivious. She lit up, one arm draped over the fence. Casual. Just three neighbors chewing the fat. "Been thinking about what you said."

The blades of Sam's pliers stopped midclip.

"The radishes."

He looked up.

"I got some seeds. Thought you could come by again."

"That right?" I squeaked. The hole Sam was boring in the side of my head was nearing the size of Alberta. I'd been caught, a trap I'd set myself.

"Alrighty," I called out slowly, conciliatory, the way you'd talk to a child, a drunk. "Good luck with that." I turned back to my mending, but not before her eyes caught mine. They looked wet.

She scoffed, muttering something before mashing her cigarette against the top rail and flicking it over onto our side of the fence. The screen door rattled as it slammed. Soon, it was quiet, birds chirping overhead. Like nothing had happened. I brought a thumbnail to my teeth. I should have warned her. But how could I have phrased it? *If anyone else is around, keep mum?* As if she were poison, contagious— a menace.

"'Come by'?" Sam's voice cut in on my introspection. "'Again'?"

"It's nothing," I whispered. "It's a long story." That much was true. He was silent.

"We were making small talk. Our yards are so close." I was struggling. "She needed help. With a ladder." It was the first thing that came to mind.

What Nana would complain about when it came time to change a bulb, tasked with checking off her list herself. Single women, with no one to spot them, stepping further and further toward heaven.

"She had a mouse in her gutter."

"A mouse," he repeated. He wasn't making it easy.

"It took five minutes."

I looked out at her yard. She'd taken one, maybe two, drags of her cigarette before crushing it. What a waste. Everything.

"It's not a big deal."

"Who said it was?" Sam turned, resuming his clipping.

I knew what came next. The bricks laid with precision. Sam didn't insist, but he didn't just forgive either. He buried. Next argument, there it'd be, cold as the earth, waiting to be dusted off.

We ate leftovers for dinner, him upright in the recliner, me curled on the far end of the couch, the shifting light of the tube washing over our plates of reheated spaghetti.

There was a spot on the news, a local psychic who claimed that Beth was safe. She'd had visions of her, down in Vancouver, an airy, yellow house near the sea. She'd come back once the danger passed. What danger, the psychic didn't say. Or when. It was coming on a month since she was last seen. Our thoughts and prayers as useless as they'd seemed.

Sam had killed all the lights and closed the door to our bedroom while I was still flossing. I'd left the TV on, a commercial for Arm & Hammer whitening gum. I went into the living room to switch it off.

As I reached for the remote, a waver of light hit my forearm. I squinted at the window. I'd assumed she'd turned in early, but I could see then that I'd been wrong.

She was there, but I could no longer see her. Her blinds were drawn down again.

The next morning, I woke with a sinking feeling, as if I'd been hollowed out, the dull ache of regret. Stepping into the kitchen, putting on the coffee, cracking the eggs—I was barely present, kept craning toward the window in hopes of any sign of her.

The blinds in her kitchen had been drawn down, too. It was like staring at a wall. Around nine, I saw movement, the first of the morning: a hand cracking the window, the blinds left to clatter against the frame. She'd stayed inside for her first cigarette.

The phone rang, and my heart leapt into my throat. I was jumpy, guilty, waiting to be told off. It was almost as if I'd expected it to be her on the other end.

Missy's rasp yanked me back to reality.

"I have news," she said, Missy-speak for when she needed something. "You want to come over for lunch with Annie?"

Sam hadn't said more than a few words to me since the run-in. Lunch was an unnecessary lure. I would've agreed if she'd have asked me to come hand-wash Jim's drawers. Happily.

Missy lived north of town, where the money lived, a sloping hill out of reach of the worst of the dank. I took the scenic route, the road that ran alongside the Nechako, passing spruce, pine, ropy telephone line, dipping down as if to girdle all that green and fuchsia in. The first of the fireweed was in bloom, the countdown—as the old adage cautioned—to winter commencing. How something could signal its utter opposite, I never understood. Fireweed always felt like the epitome of summer, its pink carefree, effervescent.

I used to never want that time of year to end. Now, I dreaded it. The inevitable way the flowers would brown, strangled by seed tufts, dense as quilt batting. A reminder of that summer: all that'd gone south.

Missy's house was imposing—the asphalt moat of a driveway, the jumble of turrets and columns and gables, flanked and studded with windows that appeared to have been painted on. The glass had been treated, a special technique, so that they could see out, but you couldn't see in. It looked like something from a toy catalogue.

Peach-colored gravel was shoveled into brick-lined islets, a three-tiered fountain dribbling in the center of the circular drive. I parked next to it, behind one of Jim's Harleys. Missy had made it. Sort of.

Three years later and it looked like they were still moving in, the only rooms with any furniture the bedroom, the kids' rooms, the living room, and the kitchen, leaving four other rooms and an aboveground basement that were, as Missy put it, *taking shape*. Your voice would echo in the entrance, wires dangling from a fist-size chasm, the chandelier that was due to be delivered any day. Folding chairs were gathered around the oak kitchen table, the windows mounted with curtainless rods. Whatever it was Jim did, money wasn't coming in fast enough.

Paris wasn't built in a day, Missy would say. No one ever corrected her. She had the type of deep-dyed confidence that comes with getting something from nothing. It's not like she'd worked to be hot.

We sat on the folding chairs, the steam from the half dozen aluminum containers a heady cloud. Shards of chicken and bundles of spinach surfaced above the marbled pools of slick fat, colors ranging from tomato, to lemon, to acid. The kids were camped out in front of the big screen with a large cheese pizza and a roll of paper towels. Missy's dogs, two Pomeranians named Ginger and—confusingly enough— *Misty*, were dashing to and from the pizza to the table, raising their heads and whimpering and wagging their tails.

"They call this naan." Missy tore a piece off the charcoal-flecked bread, dipping it into the sauce. "Jim put me onto it. Their churches are ass-ugly, but the food ain't half bad."

Sauce dribbled down her hand, staining her square-tipped white acrylics red. I noticed two were missing, her middle and ring fingers, the pockmarked nails chewed ragged.

There were a lot of them in PG. East Indians as opposed to the other kind. Like the Chinese, they had a restaurant in every plaza, including one at the mall. Tandoori Nation. I stuck to KFC.

"You hear about the search party for Beth?" Missy asked, rotating her hand, the tattoo on her inner wrist, a bunch of blurry cherries, made into even more of a blob.

The sore wrist, the missing nails. She and Jim must have had it out. She stood, opening a French door and flicking her lighter.

"It's Saturday," she said between drags. "They're going to search all the logging roads, the ones that cut straight up off 16. They need volunteers."

"Jesse was talking about it." Anne-Marie spooned more rice onto her plate. "We were thinking it'd be good to go."

She'd been nauseous well past the first trimester, barely able to keep down anything she was used to, let alone all that oil and spice.

"If my mom can watch Tanner. You going?"

"Was thinking about it." Missy eyed Anne-Marie's spoon. "For fuck's sake, just make yourself a kiddie plate." She jerked her head toward the pizza. Anne-Marie went red.

"I'll go," I said, maneuvering around Missy's barb.

Maybe I could even convince Sam to come, bypass the silent treatment, at least for a day. This was bigger than us. This was about Beth. *Who knows?* I remember thinking, my heart starting to quicken. *We might even find something.*

"We'll all go," Missy decided. "I'll pay for a sitter." She winked at Anne-Marie, who nodded, rice dropping from her spoon onto her baby-pink zip-up terry that matched her elasticized pants.

Missy stamped out her cigarette and walked over to the counter, the cardboard boxes stacked high. *BetterYou Nutriceuticals Inc.* was printed on the sides.

"Now," she said, lifting up a white bottle, "I wanted to take a moment to share something with you."

First it'd been Avon, then lingerie, then those scented candles with names like *Fresh Laundry* and *Stress Away*. Exciting opportunities to be your own boss, to grow your own business right from home. Anne-Marie had signed up with the candles, supplied with enough last-minute Christmas presents for the next decade.

On cue, Missy smiled, bottle rattling in hand. "What if I told you your dream life was only one small down payment away?"

five

There were at least a hundred people that morning, swarming at the junction between 16 and 97, netted under Mr. PeeGee's tall shadow, Canadian flag limp in his saluting hand.

He'd been fashioned from real wood once, back in the fifties, by whichever mill first had the idea to give our town a mascot, but it kept rotting through. Only made to look like wood, his barrel-shaped body was, in fact, a steel septic tank—shellacked a variegated brown.

"Wouldn't be surprised if the shit was still in there," Anne-Marie's husband, Jesse, said, his baritone as anomalous as the first time I'd heard it in middle school.

Working the mill had given him some muscle, but even so, Jesse was slight, his fine-boned face freckled and wan. A loner, he'd always been different—*special*, the other boys would lisp, even though he and Annie had been together since sixth grade. When he cracked the rare, toothy smile, his boyishness gave way to rough-hewn lines, an oyster knife taken to a hunk of tin. A weariness, or maybe wisdom, that was otherwise unapparent, at least at first glance.

It was just the three of us. Missy had a headache, and Sam was at the farm. Had been all week. On Monday, I'd come home to an empty house. The door opened just as I was lifting the lasagna from the oven. Sam with an A&W bag in hand, a spicy chicken sandwich for one. He'd gone to bed before nine P.M., getting an early start. "Good luck," he'd muttered about the search, letting the door slam.

I squinted up at Mr. PeeGee's round head, the log that protruded from his face like Pinocchio, the big dumb eyes shaded beneath the jaunty little cap. His smile felt baleful, considering.

The search extended as far west as the highway—to Vanderhoof, to Burns Lake, to Terrace, all the seven hundred or so clicks to Prince Rupert, land's end. Any place big enough to be called a town.

"She could be anywhere by now." A woman in a black windbreaker embroidered with hot-pink lettering said to no one in particular. *Forty-Eight Racing Team*, the letters read. The man standing next to her nodded his head.

"Between the bears and the cougars, I don't see how there'll be much of her left."

"At least we'll know what happened," another man replied. "Catch the bastard who did it." The first man nodded again.

I adjusted my backpack. It hadn't dawned on me until then. What it was we were really looking for. Not a girl—but a body. A clump of hair, a mud-spattered sock. A hastily covered ditch. Evidence. The sleeve of Double Stuf Oreos I'd packed for a picnic suddenly seemed in poor taste.

They split us into groups, each assigned a resource road to plumb. We'd been lumped with a middle-aged couple from Vancouver and their teenage son and directed to RR7. All the resource roads were unpaved, rutted channels diverging from the broad expanse of the highway, none any wider than a parking space. We took separate cars, the family in their '02 Jeep Cherokee at the head, parking single file on the RR's incline.

"It's just awful what happened," the woman said, tightening her hiking boots.

"Awful." The man shook his head in agreement. Their son lifted his sweatshirt's hood over his head, fiddling with the volume on his Discman.

The family had heard about the search party on the news. They'd never been so far north before. Figured it'd be an adventure. The nine-hour drive, the woman kept repeating, had been absolutely stunning. *Stunning*, she'd practically sing.

In one day, they'd seen more of BC than I had in twenty-four years. A cactus flower, the northern lights, a speck of a woman beside a mammoth tree—the postcards Erin sent the closest I'd ever gotten to the patchwork landscapes of our province.

"When we first heard the story, we knew we had to do something," the woman said, giddy. There was a straw attached to her tiny pack, and between every sentence, she'd suck on it. The man had already taken off, was marching far ahead.

"We think about if we had a daughter, how we'd feel."

They were both dressed in gear, high-performance material, pants that zipped to shorts, moisture-wicking technology. Walking with them, I almost felt like we were hiking: the sun-warmed path, the sweet, pine-imbued air. For a moment, I forgot what it was we were doing there.

"What's this?"

The woman crouched, her blonde braid brushing her ass, small and hard as a nut. She must have been Mom's age, but she was in better shape than me. She pointed to an object no larger than a penny. It was caked in dirt, but it looked like it'd been white once.

"Looks like a tooth," Anne-Marie said, one hand shielding her eyes, the other buttressing her belly.

"Don't pick it up," the man shouted, jogging over. "We don't want to tamper with the evidence."

The light refracted, and I remembered. We weren't out on some trail. We were looking for human remains. Beth. Or what was left of her. And we'd found something. I felt faint. What could have happened to oust a tooth? She must have fought back. I swallowed, throat cotton. Her last breaths might have been taken right here, the pines the only witnesses to her futile screams.

RR7 wasn't but ten clicks west of town. Her killer could easily be from PG. The man in the pickup stopped at the light, the one sipping coffee at the counter. A worker at one of the mills, someone Jesse knew. I squinted over as he fiddled with his lighter. Someone I knew. The smell of smoke, the taste of fire. I'd never drunk anything hard like whiskey before, the tube top so flimsy, it'd ripped right in half. My breath thinned, and I had to steady myself on a branch.

"It's a dog's tooth." Jesse pawed it into the light with the toe of his skate shoe, puffing handless on his cigarette. He lifted the tooth up, its tip narrowing to a curved point like a sickle. "See how pointy the end is?"

Anne-Marie sidled over, squeezing my shoulder. "You okay?" she whispered. I nodded my head. I'd never told her. I'd never told anyone, but Annie had always had a sixth sense.

"I still think we should take it in," the woman cautioned, standing back up. "Just in case."

"Definitely." Her husband nodded, hands on his hips, the authority. Their son was kicking a hole into the earth, death metal clanging from his headphones.

Jesse went quiet, shaking another cigarette from his pack. The man was already scooping the tooth into a freezer bag with a trowel. They really had come prepared.

"Your call." Jesse shrugged, walking to the edge of the road, taking a seat on the stack of lumber that was waiting to be hauled out.

"They said to bring forth any evidence ASAP," the man said. "Back to the cars?" He'd directed the question at me, a hand in his pocket, jingle of his keys. My Buick was blocking their Jeep in. I felt Anne-Marie squeeze again.

"Sure," I croaked. I was still feeling queasy. As soon as I'd replied, the man had taken off in a near sprint, freezer bag wagging in hand.

"Just as well," Jesse muttered as we lagged behind them. "It's been, what, a month? Was probably the most interesting thing we'd have found."

Thankfully, I remember thinking. I wouldn't have been able to stomach much else.

We were all at our cars when the woman approached us, asking for dinner recommendations.

"There's the Indian we had the other day," Anne-Marie suggested. The woman wrinkled her nose.

"Isn't there something more local? You know, homey?"

"Like where you'd go." The man's hand was back in his pocket, impatient jingle.

I could tell what they were after. The far Northern experience, Quaintsville, BC. Checkered tablecloths and lacy curtains and waitresses who knew every customer by name—topping off coffee, serving up pie, the berries picked right out back. Millworkers and cowboys and the town beauty queen tucking into plates of grandma's meat loaf and gravy, root beer floats capped with hand-whipped cream from the farm. A PG that hadn't existed in decades, if ever.

The North, to them, a place wild and pure, unadulterated as a salmonberry. I could see it already, the surprise on their faces, like Michael at our wedding when he learned of Sam's plans. As if the coking coal used to fuel steel plants was mined not by his fellow Canadian citizens but forest gnomes. Tumbler Ridge, where the Murray River mines were located, was a town born of industry. Not unlike PG.

"There's a Denny's," I said, opening my car door.

There were other places, of course, but Denny's was by far the most popular, where most of us *locals* went. Food was consistent, plus it stayed open late. If she really wanted the PG experience, that was it.

"A Denny's." The woman didn't hide her disappointment.

A horn blared, her son's face at the window. She regained her composure.

"Hey, look at us." She did a little jig. "We did it!" I felt her palm slap against mine.

Sam came home Sunday morning, packing his duffel with his washed jeans and washed shirts and leaving without so much as a glance in my direction, let alone a peck goodbye. Six days later and he was still fuming. A new record.

I wasn't dim. It's not like I couldn't see his side. Sam was the normal one. He just wanted what everyone did. To keep the drive shoveled, the lawn mowed. To drag in the trash bins on time. To leave nothing for the neighbors, or anyone, to comment on. Blinds strung up, the windows spotless.

While he was out busting his ass, I was at home sitting on mine, making a fool of myself, of him, for what? A cup of coffee with the welfare mom? If I wanted attention, there were subtler methods, like lighting my hair on fire, for one.

"Always got to be different," I heard Sam mutter, the door slamming, the stench of tar tingeing the air. He'd left the coffee maker on, had drained the pot into his thermos. Usually, he'd leave a fresh pot waiting for me. It wasn't carelessness, I knew. It was payback. I dug a spoon into the Folgers tin, dust whirring in the air. *There were worse methods*, I remember thinking. When Mom was with André, her split-open lip. Missy and her missing acrylic nails.

The coffee dripped, and I found my eyes lifting toward the window again. It'd been exactly a week since the incident, and I hadn't seen her once, the only sign the spectral glow leaking through the slats of her kitchen's warped blinds.

I'd driven by Tuesday on my way home from work to see if I could catch a glimpse of any life out front. A webbed lawn chair had been splayed under the shade of her mountain ash, a Hula-Hoop forgotten in the grass. Seeing that chair, it got me mad. Like she thought I was the one to be avoided. She hadn't even given me the benefit of the doubt. *Look at her, with her nose in the air,* what Missy had said once after Rachelle had gone back in from her yard. *Thinks she's pretty, living in that squalor. Miss Squaw, Canada.* We'd all laughed. Missy was right. She was haughty. *Forget her,* I remember thinking, and I did. For the rest of that week, at least.

The photomontages, the home movie footage, the teary-eyed interviews with her parents, her sister, her schoolteachers, her friends; every night I buried myself in Beth. In the days leading up to the search, she'd been everywhere. Soon, it really felt like I'd known her for years, as if she'd lived next door, like a childhood friend.

Beth was funny and bright, always smiling, a giver. Always willing to lend a helping hand. She wanted to be a veterinarian. She'd volunteered in Africa. A straight-A student, she'd had so much potential. She was a good girl, the best.

On Saturday evening, they'd made an announcement. The findings from the search were inconclusive.

"We're just getting started," the Royal Canadian Mounted Police officer had said. "We're not losing hope yet."

I poured myself a cup and went into the living room, flicking on the tube to kill time. I picked up the remote, pausing on MuchMusic, Britney Spears's midriff undulating atop a glittering star. I was due to visit Nana that morning. We both were—always did every Sunday Sam was home. He hadn't forgotten. More payback. He knew I hated going alone.

I stopped at the Timmy's, as was tradition, picking up half a dozen jelly doughnuts (Nana's favorite) and two double-doubles, hers extra large. I pulled up to her condo, sliding the key out from under the fake rock and letting myself in.

"Fi?" Nana shouted, her feeble voice barely audible over the blare of the TV.

"It's me," I called back, slipping off my shoes and heading straight toward the den.

I used to visit more, back when she was better, when she still lived west of town. The farmhouse wasn't pretty, but she'd been born there, every nail hammered by my great-grandpa's hands. The 160 acres he'd come over from Scotland to claim at the turn of the century lopped, in Nana's lifetime, to ten.

The Dominion Lands Act, a call to the Scottish, the German, the Welsh—what settled much of the prairies, the great West. For just a ten-dollar administration fee, the Canadian Dream in reach of any able-bodied man who could work a tiller. Those newly Canadian grew what they knew: barley, wheat, oats, each crop flourishing as if by magic, the soil far more amenable than the long-tilled parcels of their homelands. It was the collapse of grain prices following the war that forced my great-grandparents to start divvying up their dreamland.

Anyway, after Nana my great-grandma's body proved uncooperative. She never bore any more children—forget about the boys, with strong hay-pitching forearms, my great-grandpa had been praying for. By the time Nana was grown, my great-grandma had sold almost everything.

In Nana's old age, her inheritance proved to be about nine and a half acres too many. But she was stubborn, and she insisted, and up until the accident, she'd managed. She'd been pruning an apple tree when she lost her balance, the postman arriving to find her flat on the grass.

That was three years ago. The move had aged her at breakneck speed. She'd never been one for frills, but Nana had always been what she called *decent*: the nylon stockings, the white slip, the lipstick that barely added any color to her often-downturned mouth. That morning, she was zipped up in the same housecoat that she'd been wearing the last time I'd seen her, red specks of jelly marring the mustard-hued flowers.

She was tuned into the eleven o'clock news. I took a seat on the sofa beside her recliner, passing her a doughnut and squinting at the small fuzzy screen.

"We're here for our sisters." A squat woman with dark braids flanking her face spoke into the microphone. "All of the women who've been taken, who've been stolen from the Downtown Eastside."

The woman was standing in front of a domed granite building, a mass of brown faces milling behind her, many of them toting signs.

ENUF IS ENUF, Find Our Stolen Sisters, Our Love Shines On. There were pictures pasted on them, some of the girls no older than twelve. *I WANT TO LIVE,* one of the signs read, the letters girly and looping, held up by two tiny hands.

Someone was chanting, someone else beating a drum. A reporter stepped into frame, smoothing back a strand of bottle-blonde hair. "We're here live at Hastings and Main in Downtown Vancouver, the Missing and Murdered Indigenous Women's Annual Memorial March."

Indigenous. A five-dollar word if ever there was one. I'd never heard it used to describe them. I knew it from Erin, a way to categorize plants. What was local to a place versus what was non-native. You could forget, sometimes, the meaning of that word. *Native.* They were here first—like the cow parsnip, the fireweed. What I'd always been taught to weed out.

Invasive was the antonym. Foreigners to a habitat with a tendency to spread, smothering out all other plant life. Purple loosestrife, which was illegal to sell, a fireweed look-alike. It affected the animals, too—unsuitable for food or shelter or nesting. Giant knotweed, a ground cover called creeping Jenny. My cheeks burned, seeing from that perspective.

Nana picked up the remote, changing the channel. "They'll call anything news today." She blew at her coffee, wobbling her head.

We watched the end of an episode of *Columbo* together, the police commissioner providing an alibi for a friend who'd strangled his wife in exchange for help offing his own.

"I just can't find him handsome," Nana was saying between sips. "He reminds me too much of Bobby." She thought I was someone else again. Those days, most of our conversations went like that, with her absent, lost in the mist of her own memories.

"Who?" I asked. Nana adjusted the frames of her bifocals.

"Robert, Fi."

"It's Jenny, Nana." She didn't seem to hear me, her bifocals turned to the screen again.

Watching her body falter had been hard, but the decline of her mind was heart-wrenching. Nana had always been sharp, no-nonsense: nothing if not efficient. She'd had to be. My grandpa died young, when Mom and Erin were small—an accident at the mill that had cost him an arm and, swiftly after, his sobriety. Disability checks dissolving like Alka-Seltzer up until the day his Chevy careened from the bridge, landing facedown in the Fraser. His blood alcohol level a full one percent, the worn story went, Mom's smirk an inversion of Erin's expression. How Nana would summarize, what Mom took to repeating, *was just as well*. He wasn't a husband or father at that point—but just another dependent.

By all accounts, Nana never missed a beat. She'd tended to her daughters (and later, to me) like she'd tended to the tomatoes that'd once been staked tall in her garden. Not with cuddles, or trinkets, or whimsy, but with plain, effective care.

"There's no man worth crying over," she'd reiterate the countless times Mom would call her, the receiver slick. It was the same adage she repeated anytime I dared to bring up my dad. Her own father had left before Nana was ten. I came from a long line of disappearing men.

Nana started snoring, the doughnut untouched in her mitt-sized hands. The same as the two folded in my lap. We looked alike, everyone said. Sturdy women, built to grip a plow. Seeing her there, her size-ten orthopedics elevated in her recliner, spittle gathered at her lips, I couldn't help but see myself fifty years down the line. The view wasn't exactly heartening.

I came home to the flicker of the answering machine. It was Mom, needing a sitter for Wednesday. I was free, wasn't I? Yep. I reached for the remote. Chronically.

The same *Crimestoppers* segment was on. By then, I'd seen it at least fifty times. "Do you know what happened to Beth Tremblay?" I mouthed along, biting into my second doughnut, the jelly landing at the crest of my sports bra.

I clicked off the TV, standing. At least Nana had had seventysome good years. Here I was at twenty-four, caught in the same loop, each day melded into the next.

I looked out the window, willing something to happen. With the blinds drawn down, Rachelle's house looked almost vacant. As if she, too, had disappeared. It felt worse than just lonesome; I'd been banished.

Women go missing every day, she'd said matter-of-factly. I thought of Erin down in Vancouver, once my aunt, now Michael's wife. Mrs.

Lavoie. How fragile they were, relationships between women. Was that all she'd meant?

The back door opened, and I felt feverish, dizzy. It was Rachelle's daughter, the older one, in a yellow bathing suit and pigtails, tiptoeing through the maze of appliances. Alone. Before I knew it, she was gone again, the pair of pink-wheeled Rollerblades that'd been strung over her elbow clacking as the back door closed. For a moment, I could've sworn I saw her peeking through the blinds. Slats upheld by a pair of tiny brown hands.

I WANT TO LIVE. I thought of the news segment. There were dozens of faces on those signs, some as young as Rachelle's eldest—daughters of the women who'd gone missing, no doubt. Enough of them to merit an annual march. A byword for 16. They couldn't all be hookers. That must have been what Rachelle was talking about.

Someone out there was targeting women like her. Like the fireweed, someone was mowing them down.

And now they were broadening their range. To girls like Beth, the dots were connecting. Dozens of faces. What made us all think this had been a one-off? *Women go missing every day.* The more I replayed our conversation, the more it sounded like Rachelle knew something. Or someone. *If you have any information that can help solve this case,* the *Crimestoppers* anthem resounded.

I marched into the kitchen and rummaged through the cabinet, energized. I ripped open a box of brownie mix and switched on the oven. I had to go back there to find out what she knew. I broke an egg against the bowl, whisking it into the batter. Until they caught who was behind this, no one was safe. Not Anne-Marie, not Missy, not Mom. Not me. Even Sam would have to understand.

Rachelle might be the key to crack the case wide open. Together, we might be the ones to solve what had happened to Beth. I had to go back there. I didn't have a choice. I lifted the pan and felt the sting of the oven.

It wasn't the first lie I told myself.

SIX

I stood at Rachelle's doorstep, an old sundress from Missy fluttering at my knees, tinfoil-sheathed Pyrex balanced in one hand. I knocked. No answer. I knocked a little harder, pressing my ear against flaking paint. Dead silence. It was ten A.M. on a Monday. She had to be home. Where else would she be?

"Rachelle," I called out, knocking again. I heard someone cough.

"Rachelle," I insisted, my voice growing louder, dogged. I lived right across from her. I'd brought brownies. She couldn't just ignore me forever. "Rachelle!" At that point, I was practically shouting.

The door cracked open, a sliver of face. "Are you nuts?" Rachelle whispered, her tone snippy, terse. "I just got Beth down."

"Shit," I blurted, still too loud. Less than a minute in and I was already floundering. "Sorry." I lowered my volume, composing myself. "I just wanted to come by and check in."

"'Check in,'" she repeated, dry as bread. A puff of smoke blew past the door, acrid tang swimming into my mouth. I stepped back.

"I brought these." I thrust out the Pyrex. The door didn't budge. The pan so tightly wrapped that, in her eyes, I realized, I could have been handing her anything: Nanaimo bars, meat loaf, Spackle. "They're brownies," I clarified. One dark eye stared back.

I cleared my throat. The chances of the door opening were dwindling every second. I was desperate, though at the time, I couldn't pinpoint why. Maybe it was premonition. I only knew that I needed to find something—anything—to keep that door cracked.

"I'm taking care of my mom's kids on Wednesday." I tucked the Pyrex back under an arm. "Well, her boyfriend's kids. Was thinking we could have a playdate."

"A playdate." I could hardly believe the words myself.

"Maybe plant those radishes?" Apparently, I was trying everything. She responded with another gust of smoke. I could only make out the one, but I could feel both her eyes hot upon me. I turned, evading them. It wasn't like Rachelle was new to town. She'd been handed the same user's manual—the well-oiled machine, *us v. them*. If our roles were reversed, would she have acted any different?

If our roles were reversed, would I have?

I'd been hoping she would just breeze past it, interpret the brownies for what they meant, but that wasn't fair. I knew what I owed her, but the words were refusing to leave my mouth.

"Look, can we talk?" I stepped back toward the door.

"I'm busy." She started to close it.

Without thinking, my arm flung itself up and out, wedging the door open, hand knocking into hers, the red-burning tip of her du Maurier. The brownies dropped to the ground.

"Fuck." I retracted my arm, shaking my hand in the air. What was I doing? She was right. I was nuts. The Pyrex had split into two even pieces, the foil undisturbed, as if someone had placed it there intentionally to cover the splatter.

"Christ, Jenny." She swung open the door. "Five minutes, okay?" She mashed the cigarette against the jamb. "You can run that burn under some water."

I stood hovering over the tower of dishes in her kitchen sink, babbling over the rushing sound.

"I feel terrible," I said, and I meant it. "I didn't have time to tell Sam I'd been over. He'd just gotten home from the mines." Her back was toward me; she was pouring two cups of coffee, hospitable in spite of everything. "You know what it's like."

"Yeah?" She stopped midpour, turning. "How's that?"

"Just." My face went pink. How could I put it? "The way men get. They need to know everything. And they say we're nosy." I forced a laugh.

"Hm." She took a seat at the table, fishing out another du Maurier from her pack. Her head had turned away from me again.

It wasn't supposed to go like this. I'd meant to row us out of the shit, but instead, I'd lost both paddles. If the roles were reversed . . . But they weren't. I'd only ever heard what the neighbors all said. She'd been on the receiving end.

"I'm sorry." It's what I should've opened with. "Really, I am."

She was leafing through an old copy of the Bargain Finder. She didn't look up. "Your coffee's going to get cold." She nodded toward the seat next to her. "Let's take a look at the damage."

I turned off the tap, patting my hand against a nubby tea towel, a snowy white perched on an evergreen branch. Her cigarette had dragged down the pinky-side of my hand, and the burn was lopsided, a backward, elongated *C*, one half of a heart. I sat beside her, holding out my hand. To my surprise, she grabbed it.

"Doesn't look too bad." She guided my hand into the light, and I went still, quieting my breath, minimizing myself as if a hummingbird had landed near, like when Kayden would start playing with my hair. It felt special, that moment. I didn't want it to end. "You should put some butter on it later. It'll help." Before she let go, she patted my hand.

"Okay." I sipped my coffee. *World's Greatest Mom*, a teddy bear in a floral sundress not unlike the one I was wearing was propping up the letters with a paw. She'd given me the same mug the last time. My mug here. I stifled a grin.

The phone rang, rattling against the kitchen wall. They didn't even make phones like that anymore, ones where you were tethered to the receiver, with dials that required a full finger swoop. Even Nana had a cordless. Wouldn't be long, I couldn't help but think, before this made its appearance among the other relics in Rachelle's yard. *Shut up, Jenny*, I scolded myself. Rachelle stood, picking the phone up.

"Hello?" She stood with her back against the wall, twisting the cord around a finger, just as I'd watched her do countless times before from afar. My ears perked up. So this was the mystery caller. I leaned forward in my chair, trying not to be too obvious. Five minutes in and I'd already forgotten all about Beth.

"Shit," Rachelle was saying. "Where is she?" She stepped over and opened a drawer, her voice taut as the phone's cord. "Can you keep her there a couple hours? I got to find someone to watch the kids." She pulled out a legal pad and flipped through its pages. "Okay. Yeah. Two hours, tops." She clacked the phone down.

"Sorry." She turned toward me, elsewhere. "I've got to figure this out."

"Everything okay?"

"It's nothing," she said, eyes starting to drip. She looked as if she'd swallowed a dart. "My sister. She's in Vanderhoof. I need to call someone for the kids." She picked up the receiver and started the roundabout process of dialing.

"I'm free all day." This was it, the opening. "I could watch them." A way to show her that I wasn't that person who'd snubbed her, that I was different. Better.

"I couldn't ask that." Her head was shaking, but the dialing had stopped. She was considering it.

"I'm already here," I chirped, my voice syrupy, mawkish. "The sooner you leave, the sooner you'll be back, right? I babysit my mom's boyfriend's kids all the time. I'm practically a professional." I chuckled. I was trying too hard, but Rachelle was too distracted to care.

"Okay." She was nodding. "Okay. If I leave now, I should be back after lunch." She set the receiver back down. "You mind staying here? There's plenty of food. Might be easier for the girls."

"Not at all," I answered, genuine. That time, I didn't have to hide it. My big, idiot grin.

I followed Rachelle to the girls' room, tiptoeing behind as she navigated their floor.

"Girls, Mama's going to Auntie's for a bit." Little Beth was propped up in her older sister's arms, a book spread out in front of them on her narrow bed.

"You remember our neighbor Jenny?" I lifted a hand. "She's going to stay with you, okay?"

"Okay," the older girl said, her eyes on her mother's, turning a page. Her baby sister started to squirm. "Shhh," she whispered, her voice raspy. "Mama'll be back."

"You're my big girl." Rachelle bent over, planting kisses on the tops of both of their heads. "Be back soon." She gave her eldest one final squeeze.

"Thanks again." She leaned in toward me. "They're easy. You'll see." She blew them a kiss before rushing out their door.

"Hi." I inched closer. "I'm Jenny." The older girl looked up at me, unimpressed. Little Beth was attempting to worm her way off the side of the bed.

"What's your name?" I squatted down.

"Destiny," she said, wrangling her sister.

"Destiny. How pretty." Destiny bunched up her mouth, thumping a foot against the bed.

"This is Beth." She smoothed back her sister's black hair. "You like dogs?" She picked up a tattered stuffed animal that was lodged under a pillow, presenting it to me. I nodded, making him dance. Destiny grinned, tongue poking through the gaps left by her two missing front teeth.

I went to sit, and a Barbie doll's arm stabbed me in my rear end. Their room really was a sight. Somehow Destiny seemed to know where everything was, a sense of order in the chaos. It must have been like that for a while. She switched on the TV. An old episode of *Road to Avonlea* was on, fair-haired girls in prairie dresses bickering in the reeds.

There was a laundry bin in the corner, the same bloodless color as a dish rack, all those household items that weren't supposed to draw attention—a toilet brush, a mop—like the chores themselves. Someone had taken a few fistfuls of the mess from the floor and dumped them inside it. A pair of goggles and a half-dressed doll were interspersed with the leggings, the T-shirts, the onesies. I tilted the bin upside down and started to pile all the clothes I spotted inside. If our house plans matched exactly, Rachelle would have a washer-dryer unit in the basement. It wasn't much, but it was a start. The girls were glued to the tube anyway.

I went into the kitchen to start lunch, swinging open the fridge and scanning. Two-percent milk, two cartons of eggs, I Can't Believe It's Not Butter, half a loaf of Wonder Bread. A jar of mustard, a lone pickle in its foggy brine, ketchup packets from A&W seeded across the plastic egg tray. A head of iceberg lettuce rolling around the crisper, a few shrunken apples pocked brown.

There had to be more. I opened the freezer. Bingo. Swanson Dinners, ground pork, bags of frozen peas and corn and carrots. Lean Pockets, Tater Tots, fish sticks, a whole honey-baked ham. Everyone was a freezer person come winter. Some people kept the habit year-round. I popped open a bag of sliced carrots, orange pucks clanging like hail as I emptied them over a pot. I was whisking together three eggs when Destiny appeared, her head peeking around the kitchen door, Little Beth crawling beside.

"Where's your son?"

"Who?" I scraped the eggs from the top of the pan toward the bottom, marbled froth firming up nicely. "Oh, Kyle." I turned off the heat. "He's not mine."

"Who's his mama?" She hadn't moved from the doorway, was standing there fidgeting with the hem of her nightgown, Barbie with her Dreamhouse splashed across it.

"His daddy's my mom's boyfriend." I opened a cabinet, looking for the plates.

"Next one over." She pointed to my left. "I can help if you want." I lifted two out, turning back toward her.

"Almost ready." I was mashing the carrots with the tines of a fork, the way Erin used to do when she'd watch me. "Just come here and wash up." Saying those words, I felt Erin with me. Like I was a real fake mother.

Rachelle hadn't been lying; the girls really were easy—Destiny so thoughtful, playing mama to her sister, making sure Beth was eating before she even looked at her own lunch.

I took them outside, out of sight in the shade behind the pickup, fencing Beth in between my crossed legs, Destiny in a pair of jammed-on runners, attempting handstands over the dandelion stalks. Back in May, there'd been yellow: the fluff carried by the wind, spiking sales of Weed B Gon for at least a few houses down. By September, the fireweed would shoot straight past Rachelle's head.

Her garden was there, right beside us, fallow, technically speaking, and, at the same time, teeming with life. Sorrel, plantain, shepherd's purse, thistle. What hadn't been planted but was there all the same, stretching toward the light.

Hemostyptic. I still remembered the word Erin had used, plucking a spindly stalk of shepherd's purse from her yard, seeds flickering like a dozen tiny hearts. It stopped bleeding, she'd learned from one of her textbooks. The course in ethnobotany had been among her favorites. *The difference between a plant and a weed,* she'd recited, *all depends on your perspective.*

I hoisted Beth up and padded over, snapping off a stalk and twirling it in the sun. I eyed the garden. I'd need to bring over my spade if there was any hope for those radishes.

The phone rang around three. She was going to be late, Rachelle apologized, voice spent as if she'd been talking—or shouting, or crying—for hours.

"I can call someone if you need to go." She sounded close to crying again.

"No rush," I told her. "Take your time."

There was still a load of clothes knocking around the dryer, and I'd just started stacking the girls' books in a corner I'd cleared. Destiny had been helping. It was like a game, a scavenger hunt. All she needed to organize the girls' room was a few more bins, maybe a shelf. I could bring a bin over with the radish seeds. Maybe a bigger pair of runners for Destiny.

"I'm just happy to make some use of myself," I said. "Sam left yesterday morning. I'm not in a rush."

"That right?" she said. My ears burned. I hadn't needed to tell her. She'd been handed the same user's manual. On the receiving end.

"I appreciate it." She changed course. "I put Beth down at eight. Destiny can stay up a bit later. She's old enough now, she'll tell you." She paused, clearing her throat. "Sorry again. This hasn't happened in a while."

She spoke as if I knew what *this* meant. I didn't, but I could guess. We all knew what became of the girls reared in foster homes. It'd been the subject of the latest episode of *Dateline*. It made Rachelle even more exceptional—to think of all she'd maneuvered past. Her sister hadn't been as lucky. Maybe her sister had never found her own Al.

"What's for dinner?" Destiny's garbled voice brought me back to where my feet were planted. *Breakfast All Day*. I'd let her choose, poking holes in the plastic before wedging the trays into the microwave. Sausages the size of cocktail wieners, three mini-pancakes, maple syrup product that was microwavable, too. I ate what the girls didn't finish. I changed Beth's diaper and snapped up her footie pajamas, lifting her into my arms and swaying the way I'd seen Rachelle move. I even tried an imitation of her song but felt stupid and settled on Tom Petty.

Destiny had already nestled herself in, was flipping through the pages of an outsized book when I finally set a sleeping Beth down and picked up the girls' hairbrush. The book was a picture version of *Anne of Green Gables*, the page turned to Anne's first day at the farm. On the cover was a close-up of Anne, a smiling portrait that reminded me of someone. Beth, I realized: the sweetly upturned nose, the eyes wide and innocent as a doe's.

"I wish I had freckles like Anne." Destiny set the book down on her lap and burrowed her face into a pillow. "And light hair like you." My heart thumped. Was this what it'd be like? I moved a brush through her inky hair, smoothing my work with a hand.

I'd shoved what laundry I didn't get to from one end of the couch to the other and was half dozing, half watching a rerun of *Jeopardy!* when Rachelle opened the front door. I glanced over at the numbers on the VCR. Ten forty.

"I'm so sorry," she said breathlessly before even stepping foot on the carpet. She slid off her sneakers in two seamless motions and started toward me. "I owe you one." Her face was wan, swollen under the eyes. I could see it'd been a long day.

"It's not a big deal."

She nodded, collapsing onto the couch beside me, right on top of a pile of jeans. It really wasn't. I hadn't even noticed it'd gotten so late until I'd heard the door. Maybe it was just that our floor plans were identical, all that familiar emerald green, but I'd felt at home almost immediately, as if I was slumped on my own couch, beside my own cluttered coffee table, as if I'd just tucked in my own two daughters and flicked on my own TV, spent. Or maybe it was all that looking in. I'd watched this exact day play out.

"It was fun," I said, looking over at her. She hadn't budged since she'd flopped down. "Your girls are sweet." She was quiet. Was she sleeping? I stood, looking for my things before remembering that I'd come with nothing, just a now-shattered Pyrex. I started toward the door.

"Let's do that thing you were talking about. The, uh . . ." She trailed off, her body in the same slack position, her eyes still closed.

"The playdate?" I had my hand on the doorknob. She hadn't checked in on the girls, hadn't seen the dent I'd made in the mess.

"Yeah, the playdate." She turned her head toward me. "Wednesday, right?"

I nodded. She hiked up her thumb. Her eyes had closed again.

"Sounds like a plan," she managed to say, her voice drifting away from her like smoke.

seven

Her blinds were up again that next morning, welcoming in morning light, spiny needles of rangy pine, and me in one of Sam's fraying flannels and bare feet. I'd been forgiven. I flipped on the coffee maker. I couldn't help but beam.

Rachelle was stooped over her stovetop, her back toward me, pot of eggs gurgling on the burner, sweatshirt pushed to her elbows, makeshift puffed sleeves. I turned to take the milk from the fridge, topping off my coffee, and when I looked back, I could've sworn I saw her head whip around. It was further confirmation of what I'd felt since the day she stepped into my garden. Mug of coffee, fried egg and toast, red-checkered flannel, freshly combed hair: she'd been taking note, too, the light from my side just as magnetic.

I went out to take the washing down. The sheets were still cool from the night, crisped up in the strong morning sun. It rose at five come late July and didn't quit until after ten. I'd stashed my yard shoes in the hall closet, the grass plush beneath my feet.

I guided the ends of a sheet together, piling it into the basket, clothespins fastened to the hem of my shirt. Rachelle came out, thump of carton against palm. She waved. I waved back.

"Still on for tomorrow?" she asked.

"You bet." I unpinned a pillowcase, shaking it out in the air. She smiled, the other hand raking her long hair back. I smiled, near delirious—the ease of it all intoxicating. It was as if I'd never fumbled, as if we were more than just neighbors. *Friends.*

I propped the basket against my hip and started back toward the house. I didn't know what would happen when Sam came back, but in that moment, I didn't care. I was back in. For the next couple weeks, that was all that mattered.

I had the morning shift. I wasn't looking forward to it. The mall had been dead since Canada Day. When you bear the weight of an eight-month-long winter, you make the most of your summer, Sears be damned. There was the occasional breeze of preteens or grandmas maundering the length of the concourse, the grannies on their motorized carts, the teens with their hands jammed in their pockets (or the pocket of someone else, depending), none with any cash to spend.

The competition didn't help. The store that'd been under construction for the better part of that year had recently opened smack across the concourse, a clone, but better, newer, with the same foot creams and body sprays lining their shelves. Only the names were different. Our *Spring Drizzle* was their *April Showers*. *Fresh-Cut Grass* became *Freshly Mowed Lawn*. With some, all they'd done was switch the words around. *Watermelon Mint, Mint Watermelon*. It didn't seem legal or fair.

Our bath bombs were wrapped in cellophane; theirs were piled lose as apples in shallow wicker bins. Our bottles of shower gel were an ivory plastic; theirs were see-through, the rainbow contents—insulation pink, glitter-flecked green—mouthwatering, like frosting on a spongy cake. Their prices were cheaper, too. Otherwise, it was as if they'd erected a mirror that spanned the length of our store. There was even an employee who looked like me. No tits, the same slouching frame, the same empty, outsized hands. Her hair was darker, but it was twisted in a low bun just like mine.

In the whole four hours, I had made only one sale. A man, Mom's age or so, with a prewrapped gift basket under one arm and a tube of body glitter in hand. Obviously he was shopping for someone else. His wife, maybe. Or daughter. I couldn't stop watching him. He was tall, and his hair, although short, was dark. Tar black.

It was knee-jerk, as involuntary as a heartbeat. When he handed me his credit card, it took me everything to keep from blurting it out, the word less a coherent thought than an impulse, a tic. *Dad?*

I'd never outgrown it. I wasn't looking exactly, but I was never not looking either. *We're better off*, Mom's remorseless refrain. It had to have been her, what pushed him away. Sometimes, after she'd really blow up, I'd dig at it, the wound that refused to scab. The image of him swooping in as if winged. *You can't keep me from her any longer*, he'd say. I dug at the wound in other ways, let it fester, *was just as well.* The chair beside Mom either empty or filled—not with a father figure but a foul smell.

He was American, Mom had revealed back in middle school the first time I convinced myself I saw him. Sitting in front of us in the bleachers at the hockey game, the sheath of dark hair. A cowboy, I'd imagine later. Bruce Springsteen with long hair. My dad was from Washington, Mom had relented, or North Dakota, or Montana, or one of those other roomy border states. The point being that he'd left and was far, far away. *End of story.* But Mom's stories had always been changeable as the clouds. For all I knew, my father might still live in town.

I handed the man back his credit card and found my hands trembling. His eyes lifted. My heart sank. They were blue—startlingly so, like Windex. Stupid as it was, it still hurt. For a moment, I could see him, the type of father to not only remember a birthday but deliberate over which scent suited his daughter best. For a moment, he was real, not just another invention. It was why it was better. *Was just as well.* If I let myself care, it was like I kept losing him. Over and over and over again.

Sam needed a few shirts for work, so I stopped at Value Village on my way home. He wore through his clothes quicker than anyone, more so since starting at the mines. The work was so physical. He blasted through any repairs.

Sam never bought much new. Neither did I. Underwear and bras, a bathing suit come summer, socks, flip-flops—what wouldn't be hygienic used. Most of what I owned had been handed down from friends. Even Mom would come over with a pile, most of which was passed on a second time. She was a whole two sizes smaller on bottom, and I wasn't exactly a skintight and bedazzled girl on top.

Not to say I was fussy. In my head I dressed differently, deliberately—eyelet blouses, brushed suede, a page ripped right from the Gap catalogue. But the reality was that my style would have best been described as miscellaneous, my closet an inventory of what other people liked. So much so that even when I was given something new, it was never anything I would have picked myself. Like the coat Sam had wrapped up one Christmas, yellow as an Easter egg and puffy as a pack of hot dogs. It even squeaked when I walked. I remembered how Missy had smirked when I'd first worn it. *What, you lose a bet?*

I pushed against the revolving door, stepping out under the glare of the fluorescents. I coughed, picking up a shopping basket. The stench still surprised me. It wasn't as noticeable at home, but there, with all of Prince George's discards stockpiled, aisle after aisle, the dank was concentrated, like riding with a smoker in winter or putting a lid on a sputtering pot.

I found a few shirts in Sam's size, quilted flannel, in near new condition. Days were hot, but nights up at Tumbler Ridge dropped way down, and it wasn't like camp was heated. The men found other ways to stay warm: the illegal fires they'd build in the bed of someone's truck, the handles of whatever booze was cheapest, also illegal, as camp was— or at least was supposed to be—dry.

The jewelry section was against the wall near the registers. Most of it junk: tin claddagh rings and rhinestoned brooches staked to pegboard in those little sandwich baggies. A hemp bracelet, clip-on studs, a mood ring stuck on murky blue. A pendant missing its chain, a puffy pink enameled cross. I thought of the glint below Rachelle's neck, the silver rings flashing from her fingers. She wore earrings, too, a pair of dainty gold hoops. Too delicate to have seen at a distance, what I'd only noticed that first time in her yard.

I picked up a bag and opened it. Earrings, not dissimilar to Rachelle's. I fished them out onto my palm, scratching at the surface with a thumbnail. Not painted. No greenish tinge. They were gold. Real. I never wore much jewelry—just my wedding band—but it's not like I was immune to the appeal. I looked at the stickered price tag. 12.99. Two steaks. I hung them back up. Where would I even wear them?

The key was already in the ignition when I tugged it out, jogged back in. I pulled down the sun visor, flipped open the mirror. It took some finessing, but then they slid right in, glimmering as I turned my head. I smiled, raking my hair back.

I took the long way home, turning onto Rachelle's street to loop around back to mine. The lawn chair was gone, I couldn't help but notice—but there was something else. A white pickup was parked in her drive.

I eased off the gas, idling. The body was as pitted as a shooting target, its fender unhinged, nearly off. *Wild Rose Country.* Alberta plates. All the front blinds were lowered.

I raced home, hoping to catch a glimpse of something. I switched on a burner, sliding some butter into a pan. I'd gotten a slice of pizza at the food court earlier, but while I was walking back to the store, it'd slid off my plate and landed on my Keds. I was starved. I shook two slices of bread from the bag, peeling plastic film from the Kraft singles. Her living room and kitchen were empty. Whoever was visiting, they were in her bedroom. That truck could only belong to a man.

I cracked open a Coke. I felt queasy, and it wasn't just on account of having missed lunch. Maybe it wasn't even the truck, I remember convincing myself. Something new was happening, finally, and I'd been shut out. Maybe it was just that.

Why didn't I trust that sinking feeling? Why didn't I trust the urge to act? Ask for some sugar, an egg, batteries, anything. Intervene, be the tree felled in the tracks.

Instead, I just stood there, flipping my grilled cheese, watching the butter sparkle and crack.

When I came out of the shower, it was dark. I looked out the window and realized: someone had yanked the blinds down again.

Her house was still shuttered when I woke the next morning. Whoever was there had spent the night. It was Wednesday, the day of our play-date. Maybe I'd even meet him. This mystery man. I went into the washroom to brush my teeth, assessing my reflection in the mirror. Wasn't a beautiful face, but wasn't completely hopeless either. I dug in a pouch for some eyeliner, screwing in the gold hoops.

Mom was late dropping off the kids, forgoing the doorbell for her horn—three consecutive shrill bleats, as if she'd roped a goat in my drive.

I stepped outside and was greeted by the lime-green lace of her thong, one pale foot slipping from its platform flip-flop. Her hair had been banded at the top of her head, nub bobbing as she wrestled Dawn out of her car seat. "Fuck," I heard her mutter. I checked her arms.

Sure enough, it was there, adhered to her bicep, the flesh-colored patch that'd appear every couple of months, never lasting longer than a workweek. The explanation for the unwashed hair, the flip-flops, the frustration. The near half hour behind schedule. Mom was usually a stickler for time.

"For Christ's sake, Kyle, would you hurry the hell up and give me a hand?" She gnawed at a strand of red licorice. "You know I don't know how to work this damn thing." She clicked at the car seat buckle. Dawn squirmed, kicking her legs. "Fuckin' hell."

It always went like that when she gave up smoking, as if the cigarettes were like a pressure valve.

"Kyle!" Her voice was hoarse, swelling at the second syllable and cracking. She must have been going all morning. Kyle squatted on the seat cushion, facing the plush of the headrest, attempting to untangle his sweatshirt's sleeves from around its raised shafts. Mom marched over to his open door, shoving his hands away.

"I told you not to play with that." She tugged at the sleeves.

I started toward them. "Hi, Mom," I said, her back toward me. She stopped what she was doing, cocking her head.

"Cut the attitude, Jenny." She took a pull from her licorice, chewing aggressively. "I can't with these kids today. I can't."

I looked over at Kyle, his face drained of its color, his eyes damp and red. It was all too familiar. The rage that gutted everything in its path. Missing the bus, spilling juice on a dress, wetting the just-changed bed. I never learned. I never listened. I only existed to make her life hell.

"Let's figure that out later." I crouched down to his level. "Why don't you head on in? There's doughnuts on the counter. Want first pick?" He nodded, jumping up from his seat and practically sprinting toward the house. Mom was still chewing, her arms crossed, flip-flop tapping.

"Bye to you, too!" she called out after him. "So ungrateful. His mom don't teach him nothing, no manners." She took another pull.

I went over to Dawn, leaning over her car seat, keeping my thumb on the buckle as I gently pulled back the belt. It eased right out. "There we go." I lifted her up, her wet cheek against mine.

"Well, ain't you something," Mom said sarcastically, slamming Dawn's door and stomping back to the driver's side. "What." She must have seen my expression. Her eyes darted to mine. Dawn was nestled against me. It wasn't worth it. "Nothing." I said. Mom paused, starting toward me, looking me up and down.

"You know, sweetheart, you should really come in." She'd stopped just an inch or two from my face, was twirling a loose strand of my hair. "Color's dull, ends are fried." Her voice was false, sticky-sweet. I could sense what was coming. "I know money's been tight." There it was, the last word. "Don't worry, I'll give you the family discount." She winked.

"Okay, Mom." I stepped back, biting my tongue. *No winning,* I reminded myself.

"See you at eight." She slammed her door, smearing on lip gloss before wagging her fingers, her car lurching back.

We sat on the couch watching *Care Bears*, Kyle on his second doughnut, Dawn squirming in my lap. I checked the changing numbers on the VCR. Twelve forty-five. Only five minutes had passed since I had last checked.

I was restless. I'd told Rachelle one—an hour after Mom was due—not wanting to take any chances.

I went into the kitchen, poured another cup. Rachelle's blinds were still down. Kyle had left the box of doughnuts open, the granulated sugar glistening in the light. I'd gotten a dozen, enough to share. If I wanted to catch a glimpse of him, the mystery man, maybe showing up early was my best bet.

"Let's go for a walk." I switched off the tube, shooing Kyle from the couch. I helped him lace his shoes, knotted the strings of Dawn's floppy hat.

Dawn charged herself with carrying the Timmy's box while Kyle ambled on up ahead, pausing in front of every other driveway, hands on his knees, inspecting.

The mud-splattered ATVs, the four runners, the dirt bikes, the boat trailers hitched to nothing, the jon boats docked on grass, the pickups with their hoods flung high, orange wires snaking down like spaghetti: all the toys, the fix-up projects that were stashed come winter, rolled out with the dry weather, the twelve hours of good light. The time of year nearly everyone's driveway was full.

Except Rachelle's. Every crack in the faded blacktop in plain view. The white pickup had gone.

"This where your friend lives?" Kyle asked, hiking up his shorts. I nodded, guiding us toward the front door.

I knocked, glancing down. The Pyrex had been swept away, but the brownies had left a stain, a muddy splotch the size of a startled cat. No answer. Her front blinds were drawn, the lights all off. I knocked again, pinning my ear to the door. It was early still. Maybe she'd stepped out.

"You sure this is the right house?" Kyle was already at the end of her drive, feet pointing farther down the road.

"Yep." I took a seat on the step. I was early, but only by ten minutes. It wouldn't be weird to wait, would it? I adjusted the brim of Sam's Canucks hat.

Kyle had found the Hula-Hoop in the grass. Dawn was poking a finger in a Boston cream. Ten minutes came and went. Then another ten. Then another. *Indian time.* I cringed—the popular saying just popped into my head. Mom was late this morning, too, but there wasn't a saying for it. A late Canadian was just that. Not on time.

"Can we go home now?" Kyle crossed his legs and squeezed. "I have to pee."

"Okay." I stood, looking back one last time. Had she forgotten? Lost track of time? Maybe she'd had another emergency. Had gone back to Vanderhoof, brought her girls along. Maybe the pickup had given her a ride.

I caught a glimpse of something, movement, from the corner of my eye. "Just a sec." I handed Kyle the doughnuts, pacing to the side of the house.

The dingy lace of a curtain quivered in the wind. I stood on my tiptoes. The washroom window was ajar. The interior was dim, clouded with the lace, but it wasn't difficult to see in. From the tiles to the toilet, her washroom was done in the same frosty blue as ours was. The seat was up, and I could almost smell the spray that was surely there, splashed around the rim. There were different degrees of consideration men showed in the washroom. That they'd leave the seat up was a given, but some didn't even bother to flush. There was even a phrase for it, what Anne-Marie would gripe about. *Boy smell.* I brought my nails to the back of my neck like a penny to a Scratch 'N' Win. The eczema that waxed and waned come summer was pricking up again.

"Jenny?" Kyle called out, standing behind me. He was turned toward the rosebush, starting to unzip.

"Right here." I dropped to my feet. "Cut it out, Kyle, we're going."

As I ushered them home, I kept finding myself turning my head back. Watching, listening. Waiting. Like I already knew.

Like I was already looking for clues.

eight

Mom arrived at eight on the dot, her mood markedly improved, a caustic cloud of tobacco wafting from her Ford Fiesta.

"Thanks a million." She'd smirked, hurried the kids into the backseat, and put her car in reverse, gone as quickly as she'd came. She was allergic to my place, too.

There'd been no sign of Rachelle all day, at least not from the back. It was déjà vu, the slats of her blinds like poured concrete, sequestering. I'd been shut out again, but this time, I hadn't done anything. This time, it felt different. Alarming.

I was too electric to cook, so I decided to go for a drive and a bacon cheeseburger to check if anything had changed out front. I eased off the gas as I passed her house, its lightlessness salient against the darkening sky. Wherever she'd gone, she was still there, maybe even planning to spend the night.

I sat awash in the sepia blaze of the A&W parking lot, licking sauce from my fingers, dunking onion rings into ketchup. I tore open another packet, spattering grease-rung carton red. My engine was off, but the radio was on, that Sarah McLachan song that always made me cry. I cranked the dial clockwise.

"Building a Mystery." I knew all the words by heart. As I sang, something in me surged, washing up what'd been buried, my eyes starting to leak.

I couldn't shake the feeling that something had happened, the white pickup a harbinger, the hairs on the backs of my arms shooting up as soon as it'd come into view. Something was off. Rachelle never left home—not for that long, anyway. And why had she drawn down the blinds? How come I'd never seen it before, the white pickup? Even if Rachelle had received another call from her sister, we had plans. She would've at least thought to leave a note. Right?

Maybe. Maybe not. I'd only ever been over there twice. I wiped the wet from my eyes. The truth was I didn't know her that well.

All my worrying was conjecture, really, the sum of the limbo I was fixed within—we were all fixed within that summer, the summer of Beth. *Missing*, the very word incomplete, imbued with the anticipation of its opposite. There was no missing if there was no looking, no waiting to find or be found.

As long as Beth waited, we waited, too, pushing away the possibility that someone like her could meet a fate like, well, like what we all imagined. Every inconsistency we came across incriminating, suggestive of something dark, dire.

I was rattling my root beer, rooting straw around crushed ice for those last watery sips, guiding the wheel with the tops of my knees when I saw a car in Rachelle's driveway, high beams flooding her door. I sighed, relieved. There she was, safe and sound. I knew I'd been getting ahead of myself. *Something came up*, she'd apologize from across the yards. We'd talk over coffee and day-old doughnuts. I'd forgive her instantly. We'd make new plans.

As I drove closer, I realized—that wasn't her car. She drove Al's old Fleetwood. This was a Dodge, a minivan. Whoever was at her front door, it wasn't Rachelle. I killed my lights and cranked the passenger-seat window down.

"Hello!" a woman's voice called out, knuckles rapping against the door. "Mrs. Murphy!" I shifted to park, climbed out. "Mrs. Murphy!"

"Hey, there." I'd meant to sound sunny, disarming in my approach, but my words arrived in two croaks. The woman jumped. I cleared my throat. "Sorry to startle you." I pocketed my keys.

"Are you Rachelle Murphy?"

The woman was older, in her late sixties at least, her perm an ashen halo under the van's unforgiving glare. Her blouse was tucked into a pair of pressed slacks, bulges from her compression stockings erupting between her ankle and the lips of her shoes—those colorless moccasins made for the elderly.

I lifted a hand self-consciously to my ears, the hoops I'd bought still threaded through my lobes. Rachelle must have been wearing the same ones that morning. I couldn't help, for the smallest moment, but feel flattered. Rachelle was probably about fifteen pounds lighter and beautiful, as I mentioned, by anyone's standards.

"No," I said, and the woman stomped a moccasin, arms linking to shield her chest, that momentary feeling evaporating under the rays of her stare.

I recognized that stance. The woman stood illumed, but I moved in the night. In the dark, she couldn't see the color of my skin. In the dark, I could've been as brown as Rachelle.

"Well." She sighed, her irritation palpable. "You know where she went?" If she'd had any patience at the start of her day, by then, it was all spent.

"I was just going to ask the same question."

"Great," the woman muttered. "Just great. You know, I got her kids in my van." She flung an arm out toward her Dodge. I looked back.

There, half in shadow under the weak dome lights, was Destiny, strapped in the backseat, twisting toward the window. Rachelle's girls weren't with her. I felt the ground go marshy.

"She dumped them at New Caledonia this morning." The trade school over by the electric supply store. They had a program in early childhood development. Anne-Marie had wanted to enroll before Tanner. They were the only day care that took drop-ins, hands-on experience for the students.

"I told her like I tell everybody: we close at eight, no exceptions."

So it wasn't just conjecture. We may not have been friends for long, but I'd seen Rachelle around her girls. There was no way she'd just ditch them. Something must have happened. Something bad.

"She's got a contact listed. Al Murphy. Heard of him?"

"He's her husband." I shooed the panic from my voice. I didn't want to spook the woman. Her face brightened. "But he's gone." She cocked her head. "Dead." I spelled it out.

"Well," she whinnied, clopping down the steps. I sidled backward, keeping pace.

"What time did she drop them off?"

"Seven A.M., soon as our doors opened."

Tap-tap-tap.

Once, when I was nine, Mom had forgotten me—not at day care but at the neighbor's. Sue. Mom never really had any female friends. Sue was the sole exception. Not just considerably older, Sue was ugly, her face pinched and red as a sausage, her arms winged with jiggling fat. No threat. I remember sitting in a squeaking vinyl chair at her kitchen table, my hands folded in my lap, trying hard as possible to minimize myself. Sue was on the phone with a friend. "Guess I'm stuck with her." She'd been flipping through the pages of a wrinkled magazine. The shame I'd felt just for existing—it all came rushing back.

I stepped into the light. "I can stay here with them until she's back."

The woman paused, turning toward me. The smattering of freckles, the hair combed into sandy plaits. The innocent eyes, brown as a rabbit. Her shoulders eased down from her ears. Revealed to be as harmless as she was. I might have even reminded her of a granddaughter, a girlhood friend.

Tap-tap-tap.

"Oh, honey," she said, aggravation softened, so different from when she assumed I was someone else. "If only it were that simple."

Tap-tap-tap.

That sound, I realized, was Destiny, her fingers at the glass. Before the woman could stop me, I stepped toward the girl, sliding open the rickety door. The radio was on, the country station Nana liked, flaccid Jesus rock, as Mom called it, *bringing good news to Canada's people.* A woman's thin voice singing out:

For in a world of sin and vice you must start to see
How to grow and tend your family tree

"Hi." I crouched down, forcing a smile. Destiny's face was wet, snot bubbling in her nostrils. One hand was gripping her sleeping sister's ankle. She clasped the other around mine.

"Where's Mom?" Her nails dug into my palm. I wished I had an answer. Instead, I just hovered there, useless as a pricked balloon.

"Mommy's fine." The woman elbowed her way between us, parting our hands. "Everything's fine. Just give us a minute, okay?" She pitched the van door shut.

"You know," she said, pivoting toward me, any sweetness in her voice curdled. "You're not helping. I'd just calmed her down."

"What's going to happen to them?" I asked. I knew before she said it, shrugging.

"They're in the province's hands now."

Foster care. Like Rachelle and her sister. What a cruel joke, history repeating itself. I looked back at Destiny's crumpled little face and thought of the sign, those tiny brown hands. *I WANT TO LIVE.* We had the spare bedroom, my mind raced. They were kids, the youngest still a baby. I could borrow a crib; a pack of onesies didn't cost much. Take care of them, until she was back. In that moment, I wasn't even thinking of Sam.

"I could take them," I found myself saying. "I know them. This isn't like their mother. There must have been an emergency. I live right across from them. I'm sure she'll be back."

The woman hadn't heard a single word I had said. She'd opened her door, was heaving herself into the carpeted seat and buckling herself in.

"Look," she told me, one hand groping in her handbag. "I'm sure *she'd* be fine with whoever watching them, but the only person *I* can entrust them with is the name on my list. And unfortunately, that person is"—she slid down to a whisper—"dead." She tore open a brick of silvery gum and folded it into her downturned mouth.

"Mom can pick them up when she's back from . . ." She trailed off, wad of blue between her gums. "Wherever she went." She didn't have to specify. Anyone would've known what she meant.

"Alrighty." She started her engine, reaching toward the door handle.

"Jenny!" Destiny shouted, her desperation tugging at my heartstrings.

I blocked the woman with a knee. "Couldn't you just add my name to the list?" I leaned in close enough to taste spearmint. "Just give me your number. I'll call you as soon as she gets back."

"And risk arrest? No thanks." She turned on her ignition. "I still have a long night ahead. If you want to help, why don't you go on home and figure out where your friend went." She had to shout. Destiny's cries had woken Little Beth.

"You're sure there's no way you can . . ."

"Good night." I felt a surprisingly strong arm prodding me back. The door slammed.

Destiny craned her head toward me as the van pulled away. Her mouth was open, but I could no longer hear her. I was left alone, in the dark, deaf.

I drove home, shaking. The tears were back. Those poor girls. Rachelle. There was only one thing to do. I parked my Buick and marched straight to the phone, punching in the three numbers. *Nine-one-one.*

"I'd like to report a missing person."

"Okay." It was a man on the other end of the line. "Can you back up for a second? Who's calling?" I gave him my name, then Rachelle's.

"And how long has she been missing?"

"She was last seen this morning at a day care center," I started, then hesitated. I didn't want to fudge the timeline. "But I last saw her yesterday. She had a visitor, a man, a truck I've never seen before. White, with Alberta plates. All her blinds are down again."

"I see." The man's voice was clinical, untouched by the urgency in my own. "So you're not sure when you last saw her." It wasn't really a question. "You know, usually officers wait at least twenty-four hours before filing a missing person's report. I assume you've tried calling her?"

"Yes," I lied. It didn't matter that I didn't have her number. It's not like it would have been any use. Her phone was there, nailed to the wall, and she was someplace else. "Can't reach her."

"I see," the man said. "And have you reached out to her family, any mutual friends?"

"No." My face flushed. "I mean, not yet."

"'Not yet,'" he repeated. "Look, sweetheart." His tone had warmed. "I know with what's been going on, it's scary. We've been getting a lot of calls. I'm sure your friend will be back in the morning. And if she's still gone after twenty-four hours, you give the station a call. Simplest answer's usually the right one. These things have a way of shaking themselves out."

"Okay," I said, wanting to believe him, my eyes at the window, peering into the dark. He was probably right. It was probably nothing. *These things have a way of shaking themselves out.*

I didn't sleep that night. Staying calm was easier said than done, and I kept finding myself drifting toward the living room, willing a light to switch on. After the fourth waking, I gave in, setting tent on the couch, flipping through the infomercials, a symptom of the hour when only the lonely, the desperate, were awake. Like Nana.

I thought of her dwindling pension, all the boxes barricading her front door. The Slap Chop (*One slap, you've got big chunks for stew; two slaps, home fries in one second*); the ShamWow (*This cloth is for the house, the car, the boat, the RV*); the Flippin' Fantastic, a plastic mini-pancake mold so flimsy, it looked like if you glanced at it wrong, it'd snap. Never mind that Nana never made home fries or pancakes, that she lived in a condo, not a house. The Chia Pets, the clip-on earrings, the Thigh-Master, the knives forged in "Japan"—all stuff no one actually needed. Stuff to shoulder the weight of passing each long night alone again. I pressed mute.

I woke to the worst infomercial of all, the *Girls Gone Wild* VHS sets, a montage of glassy-eyed coeds lifting their shirts to reveal bejeweled belly buttons, those scrambled bras of TV static. I switched it off, the feeble blue of daybreak ladled in through my window in the tube's stead. I glanced out it. Still no sign of Rachelle.

I dozed off again, waking at noon, ridged pattern from a needlepoint pillow impressed across the side of my face. I went to put the coffee on. The fireweed against her side of the fence lurched in the breeze, but that was it. All else was quiet. Dead.

I drove by her house on my way to the mall. No sign out front either. There was still time, I told myself, unpacking a box of foot cream. *Simplest answer's usually the right one.* I went through the possibilities. I doubt she'd had her car serviced since Al passed. Maybe it'd broken down. She'd tried to phone the day care, but the office had closed for the night. Her AAA was expired. She'd had no one else to call. It'd taken all night, but it'd all been worked out. As I was counting my register, she was gathering her girls in her arms, kissing the tops of their silken heads.

When I stepped out onto the near vacant parking lot, my knees went weak. The sun was sinking, night beginning to snuff out the assurances of the day. Mine was one of only three cars left. I crossed the dusky lot alone, quickening my pace. That foreboding feeling was back.

I turned onto 16. Most of the highway was unlit, reliant on the headlights of your own vehicle or the oncoming one. If she had broken down, she would've been stranded in pitch. The shoulder was nearly nonexistent. The road bled right into the bush. I thought of Beth, lost in daylight.

Something had happened. Something bad.

And what about the pitted truck, the mystery man? A woman has her first visitor in weeks, maybe months, and the next day, she's nowhere to be found? *Stupid dispatch*, I chided myself. I was too compliant yielding to authority. *You're searching for your daddy*, Missy liked to tell me when I'd hand in the extra credit, slam on the brakes at a yellow. What did the cops know anyway? They hadn't found Beth.

I was expecting it. Still, I felt woozy when I saw Rachelle's dark house, empty as a spent can.

I went out onto my back porch, stepping down to the cool grass of the yard, raising the hood of my sweatshirt, white flag in the soot of the night. The only light the silver blink of the stars, puny as mustard seeds, sown haphazardly, like fuzz, spit—specks of blood—ash overhead. *Wherever you go, the stars follow*, Erin always used to say. I squinted up at the vastness, wiping my eyes. Twenty-four hours was well up.

Rachelle was gone, this much I knew. And I was going to find her.

PART II

Rachelle

nine

The radio was off, but 16-W was coming in loud and clear. In billboards:

YASKOW SAND & GRAVEL: Call to Discuss Your Aggregate Needs

SKI SMITHERS: Hudson Bay Mountain Resort: The Best Skiing in Canada

CANFOR: Now Hiring

In handwritten signs posted low to the ground:

Potatoes 4 Sale

Jesus Died So You Could Live, John 3:16

In names etched across trailers:

BISON TRANSPORT
RAI EXPRESS LINES LTD
DOLE

Wordlessly, in symbols, shadows affixed against cautionary yellow— deer, moose, big rig, bear.

And there, plastered to the bumper of the pickup in front of me, the objective of the summer:

FIND BETH

They were everywhere, those stickers, stacked beside the register at the gas station, the Safeway, the liquor store. Anne-Marie's mom had gotten hers at church. Even Ray had one, slapped above the arc of urine, Calvin and his ass crack and his smirk. I still see them now from time to time, the edges dulled, the letters puckered, no longer a mission— only more noise.

I'd never been as attuned to the road as I was that morning, every sign, every bit of roadside debris a potential clue. I passed a billboard for A&W, root beer float as vast as the clouds overhead. I dug in my bag for a tube of Life Savers. I'd skipped breakfast that morning, leaving in a huff, after my call to the station didn't exactly go as planned.

It was the same officer I'd spoken to the night prior, and he must have already written me off, the imaginings of a bored housewife, his response like a pat on the head.

"Call us back," he'd said again. "After you get in touch with some of your neighbor's family or friends."

I was thinking to head west that morning anyway, but that call got me out the door that much faster. I didn't know Rachelle's sister's name, let alone her phone number, but I knew she lived in Vanderhoof, and Vanderhoof wasn't far.

"The chances of finding a missing person drop dramatically after the first forty-eight hours," the host of *Crimestoppers* had warned when Beth first vanished. It'd been well over that for Rachelle. The clock was ticking whether that officer believed me or not. I couldn't squander what little time she had left.

The sign for Sob Lake came into view. Only twenty more clicks to town. I crunched into a Life Saver, working out a plan. I hadn't left with anything specific—figured I'd just ask around. Vanderhoof was nothing if not small—a sliver of PG, sizeable only in relation to its surroundings. The ranches, the farms, the canola fields, the resource roads. The acres and acres of mountainous bush, terrain rutted as some wrinkled old skin. I looked out the window, the rush of green engirdling the highway as dense and suffocating as burlap.

No wonder no one's found the body. Jim's voice popped into my head. He'd come home early the other day, leaning himself against the counter and hefting a slice of pizza, folded lengthwise, into his lipless mouth. His eyes were glued, as they always were, on Missy, gaze breaking only to tear into a roll of paper towel and flick the slices of pepperoni he'd peeled off into the sink. He'd referred to her like that before, *the body*, as if she'd lost what had made her a person, a Beth.

Lots of places around here to make someone disappear, he'd said without inflection, sucking at an oil-slick finger. *Even with all of Vancouver coming. Ain't possible to search every road.* He'd paused. *And ditch, and cutbank, and truck bed,*

I eyed the surrounding bush with suspicion, the episode playing out on the screen in my head. The white truck pulling off onto some resource road. Pine needles stitched through Rachelle's long dark hair. I switched on the radio to change my mind. I was getting ahead of myself. Beth had been missing near a month and a half—and still, we hadn't given up hope. *We've got to keep looking,* the host of *Crimestoppers* urged. He'd stopped mentioning, long ago, those first forty-eight hours. *If we haven't found her, that means she's still out there. Waiting.* I had to focus, remain clearheaded. I pressed on the gas, passing Vanderhoof's welcome sign.

The mill there was infamous, the last in the area to still use a beehive burner, a cutesy way of saying they burned their trash. PG had a dozen or so back in Nana's day, giant furnaces that looked like inverted ice-cream cones or teepees, blotting the sun with black clouds. By my time, most of them had been razed to the ground, those remaining repurposed as shelters for livestock or underaged partiers.

Was a health hazard, even one of them, let alone a dozen, we learned decades after the fact. Not to mention what people were burning after hours.

Mattresses, busted furniture, car parts, all you'd normally have to haul to the dump. Some men brought dead animals to burn. The fire hot enough to melt steel, even before Beth's disappearance there was speculation. *Wonder what else men are getting rid of in there.* The rounded top of the beehive burner came into view, and I clicked to make sure my doors were still locked.

Vanderhoof's downtown was three clipped blocks—a hardware store, a truck-and-car wash, BC Liquor, Fountain Tire. A Petro-Canada. It wasn't until I arrived that I realized I had no destination. I switched on my blinker. The gas station seemed as logical a place to start as any.

I stepped inside. There was a lineup at the register, and I stood behind a man in a Royal Canadian Air Force T-shirt, his gray hair slicked under a faded bandana, a bottle of Mountain Dew dangling from each hand. I didn't get the impression that he'd have known someone like Rachelle. There was another man in front of him in cargo shorts and shower sandals, but he was already checking out. I'd wait to ask at the counter.

My stomach growled. I'd run out of Life Savers. To the right of the till was a glass case of fried chicken, the breaded meat organized in sections: *LEG, THIGH, WING, RIB, BREAST.* Rib? I stepped one foot out and squinted over.

"Next," the cashier called without looking up. My hands were empty. I went for the nearest thing. An XXL Slim Jim.

"That it?" she said, her eyes pointing downward. Her long black hair was suspended in brown mesh, her moon-shaped face pitted with acne scars. She was wearing a polo shirt with *PETRO-CANADA* embossed over her heart. The color of her skin was the same shade as Rachelle's.

"Yeah," I squeaked. I wasn't sure how to phrase it. I'd spent the drive rehearsing, but now that I was there, face-to-face with someone who very likely knew her, I choked.

"I'm looking for someone." I cleared my throat. "Do you know a woman with the last name *Murphy*?" The cashier lifted her head, her face blank. "She's Native?" For some reason, I'd phrased it like a question. "I need to talk to her about her sister, Rachelle."

"'Murphy,'" the cashier repeated, scratching a cratered cheek. "I'll be straight with you, I just moved here last month. Maybe he knows. John?" She craned her neck toward a teenage boy who was restocking the potato chip aisle. "She's looking for someone. Rachel Murray."

"Murphy," I corrected. "Two sisters?"

"Murphy," he drawled, as if elongation might jog his memory. "Murphy," he said again, and it dawned on me. Murphy was Al's name. Her sister's would be different. Once women were past a certain age, there was no accounting for them. My mom, Erin, me—none of us were McCarthys.

"What grade are they in?" the boy asked. I winced. Vanderhoof was small, but not that small. I didn't even know her sister's first name.

"Never mind," I muttered, handing over a toonie, a two-dollar coin, and stepping back out onto the parking lot.

I leaned against the door of my Buick, checking my watch. Eleven twenty—not even noon and I'd already run out of ideas. Was no asking around when you didn't know what you were asking. My stomach yipped. I looked down at the Slim Jim, rancid meat baton. There was a Chinese restaurant across the street, its golden letters glinting. Fortune Palace. I'd already driven all that way, I remember thinking. Lunch would give me some time to devise a plan. I crossed the highway, bell tinkling as I swung open the smudged glass door.

The palace was dead, save for an elderly man polishing silverware silently in the corner. "Anywhere you like," he said, rubbing a red napkin against a fork.

I slid into a booth, vinyl upholstery sticking to the backs of my thighs. The man set down a laminated menu.

"To drink?" He pulled out a small notepad from his apron pocket. His accent was strong, his face wrinkled as a dried fig.

"Just water." I eyed the prices. I'd spent enough on gas.

I ordered a number twelve, chicken lo mein, the cheapest option on the menu, struggling with the chopsticks before switching to a fork. I ate, watching as the man set the other tables, his feet shuffling against the carpet, patterned crimson to hide the stains—and about as ancient as he was. He must have been Nana's age at least. Asking him about Rachelle would've been as naïve as expecting her to strut in, place an order for the General Tso's.

I was stumped, couldn't work out an in, was racking my brain for someone else, anyone, who was connected to Rachelle. If she'd had a job, I could've poked around there, but as far as I could tell, she was housebound. I'd never seen a friend come to visit (excluding that white truck), and even all the photos on her fridge had been of her girls, or her, or Al. Al was her emergency contact, the woman from the day care had said, more than a year after his death.

Her sister wasn't just my only lead. She must've been the only other person who really knew Rachelle. I had to find out her name. But how? I cracked open my fortune cookie, as if that'd help.

Life is not a problem to be solved, but rather a mystery to be lived.
I bit into a waxen shard, rolling my eyes. *Tell that to my mortgage.* I crumpled the paper, pushing open the door.

I sat in the driver's seat of my Buick for a while, dejected, staring at the green numbers on the digital clock as they switched. I was a fool, driving all that way for some soggy lo mein. There had to be an official document linking the sisters, but that wasn't something anyone could just see. What would Columbo do? I thought of all the other detectives I knew. Nancy Drew was the first female that came to mind. Stephanie Plum, Agent Scully. Sergeant Alison McCormick, the only Canadian. The dozens of cases I'd watched her crack in Vancouver, all those episodes of *Cold Squad.*

There was a formula to the episodes and to police procedure. Every investigation started at the scene of the crime. Rachelle had disappeared at home, after that white truck's arrival. That's where I should have gone first. I remembered something—ashen lace quivering in the wind. Her washroom window left wide open. Climbing in would be as easy as scaling the fence. I was sure to find her sister's name somewhere, if not something else. Some clue, some proof, irrefutable evidence. I started my engine, heart quickening.

It's strange to think now how excited I was, my windows rolled down, the wind in my hair, as if setting out on a scavenger hunt. It didn't cross my mind as I pulled out of that station—or maybe it did, that feeling, near giddy, that came with every opening scene of *CSI*—the gruesome possibilities of what I might find.

I drove back with the radio blasting, tuned into a country station's non-stop lunch hour, Buick charging past the spruce and the pines. There was less traffic running east, and most of the billboards were neglected, plywood underpinnings as mute as some felled logs. Once the truckers hit Rupert, they shot straight down to Vancouver, rounding their way back up to PG. A circle, a loop, like the felling, the replanting; another snake eating its tail. Lumber, coal, oil from McMurray—it was all hauled west, packed onto freighters pointing toward China or driven down south to the States.

That made it all that much more impressive, what was still new back then, one of the dozen or so billboards they'd erected along the length of 16.

Hovering above the highway like an angel or a Big Mac, the giant face of a smiling Beth. The details of her portrait so immediate, you could almost taste the fuzz of her sweater. The reward money printed beside her, the red of poppies, of ketchup, of blood.

It was an omen, I see that now, but back then, I just sped on by, belting stupidly into a Surge can to "Achy Breaky Heart." The record didn't just scratch; it shattered—faced with what I'd thought I wanted to find.

There, brown as mud, stalled on a particularly weedy section of shoulder, was Al's old Fleetwood. Rachelle's ride. Was it? I switched off the radio, my heart thumping in my throat.

I pushed on the brake, easing up behind it. On the bumper, a white sticker: *Driver Carries No Cash, He's Married.* A trucker's joke. It was Al's, no doubt. And by the looks of it, empty. Could I really have missed it before?

I stepped out of my Buick, walking toward the car. The hazard lights were off, with no sign of any of those little orange warning flares. The hood was down. We'd always been taught to pop it if we ever had to leave the site to call for help. If she had broken down, it didn't look recent. I'd been attentive to the road but more so to my side. The way it was parked, the car was almost camouflaged.

I started to circle around. Not a nick on the body. The tires were fine. No leaking fluids, no off smell. Assuming there'd been an electrical problem, why hadn't she gotten it to a garage?

I tugged at the metal handle. Locked. I cupped my hands around my eyes and pressed my nose to the window. The interior was spotless. Not a single coin, or crumpled receipt, or any of the signs of life, of routine use—the straw wrappers, the hair elastics, the Timmy's cups, the coupons—the chaff that'd collect over time. Dangling from the rearview mirror, a preternaturally blue maple leaf. *New Car Smell.* The floor mats even looked vacuumed. I circled around again.

Al had taken pathological care of that car. Whenever I'd seen it stopped at a traffic light, plugged into a fuel pump at the closest Esso, it was the definition of spic-and-span. I'd only seen it once since he passed, in the parking lot of Safeway some months back. *CLEAN ME*, someone had scrawled on the rear window. It was unsettling how pristine it was now. Suspect.

I stepped back, taking in the area. Nothing but bush around. I was at least twenty clicks out from Vanderhoof. Fortysome back to town. It was strange to think, but the way I'd found it (spanking clean, no outer signs of damage), it was almost as if the shoulder had been her destination. As if she hadn't stalled but parked. Or someone else had. My heart was back in my esophagus.

If someone had wanted to ditch her vehicle, 16 would've been just as good a place as any. I'd found it, irrefutable proof. Something had happened. Something bad. I jogged back to my Buick, hooking a U-ey. There was a Chevron with a pay phone some clicks back.

I dug out the quarters from the bottom of my cupholder, feeding them into the pay phone's narrow slot. I'd written the number of the PG station down, but it was hanging on my fridge. Nine-one-one would connect me to Vanderhoof, the nearest town, but maybe I'd have better luck with one of their officers anyway.

"Nine-one-one, what's your emergency?"

"I called before. It's my neighbor. She's missing." My voice cracked. Saying it out loud, it hit me, the weight of it. "I just found her car," I gasped, out of breath.

"Let me transfer you to an officer," a woman's voice answered. "Just a minute, hun." I wiped my eyes, steadying my breath. *Focus, Jen.*

I started from the beginning—the appearance of the white pickup, the mystery man, how the blinds had been suddenly yanked down. The plans we'd made, her house empty that morning. The woman from the day care, Rachelle's daughters strapped in the van.

"Her car's just sitting there, on the side of the highway. It really doesn't look like she broke down."

"What'd you say your friend's name was again?" This officer sounded younger than the one I'd spoken to in PG, less jaded, more earnest, or so I hoped. I could hear the patter of a keyboard. He was getting everything down.

"Rachelle Murphy."

"Murphy," he said, and I heard him punch in the letters. "And you said you last saw her on Tuesday, that right?"

"That's correct."

"Can you describe her?"

"She's taller than me, maybe five foot nine or so. And skinnier. Maybe one hundred thirty, one hundred twenty-five pounds. Brown eyes. Black hair. She's Indian." I caught myself. "Native. I'm twenty-four. She can't be much older than I am."

The line went quiet. Just as it had, it dawned on me, after I'd described her to first officer. "First Nations, eh?" he'd said, clearing his throat. "How well did you say you knew her again?"

First Nations. You never heard that term spoken. It was the official one, but there was really only one place you saw it. In the *Crimestoppers* section in the paper, what was printed below the mug shots. *AGE, DOB, DESCRIPTION.* More often than not: *FIRST NATIONS, MALE.* And occasionally, their faces sallow, their eyes dead: *FEMALE.*

"I've lived across from her for five years," I said preemptively. I no longer heard any pitter-patter.

"I called the other day." I was getting impatient. "They said to call back. She disappeared two days ago, nearly. The chances of finding a missing person drop dramatically after the first forty-eight hours," I recited. He had to know that.

"Just calm down," he said, a change in his voice. I could almost see him leaning back, his feet up, his arms crossed behind his head. "She party?"

"She what?"

"She a drinker? Any drug use? Different men around, who come and go?"

"She's a mother. She was married. She's got two young girls." Her sister, I remembered. The mystery man. But he was singular, not plural. I'd already told him that. The questions he was asking, it was almost as if Rachelle were a suspect in her own disappearance. Not a victim but the one to blame. Clearly he didn't understand.

"I'm telling you, this isn't like her to just up and vanish. I just found her car on the shoulder of 16. Not a single sign of damage. In fact, it looked like it'd been recently cleaned. Shouldn't you at least come out and investigate?"

"'Investigate,'" he repeated. "Tell you what. Wait a few days, and if the car's still out there, give us a call and we'll *investigate*." He said the last word as if it were a punch line. But then what was the joke? Me? Rachelle? His approach was different, but the sentiment was the same as the PG officer's. *Call back.* This wasn't how it always went.

Missy's neighbors had called the cops once. Domestic disturbance. The shouting so loud, it had roused three of their neighbors. Jim had hurled a blender through a French door, and Missy had sliced her foot up in the shattered glass. The RCMP came right away, calling every few days after to check in on her. The scene had looked a lot worse than it was, on account of all the splatter. One of the officers still came knocking when his patrol took him nearby. "Think he's got a little crush," Missy had said, patting concealer onto the bruises that'd lingered, scraping out the flesh-hued cream that'd gotten lodged under an acrylic with a butter knife.

"I'm sure she's fine. Sometimes, these people"—the officer's voice drifted—"we don't know what they get into. She probably just took off for a, uh, long weekend." He didn't have to say the word. *Bender.* Just like with the woman at the day care, I knew, immediately, what he meant.

"She'll turn up," he was saying. "Always do." I lowered the receiver from my ear.

"Okay," I said to no one, hanging up. There was no use in convincing him. The men might've been lousy, but the women, as anyone could tell you, were worse. *Indian women, working the highway*, babies abandoned for the thrill of the needle, the night. He didn't know Rachelle was different. How could he? PG, or Vanderhoof, or Quesnel, or Smithers, they dealt with them daily, saw the evidence firsthand. The RCMP wouldn't be any help.

I switched on my blinker, turning back onto 16-E, Rachelle's car appearing before fading again, a blip in my rearview mirror. I was on my own. That call had confirmed it. I had no choice but to find her myself. I turned the radio up. ". . . Baby, One More Time" blared out.

I was scanning to find something better when a flash of white floated up to my right, pink flicker far brighter than the fireweed. No one was behind me. I slowed to a halt, rolling down the passenger window and squinting.

Two tiny white crosses were staked in the earth, a spray of fake roses nailed to each one, petals rigid as tire irons. A name was painted in black lengthwise down one. *JADE.* I couldn't make out the name on the other, only the bottom two letters: *IS.*

Stolen sisters. I thought of the women on the news. Even if they were selling their bodies, no one deserved a fate like that—to end up among the beer cans, the A&W cartons, the thistle, the hemlock, all the litter the highway's shoulder housed. I'd almost missed it, this memorial, white paint browned with the passage of time. These were far from new. I must've driven past them an untold number of times.

PG's cutback soon came into view, followed by the first billboard, what still stands erect. *BETH TREMBLAY.*

Her face may have faded, but those letters, *MISSING,* still loom as large as the ones on the Canfor ads. Red-urgent as ever.

ten

It wasn't hard getting in. Rachelle's street was as quiet as ours was during the day, with most neighbors out working and the rest shut in, occupied—tackling the laundry pile, spoon-feeding the baby—or otherwise, with stony faces set toward the screen. As a rule, people didn't pay too much attention to Rachelle's, as if it could be willed into nonexistence through continued disregard.

Still, I was cautious. Parking at home, walking from my place to hers, just in case. Tucking my hair beneath Sam's Canuck's hat, sporting Nana's old sunglasses, ink-hued and outsized. I brought a stack of magazines with me as a cover, as if I were going door-to-door. I made a whole show of it, knocking on her front door, ringing the bell, waiting before ringing again. I glanced around. Checkered print, heavy lace, venetian blinds, velvet. Even if any of Rachelle's neighbors were home, it didn't matter. There wasn't an unobstructed window in sight. I saddled casually around to the side of her house, stopping in front of the washroom window that'd been left ajar.

I dug into my JanSport. I'd brought a few things along I thought I might need: a disposable camera, a pair of thick winter gloves, one of those legal notepads. Bear spray.

I slipped on the gloves and gripped on to the window's ledge. It was low, coming up to my chest, and it didn't take much to hoist myself up and in. At least not physically.

Mentally was another story. I caught a glimpse of myself in the spotted mirror, the figure frozen, her mouth gone tight. If there was a point of no return, I'd hurtled past it, landing like a stray cat on the blue tiles of Rachelle's washroom. *A possible crime scene*, my shallow breath reminded me. I dug around for the bear spray and kept it firm in hand.

I ditched the sunglasses and scanned around. Despite the layout (and all that tiresome blue), the room couldn't have been less familiar. It was dingy, claustrophobic, felt smaller than it was. Like Anne-Marie's place after Tanner. There was no keeping up with it—the toothpaste spatter, the fingerprints, the puddle piles of laundry, the relentlessness of the diaper bin. What little Formica countertop there was, Rachelle had maximized: the makeup, the bobby pins, the Band-Aid boxes, the soap dish with a sense of humor. Bubblegum-pink mermaid posed atop goop-glommed shell. I took off a glove, poking at the goop and sniffing. It was the same sap green as our *Pine Breeze*. To think—all that we had in common, what could have been. It was my favorite scent, too.

My eyes met the mirror again. The baseball hat, the zipped-up hoodie—I was reminded of my mission there. The clock was ticking. *Focus, Jen.* I slipped the glove back on and batted back the shower curtain, bracing myself, as if I expected someone to pop out.

Herbal Essences, Mr. Bubble, the ringed tub a container heaped with those toys that came with Happy Meals. A steak with a mustache, a winking container of low-fat milk, a googly-eyed McNugget in a cowboy hat, a lone hot-pink Barbie heel.

Something sour in the air. I turned toward the lifted toilet seat, yellow tingeing the bowl. *Boy smell.*

Reflexively my hand raised itself toward the handle. As the water swirled, I kicked myself. It was evidence. They could've tested it, like on *Cold Squad*. Trace the DNA. I pointed the camera at the bowl. *Click.* There was always a photographer, the scenes that would start with the sound of the flash. You never knew what could prove to be useful.

The door was closed, and I opened it apprehensively, holding the bear spray in front of me as I stepped out into the hall. How could I know the house was really empty? Something clacked, and I practically pissed my cutoffs. It was the door to the girls' room flapping against its jamb. I took a deep breath and started toward it, my index finger on the nozzle of the can.

I kicked the door open with a foot. No one was there. It was the window, I realized, left slightly open. The breeze blowing in through the blinds. I sighed.

The mess was still there, the books I'd organized since toppled, scattered across the floor. The laundry bin had returned to being a net for whatever—VHS tapes, a clawed-open bag of Pampers, the tattered angel wings—it happened to catch. Destiny's bed had been made with care, the quilt's edge folded over, the dog she'd clutched to her chest. She hadn't been able to take him with her. They hadn't been able to take anything. Just the clothes on their backs. It felt like evidence, two other lives lost. I pulled out my camera. *Click.* I stepped back out into the hall.

The door to Rachelle's room had been firmly shut, and as I reached toward the handle, I lost my nerve. I could feel her presence, the dark thoughts crowding in. What if she was there? The scene made to look like an accident. I squirmed at the sight of a squashed mosquito. Why hadn't I thought of that?

If she was there, who else would find her? I thought of the stories on the news, the women found days, weeks, months, years later, decomposing like heaps of trash. Now or never. I pushed the door open, holding my breath as if preparing to dive.

The room was vacant, thank God, and clean. Sparkling, considering the rest of the house. I thought of the Fleetwood. Maybe she'd been the neat one. Maybe this whole time, the mess had been Al's.

But neat freaks never just confined themselves to one room. I ran a gloved finger across the surface of her bureau. It was spotless. I thought of Mom, who, twice a week, would scour the apartment, knees bent at the coffee table, hiss of her canister, furiously wielding a rag. I inhaled. Beeswax and turpentine. The room had been recently cleaned. Like her car.

I opened the top drawer. Coins, lipstick, one of those hairbrushes with bristles all the way around. Bobby pins. A stained foundation sponge. Something special, wrapped loosely in pink tissue paper. I folded the top layer back. It was a pair of intricately beaded earrings, each broad as my palm, in fiery colors—red, orange, gold, black. They were birds, I realized, but not like ones I'd ever seen.

An oval mirror was propped on the bureau, a scarf—carmine gauze—draped over its arc. I held an earring up to my ear, eying my reflection, my face washed in red. The bird nearly came down to my shoulder. They were extravagant, a costume. I couldn't imagine them on Rachelle in her T-shirt and jeans. Maybe they were from a powwow, the robes they wore to twirl and drum. I wrapped them back in their paper, closing the drawer. Socks, underwear, long johns, nightshirts. The earrings were the only item of note. I opened the drawer again, pulled out my camera. *Click.*

I stepped over to her bed, catching my reflection again. Rachelle had the same closets as we did, the two mirrored panels: his and hers. I slid open the left one. Al's side. The smell musty, old sweat. It was as sparse as Sam's was: a few work shirts, a couple hoodies, a pair of slick waders still rolled at the cuffs. A white dress shirt, embalmed in plastic, the bright stub from the cleaners safety-pinned to its tag. The date read '96. She'd hung on to all of it.

I slid open the other side, and a pile of sweaters came tumbling down. Her closet was stuffed, the scant rack bursting. All that clutter, it made Al's clothing look even more disposable. For practicality's sake.

Maybe the rumors weren't true. Maybe she really had loved him. I'd never seen them together much—a long-hauler, Al was gone more often than Sam—but there was that one morning a few springs back, her gesture still seared in my memory. I was out early, tucking cabbage seedlings into the soil, Rachelle fishing for a cigarette in her pack. Al had come out to bring her a lighter, and she'd wrapped an arm around the back of his head, rubbing his lips with a finger. I felt embarrassed to have witnessed that. A moment so intimate, it felt like I shouldn't have been there in my own yard.

I slid the door closed, taking a seat on Rachelle's neatly made bed. Her quilt was embroidered, two branches of dogwood in bloom, intersecting hoops like the number eight, the infinity symbol. I thought of Missy and Jim's matching tattoos, his on his forearm, Missy's in the middle of the small of her back. *It means forever,* she'd explained. *Target practice* was what Jim had said.

My foot bumped into something, what had been shoved underneath the bed. I reached down. It was a pair of platform sandals, silver, and with heels at least four inches high. Size seven. I held them up against the soles of my Keds. Mine were tens.

The shoes were flashy, slutty even, their varnish dulled, the bottoms caked with dried mud. There were women, like Missy, who wore heels to bush parties, but those women wore heels everywhere. Rachelle wasn't that type. Unless—the other rumors were true. I glanced at the bureau. Maybe that's what those earrings were for. Impossible. I shook my head, taking my camera out. *Click.*

I walked through the living room, the explosion of toys, the laundry still mounded high on the couch. I went into the kitchen. The coffee maker was on. I switched it off, the handle so hot, it singed my gloves. I poured the liquid down the sink. Burnt tar. She must have forgotten it. Or else she hadn't expected to be gone long. It was a miracle there hadn't been a fire.

There was a notepad on the counter, its pages blank. When she was on the phone the day I'd come over, she'd written something down. I'd seen it before, the old detective movies André would watch. *Columbo* had been his show. You could shade the first page in with a pencil and sift out the imprint of what had been written before.

> *milk*
> *shreddies*
> *eggs*
> *chikin nugats*
> *pees*
> *OJ*
> *jiffy*

Groceries. I crumpled it. Only thing that proved was Rachelle wasn't a speller. She must have had a list of emergency numbers somewhere. All moms did. Anne-Marie's and Missy's were tacked to their fridges. I scanned hers. Not there. I opened the cabinet drawers. Utensils, rubber bands, rolls of foil. I started to leaf through the papers on the table. Coupon inserts from the *Citizen*, third notices, the acid yellow of the *PG Xpress.*

A pink envelope gashed open, the letter inside gone—the only piece of personal mail. Rachelle's name and address had been written in hesitant letters, a child's looping scrawl. *Rhoda Bluecloud*, the return address read. *Bluecloud.* It was a native name. *351 McLeod Road, Vanderhoof VOJ 301.* Bingo. That had to be where her sister lived. Rhoda must have been Rachelle's niece.

I took out my legal pad and jotted down the address, exhilarated with what I'd accomplished. It was a Friday; the timing was perfect. I could head there first thing the next morning. Saturday—when Rachelle's sister was sure to be home. I wasn't about to waste another half tank of gas.

I was turning the handle when I caught myself. Detectives didn't just leave through the front door. I padded back toward the washroom, launching from the window's ledge, smile flitting across my face as I slipped back out onto her street—unseen, and with a destination in hand.

Looking at it on the map, I couldn't see how deep in the boonies McLeod Road really was, at least twenty clicks north of Vanderhoof's already dinky downtown. The road was unpaved and badly rutted, sending my Buick skyward, even with my foot off the gas. *Must be a real bitch come winter,* I remember thinking, skidding to a stop across from the Blueclouds' modest house.

Modest being the polite way of putting it.

Shithole being the more accurate.

It wasn't that I had anything against trailers. Anne-Marie lived in a modular, her place as nice as any. But there were trailers, and there were *trailers.* This was different. This was depressing. This place had all but thrown up its hands. The clapboards warped, the latticed wooden deck caving in on itself. In fact, the whole structure looked one storm away from collapse. The roof was staked with a rusted-over satellite dish, hovering in blue like some ominous blood moon. All the junk out front— what the wire fence hemmed in from the road, the busted dryer, the tire spokes, the giant faux-wood-paneled speaker that looked like it'd been slashed at. A sun-faded trampoline was wedged in between one side of the house and the fence, its sagging webbing blanketed, a replacement for the dryer, the array of frilly girls' bathing suits laid to bake.

I wasn't sure what I'd been expecting. I knew her sister was in a hard way, but the truth was, I'd never really known someone like *that.* Like what all the other neighbors imagined Rachelle to be. Strung out, tatty. Desperate. If she was anywhere near as pretty as Rachelle, I'm sure she was popular. Rachelle had been trying to help her, get her off the highway. The story pieced itself together. Maybe those were her sister's heels, what Rachelle had stashed under her bed.

A dinged-up Ford Escort was parked in the driveway. A light on in one of the windows. Someone was home. I chewed on a thumbnail, glancing back at the clumsy writing on the envelope. I thought of Destiny, Little Beth. Whatever Rachelle's sister was, she was still a mom, I reasoned, fanning up my resolve. I took a deep breath and stepped out of my car, locking the door behind me. Mystery wasn't going to solve itself.

As soon as I'd crossed onto their lot, a dog erupted, bark guttural and frenzied as a chain saw. *Fuck.* I froze. There were dogs, and there were *dogs.* I really hadn't thought this whole thing through. I stole a look back at my Buick. In any case, the bark was coming from inside the house, not out. *Go on*, I coaxed myself.

I pushed in the doorbell. It was barely audible. The dog must have been right up against the other side.

"Daisy!" I heard a woman's voice call. That bark didn't sound like it belonged to a Daisy.

"Quit your yapping, girl, I'm coming." That voice didn't sound like it belonged to any sister of Rachelle's.

The door swung open, and Daisy's owner appeared, one hand holding the dog back by her collar. Daisy, I realized, was no bigger than a fanny pack.

"Yeah?" the woman grunted, her eyes focusing past me, no less gruff than she'd been through the door. A ratty bathrobe was cinched around her waist, her dark hair yanked into a nest at the top of her head. I'd woken her up. It was a Saturday, granted, but it was well past ten A.M.

"Hi," I said, stretching out my hand. The woman looked down at it as if it were covered in ticks—disgusted. I lowered it. Who even was she? This woman as dark and rough-hewn as a work boot, the slanted furrow above her penciled-on eyebrows a result of what must have been a perpetual scowl. If Rachelle was soap, this woman was gristle. There was no way they were related. Was it possible I'd stopped at the wrong house?

I took a step back, scanning for the address. *351*, the mailbox confirmed. Maybe she was a cousin, a neighbor, charged with watching Rachelle's niece. Whoever she was, she knew the two sisters. She could still help.

"I'm looking for someone," I said, starting over, smiling, as if that'd disarm her. "Does Rhoda Bluecloud live here?"

"What?" The woman crossed her arms, mouth agape.

I should have said Mrs., I realized too late. Rhoda was a child. *Who goes around asking for a little girl?* The dog, sensing the tension, started growling again. She tried to wrangle free from the woman's grip by yipping and baring her teeth, nipping at the woman's hand.

"Stop it, will ya? That's enough." The woman yanked the dog up by her throat. "Enough," she commanded, fists locked around the dog's face, tamping bark down to a whimper. "Good girl." She let go of the dog's collar. "Good girl." The dog turned in two circles before folding herself in at the woman's feet. The woman rubbed at an eye, looking back at me. "Who's asking?"

"I'm Rachelle Murphy's neighbor. Jenny Hayes. I think, um. Is Rhoda her niece?" She blinked. "I'm looking for her sister. Mrs. Bluecloud? Does she live . . . here?" By the last word, my voice had gone meek. It wasn't unlike talking to a television set. The woman was wholly unresponsive—eyes vacant, like the mug shots in *Crimestoppers.* Had I seen her there?

"I'm Rhoda," the woman said after an eternity. "Her sister. Rachelle don't got no niece." Now it was my turn to go walleyed.

"I'm older." She cinched her robe tighter. A whole head shorter than me and apple-shaped; the punch-red terry was a misguided selection. To have a sister so lovely, looking like that. Rhoda must have been used to my type of reaction.

I thought of the pink envelope, those crudely formed letters. Script, when I thought about it, not dissimilar from Rachelle's grocery list. I'd only ever heard about them, the ones reared in the bush, adults barely able to sign their own welfare checks. Maybe the sisters hadn't been raised in foster care. Maybe they'd been raised in the wild.

"So?" Rhoda huffed, one hand ready to close the door.

"I'm looking for her," I blurted. "Rachelle. I thought she might be here."

"Here?" she repeated. "No." She cocked her head. The furrow deepened. "Why?" She seemed angry I was even asking. It wasn't exactly the response I'd pictured.

"I know she came by here the other day. I just thought maybe there'd been another emergency . . ."

"Hey," Rhoda interjected, her eyes narrowed, defensive. "How'd you say you got this address?"

"Rachelle did. Give it to me. Gave." I'd always been a shit liar. "An emergency contact when I'd babysit her girls. That's how I knew about the . . ."

"Hm," Rhoda interrupted again. "And you always just keep that list handy, eh." It wasn't a question. My face went even redder.

"Yeah," I muttered. The conversation halted. This was it, my first and last chance. "Has your sister been by at all this week?"

"Nope," Rhoda answered, arms shielding her chest.

"So you last saw her when?"

"I don't know. Last week." The day I went over. When Rachelle had to leave.

"So last Monday, then?" I said. Rhoda shook her head.

"I don't know, maybe. I'd have to check a calendar." She scratched at her temple, her nails long and yellowed. "What are you anyway, some kind of a cop?"

I looked down at my Keds. In OshKosh overalls and a striped T-shirt, I couldn't have looked less official. Maybe a cop's daughter, if that. "I work at the mall," I said quickly, before catching her tone. She was obviously being sarcastic.

"I live across from your sister, Rhoda," I told her in all earnestness. "We were neighbors." Rhoda blinked. "Are. We're friends."

"Something happened." It wasn't a question—Rhoda's voice clinical, as if she were stating a fact. "Did something happen?" It frayed, faltering at the end. Her eyes met mine for the first time. They were big and brown, like Rachelle's.

The phone rang. The dog jumped, starting up again.

"I should get that." Rhoda gathered the dog in her arms and started to close the door. The way our conversation had gone—I doubted she'd be back.

"Actually," I blurted, "can I use your washroom? I really need to go." I crossed my legs, insisting. She looked genuinely caught off guard. The phone rang again. "It'll only take a minute."

I could corner her after, sit down for a coffee, start from the beginning, leave nothing unsaid.

"All right." Rhoda sighed, probably figuring it was the easiest way to be rid of me. "But make it quick."

The hall was dim and musty, the faint smell of Pine-Sol in the air. Dark wallpaper and wood veneer. The first thing I noticed was the hill of shoes in the corner. Just like at Rachelle's. Runners in a few different sizes; little red rain boots; a new pair of men's Timberlands; one lone, sodden pink flip-flop. Was it the mate to the one in Rachelle's yard? Rhoda cleared her throat. "Washroom's just over there." She pointed down the hall. I turned on the faucet, leaving the door slightly ajar. "Hello." I heard her pick up the phone. "Hey, Shirley. Okay. How's it going with Bill?"

I looked around. The floor was linoleum like the entrance, the washroom done in chipped yellow tile and more wood veneer. Cheap as it was, it was spotless, clutter-free, with only a soap dish in the sink, what looked like a fresh bar of Dial. A drinking glass stood on the shelf below the mirror, patterned with an outline of Vancouver Island. It was filled with four toothbrushes, two of them stunted. Barbie pink. I thought of the bathing suits, the pint-sized Nikes. *Rachelle don't got no niece.* Rhoda was lying. But why?

"It's like I told you," I heard her saying. "Now you've got two babies to take care of." She laughed, her tone easy.

Her sister was missing, and there she was, shooting the breeze with a friend. If Rhoda was worried, it sure didn't seem like it. Or maybe it was more that she didn't know all the facts. I flushed the toilet and turned off the faucet. I'd just have to be more direct.

I followed the sound of Rhoda's voice. She was seated at a small round kitchen table, a cordless phone tucked under an ear. The room was dark, the shades drawn, her feet raised on a pulled-out chair. She must have heard me approaching, but she didn't bother turning.

"Shirley, I need to call you back. All right," she said. "Five minutes." She clacked the phone down, craning her head, her eyes narrowed like before. "Yes?"

"Rachelle's missing." The two words tumbled out. How was that for direct? "It's been a few days now. I thought you might know where she went."

"'Missing'?" Rhoda repeated, her voice thin again. She'd turned away from me, but I could still see her in profile. Her jaw was tightened, the furrow bent.

"I found her car yesterday. On the shoulder of 16-E. Thirty or so clicks from town. You're sure she didn't come here?" Rhoda was quiet. She shook her head.

"She left her daughters," I continued. "At the day care center. That was on Wednesday. On Tuesday someone came. A white truck I'd never seen before." Rhoda stood abruptly, expression inscrutable, her hands limp at her sides like hooked fish.

"It was gone the next morning. So was she."

Rhoda stood at her counter, topping off her coffee with what looked like a fresh pot. She hadn't even looked in my direction once since I stepped into the kitchen. Was more chance, I realized, of her sprouting wings than inviting me at the table for a cup.

"This isn't like her." I took a step toward her. "Something happened. Something's off. I figured you might know what to do next."

Rhoda didn't make a peep. I didn't get it. None of us had actually known Beth. We'd all still cried. Rhoda was emotionless, the same nothing look on her face as before, leaning against the counter, blowing at her mug. Maybe she was in shock.

"Can I get your number? So we can stay in touch?" Rhoda blinked. "In case you hear anything." Maybe she was just wary.

"Or, at least, I can give you mine." I made to search my pockets, even though I knew they were empty. "If you have a pen?"

I heard the front door open. Her shoulders tensed. "Rhoda." A man's voice boomed through the house. Or maybe it was something else.

"Whose car is that?" A man towered at the kitchen's entrance, his head nearly skimming the trim. A long dark braid trailed down his back, stopping just short of his Wranglers. He was older, in his late fifties, but still in shape—strapping even, clenched muscle, a rugged silhouette. He was much better-looking than Rhoda. Remarkably so, the inverse of Rachelle and Al.

"It's hers." Rhoda nodded in my general direction, her voice small, suddenly compliant. She was a different woman, this Rhoda, than the one who'd opened the door.

"Who?" The man didn't seem to see me. His scope zeroed in on Rhoda, like how Jim was with Missy, like a nail he needed to hammer.

"Jilly." Rhoda busied herself, opening a cupboard, scanning a drawer for a spoon. "She's Chel's neighbor." *Shell* was what I heard until I realized. *Chel.* Rachelle's nickname.

"Coffee?" Rhoda was already pouring it. The gold band around her ring finger clinking against the mug. So they were married. I searched for the man's band, but his hands were jammed in his pockets.

"That right?" he said, cold as night.

Something sharp dug into the toes of my Keds. I yelped, jerking back. A white rabbit, three times the size of the dog, hopped away from the kitchen and out of sight. Had it been there the whole time? I clutched my hand to my chest. Neither one of them flinched. It was like they didn't see me. Like I wasn't even there.

"She hasn't been home," Rhoda was saying. "Jilly said she saw her car on the highway."

"Whose car?" The man turned away, was riffling through an opened cabinet.

"Chel's." Rhoda placed a hand on his back. "Sugar's on the table, baby." He shrugged her off.

"Well, what'd ya move it for?" He dug his hand into the box, pitching three cubes into his mug before lumbering past me, out of the room. The clink of his spoon, the gears on his recliner—I heard the TV switch on.

Rhoda just stood there, staring at not even the window but the scuffed wall. It was like she'd been powered down. I knew that look. How Mom would get after she and André had had it out. I'd come out of hiding as soon as I heard the front door slam, just to make sure it wasn't her who'd left. I'd find her slumped in the same chair, bag of frozen peas in hand. I thought of something. Rachelle's grocery list. *Pees.* Maybe they hadn't been for her.

I stepped into Rhoda's eye range.

"A pen?"

"Oh." She turned her head. "Yeah. We're listed anyway." She tore a sheet of paper towel and started to write, pausing midscrawl as if she'd forgotten her own number. The TV was loud, a Western. *Bang bang bang.*

"Here." She handed it to me, and I tore off a corner, writing mine down. I went to pass it to her, but she'd already turned away, starting the faucet and scrubbing out her mug as if it'd been tainted. I left the paper on the table.

"Okay," I said. "I guess. Call if you hear anything?"

"What?" She kept scrubbing, the back of her head my answer. "Sure, okay." I let myself out.

A red-and-white Chevy Silverado had appeared in front of their house, the tarped-over bed blocking the view of my car. The man's, no doubt. I'd already strapped myself in before I realized: no keys. I must have left them on the counter.

I stepped out of my Buick, the barking no less unnerving the second time around. I pushed in the doorbell. No answer. I rang again. And again. They were in no rush.

"Yeah," Rhoda answered after the tenth or so ring, her eyes watery, rubbed pink. She'd changed out of her robe into a yellow sundress, her arms cradling the dog like a newborn, tawny fur clutched to her chest. I saw something then, what had been concealed before. Her forearms were punctured with scabbed-over holes. Track marks, I'd learned from *Cold Squad*. She wasn't and was exactly what I'd expected.

"S-sorry," I stuttered. "I forgot my keys." She didn't budge. "I think they're in the kitchen." She sighed, stepping back to let me in.

"We don't have all day."

I tiptoed past her, trying to take up as little space as possible. The TV was off—the house had gone quiet. The calm after the thunderclap. I scooped up my keys, scanning the counter. The scrap of paper towel I'd written my number on was gone.

As I turned back into the hallway, I caught a glimpse of the man in the dim light of the den. Bolt upright in a recliner, smoke heavy in the air, white fur clasped between his fingers. He was facing the muted television but kept one eye trained on me like a lizard or a snake, waiting to strike.

"Thanks again." I scooted past Rhoda, breath quickening.

"Yeah," Rhoda croaked, closing the door. I heard her lock it behind me. Twice.

I pulled into the Petro-Canada station, a knot in my stomach, the arrow on my gas gauge horizontal, hungry and thirsty and even more frustrated when I realized that I was parked in the same damn spot as the day prior—and no further along in my search. I was basically burning cash at that point. I trudged into the station, a twenty in hand.

It'd be worth it, I figured, optimistic that morning. I could scrimp on the shopping, buy the no-name brands. Use my car less during the week.

But to have driven all that way for . . . *that*? I wasn't dumb. It's not like I was expecting Rachelle to open the door, but at the very least I'd thought that her sister would know something. Who to call, where to start. At the very least I'd thought that her sister would care.

Rhoda had been crying after I'd left—but whether her tears were for Rachelle or something else was impossible to tell.

It had been stifling, the atmosphere. Familiar. The way André used to siphon all the oxygen from the air. He was a manual tree feller, highly skilled with a chain saw. Built exactly like the Man with the Braid. The violence tracked in, even after he'd kicked off his work boots. It followed them, men like that, to the game, the bar, the kitchen, the bedroom, the backseat, the bonfire—everywhere.

I dug in my bag and counted out enough quarters to buy a can of Pepsi and a bag of peanut M&M's. The cashier was a different woman from the one from the previous day, freckled like I was, her eyes muddled blue like Beth's. *FIND HER*, the sticker from the top of the pile urged. Beth, Rachelle, the white crosses on the highway. There might as well have been a follow up sticker: *WHO'S NEXT?*

I stepped outside and lifted the fuel dispenser. The more I thought about that morning, the tighter the knot in my stomach was wrenched. There was something off about them, Rhoda and the Man with the Braid. A marriage of concession—at least on his behalf. The kids must have been his, needing a mother. A role Rhoda had been happy to play. She knew something. Was protecting someone. If I were making a suspect list, that man would be on it. Right after whoever owned that white pickup. *Bluecloud.* The very name sounded invented. I wondered if it was his or if Rhoda had kept her maiden one.

The fuel dispenser clicked, and I drained the dregs of my can. I had Rhoda's number. A potential suspect. The morning hadn't been a total wash.

———

I stopped at the Safeway on the way home. Sam was due back that evening. I didn't feel much like cooking, so I bought a rotisserie chicken (on sale, the weekly special) and a box of those ready-made mashed potatoes. *Just add water.* Almost home-cooked. Not that Sam cared. He always told me not to trouble myself, but I'd insist. I might not have been able to make us a family, but dinner was always hot (or at least ready for the microwave) when he came home.

I was walking back to my Buick when I spotted Mom, her back toward me, unloading—more like flinging—the items from her cart into her trunk's opened maw. Muttering, as she often did, to herself as she lunged bottle after bottle of Diet Pepsi like some jumbo artificially sweetened grenades. She must have had it out at the salon again. I lowered my head as I approached, quickening my pace. The owner, a client, another hairdresser. Conflict to Mom was like a heartbeat. Automatic.

"Fuck," I heard her sputter. "Fucking goddamn, fuck."

Legs so starved, they looked about to splinter. Spine jutting from her skin. I could pity her, at a distance. More than pity—I could've sobbed. Like the moments—even when we were fighting, especially then—when that impulse would take over. To touch her face, to take her hand. I never did. She'd never let me. I stopped, turning back. I'd always been too mad.

She was digging in a pocket of cutoffs so shrunken, they were basically jean underwear, when her head turned toward me. The face formed strangely, alien. It wasn't her. Just another anorexic driving a taupe Ford Fiesta.

"Fucking goddamn motherfucker." The stranger slammed her trunk, gripping the handles of her cart, winding it up and launching. Her eyes caught mine, glaring. "What?" she jeered.

"Sorry," I muttered, turning again.

"That's what I thought, you stupid little bitch," she called out, laughing. Her words, like her doppelganger's, lodged down my throat. What I'd repeat back to myself, rote invocation. Thoughtless as prayer.

eleven

I woke the next morning with Sam's breath in my ear, his arm angled around my chest. Everything back to the way it was. Well, almost.

I edged out from underneath Sam, tiptoed into the kitchen, and started a pot, staring out the window at the yard. The first strawberries were long gone, and the summer squash were just about ready, waiting to be snapped from their prickly vines. August was here. Summer barreling closer to its end. The porch across from me empty. The garden behind the rusted truck fallow. Maybe forever.

"Taking in the view?" Sam came up behind me, pecking the top of my head.

His height was his best feature, no question. Sam had a good eight inches on me, and when he put his arms around me, he could wrap me up completely, a barricade from the rest of the world. *Strapping young fella ya got there,* Ray liked to say every time he saw us together. Sam towered over him. Ray and Mom were the same height. *It's the small ones you've got to watch out for,* Missy would caution. *Something to prove.* I thought of the Man with the Braid, two Rays stacked on top of each other. Small or large, it didn't seem to me to matter. You just had to watch out.

"It's weird," I said, eyes focusing on Rachelle's yard. "I haven't seen her all week."

Since Tuesday, more accurately, but I didn't want to be too accurate. I was tapping one foot, testing the ice. Sam stepped away from me, toward the fridge. He'd gotten in late, after I'd went to bed, and the plate I'd made for him was still sitting there, untouched. Cellophane taut over congealed chicken breast, beige potato lump. It didn't look appetizing to me either. Sometimes it felt like I couldn't get anything right.

"You fixing something for breakfast?" he asked, scanning the shelves. "I'm starved."

"Scrambled eggs and bacon?" I knew better than to push. Sam wasn't the type to poke around in other people's business, especially not the business of the only Native on the block.

I turned away from the window and back toward my kitchen—the hum of the refrigerator, the sputter of the coffee maker—back toward my husband, the crinkle of the *Citizen* between his sure hands. I glanced at my own: cracking eggs, unwrapping bacon. Busied fingers blanched under the wan morning light. For a moment, maybe longer, I wasn't sure whom, exactly, they belonged to.

Sam drove like he always did when he was home, the strip malls and the casino and the used-truck lots giving way to backcountry, rutted dirt road, dust kicking up around us like a shroud.

We were headed to a bush party, thirty clicks north of town. Forestry land nestled right between two boating lakes. Missy's family had been out there since May Long, campers linked like daisy chains in the clearing, securing the location, primo as it was, from any interlopers.

Some people spent their whole summer like that. Every weekend, out in the bush, the men comparing toys—motorboats and ATVs and four- and six- and eight-wheelers—the women restocking the coolers, wringing out swimsuits, scaling trout. Rain or shine or wildfire warning. Summer was as short as winter was long. Every Saturday had to count.

Missy had stopped inviting me years ago, saving me the excuse. I'd gone only once, back in high school with Anne-Marie and Jesse. We'd arrived before noon, but the heavy drinking must have commenced at sunrise. Everyone was too piss-faced to notice when we'd snuck off before lunch, ordering bacon cheeseburgers at the A&W and wolfing them in the bed of Jesse's trunk. They were straightedge back then, and I never drank anything harder than beer—not after what happened. Wasn't much to do at a bush party sober, unless you were one of the children.

Jim had called to invite Sam that morning. "To talk business," Sam had said into his coffee. "Should be fun." I doubted it. Even Jim usually avoided them. Missy always griped about having to drag him by his feet. He'd tell her, *Your family, your problem.*

I couldn't disagree with the sentiment.

Even outside the booze-drenched parameters of a bush party, I wouldn't willingly choose to spend the day with the Andersons. The dad was a hard-ass; the mom's brain pickled; Scotty, Kieran, and Eric, Missy's three older brothers, Irish triplets, neck and neck and neck in a lifelong pissing contest, a choke hold their idea of a good time.

We arrived just as the boys were coming back from the lake. Fishing rods hoisted, ice coolers in hand, pink banded across their faces, around the backs of their necks, as if they'd set themselves on the grill, between the hot dogs and the trout. Kieran was shirtless, his shoulders sure to blister. It was almost impressive how burnt men were willing to get. As if the sun were a provocation, another arm to thump down.

"Well, howdy-freakin'-do." Missy spotted us from afar, hollering and raising her red Solo Cup. She was sitting cross-legged in a lawn chair, a cigarette in her mouth and one tucked behind her ear, face redder than the sheeny fabric of her bikini. Her eyes were glassy, her words crowded together. It wasn't even eleven.

"Look who decided to grace us with her presence." She grinned, her lighter slipping from her hands. "Goddamn it," she muttered, using her toes to search the ground.

"Here." One of her sisters-in-law tossed her a BIC. I'd met all three of them before, but I could never keep the wives straight. Each bottle blonde with frosted lips and dark lip liner, preoccupied, always, with a baby or toddler or Popsicle-sticky child, their voices hoarse, primed to carry.

"Kim." Missy waved a hand at another sister-in-law. "Grab them some chairs. Come," she bid sarcastically. "Gather round our 'fire.'" She flexed a flip-flop toward the smoldering half barrel that was set in the center of their semicircle. Stuffed to its gills with charcoal, the smoke blowing right in our direction.

"Can you believe this fuckin' fire ban?" she asked, cigarette clenched between her teeth, flicking the lighter. It'd been on almost all summer. It was becoming the norm, campfire-less seasons: too little rain, the risk of combustion too high.

"I heard it's the beetle rot," a third sister-in-law chimed in. "My brother's a feller, says they can't haul the dead wood out fast enough."

"And pine burns quick, too," the first one agreed.

We'd celebrated the pine beetle years back—the boom it ignited in the industry, all those forests falling in on themselves, lumber waiting to be fed under saw. The planes came out squiggled blue, the same shade as a line on a pregnancy test, but the Chinese market didn't mind. The cash rolled in, and with it opportunity, until demand evaporated, eviscerating all those new jobs along with it. The dead trees, a ticking bomb.

It was the monoculture that was the real problem, Erin had taught me during the first wildfire season I can remember, on a hike we'd taken up near Salmon Valley.

A century ago, this place would have looked completely different, she'd said, gazing up at the canopy. *It's not sustainable. Planting row after row of pines.*

Forests needed variety, diversity, to thrive. Otherwise, they became like a body fed solely on potatoes or polished rice. Deficient. The mealy bugs and the stem borers and the beetles given not just a window but a swung-open door. The industry didn't take that into consideration. After clear-cutting, they planted fields of their highest yielding crops. Spruce, mostly. And pine.

"Drink?" Missy asked. She was refilling her own. Glug of Jack, glug of Diet Coke. Another glug of Jack.

"Sure." Sam took a cup off the top of the stack.

"There's some stuff you might like at the bottom of the cooler, Jenny." Missy looked over at me, still pouring. Her cigarette tumbled from her mouth as she attempted a wink. It landed lit side down on her thigh.

"Motherfucker!" She jerked the bottle sideways, whiskey watering the grass.

"Whoa, whoa, whoa!" A man sprinted over, rescuing the bottle from Missy's hands. He was wearing a pair of DayGlo basketball shorts and aviator sunglasses. No shirt, no shoes, just a scar that looked like a bullet wound on the back of his right calf.

"Waste not, want not." He raised the bottle to his lips and chugged. I'd never seen him before. Jim appeared next.

"Sam," he said, nodding in our general direction.

"Jimmy." Sam jumped up. "Hey," he said, slapping his hand.

"Let's talk." Jim jerked his head, and his ponytail swayed. It was sectioned into quarters by a set of thick black rubber bands. On anyone else, the style would have seemed ornamental, feminine even, but on Jim, it was as macho as a Randall knife. He turned away from the circle, Sam trailing behind him. *Jimmy.* I thought of our conversation the other week. As far as I knew, they'd never said more than a few words to each other. Since when were they friends?

"Some weather we're having, hey?" Mrs. Anderson leaned over, grinning, the lenses of her rectangular frames specked with charcoal, her breath harsh as shellac. I hadn't even realized she'd been sitting there. A wisp of a woman, she was easy to overlook. Her brain so nuked from vodka, it was like she was only half there.

She'd always had a hand glued to a bottle, but it wasn't until the previous summer that she really began to deteriorate. She was one of Mom's clients; I'd been pestered into a cut. I'd asked her how she'd been, and her face clouded over, like she hadn't understood the question or could no longer figure out how to get the words out from inside her head.

"Yes," she'd finally managed after a considerable pause, the gelled curls of her mountainous perm quaking.

"Wet brain," Mom had summed up, fishing a comb from the blue jar of Barbicide. "The brain cells don't renew anymore. Same thing happened to Sue's brother. Sad, sad," she'd said brightly. Pity was one of Mom's most prized sentiments.

"Sure is, Mrs. Anderson." I smiled back. She set down her cup and reached over, taking my hand.

"Tell me, sweetie, which one are you again?" Her hands were freezing. She must have been cutting with ice. "Kieran's?"

"That's Jenny, Mom," Missy hissed, her chin tucked toward her chest.

DayGlo Shorts was standing behind her, kneading his knuckles into the back of her neck. The man couldn't have been any taller than I was, but he was sturdy, biceps flexing as he dug into Missy's flesh. His left forearm was blanketed, tattoos clearly drawn with his right hand. A biohazard symbol, a piece of barbed wire, *Fuk Off*, a skull. A swastika.

I'd seen them before on the arms of Jim's friends. *A jail thing*, Missy explained airily. *All the white guys get them.*

Missy propped her elbows onto her knees, edging forward, the man's hands roving down to her tramp stamp. "You've met her, like, I don't know, twelve dozen times."

"Yeah," Mrs. Anderson said vacantly, grip loosening from my hand. Then, out of the ether (or maybe ethanol), a flash of recognition. "Hey, honey, how's your mom?"

"She's good," I said, voice lifting an octave.

"That's good," she echoed, sucking at her drink. "And your dad?"

Her eyes were buttons, her mouth a stitched line, the woman a husk, a half-wit—more like a quarter—but still, despite myself, my face burned red. She'd forgotten again. Whom she was talking to. *He's missing*, I said to myself in my head. *He's not in the picture*—what I would have actually said, the response at that point reflexive.

"That's *Jenny*, Mom." Missy sat up, vexed, her own mother like a third, pea-brained Pomeranian. She repositioned the scant flaps of her bikini, puffing on her cigarette. "You know her dad left."

My teeth met the inside of my lip, drawing blood. I hated whenever anyone put it like that.

"Oh." Mrs. Anderson brushed the bangs she no longer had from her eyes, which were aimed not at me but at a rusted-out camper. "Nice to see you again."

"Who needs a beer?" DayGlo Shorts had moved to the cooler. Missy and her sisters-in-law all threw up their hands. The man slinked around the circle, doling them out.

"You hear about the girl they found?" He held one out to me. Molson was more like water than beer anyway. I cracked it open. It was warm.

"What girl?" I'd just realized what he'd said.

"You mean Beth?" a sister-in-law suggested.

"*Pfff*," Day-Glo Shorts scoffed. "No. This was some Indian. Over by the golf course, in a ditch off Northwood Road." He was back behind Missy, working a knot in her shoulder between sips of beer. She swung around her head.

"Shut up," Missy said, slapping his gut. "That's right by our house." Beer spewed from the man's mouth onto his chest.

"No shit," he said, belching. He wiped the foam with the back of his hand. A spiderweb was girdled around the point of his elbow, degraded and blurry, as if he'd leaned into some dung. "Where'd you say Jim was again last weekend?"

"Do they know who?" I asked, breath rapid. Rachelle. *The first forty-eight hours are the most important.* Was this how it'd end? DayGlo Shorts was on round two, his mouth glued to the can. I took a sip of my own to try and calm myself. I felt like I was going to hurl.

The can dropped to the ground, and the man let out another prolonged burp before stomping it, with the bare sole of his foot, flat. "Some chick. I don't know." He placed his hands back on Missy. "Ask Jim." Missy made to whack him in the groin. He maneuvered away just in time, cackling.

"How old was she?" I tried to steady my voice. It was louder than I'd intended. "Was she from PG? Do they know what happened?"

DayGlo Shorts stopped dead, his eyes, pink as shrimp, latching onto mine.

"Someone's curious," he said, wetting his lips. "Someone's morbid. Wants all the gory details. She likes that. Hey, Missy." He snapped the band of her bikini. "Why you ain't introduce me to your friend?"

Missy lurched back, crushing his fingers against the chair. He wagged them in the air, running in a circle, the wheezing sputter of his laugh.

"She's married." Missy straightened, fumbling for the cigarette she'd stashed behind her ear.

"Ain't never stopped you."

Missy flicked on her lighter, swinging it toward him. Flame fluttering as she jerked her arm around.

It was a well-worn bit, a role Missy played effortlessly. The woman who didn't take no shit, who wasn't afraid to hit a man where it hurt. *Men like a woman who puts up a fight.* I thought of Mom, the bag of frozen peas against her cheek. Rachelle. Thrown in a ditch like an old mattress, another broken appliance. Had she fought back?

DayGlo Shorts had snatched the lighter and was holding it behind him, setting his farts on fire. I was doing everything I could manage to hold back tears.

A little girl waddled over, climbing into one of the sisters-in-law's laps. I thought of Destiny, Little Beth. Lost forever. Their mom disappearing like some cruel trick. The little girl nestled into the crook of the sister-in-law's neck. She was Eric's, the youngest of the three brothers. He came over next.

"Tina, have you seen my hat?" Eric's hair was buzzed and bleached yellow, his wifebeater streaked with mud. His elbow had opened, his knuckles roughed up. I must have missed the customary Anderson brother tussle. All in good fun until it wasn't. I crossed my arms over my chest.

It was Eric's friend who did it, what happened at the bush party. If Eric remembered, he never let on. We'd all been drinking. Missy had already zipped herself up in another boy's tent. Before I knew it, we were the last three by the fire—and then Eric left. No one saw me stagger-ing, the seat of my jeans blooming red. Still, I hated seeing him. It felt like I was back there, pinned in the dirt, pine needles stitched through my hair. I took another sip of my beer. And another.

"How do they know it's not Beth?" Tina insisted. "What if it's too early to tell?"

"Too early to tell white skin from brown?" Missy rolled her eyes. "Hey, Eric, toss me another beer." She spread out her hands, the can thudding to the ground. She didn't wait to open it, the lather fizzing down her thighs.

"Nice catch." Eric walked over toward the grill, cranking the knob on the propane tank clockwise.

"I already told you, it was a nobody." DayGlo Shorts hocked a loogie and spat. "Some squaw bitch. Shit like that happens all the time. Except usually they do a better job of hiding the body."

He went to the grill. Soon enough, all the men would be huddled around, drawn to the barbeque like flies to a bowl of stinking fruit. Mr. Anderson must have been up at the mines. Otherwise, he'd have been at the helm.

"Been dead since winter, they're saying. Some dumbass tried to bury her under the snow," he continued. "Dog walker found her. Hey, Fido, what's that? A human arm? Fetch!" He launched the imaginary limb in the air. Missy snorted.

Since winter. So it wasn't Rachelle.

I should have felt relieved, but instead, the pit in my stomach widened. It wasn't Rachelle, but it could have been. Whoever it was, she'd been missing since winter. None of us had even known she was gone.

"Good looking out." I heard Jim say to Sam, their faces serious, something brewing. They pounded fists. "Alistair." Jim looked over at DayGlo Shorts. "Let's move." *Alistair?* The name didn't exactly fit the bullet wound.

"Already?" Alistair was flipping sausages with his fingers. Jim didn't respond. He just turned and started walking toward the road.

"All right, boss, whatever you say." Alistair plucked a half-cooked sausage from the grates, jogging to catch up with him. "See yous later." He turned toward our circle, raising his free hand in a salute.

Jim's boys was what Missy called them, the men dogtrotting behind him, trained to follow his every command. *More like Jim's pets*, I remember thinking, trying to get a read on Sam. He'd taken over Alistair's place at the grill, his attention turned to the sizzle and pop. The smoke was there, right in front of him, but he couldn't see it.

Wasn't that the way it always went?

twelve

Sam had an extra week off before his next shift. I learned—that next morning—it would be his last. Jim had hooked him up with a job as a contractor. *With all sorts of strings attached.* I filled in what he'd omitted.

"You're trained to do that?" I asked, staring at the ceiling. We were still in bed, my head resting against Sam's heaving chest.

We rarely did it in the mornings, but we had to make up for the previous night. I'd drank too much at the bush party and couldn't stop seeing Alistair every time I closed my eyes to kiss Sam. *She likes that.* He'd morph into someone else, the words the slack-jawed boy had kept repeating, convincing himself. Eric's friend. *She likes it, huh, she likes it.* His palm sealing my mouth, driving my head deeper into the dirt, another girl, a former self, lost in a ditch. Still buried.

I'd told Sam I felt sick, locked the door to the washroom and leaned against the toilet, reaching over and flushing every couple minutes, pretending to heave.

I was at the end of my cycle, my breasts pumped like tires, waiting to bleed any minute. The possibility of conception so far off as to be imperceptible, a pebble in a river viewed from the clouds. But there was no use telling Sam. He was nothing if not persistent. Dogged even.

"I'll learn," he said. He knew the rumors as well as I did. As everyone.

"It's just." I had to be delicate. "What about Murray River? The money's not bad."

"Jim gave me a better offer." He shifted, starting to sit. "Based here. You really want me gone two-week stretches for the rest of our lives?" He looked back at me. Hurt.

"Of course not." There was no arguing with that. I sat up, pulling my hair back. I had to wash it. Even without an open fire, it still reeked of smoke. "I just want to make sure you know what you're signing up for."

As soon as I said it, I regretted it. He couldn't think I was questioning him. Sam was sweet, but like I said, dogged. Proud as any other man. There'd be no reasoning with him after.

"I can't work the mines my whole life, Jenny." He stood, pulling a T-shirt over his head. He moved toward the door.

"Besides." He turned, looking straight at me. "Missy's your friend." Emphasis on *your*. "Don't you trust her?"

"Of course," I said softly, his logic a snare.

Sam wouldn't even know Jim if it weren't for me. Missy was *my* friend. *My* fault. Whatever it was Sam had agreed to, he'd made himself clear. The engine was running, and though I may not have been the one behind the wheel, I'd provided the keys. Whatever it was Sam had agreed to, we were in it together, strapped tight.

The only way out was to jump.

I had to comb through the *Citizen* twice before I found her—the woman they'd found off Northwood Road. A girl, really, just fifteen years old. A runaway from a foster home in Terrace. Her body had been stuffed in a duffel bag. Dead since winter, just as Alistair said.

Delphina Thomas. Or was it Thompson? In the time it took me to drive to work, I'd already forgotten her surname. It'd been a blip on the back page of the paper. *Woman Found Dead*, the title read. Given no more attention than a snowfall warning or a vehicle incident. They hadn't even included a picture. No teary-eyed quotes from the people who'd known her. No community rallied. No thoughts, nor prayers. *First Nations woman* was as far as the description went.

I passed the Roll-A-Dome, the looming portrait of Beth. You'd have to be dim not to notice the discordance. The discovery of Delphina's body was the first anyone had heard of her disappearance. Was that the fate waiting for Rachelle? Unearthed seasons—or years—later? By chance? A dog rooting for a bone.

I should call Rhoda, I remember thinking, pulling into the mall's parking lot. My only lead. I'd discounted her too soon. She probably just needed some time for the news to sink in. People reacted in all sorts of different ways to grief. She had my number. Maybe she'd even call me. It'd only been two days since my visit. It just felt longer, as if it'd been another version of me that'd been standing in her kitchen. A Sam-less me, a me free from other people's opinions and expectations. After all, Rhoda didn't know me from Adam. Or whatever the female equivalent of that saying would be. Eve.

Was that why I'd been so drawn to Chel? I pinned on my name tag and stepped out of my car. Even though we were neighbors, we were still strangers—able to be whomever we wanted without even leaving our suburb. It was invigorating, that feeling. Freeing. And now it was gone.

I punched in in the break room, stashing my sack lunch in a locker. I'd already spent too much on gas. I couldn't justify burning any more cash.

Elyse was there, hunched over the counter, extracting a clump of mascara that'd lodged itself in the corner of her eye. Fresh out of high school with a slapped, ruddy complexion, she spent more time on her makeup than on any actual work. Not that there was much anyway.

"Been dead all day." Elyse glanced up at me, wad of gum glinting in her mouth. We were supposed to wear khakis, keep our company polo shirts tucked in, but Elyse was in cutoffs so short, they were just visible beneath the hem of her polo. Anytime she bent, her ass cheeks fell out. I wasn't sure why she'd been hired. Following protocol, I guessed.

Vita, the other part-timer, had left in June, as soon as she'd started to show. "Your turn next," she'd said, hand safeguarding her belly. Vita was two years younger than me, had been hired at the same age—eighteen—as Elyse. Before her, there'd been Megan. And before Megan, Angelique. Upon leaving, they'd all said those same words to me, like some sick sort of a curse. I looked at Elyse, her lip-liner pencil in hand. She was snub-nosed, her eyes sleepy, like a child's. No amount of makeup would make her look less young. The moment she uttered those words to me would be the moment I quit.

But then, what else would I do?

"It's too fucking small." Elyse was on another tangent, slathering her legs with *Boysenberry Bliss*. I was dusting the shelf of roll-on body glitter. "There's not even a mall, did you know that? I mean, Jesus fucking Christ."

"That right?" I answered automatically. Elyse salted all her sentences with cusses, our conversations alternating between how shit it was here and how great it would be someplace—anyplace—else.

"Sometimes I can't even believe I'm from there. At least PG has a Sears. Vanderhoof. Vander-*hoof*. What kind of a fucking name is that?"

Vanderhoof. I tuned back in. I'd almost forgotten; she'd just moved here. Elyse was obviously a whole generation removed from Rhoda and the Man with the Braid, but their daughters—they might've been in school together. Maybe there was a reason Elyse had been hired. Just how small *was* Vanderhoof?

"Hey, do you know anyone with the last name Bluecloud?"

"'Bluecloud'?" Elyse repeated, spritzing the air with a body mist. *Tahiti Dreams.* She shook her head. "Sounds made-up."

I stopped at the Esso on the way home. Sam would flip if he saw my gauge on *E* again. Since Beth, he always insisted on keeping at least a quarter in my tank. Only stopping once I'd arrived where I was headed. Never hitching, no matter what. Not that I needed Sam to tell me that.

He wanted to get a lease on a new car, one that was more reliable than my Buick. He could save up once he started his new job. Jim had a friend who could get him a deal. Jim was everywhere all of a sudden, solving all our problems, left and right.

I pulled up next to pump number seven. A woman crawled out of the dinged-up station wagon at the pump in front of me, stepping around to the passenger side. Close to Mom's age, she had stringy hair that was dyed an acidic orange, her earlobes perforated with tiny hoops and studs. She swung open the door to the station's store, one arm latched around the shoulders of a little girl.

The glossy black pigtails, the dot of a nose. From that distance, I could've sworn it was Destiny. The woman was white, her skin splattered with freckles. Could the girls have been placed in foster care so soon? My heart lurched as I followed behind.

The woman stood at the counter, pointing to a pack of Player's Lights—the cheap stuff. She didn't have on any pants, just a tie-dyed shirt that could've fit three of her, spiral of bears undulating as she dug into her tattered bag. She was paying in change.

It always went like that. If you were really hard up, you could always take in a ward. There were enough of them.

Only two types of families fostered, neither one of them virtuous. If you were lucky, you'd be placed with the zealots, Bibles stacked beside bunk beds, ten—sometimes more—of their own children to mind, to discipline, leather belt a multifunctional device. The others were beyond the pale, no book to guide them, their sole motivation the check at the end of the month. Desperation patent, insidious as a gas leak, those wards better off in a group home or even in lockup, where at least they were guaranteed three square meals a day.

I'd known one family like that. The Bouchers. One of their daughters was in my grade. June. She never said much, always sulking toward the back of the classroom, her spine curled, her sleeves yanked down around her fingers as if her sweatshirt were a shell. Once, in sixth grade, I caught her with them rolled up, the rush of the faucet, the drone of the lights. I thought they were shadows at first—what was braceleted up and down her forearms—like a finger painting in shades of purple, bile green, dusk.

The mom would drop them all off in a minivan with a crumpled bumper, the rear lights readhered with packing tape, the fissures in the windshield fracturing the woman's square face. It was always red, as if she were perpetually on the verge of eruption, her voice blaring, more of a bleat.

There was always someone new in the backseat, another dark face, indistinguishable from the last or the next. They never made it past a month, their wards. Delphina could have easily been one of them. Had anyone even asked why she'd run away?

The woman's bronzer fell from her bag and clattered to the floor. "Shit." She squatted down, scooping brown powder back into its case. I looked for the girl, but she was gone. I started down one of the aisles.

"Destiny," I said in a low voice. "Destiny?"

Seated cross-legged near the pop dispenser, the girl had her back toward me, poking her fingers inside a cage. Two rabbits, one sucking at a bottle of yellow-looking water, the other on its haunches, its eyes fixed, black.

"Destiny," I said, my blood quickening. The girl turned her head.

"Mallory." The woman was behind me. "Time to go." She stood with one hand on her hip, clutching her keys and the pack of Player's in an upturned claw.

"Look, Mom," the girl was saying. "Bugs Bunny."

She was at least four years older than Destiny, I realized, a preteen even, the metal of her braces glinting under the fluorescent lights. Her eyes were green, her hair not black at all but chestnut, more like sandy brown.

"I said, it's time." The woman tapped her flip-flop, eying me.

Delphina. She'd gotten to me. I was projecting, seeing Rachelle everywhere. Assuming the worst. I'd even been so desperate as to imagine that Elyse would somehow know them, Rhoda and the Man with the Braid. Now here I was, pestering a random little girl in a gas station convenience store. Is this what it'd come to?

There was no more putting it off. Even if Sam was home, I'd call Rhoda. I had to. For the sake of my sanity. I was on my own—the only one looking.

And Rhoda the only one who might be able to help.

Lucky for me, when I got home, Sam was already conked out on the sofa, the TV turned to the hockey game, puck skittering into net. I clicked off the screen, eying the clock on the VCR. Eight wasn't too late. I took the phone and marched into the washroom, unfolding the piece of paper towel from my purse. *Rhoda*, she'd written, the same unsure letters as on the envelope. It rang, and rang, and rang again—and kept ringing. The answering machine hadn't been set up. I hung up after about the thirtieth peal, dejected. Another dead end.

I went into the kitchen and stood over the sink, picking at what Sam had left on his plate, squirting ketchup over bites of cold steak and potatoes. Rachelle's lightless house a beacon, a blight; the sole dead bulb on the string. Everyone, even those who'd left on vacation, kept their lights on, at least out front. I'd driven by again on my way home, just to make sure. Dark.

The kiddie pool, the washer, the rusted-out truck—even in the night, you could still make out the mess. It'd all be cleared soon enough, left to fester in the city dump. Rachelle would decompose sooner. *Stop it*, I scolded myself. I thought of the officer on the news, a full month after Beth's disappearance. *We're not losing hope yet.* I could try Rhoda again in the morning, all day if I wanted. Sam was due in Mackenzie to help with the potato harvest. He'd be out of the house by six A.M.

I used to go every year, the week of twelve-hour days, but I'd opted out that summer. To be honest, I couldn't stand the farm. I wasn't afraid of getting my hands dirty, but it was nothing like my garden, all those endless acres of potatoes—sea of brittle husks. It looked like the earth had been scorched. Killing the tops made it easier for the machinery, windrow harvester gashing the soil, spitting out spuds, rapid as a machine gun. The women used to do the sorting—the potatoes from the rocks that would invariably make their way into the bins—but there was another machine for that now. Instead, they made lunch.

Sam's mom wouldn't have minded another set of hands in the kitchen. A true farmer's wife, always buzzing from task to task, she was friendly enough. I just couldn't stomach the disappointment every time I had to tell her that her prayers weren't working. No miracle was on its way—not now and, most likely, not ever.

My heart skipped. I almost choked on my steak. For a moment, it seemed as if a light had been switched on in the truck. I stepped outside to get a better look. It was gone. *What?* I stepped closer, and the light appeared again. Cylindrical—this time on the handlebars of one of the kiddie bikes. I heard whispering, someone laugh. I squinted toward her neighbors. Their grandkids must have been over, passing a flashlight back and forth between their hands.

That's it, I realized. *Her car.* I'd seen Jesse open Anne-Marie's minivan with a shoelace once, when she'd lost her keys in the Safeway. He'd made a loop and shimmied it through the crack in the door, hooking one end around the lock and tugging. It didn't seem that complicated.

There must have been something—in the glove compartment, the center console—Rachelle had left behind. Something to explain what had happened. Or at least point me in the right direction.

I could try Rhoda again, after I checked out Rachelle's car. Maybe we'd have more to talk about. I could even stop by. It wasn't far. Two birds, one tank of gas.

I caught my reflection in my kitchen window, my eyes brightened, mood lifted by my plan. I wasn't losing hope yet.

thirteen

I thought it'd be simple, getting into her car. Had convinced myself, hands firm upon the wheel, that it couldn't be hard.

That sort of willful, unearned confidence carried me along 16-W, up to the Chevron that wasn't but a few clicks from Rachelle's Fleetwood. Maybe it was the sight of the phone booth, a reminder of my failed attempt to involve the cops. Or maybe it was the sudden realization that I'd forgotten the shoelace—the one morning that I hadn't just slipped on my Keds. Instead, I was wearing a pair of sandals, off-brand Dr. Scholl's clogs.

Whatever it was, any faith I had vaporized. And for some reason, I wasn't seeing her car. Then, like a sledgehammer, the Vanderhoof welcome sign. I'd gone too far. My eyes had been trained to the shoulder. There was no way I could've missed it. The highway calm, with few passing vehicles. Unless—it was no longer there.

I hooked a U-ey, switching off the radio and focusing, just to be double sure. A semi rattled by. My clog on the brake pedal, my neck craning to see. Nothing but the indifference of the fireweed and the pines. The Chevron came back into view. The Fleetwood had vanished.

I cranked the wheel and turned into the station, pulling up next to the phone booth. Maybe the cops had come after all, towed it in as evidence. The officer had said to call back if the car was still there after a few days. What about if it went missing? Its owner still AWOL. I stepped into the booth and picked up the receiver, punching the metallic buttons. *Nine-one-one.*

"Nine-one-one, what's your emergency?" a woman's voice asked.

"Hi," I squeaked. *Emergency*—I wasn't sure this qualified. I really just needed to talk to that officer.

"Could you transfer me to the Vanderhoof station?" I asked. "I need to follow up on something."

"What's your emergency?" the operator said flatly, ignoring my request.

"There was a car," I started, "on the shoulder of 16. It was here a few days ago, and . . ." I trailed off. "Now it's gone."

"'A car,'" she repeated. I knew how it sounded. "I'm sorry, was this your vehicle?"

Just then, a hatchback skidded its way into a parking space, the passenger door swinging open before immediately slamming shut. A small man in an outsized T-shirt aimed himself toward the convenience store. *NO FEAR*, two eyes glared from his back. Spitting a wad onto the concrete, he rubbed a palm over his buzz cut before disappearing beyond the streaked glass. That's when it registered, the hatchback's color. Greenish-yellow.

"Ma'am?" the operator was saying. "Are you referring to your vehicle?"

"What?" I croaked, mouth sapless. *If anyone has any information.* "I'm sorry, but I'm here at the Chevron, and I think I might have just seen . . ."

"Plate numbers," she interjected, clearing her throat, her tone taut, sharp as a tack. *Plate numbers.* I stepped out of the booth and squinted at the hatchback. The sun was blinding. I couldn't make out a letter.

"I don't." My face flushed. "I'm . . ."

The man exited the store, and I yanked the cord as far as it could travel. As he snapped back the tab on a can of Surge, I realized: he wasn't a man but a boy, with slight shoulders and a greasy sheen to his skin, firmly adolescent. There was smoke blowing out from the gap in the driver's window, a woman's hands upon the wheel. His mom.

"I'm not sure." I switched the receiver from one ear to the other. First the girl at the Esso, and now this. I really was starting to lose it.

"It's my neighbor's car," I said, jolted back into action. "Rachelle Murphy. She's been missing since Wednesday. I'm just wondering if maybe they took it in. I . . ."

"Plate numbers," the operator interrupted again.

"I don't—they didn't ask that before." I heard her tongue clucking. I could almost see the thought bubble—*Idiot.* "Couldn't you just transfer me to the station? They said to call back after a few days."

"You are aware that it's illegal to call this number unless there is an actual emergency, correct?"

"No. I mean, yes. I . . ."

She sighed, vexed.

"Sorry." I stared down at my clogs as if they'd have the answer. I could see it was useless. "Never mind," I muttered, hanging up. It was just like all the other times. She wasn't wrong. If I wanted the RCMP to take me seriously, I'd have to hand over more concrete information. Maybe Rhoda had Rachelle's plate numbers written down somewhere.

I dug in my purse for the piece of paper towel. It wasn't there. *Shit.* I could've kicked myself. I must have left it in the washroom, the pocket of my work pants. *Idiot.*

I went into the store and bought one of those tall cans of Arizona iced tea and a bag of barbeque-flavored sunflower seeds. I sat slumped in the driver's seat with the door flung open, spitting shells onto the sunbaked pavement. I'd lost my nerve. Going to Rhoda's without contacting her first, it felt foolish—if not downright risky. She'd paid, I was sure of it, for my last visit. The Man with the Braid was André the sequel—the same dormant rage, lid clattering, clamped tight. His energy as oppressive as duct tape. I didn't have any proof—it was only a hunch—but if I were making one of those bulletin boards they used on *Cold Squad*, his picture would've been the biggest, linked to Rachelle with thick red string.

I stared at the constellation of mangled shells. A wool glove, with its fingers warped and pointing in opposite directions, was plastered to the pavement just a few feet away. Probably lost last winter, surfacing after having been buried by feet of snow. Like Delphina. My stomach dropped.

It was then that it hit me. I hadn't thought to search the vicinity. The glove they'd found in that famous football player's trial. The Fleetwood was gone, but someone might've left something else behind. I wasn't sure exactly where her car had been, but I could ballpark it. I started my Buick, flicking on my blinker and turning east.

If I remembered correctly, it was after that second dip in the road, the handwritten sign: *Farm-Fresh Eggs*. I dipped once, twice, and hooked another U-ey as I passed the sign, pulled over, and stepped out of my car, locking it behind me. I slipped the jagged end of my keys up between my ring and middle fingers. It was the middle of the day, but you could never be too careful. That football player's ex had been nearly decapitated. I walked along the shoulder, scanning the ground.

Something silvery caught the sun, half buried in the dirt. A weapon? My heart thumped. I looked over my shoulder, bending down. An emptied bag of all-dressed, treaded with the indentations from a tire. I sighed. Another dumb idea. The whole morning a waste of more gas. The wind picked up, the pines swaying overhead. Any prospect of finding Rachelle carried with it, blowing further and further out of reach. I closed my eyes and listened to the whoosh.

"Everything all right?" A voice strained over a sputtering engine.

A black four-by-four had pulled over, its passenger window rolled down. A man in the driver's seat, his meaty paws on the wheel, a pair of wraparound sunglasses tilted atop the brim of his Canfor hat.

"Yeah," I shouted over the thrum. His muffler must have crapped out. "Thanks."

"Looks like your car broke down. Need a lift?" His plaid shirt was buttoned to the top button, the folds of his neck bulging over the collar. He didn't smile. The flash of orange. A hunter's vest was piled on the dash.

"No," I said, stepping back. "Thank you." He didn't budge. I squeezed my hand around my keys. "I didn't break down. Just taking a walk."

"You're still looking for her, huh?" the man said, incredulous, and my mouth gaped open. How did he know? He was saying something else, shaking his head.

"Beth," he repeated. "Poor girl." Beth. Of course. Beth. For a moment, I'd almost forgotten about her. "Trail's back that way." The man pointed behind him. "God bless." He lifted a hand up and out of his window as he drove off.

Trail? I turned back. So maybe the spot hadn't been random. Maybe Rachelle had pulled over for a reason. Maybe she was going somewhere. Or being led.

The path was unmarked and narrow with the bush edging in, untamed tunnel, poorly suited to my choice of footwear. It had been a logging trail once, the overgrowth signaling that it'd long fallen out of use. It went like that after they cleared what they needed, all those trails and resource roads leading nowhere, veins hitched to an inanimate heart. My breath quickened as I treaded uphill, fist still clutched around my makeshift weapon. What would've brought Rachelle out here?

The trail plateaued, opening to a clearing. To the left stood a circle of spruces, each trunk marked with white. A symbol scrawled upon bark, like an *E* but with three extra dashes. I'd never seen it before. The path stopped there, suddenly, with nothing but bush beyond.

I stepped into the circle, the hairs on the backs of my arms pricking up. The sun had shifted—the light had gone flat. The air was still. I was alone, suddenly hyperaware of myself, mosquito-bitten arms and legs, all that vulnerable white flesh. I unfolded the band of Missy's old cheer shorts. I should have worn jeans, a trench coat like Columbo. In my clogs, I couldn't even run. I stumbled backward into a pile of soot, hock of charred wood disintegrating under my chunky wooden sole. There'd been a campfire in the center of the circle. Within the past week or two, by the looks of it. The fire ban had been on since June. The fine was no joke—345 dollars for every head gathered around. If you were really unlucky, they took you to court. People were more scared of the conservation force than they were of the RCMP.

Speeding ticket? Who gives a flying fuck? I remembered Missy recounting what had happened when they'd pulled over her dad, a doe in the bed of his truck. Off-season. *Roadkill*, he'd tried to convince them. It was the first and only time she'd seen her dad's hands shake. *Take away a man's hunting license, that's power.*

Whoever had been out there was either stupid, or delinquent, or a winning combination of both. I squatted down, brushing the ash from my heel. The light shifted again, and an object winked from beneath the pile. This was no chip bag. I poked at it with a twig, lifting a threaded chain, cross hanging limply from one end. Gold. Rachelle's necklace. It was my hands that were shaking now.

I held it like that, the necklace, hooked around the twig like a fishing lure, the whole walk back to the car. It was evidence—someone had tried to melt it down. I steadied my breath. Their prints might still be on it. There might be a way to trace them. I might not have had her plate numbers, but this was bigger. This was proof nobody could deny.

Something had happened. Something bad. She still might be out there, somewhere, waiting. *Dead since winter.* I shooed the thought from my head.

I raced back to town, not stopping even when I felt that familiar spurt, red blossoming between my legs. Sam would be disappointed. He never said it; he didn't have to. *That's okay.* He'd pat my leg. *We've got time.* It was a phrase less true with each passing year. He knew it, as well as I.

I pulled into the parking lot of the RCMP headquarters, the low-spanning beige brick as insipid as the double-doubles passed through the drive-through window of the Tim Horton's beside. The jokes were too easy. *Which came first? The cop shop or the Timmy's? Think they're building 'em in pairs?*

Whoever had built it hadn't been very strategic. Flung on the far edge of town, it was hedged in by a strip mall: a Timmy's, Dollar General, Spruce Capital Feeds, a mammoth Canadian Tire. Removed from any action, so to speak.

Twig and necklace aloft, I marched right up to the main desk. The receptionist was on the phone.

"I told her it wouldn't be easy." She was picking at the top of a blueberry muffin, her fingernails painted a cherry red. "I know." She held one up toward me. "I know. Look, sweetie, I have someone. Okay." She laughed, her ample frame jiggling. "You, too." She placed the phone back in its receiver, looking up, eyes darting from my face to the twig and back again. "Sorry about that." She cleared her throat. "What brings you in?"

"This." I shook the necklace off the twig and onto the desk. "I didn't want to tamper with the evidence." *Tamper.* I thought of the family from Vancouver. It sounded professional. I straightened my back.

"I see." The receptionist nodded, eying the cross. Her lipstick had smeared onto the arch of her chin. She took a sip of her coffee. She'd probably just come back from lunch.

"It's Rachelle's? Murphy? The missing person?" My voice kept lifting, as if even I wasn't sure what I was on about. "I've called here before." I weighed the last word down, definitive. "It should be on file."

If the receptionist had any inkling about Rachelle's case, she didn't show it. Her face inscrutable, bored almost. She placed a hand on her cheek. I noticed her ring finger was bare.

"She's been missing near a week," I continued. "I just found this where her car was. I think someone tried to burn it. The necklace. Not the car. Did they take that in?" Everything was coming out jumbled, my hand still clasped around the twig. I must have looked ridiculous, a little girl and her magic wand. I set it down.

"I've called three times now," I said firmly. "They keep telling me to call back, that she'll be back. But she's not back. I live right across from her." The receptionist was nodding, reaching over toward her phone. "I'd know." I eyed the necklace, gold dulled from the ashes. "She's gone."

Saying it aloud, it hit me. I lifted my hand to find that my eyes had gone wet. So much for professionalism. The receptionist picked up her phone.

"Mick, can you come out here?" She spoke in a hushed tone, shielding her mouth with a hand. She glanced back up at me, forcing a smile. "Why don't you take a seat." It wasn't a question. She gestured toward a row of folding chairs. "Officer Mick will be out in a jiff." I nodded, wiping my eyes. I took a deep breath. I didn't want to look like I'd been crying.

A man came bounding through the glass doors of the main office, his pace measured, his stance wide, as if he'd just dismounted a horse.

"What's shaking?" He planted his elbows on the receptionist's desk, set down a coffee mug. Her face lit up at the sight of him. They were laughing, casual—him twiddling a pen, her fluffing her perm. He hadn't seemed to notice the necklace.

The receptionist said something I couldn't make out, and the man turned his head toward me, brushing his blonde hair from his eyes. He was young, close to my age, and I could tell that he thought he was handsome, that I should be impressed. The receptionist certainly was.

"Howdy." He walked over toward me. "Officer Mick." He held out a calloused hand. His grip was airtight, more pump than shake. "Why don't we chat in my office a while?"

"Okay." I stood. "The necklace." I pointed toward the desk.

"It's safe with Patty." He gave the receptionist a wink, rapping his knuckles against her desk as we passed.

Officer Mick didn't really have an office; it was just a desk in a room full of desks. I took a seat. A postcard with a blonde, supine in a lounge chair, striped towel positioned strategically around her bare breasts, was propped against the back side of his phone. *FLORIDA*, the letters above the woman read. I looked around. There wasn't a single other woman in there. Bullpen was pretty spot-on.

I started from the beginning, the dented white truck, the woman from the day care, the first call I'd placed, the second. Finding Rhoda, the atmosphere there. The strange way she'd reacted. The Man with the Braid. The more I explained, the less real it all sounded, like Rachelle were a character, somebody else's neighbor, a story I'd read or seen on TV. I glossed over a few parts—the leap through her window, the hours I'd spent watching her from my own—but otherwise, I left no detail out. He listened intently, fingers tented together, lips pursed in concentration.

"It's her necklace. I'm sure of it. It was right near her car." I crossed my legs. Another spurt. I was hoping there'd be one of those machines in the washroom, but the only option was to wad up some one-ply toilet paper. It always seemed to come at the worst moments: gym class, the first swimmable day of summer, while wearing the skimpiest shorts you owned.

"Is it here?" I hadn't seen the Fleetwood in the lot. They must have had a warehouse somewhere. "Did you find anything?" Officer Mick's hands had parted, his fingers moving through the sides of his hair.

"Stormcloud," he said after a considerable pause. "That's an unusual name." His eyes narrowed, zeroing in on mine. Did he think this was all some sort of a joke?

"Bluecloud," I corrected him. "That's her sister, Rhoda. Rachelle's last name is Murphy."

"Murphy." He nodded, leaning back in his chair. "And what'd you say your name was again?" His tone leisurely, focus dimmed, if not entirely extinguished. He'd never asked in the first place.

"Jenny."

"Jenny . . ." He retrieved a pen.

"Hayes." It was the first thing he'd thought to write down.

"'Hayes,'" a voice repeated, the desk near Mick's. This officer angled his neck toward us, wheeling his chair closer. "Sam's wife, right?"

He was a bear of a man, as wide as my refrigerator and, from the looks of it, just as dense. His face crudely formed, like random thumbprints in a log of cookie dough. I knew all of Sam's friends. I'd never seen him before.

"He's friends with a buddy of mine." He must have read my expression. "Jimbo." He grinned, flashing his gums. "Sinclair. Heard you're palsies with the wife."

The phone at his desk started ringing. He didn't move, his pinched, little eyes sweeping the length of me before meeting Officer Mick's again.

"You take good care of her, buddy." He wheeled himself back, picking up the phone with one hand and resting the other on the top of his head, pit stain a lake of damp darkened blue bleeding all the way down to his chest.

Jimbo. How the hell was he *palsies* with a cop? I looked back at the man. He was thrumming a pencil against a hulking thigh, his fingernails nubs, bitten to the quick. Jim must have had something good on him. I wondered how long he'd been listening in.

"Okay, Jenny." Officer Mick finished typing. "Let me walk you out." He stood.

"That's it?" I stayed in my chair.

"That's it," he answered, smiling. I noticed his teeth were exceptionally white. He must have used something—those whitening strips, a special toothpaste. Bleach.

"Isn't there a form or something?" I looked up at him. "Something I should sign?"

"'A form,'" he echoed, smile still pasted on. "All the paperwork is, unfortunately, on our side. I'll punch in the details at the end of my day. Consider the report filed." He patted the back of my chair. I stood—what else was there to do?

"You done good." He nodded. "Now get on out of here and go enjoy this beautiful weather." He was waiting for me to start walking, but I didn't want him behind me. I was sure all he'd see was a big red blot.

"All right," he said, smile dimming. He led the way.

We passed Patty's desk on our way out. The twig was gone, but the necklace was sitting right where I'd left it. The last of her.

I hesitated. I didn't want to leave it there. It felt too final. Like the next time I'd see it would be at Value Village, sealed up in a sandwich bag. *4.99.* I stepped back toward the desk. Officer Mick swung open the exit door.

"All right," he repeated, ushering me out. He didn't seem worried. I wanted to believe it, his confidence. *These things have a way of shaking themselves out.*

"You think . . . Is there still a chance she's okay?" I stood at the threshold, one foot on the carpet, the other on the cement.

"Rachel?" He thumbed a cigarette out from his pack, sticking it in his mouth, his words garbled as he spoke. "I'm sure of it."

Sam's truck was in the garage. He'd come home early. One of the harvesters had crapped out in the middle of a row just before lunch. A whole half a day down the shitter. He'd shaken his head.

"Where've you been?" he asked, facing the tube. He'd muted the sound, dirt bikes emerging from tawny mist silently, near graceful without the threat of their engines. A can of Molson was sweating atop the coffee table in front of him, another white ring I'd never get around to polishing out. Housework was like that; the quicker you shoveled, the faster the snow fell.

"At Nana's," I lied, kissing the top of his head. Nana wouldn't have remembered, anyway, even if I had visited. He stayed in his recliner, wrapping his arms around my waist, face still turned to the screen.

"I got to pee." I slipped from his grip, stepping toward the washroom.

I plunged my shorts and underwear down into the sink, lathering them up with a bar of Ivory, wringing them out under the running faucet until the water in the basin ran clear. I went out and hung them on the line—a small white flag, a bigger green one. I squinted out at Rachelle's deserted yard. The chimes on her back porch were clinking in the breeze. *Every time a bell rings, an angel gets its wings.* The tears were back. Soon it'd be all over the news. *Necklace Found from Missing Woman. Two Young Daughters Left Behind.*

But there was nothing that night, or the next, or the night after that. A man in Kamloops had been shot dead in the middle of the day, bullets shattering his front window, eviscerating the stuffing from his couch. No one had seen anything. The perpetrator was still at large. It was the top story. *If anyone has any information . . .*

The picture they showed of the victim, with one arm draped around someone who'd been cropped out. Smiling, unaware of what was to come. Twenty-two years old, he looked twice that, his eyes sunken, his skin loose, as if there were too much of it, as if he were inflatable and all the air had been let out. Drugs were involved. Foul play was a given. The footage of his body being carried from his house, black bag in the background, his father in the foreground, his mother somewhere off-screen. *He was a good kid*, his father had spoken into the microphone. *Got mixed up with the wrong crowd.*

It wasn't in the paper either, even the back pages. I'd triple-checked. I don't know why I was surprised. Her necklace had probably been brushed into the trash as soon as I'd left. Officer Mick hadn't even remembered Rachelle's name.

Some squaw bitch. How Alistair had described Delphina. A nobody.

I thought of Missy, all those other unnamed women vanishing along the Highway. *Occupational hazard, I guess.*

Women go missing every day. Out of Rachelle's own mouth.

Sam didn't try that night. He must have noticed the washing. Sometimes he was more observant than he let on, not saying much, just squeezing me extra tight before switching off the lights and turning over onto the other side.

He was there beside me, tucked under the same comforter in the same king-sized bed, but I still fell asleep with that familiar, lonesome dread. Deepened, since the snuffing out of that neighboring light.

fourteen

The coffee was dripping, the washer spinning, the frying pan scrubbed of its rimy bacon fat. The sink had been cleared, every dish put away. The dustpan emptied, the garden weeded and watered, the zucchinis grated and baked into a cooling brick of bread. I'd already pinned two loads to the line, and it wasn't even ten A.M. I was running out of tasks. We were supposed to go over to Anne-Marie and Jesse's for lunch, but Sam had to head back to Mackenzie and finish what'd been shelved. I was on my own. Again.

Anne-Marie was due in less than four weeks, and she wanted to squeeze in some time with her friends. "Chaos is coming." She looked at me knowingly, forgetful, I guessed, of my predicament.

"Sure is," I agreed unconvincingly, padding into their living room, startled, as I always was, by the sight of that crucifix. Nailed on a cross that was nailed above their big screen, blood cording down from the gashes, gorier than the rerun of *Cold Squad* Jesse was half watching from the couch. Anne-Marie was one of the few in our class who had actually kept her faith, her dad a Presbyterian pastor. Mom wore a cross, too, but it was purely for fashion.

Tanner barreled into the room, crashing into Jesse. Jesse grabbed him and stood, flipping the boy upside down, gripping onto his legs and spinning.

His days had freed up since switching to the graveyard shift, a tactical move to spend more time with the twins. When Tanner was younger, he'd often miss him in the morning, and then again when he came home at night. "One day, I looked up, and he was walking," Jesse was saying. "I don't want to miss everything again."

It was unusual, his approach to fatherhood. *Makes you wonder what he's got between his legs*, Missy would whisper when he'd leave to change Tanner's diaper.

"But when do you sleep?" Anne-Marie and I stood at the counter, the kitchen that was a mere section of wall. Her hacking into a block of jalapeño-flecked cheddar, me shimmying the bag of all-dressed I'd brought into a bowl.

"It's not so bad." Jesse shrugged off my question, the unlit cigarette between his lips wobbling up and down. He looked pallid, all the color wrung from his face. "Besides, I'm making time and a half." He leaned back against the swung-open door, flicking his lighter. "Can't fault that."

"I don't like it," Anne-Marie said, bag of grapes in hand. It was riskier, more chance of injury. Ideally, you'd get seven to eight hours when you came home, but most of the men functioned on two, maybe three.

"There's a reason it's called the graveyard shift." She dumped the grapes into a colander, turning on the sink. One of the men had sliced his thumb off the other week.

"They reattached it," Jesse said, laughing. "He had a few Franken-stein fingers, anyway. Usually it's around Christmas when the mishaps triple. That guy had a birthday. Twins." He sipped his coffee. "Us next year." He looked over at Anne-Marie, grinning.

It wasn't uncommon. You signed off on it, the valuation of your body parts laid out in your contract: a thousand for a finger, five large if you lost the whole hand. *Wasn't the worst way to make a buck.* I remembered what Ray had said when he'd told a similar story. *So long as it ain't the useful ones.* He'd held up his ring, middle finger, and pinky, jackhammering.

We ate outside, orbiting the plastic table Jesse had hauled from the porch. Theirs was a corner lot, the helping of grass generous, the view beyond the perimeter of the lot scenic—old growth spruces, craggy hill-side, an otherwise unobstructed sky. As soon as he sat, Jesse started nodding off, his head bowed, cigarette still burning in one limp hand.

"My neighbor's gone," I heard myself saying. I'd done everything I could to distance myself from the fact that morning, had tamped it down so forcefully, it was no wonder it came springing back. I hadn't told any-one besides Rhoda and the RCMP. No one I knew. Who knew me.

"She's been missing a full week now. I'm pretty sure she's dead." My voice broke. It was the first time I'd said it—what had been there since finding her necklace—out loud.

"What?" Anne-Marie said, wiping applesauce from Tanner's chin. "Which neighbor?"

"Rachelle." She squinted. "Al's wife."

"The, uh . . ." She hesitated. "Native?" Her voice lowered to a whisper. I nodded.

"Jesus, Jenny." Tanner wriggled out from her hands. "And you're sure she didn't just move? Go on vacation?"

"Positive."

Anne-Marie was quiet, somber. The first person to take me seriously. If Missy had been there, she would've gotten right to work, firing off round after round. Questions, accusations, jabs. Any hole in the story stretched further until the whole thing fell in on itself, like a frown. Annie just listened. Like always.

"I went over there a few times. Kyle hopped the fence. The kids, they got along." As I was speaking, I realized how believable it sounded. It was the truth, at least in part. Kids could befriend anybody.

"We were supposed to have a playdate, and she just disappeared. Left her girls at a day care, some lady came knocking." Then why hadn't I told that to Sam? I thought of his reaction when Rachelle had waved. How I'd ignored her. My face went hot.

"I got to know her a little, too. She wasn't so bad." *We were neighbors*, I'd told Rhoda. *Friends.* "Her house has been dark ever since."

"And you called the cops?" Anne-Marie was still whispering. Tanner started to roam over toward the road.

"Tanner! No!" She sat up, her voice suddenly forceful, stern. He froze. "Uh-uh. We don't play in the road, remember?" He turned, waddling back toward the yard.

"Twice. I even went in a few days ago. It's like they don't believe me." I picked up a grape. "Or they don't care."

Anne-Marie nodded, easing back into her chair. "Hm," she said, her hands on her belly, thinking. "It's weird. You'd think with what happened to Beth . . . And right in your neighborhood. What if it's all the same guy?"

"There are dozens of stories." Jesse's eyes were open again. He straightened himself, nudging the inch or so of ash that'd smoked his cigarette for him while he'd dozed. "Look at that girl—what's it—Marina."

"Delphina," I helped.

"Yeah, Delphina. Fifteen years old. And we didn't even know she was missing until her body was found." He picked up his sandwich. "The cops aren't looking." Anne-Marie scoffed, shaking her head.

"I found her car." I was galvanized. They seemed to get it, seemed to care. Three heads were better than one.

"On the side of 16-East," I continued. "Near Vanderhoof. It's gone now, but I think I know where she was going. Remember her necklace? The gold cross? I found it in a pile of campfire ash. A logging trail, right around where her car was parked. There was this circle of trees, all marked with the same symbol. Do you have a pen?" Jesse pulled one from his pocket, and I started scribbling on a napkin. "Like this." I held it up. "It's got to mean something.

"There was this truck, a white Ford, all banged up," I was rambling, but I couldn't help it. Once I'd started, all the clues I'd collected started tumbling from my hands. "It was parked in her driveway the day before she went missing. Her washroom window was open, the toilet seat up. It had to be a man. Her sister's got to know him. And her husband . . ."

I'd paused to take a breath when I saw it. What was supposed to have been a discreet glance.

Anne-Marie's eyes sunk to the table, Jesse flicking his lighter, his face shielded by a hand. Neither one of them would look at me. What had happened?

"I met her sister, by chance." I tried to reel in what I'd flung so haphazardly. "Rachelle, she gave me her address. If I can get her to talk, to tell me what she knows, I—"

"Enough," Anne-Marie interrupted, exasperated. My cheeks burned. I'd only ever seen her snap like that once, at high school graduation, when Missy kept hiking her robe to flash her thong.

"Sorry," she said, though I could see that she wasn't. "It's just . . ." She sighed, her mouth twisted in a knot. "You're not actually, like, looking for her, are you, Jen?"

"No," I lied, shifting in my seat, defensive. Jesse stood, taking the opportunity to sneak back into the house, to avoid whatever was coming to a head.

"Not exactly." I scratched at my neck. The red prickles were migrating to the base of my shoulders, appearing in new places—the undersides of my knees.

"It's just . . ." Anne-Marie paused, brushing crumbs from the table. "You don't know what type of people she ran with." She lifted her eyes to meet mine, voice softening. "What with Beth and all. It sounds sketchy. I don't think you should be getting involved."

"I'm not." I avoided her gaze. My eyes, I knew, were wet. "Her youngest is still a baby," I whispered, more to myself. "I'm the only one who cares."

Anne-Marie had hoisted herself up off her chair and was starting to stack the plates.

"It's sad, for sure," she was saying, placing a hand on my shoulder and squeezing, her fingers so swollen from the pregnancy that she had to wear her wedding ring looped around her neck. "But I don't see how it's your problem." She turned to face me. "You hardly knew the woman, Jenny. She just happened to live across from you."

My stomach churned. Anne-Marie was already talking about Rachelle in the past tense. I didn't respond. I just nodded, changing the subject. I knew it was no use trying to convince her.

It was innate, after all—felt, as palpable as the dank. If our roles were reversed, I probably would have said the same thing. They stayed on their side, and we stayed on ours.

No exceptions.

I came home to the blinking light of the answering machine, low mood brightened, the power of that tiny red star. *Rhoda*, I couldn't help but hope. I pressed play, and Mom's voice filled the room, commanding as a pan of scorched onions.

Tammy had the kids for the weekend, and she'd swapped her Saturday for Rita's Sunday. Ray's neighbor was reroofing his house. She didn't have a yard, as I very well knew, and they hadn't grilled out all summer.

"Can we do it at your place? Be nice to get the family together." Her request hung in the air, heavy as exhaust. *Family.* I winced. Ray, four years my senior, a stand-in for my father. "Tomorrow? Around two?" The machine beeped. I couldn't have said no if I wanted to. She'd already made the plan.

I opened the fridge. The ham I'd meant to defrost that morning was missing, still stashed in the freezer, hard as stone. I took stock: peas, chicken thighs, Stouffer's mashed potatoes, a crushed box of Eggos. I pulled them out, cracked open some eggs. Breakfast for dinner. I thought of Destiny, the mini pancakes. Where was she now?

I'd save him a plate, but Sam would probably eat up at the farm, anyway, I reasoned, pouring the eggs into the pan. His mom was always plying him—one more helping of green beans, another serving of potato salad, a third slice of meat loaf, another piece of cherry pie. I cranked down the gas and put a lid on the pan.

If I wanted to call Rhoda, now was my chance. I went into my bedroom and opened my closet, patting down my work pants. I emptied the pockets: just a crumpled-up receipt from the Chevron. Maybe I'd dropped it in the washroom. I opened the door, searching the floor, crouching down and angling my head so that my eyes were flush with tile. Nothing. *Shit.* What if Sam had found it? I bit my thumbnail. *It was just a number*, I reasoned, *a woman's name.* Maybe I'd stashed it someplace else.

The phone rang, and I turned, skidding back into the living room. "Hello," I said breathlessly. "Hello?" All was silent on the other end. "Hello?" I asked again. The response so slight, I could barely hear it. That faint rhythmic sound, someone's hushed breath.

"Rhoda?" It'd happened before. I'd dream of Aunt Erin and wake to find a postcard in my mailbox. The modes of communication were never as linear as we'd been taught. "Rhoda? Is that you?" The line went dead.

"Fuck," I muttered. Star sixty-nine. I pressed the buttons on the receiver. A busy signal. I'd wait and try again.

Rhoda's number wasn't in my purse, or my sweatshirt's pockets, or my other purse, or the junk drawer. I checked under the bed, the couch, even flipping through the pages of the book on my nightstand, a book Erin had sent me, *Cannery Row. A classic*, she'd written on the inside of its cover. I'd been picking it up and putting it down since Thanksgiving. It wasn't long—it was just like every other book Erin sent. No engine, all flourish; more a means for improving my Scrabble word score. Forty pages in and I still couldn't say what it was about. Sam had a cousin who worked at the cannery in Prince Rupert. Give me Janet Evanovich any day.

Star sixty-nine. I punched in the numbers. Still busy. I set the phone on the coffee table and flicked on the tube. The news had switched focus from the man in Kamloops back to Beth again. It'd been fifty days since she had disappeared. An anniversary of sorts. "We know she's out there," her mother was saying. The search wasn't over. Not by far.

The phone rang again, trill launching me from the couch.

"Rhoda?" I picked it up. The more I thought about it, the more I realized—I'd mistaken indifference for fear. Maybe the person she'd been protecting was herself. "Don't hang up."

"Jenny?" It was Sam. *Double fuck.* Star sixty-nine was out. "Who's Rhoda?"

"S-S-Sam," I stuttered, moving the receiver to the other ear. I smelled smoke. The eggs. I raced to the kitchen.

"Nobody," I said. The bottom of the pan was black, but the eggs were surprisingly salvageable. "The new girl at work. Her line keeps cutting out." Despite all the practice, I was still a shit liar.

"Hm," he grunted, too tired to probe. The work on the farm too demanding, wresting out every ounce of energy, both physical and mental, he had. He'd make it home in time for the barbeque, but he was staying put for the night.

I popped an Eggo into the toaster, salted the eggs, and cracked open a Coke. It was as I'd expected. Dinner for one. I picked up the remote, scanning through the channels. I settled on a rerun of *I Love Lucy*, an episode where Fred and Ethel and Ricky and Lucy all head to Europe. Lucy winds up stranded, pacing the gangplank, a hysterical Ricky screaming from the ship's deck.

I stared at the phone. It had to have been Rhoda, the stifled breath on the other end of the line. It was a signal, that call. SOS. I picked up the phone to call her, before remembering that star sixty-nine would just dial the farm.

I couldn't drive away the feeling that something was about to happen. Something bad. Sergeant McCormick always worked on intuition.

From the moment I saw the Man with the Braid, I knew he was danger-ous. Maybe even the prime suspect. And whatever he was capable of, Rhoda was next.

Lucy sat at the kitchen table, her hair in curlers, cigarette fuming from between her black lips. Alone, like me. I glanced out the window, the dark a punch to the gut.

I might've been wrong. It might not have even been Rhoda calling. Intuition was just that—a feeling, a hunch. But if it had been her, she'd dialed me for a reason. I had to go back there, I decided that night. What if I was the only hope that Rhoda had left?

fifteen

I got an early start the next morning, wipers frantic in the spitting rain. I was hoping that the weather would stick, pummeling that afternoon's plans into muck, but the storm was expected to pass by noon, a 90-percent chance of clear skies forecasted.

"So the grass'll be a little wet." Mom had called earlier that morning to confirm. "We already bought five pounds of ground."

Five pounds. I choked her words down. They were bringing friends. Or, more rightly, Ray was. Mom didn't really have any. She was more like a burr, socially speaking, tufted to the pant leg of whomever she'd paired off with, solely along for the ride. She'd never kept in touch with anyone from high school. She despised all the women at the salon. There was her neighbor Sue, but I'd never seen them together outside of the apartment complex. *Women are jealous,* Mom would gripe. *With men, it's simple.* One word to describe Ray's friends.

The station I was listening to returned from their commercial break, and I cranked up the volume, shooing the pall Mom's plans had cast. If problems were fish, the barbeque was a school of smelt in a piddling pond. The highway the ocean, my Buick hot on the trail of a bloodthirsty great white.

I turned onto Rhoda's street and parked in the same place as before. The driveway was empty, the house dark. It didn't look like anybody was home. I zipped up my raincoat and threw the hood over my head. Was only one way to find out.

I stepped past the rusted fence post, the *BEWARE OF DOG* sign— needless, now, as there was not so much as a whimper, let alone a bark. The quiet was worse, foreboding. The pelt of the rain like stones being thrown, *clang clang clang* against metal, all the junk littering her yard. I rang. No answer. It was a quarter past nine, a Saturday. She was home last time. Maybe she was still asleep. I walked around to the side of the house, shimmying past the trampoline to try and peer into the window. She might've stepped out, taken the dog for a walk. But then where was her car? I pressed my nose against the glass. Opaque white, the underside of a curtain. Maybe she'd run to the store.

"Everything okay?" a voice asked. I jumped, turning. A man had stopped at their driveway, one hand tugging at the leash of a sopping wet husky, the other manning a battered umbrella, its wires bent in every direction.

"Yes," I said meekly, wiggling back toward the drive, Keds so waterlogged, I squeaked with every step. "I was supposed to meet my friend here. Rhoda. Have you seen her?" I was improving. It was easier to lie to a stranger.

"No." The man shook his head, gruff. He reminded me of my high school gym teacher, Mr. Doyle, more boxer than husky, hair shorn right to the undercooked pink of his skin. Even the way he was chewing his gum: efficiently, aggressively. I wouldn't have been surprised to spot a whistle around his neck.

"Better to wait in your car," he ordered, jaw set. "Off your *friend's* property." He stayed put, his eyes insistent, icy as the husky's. The dog barked, the rain really starting to pound down. I wasn't as convincing as I'd imagined.

"I'm just looking for my friend," I answered, confidence withered. I wasn't guilty, but my face was burning, as if he'd caught me pissing in the rosebush, muscling one of the bathing suits from the trampoline over my head. He didn't respond. He didn't budge either.

"Fine," I muttered, stepping back toward the road. I walked past the man, and his head strained to follow, making sure I was back where I belonged. I opened the car door, too flustered to remember to take off my jacket before climbing in. The wet pooled down around me, my very own seat puddle. The man still hadn't moved. I shook my head, turning on the ignition. Anyway, Rhoda wasn't home. I could circle back later. A coffee wouldn't hurt in the meantime.

I drove back toward the downtown and pulled into a Timmy's, camping out in a booth, a wrinkled copy of the *Citizen* in my hands.

City Tackles Needle Clean-Up. Grizzly Trouble Strikes Pineview.
"World's Greatest" Pink Floyd Cover Act Coming to the CN Centre.
O'Brien Knows the Score.
I flipped through its pages, dunking the last bite of doughnut into
my double-double, sprinkles pocking the floor. *The Search Continues.*
Beth's school portrait, as regular a feature as the air quality report. I
was tired of seeing it, her perfect face, perfect smile. Perfect life—until it
wasn't. That quote they kept reusing, what her pastor had said: *a lily
among the thorns.*
Rachelle's disappearance hadn't even made the back pages. A mother
of two, a neighbor. A friend. She was just a thorn.
I nicked a wad of napkins from the dispenser and stuffed them into
my pockets. I needed to sop up my seat. The rain had stopped. The sun
was out. Mom was probably already in her kitchen, portioning beef into
patties, stabbing her thumb into the centers of each raw red mound. It
was ten o'clock, around the same time I'd gone the week before. Rhoda
was sure to be back. I turned the key in my ignition and drove, near
blithely, back north.
Even when I returned to find her house quiet, I didn't panic. I simply
shifted to park. The dog walker had gone, and I still had time. I scanned
through the radio. I sipped at my coffee. I studied my reflection in the
sun visor's mirror. I even thumbed through the cache of old cassette tapes,
the ones Mom had given me, in my center console's rack. Most were
garbage—Kenny Chesney, Poison—but there was the one I never tired
of. I cracked open the case to Stevie Nicks's *Bella Donna* and fed it into
the tape deck.
"Leather and Lace" started to play. I still knew every word by heart,
could hardly believe that flimsy film had held up—Mom and I had
rewound it so many times.
She'd gone in big on Stevie: the crushed velvet, chiffon, the Gothic
crosses. The white leather jacket dripping with fringe. Her perm tits-
long and as brassy as pennies, her bangs teased to the heavens. There
were still traces of Stevie in Mom's closet, but they'd been pushed to the
back, crowded out by the bedazzled, the low-rise, the tube dresses—
the things girls my age, Ray's age, wore.

Don Henley's verse came on. I lowered my register, crooning along. I'd always sing his lines, Mom passing the can of Diet Coke to my dimpled hands. They weren't all bad memories. I rewound again.

Twenty minutes passed, then another. Then another. The only action the two preteen boys pedaling, greasy sacks from McDonald's swinging from their free hands. I had to remember to pick up buns from the store.

"We got the meat, the sides, the drinks, everything else." Mom had been giddy that morning on the phone, hammering out her plans.

It always started like that, amnesia fogging the past, the inevitable way it would sour. It was textbook at that point. She'd arrive, smile pasted on her made-up face. *Let's all go in for a picture!* She'd usher me near, Ray's arms knotted at her navel. One big, happy family. Then I'd say something wrong. Sometimes it was more what I didn't say. If she cracked a joke and I didn't laugh, or laugh hard enough. Took about all of half an hour. Often less. *Well, I'll just shut my dumb mouth, Jenny, how about that?* Any happy moments, I realized, had been when I was too young to have any sense of self, when I was content with whatever I'd been handed—even if it was the man's verse in a love song.

I glanced at the clock. It was eleven-thirty. I'd been sitting there for well over an hour. Sam was due back home at one to get the grill ready. If I wanted to make it to the store in time, I'd have to head back. I stepped out of my car. Maybe Rhoda had been napping. Maybe the Man with the Braid had needed her car. It wasn't until I was at her doorstep that the dread finally surfaced, urgent, no longer allowing self-deception. I knocked. Silence. I knocked again, this time with gusto. It was all too familiar, that scene, me standing at the door of a shuttered-up house, uselessly banging my fist. Two sisters, gone. A family line, blotted. Could it be that I was already too late?

I leaned back against the door for a moment, wiping at my eyes, kicking myself for not driving there the previous night. I went to step away, back to my car, when something tugged me back. The bottom lip of my raincoat had hooked itself around the doorknob. I turned, jiggling at the handle to free it. In the process, the door cracked open. My heart pounded. Someone must have forgotten to lock up.

I listened. The house was quiet. I looked behind me. The street was, too, no witnesses, just the sheen of my Buick, muffled in the burgeoning light. Technically it wasn't breaking and entering, I reasoned, stoking the flames of my courage. The door was unlocked. It was just . . . entering. That wasn't a crime. I took a deep breath and stepped inside.

I slipped off my sneakers, not wanting to leave any footprints, and tiptoed in socks across the linoleum. I'd have to be quick. Rhoda could be back at any moment. Or worse—the Man with the Braid could. I turned into the kitchen. I wasn't sure what I was looking for, exactly, but it seemed like the right place to start.

I looked around. Had it always been so sparse? I'd been too distracted to notice the last time I'd stood there, homed in on Rhoda, the Man with the Braid, as if the two were under spotlights. I should have brought my camera, should have been carrying the backpack—the gloves, the notepad, the bear spray (especially the bear spray)—with me all along. I'd just have to make a mental list, use a napkin in the car to jot it all down.

Not that there'd be much to jot. The kitchen was void, aseptic, near sterile, the only personal effects a crucifix and a uniform white-faced wall clock. No magnets on the fridge, no pile of mail, no bowl of fruit, or M&M's, or salted peanuts on the table, not even a drying dishrag. Every surface was clear—gleaming even, the air vaguely scented of chemical pine. It reminded me more of Mom's place than Rachelle's.

A sole coffee mug was upturned in the dish rack. I tugged my sweatshirt's sleeves down around my fingers, lifting it up. Garfield, with his teeth bared, thought bubble floating above his head. *Never trust a smiling cat.*

I thought of the four toothbrushes in the washroom. It was hard to believe even a single person lived there, let alone a couple, two kids. The girls probably lived with their mom, spent every other weekend on the pullout couch, Rhoda with a Windex bottle and a roll of paper towel at their heels.

I started searching the drawers. Jumble of utensils, knot of rubber bands, oven mitts splattered and stiffened with grease. A calendar from '99 still wrapped in plastic, a hammer, a banana clip with most of its teeth cracked off, a spray of loose jelly beans. Some Starburst candies, a pink one. I couldn't resist. I tucked the wrapper into my back pocket, gnawing on the coral wax.

Ketchup packets from A&W, rolls of duct tape, envelopes stamped red, *PAST DUE*. Matchbooks from Shooters, Mr. Jake's. Snaking wire. A blank CD scratched to hell. *Summer*, someone had written, in thick black marker.

Something stashed beneath the dross. The photograph I'd seen at Rachelle's: the starched shirt and the bowl cut. I turned it over. *1967*. I realized I recognized the girl in the portrait. Even then, she had the same guarded expression. Rhoda. So she hadn't been raised in the bush, after all. She'd been a student at one of those schools that, by my time, had all been shuttered. What were they called again? *Reverential?*

So they had been close. At least close enough for Rachelle to keep little Rhoda tacked to her fridge. Or maybe they'd drifted, had never been bonded, the portrait the only photo Rachelle had of her. I remembered the welts notched on Rhoda's arms. Or maybe it was more how Rachelle wanted to think of her—puny, innocent: intact.

There wasn't just one junk drawer, I realized. It was all of them. They were two different people, the person who scrubbed at the grates on the stove and the one who shoved everything, slapdash, out of sight. I opened the fridge, its contents nearly toppling to my feet. Shelves laden with murky containers: macaroni salad, salsa, low-fat whipped cream, an unlabeled, still-dripping, viscous dark sauce. There was a stockpile of string cheese, one lone white egg. A half-eaten hot dog on an encrusted plate, squirt of ketchup congealed down its stunted length. A jumbo jar of Hellmann's, three bruised navel oranges, a brick of corn-yellow government cheese. I thought of Rachelle's dusted bedroom, her Fleetwood's vacuum-marked floor mats. Someone was backtracking, wiping away fingerprints, signs of struggle. Blood. I looked behind me, panic mounting. Expunging any trace of what had gone down.

I closed the fridge door. There was something on top of it, what I'd missed before. I pulled up a chair and stepped up. It was an envelope, photos from London Drugs. I checked the date. *August 2000*. One year ago to the month. I shuffled through.

The majority had been taken at a bush party: people crowded in camp chairs, hovering near the grill, arms wrangled around shoulders, beers sweating in hand. Rhoda must have been behind the camera, the only trace of her a fleshy smudge in the corner of a photo of a man with a fish between his outstretched hands.

I'd never seen so many of them in one place, save for the block in front of St. Vinnie's where the destitute ones clustered, slumped over, with palms upturned and eyes rolled back. It felt familiar enough—the Molson cans, the sausages, the fleece once the sun had set—and at the same time not. I'd have never been invited, one woman pushing her palm against a ball of dough, what the twins in my grade used to eat for lunch, the oil-spattered Ziploc bag. *Fry bread.* If Rachelle had been there, she hadn't been photographed. Neither had the Man with the Braid.

I was reaching the end of the pile when the scene changed to the side of Rhoda's house, her trampoline the focal point. One of the two girls was standing on it, the other midjump, black hair streaming around her face. The Man's daughters, no doubt. Steps back, the girls from across the road, each bungeed in air. To their left was a truck parked in the driveway. A white pickup. My heart lurched. I held the photo closer. Alberta plates. I checked behind me again.

In the next and last photo, the driver's door was swung open, a forearm visible, the back of a head. Not a shadow, what was dark, but long black hair woven into the likeness of a snake.

I folded the picture in half, hands trembling, tucking it into my back pocket. My head spun. My hunch had been right. The whole sordid tale revealing itself: the lust, the jealousy, the sneaking around, the lies. Was the Man with the Braid the real father of Little Beth? One night, a mistake, a habit Rachelle couldn't break. *It was the last time*, she'd told him that fateful night. If he couldn't have her, no one could. Rhoda had pieced it together after my visit, had threatened to turn him in. He'd taken care of her, too. I thought of the toothbrushes I'd seen in the bathroom. Two other little girls. Collateral damage. I felt like I was going to puke.

An engine droned, wheels on gravel. Someone was pulling into the drive. *Fuck.* I squatted down below the range of the windows, scampering toward the den. No back door. *Fuck, fuck, fuck.* I crawled back toward the front, breath quickening, heart about to pounce right through my chest. I really should've brought that can of bear spray. I curled into a ball under an end table, closing my eyes. Of all the idiotic plans. Walking right into the house of a murderer. I felt a hand press against my back.

I yelped, eyes damp, darting open. "Please, no!"

It was the bunny, nose twitching, his fur a true white. I caught my breath. He hopped away. No one else was there.

There was a window by the front door, and I inched my head up toward it. The driveway was empty. The car must have just been passing by.

I jammed on my Keds and slipped out the door. It was a wake-up call. If the Man had come home, if he had found me there . . . He was dangerous, and I defenseless, not even a pen in my pocket to jab at an eye.

Anyway, I'd found it. The evidence I needed. The plates were legible. The Man with the Braid was done for.

I started my engine. It was five to noon. I'd have to haul ass if I wanted to make it to the store and home before Sam was back. He wouldn't be happy, setting up the grill. *It's your mom*, he'd say, an accusation. My fault. I remembered the way Sam had shunned me a few months back following a run-in with Mom and Ray at Sgt O'Flaherty's. What Ray had drawled between slurps of beer: *Sure yous don't need a demonstration?* He'd pawed at my belly, latching his other hand on to Mom, fingers working her knee like he was juicing a lemon.

He's a drunk, I kept repeating, attempting to wipe what'd been spilled, wringing my hands.

It hadn't mattered. Ray was my mother's boyfriend. We wouldn't even know him if it weren't for her. For me.

What Sam had said the other week about Missy: *Missy's your friend.*

Women were always responsible. For what we did, what other women did. What men did—to us, because of us. For splitting open the apple, inventing sin.

You've left me no choice, I imagined the Man with the Braid telling Rhoda. *I didn't want to have to do this.* His hands wrenching around her neck.

I had to call the cops. He had to have a record. The RCMP might not have cared about someone like Rachelle, but they wouldn't miss the opportunity to nab a wanted man. I could stop by quickly on my way home from the store.

I was five or so clicks from the Safeway when my Buick came to a halt, tire iron in my plans. Gridlock, all the way to town. To my right was the answer—some sort of parade, a march, mostly women, I noticed, walking two by two along the shoulder, wavering rush of red.

Sweatshirts and T-shirts and dresses and hats: in cherry, crimson, candy apple, siren. There must have been at least twenty of them walking, twenty shades melded together, flickering like flames. It would've taken a concerted effort not to rubberneck.

The march was moving faster than my LeSabre, a few of its members toting signs. Each one featured the same school portrait. With feathered bangs and a Peter Pan collar, the girl was young, awash in the warm hues of the past—the seventies or eighties, when Stevie was on the radio, not just during oldies' hour. She could have been Destiny, some years older. Young Rachelle. *Aurelie Rose Andrews Memorial Walk*, one sign read. *WE WANT ANSWERS*, another demanded. *NOW.*

I WANT TO LIVE. I thought of the news segment, all those young faces pasted on the signs. *Memorial Walk.* Had I gotten it wrong? Could those girls have been not the daughters of the victims but victims themselves? Some of them had looked barely prepubescent. I felt sick again.

There was another photo of Aurelie, in bell-bottoms and a floppy hat. Why use such dated photos? Unless—when had it happened? I switched on my blinker and waited for the last couple of marchers to pass, swerving onto the shoulder and shifting to park. I wanted answers, too.

"Hey!" I shouted, jogging to catch up.

"A straggler." A lanky woman at the end of the train turned, candy cane stitched onto the front of her sweatshirt. I clashed, my T-shirt a sheeny lime green. "Berta's got an extra scarf if you want it."

"Hey, Berta!" The woman cupped her hands around her mouth, and another woman about a yard in front of us stood off to the side, duffel bag dangling from the crook in her elbow, fingernails glossy, like blood.

"Catch!" The scarf was launched toward me, red streaking the air. I caught it, dutifully wrapping it around my neck. It was coarsely knit—wool or an acrylic blend—and itchy as hell. For winter. I glanced at the candy cane. They must've just brought whatever red they had on hand. Had it been the girl's favorite color? Maybe it was simply precaution, a way to stay visible along the road.

I didn't have a chance to ask. I looked up, and Candy Cane was already paired off again, Berta out of sight, far ahead. No matter how fast I walked, I still lagged behind, peripheral, like a can tied to a bumper, unable to bridge the gap. The heady stench of exhaust permeated the air, an endless stream of vehicles chugging by, one four-by-four barreling dangerously close to the shoulder, hosing us walkers in a spray of gravel. Eyes glanced over and away again, back toward the road up ahead.

I should really head back, I remember thinking, my feet pushing forward. I thought of the pictures, Rhoda's bush party. I'd never been in a group like that.

There was a reason our paths had crossed. Someone had to know them, Rhoda and Rachelle. Someone had to be able to help.

The ribbon of red started to bend as we turned onto a side road, the crowd pooling, like yarn being wound into a skein. We'd arrived. I looked around. Was this it? A dirt lot—repurposed—fireweed and foxtail and some battered Labatt cans undertire, leather seats baking in the sun. A place to park. The double beep of a car door unlocking, the pop of an opening trunk. A little boy in a Spider-Man T-shirt darted toward a station wagon. "I call shotgun!" I'd missed it, the destination. They were already packing up.

A circle had formed near a Ford Ranger, Berta at the head.

"I know you all have places to be, so I'll make this quick. We just want to say thank you to all of you who showed up, who keep showing up every year. My sister was nine when we lost her on the highway."

Nine? I gulped. Had I heard her right?

"She would've been thirty this September," Berta confirmed, my jaw slack. "It's been eighteen years, and we've been walking seventeen of them. I know that even if it takes another eighteen years, we'll keep walking. We'll keep looking. We'll never forget."

I couldn't believe it. A nine-year-old lost on 16, decades back, and this was the first I was hearing of it? I thought of Melanie Fisher, the ten-year-old who'd been plucked from the Pine Centre Mall and secreted into a stranger's van. That was when it first opened, back in the sixties. I could've sketched Melanie's smiling portrait from memory.

The marchers clapped, took turns embracing, and steadily started to head to their vehicles. I perched on my tiptoes, searching for Berta. I still had her scarf. It was an opening, a chance to talk. Maybe Berta would know what to do next.

A horn beeped. I startled. A Dodge Spirit was behind me, engine humming. I stepped aside. Another car followed, and another, and another. The hands extended out of windows, the flapping goodbyes. I kept scanning. It was hard to spot Berta in that sea of red.

Before I knew it, the lot was empty. I was the only one left, my shirt slick with sweat. Eczema like a garland of fire pricked up around my neck. I wadded the scarf and left it on top of a rock, rolling up the cuffs of my jeans. I thought I'd learned my lesson—the cheerleading shorts from the other day. You suffered in clothes that covered your body; you suffered in clothes that didn't. I started back toward 16-E.

We must have walked two clicks from where I'd pulled over. I wasn't wearing a watch, but I didn't need one to know I was late. My thumb shot itself up without thinking. I lowered my arm, walking again.

Things had been simpler before. The rides we'd catch, ditching school. The highway an adventure. Once, in seventh grade, Missy and I went all the way to Mackenzie, just because. We wanted to see how far we could get.

Mackenzie. Missy had practically spat when she said it. There was less to do there than PG. *Wherever you go, there you are.* She'd shrugged, taking out the bottle of Sprite spiked with vodka she always seemed to have on her person back then.

We'd set up camp in the chamber of the tree crusher, passing the bottle back and forth. Sunflower yellow and sprawling, the crusher stood at least twenty feet tall, the machine that'd built the West, steamrolling the land like a boot over ants, clearing the way for the highways, the stripmalls, entire galaxies of cul-de-sacs. Inoperable since the eighties, it'd been dumped on the outer edge of Mackenzie's downtown, a tourist destination in concept and, in reality, a makeshift bar, with spent lighters and empties and the stray Trojan wrapper like mulch upon the cool, steel ground.

World's Largest Crusher, the wooden sign read. Actually, it was the second. The first was at the bottom of Williston Lake, a bet that'd been lost in the sixties. It had been built to expedite the creation of the lake, which wasn't really a lake but a reservoir, something drafted out, artificial as a beer can. It was part of the Peace River Power Project, the dam they'd built, 350,000 acres of forest flooded for hydro. The crusher was ineffective, clearing just under eight square miles. They left it there, on the floor of the submerged valley, like a lanced whale that'd somehow eluded its net.

The dam displaced so many people, Erin had said when we were hiking near there, around the Heather-Dina Lakes. I'd nodded, though I hadn't been sure what she meant.

I'd never felt worried in the cab of a truck or the backseat of a sedan. Trouble never found us, even with Missy out looking. Once she'd brought out the bottle in the cab of a logging truck. The driver was young, handsome in a sunburnt way, and she'd sidled over toward him, offering a taste. *It's not just Sprite*, she'd said, wiping the sheen from her mouth. He'd ignored her, keeping his eyes on the road and his hands on the wheel, to himself.

People were good, or else we were naïve—had hit upon a streak of dumb luck. It's like that when you're young, all that confidence. You haven't yet realized that the world doesn't owe you, that you can lose everything in an instant, with the click of an opening cab door.

I thought of the girl stuck in the eighties, like a fly to a strand of coiled fly strip. Aurelie Rose Andrews, forever nine years old. Where had she been going? And what about the others? We weren't that much older than her, Missy and I, when we'd caught our first ride. Things hadn't been simpler. We just knew less.

I was on the wrong side of the road, the same current as traffic. It felt riskier to cross it—someone fiddling with a CD case, gunning to make good time. I'd edged in farther toward the bush, was tramping through tansy, when a minivan came to a stop.

"Hey." It was a woman behind the wheel, the sleeves of her smocked blouse ballooning around her wrists, the fabric gauzy, threaded with flowers. Red.

"You okay?" she asked, her voice warm, concerned.

"I'm fine," I said, stepping closer. "I pulled over when I saw the march. My car's just up ahead."

"The walk?" The woman paused, reaching a hand toward her radio and lowering the volume of some Top 40 Country, switching to park. "I was with them." She hesitated again, weighing her words, her jowled face knitted in concentration. "I know you don't know me, but I'm a mom. I can't stand to see a young woman walking this road. Not today." She frowned. "Can I give you a lift?"

In all the years I'd been hitching, I'd never seen a woman stop before. I never blamed them—I never did either. I stepped closer. She was with the walk. A woman. A mom. It was safer than the shoulder, anyhow.

The woman flicked on her blinker and veered back onto the highway. Her hair was reddish, graying at the temples, and every inch of her skin was marked—freckled, as if oil were permanent and she'd been standing in front of a sputtering pan. Her eyes were blue, clear as glass, and if I'd had to guess, I'd have said she was of Scottish or Irish descent. She looked more like a relative of mine than Rachelle's. Maybe she'd married in, her own daughters brown-eyed, like Destiny, Little Beth.

"Sorry," she said, cutting in on the conversation I was having in my head. "I have to ask. No one told you about the walk? You just saw us and"—her hands lifted from the wheel, as if she'd been tossed an invisible ball—"decided to join?"

Hearing it aloud, I realized how stupid it sounded. A woman with nothing but time. *Yes*, I could have said, *I'm on a search of my own*, the two missing sisters, the Man with the Braid. Instead, I just mumbled, ears on fire. "More or less."

"Guess it's working." The woman grinned. "One curious driver at a time." *Curious*, that was a nicer way to put it.

"What's working?" I asked, bolstered by the adjective. "I think I missed where you were going."

"No place in particular. Around where Lee disappeared. There's a marker, a little white cross on the shoulder. It's just an estimate, though. Like the others." I nodded. *What others?* I wanted to ask. Instead, I clammed up. She'd assumed I'd known what she'd meant.

"That you?" My Buick floated into view. The woman pointed ahead, her sleeve billowing, the color of a hazard light.

"Yeah," I mumbled. I didn't want the ride to end. "Was red her favorite color?" It was the least charged of my questions. Or maybe not. The woman went quiet, my LeSabre close up.

"Red's the only color spirits can see," she answered after a pause that felt endless. "The walk's for Lee, but it's also for everyone. You know what I mean?" I nodded. *Find Our Stolen Sisters.* The sign appeared in my mind. That time I did.

"All right," she said, while I sat there, stuck, as if I'd not only sat in glue but swallowed it. I couldn't seem to work out a way to say it. To ask her about the picture. *Speaking of missing women . . .*

She must have sensed my reluctance, because she shifted to park. "Want one?" She presented the foam plate that'd been stashed on her dashboard, clawing through the plastic to procure a bun. I couldn't even croak out a *no*. I could barely shake my head. Wrong guess. She reassessed.

"You know, if you're interested, we're having a meeting next Saturday at the rez." She broke off a piece of the bun and chewed. "We've been trying to set up an inquiry. There's a lawyer who might be able to help." She lifted the flap of her sun visor, coupons fluttering down into her lap. She wrote something on the back of one of them.

"The address." She handed it to me. *Clorox Bleach, 2 for 1.* "Starts at ten, but you know our relationship with the clock." She winked. *Our?* I gripped on to the coupon, managing to climb out.

"Get home safe," the woman called after me, familiar valediction, how women often sent each other back into the world. I'd never heard two men say it. They didn't need to, I supposed. They were the calamities we were casting spells against.

sixteen

I drove home in a fog, mind cramped with all the new information. The cops, for some reason, had been burying years—decades even—of disappearances. The women not women but girls. Innocent. Blameless as someone like Beth. It wasn't at all like what I'd believed. Like what any of us had been led to believe. The Highway of Tears flecked white, countless lives given about as much attention as the Molson empties.

How many of them were there? Had they all been so young? And if the RCMP was keeping it hush, the question nagged: Why?

I didn't know it then, but the wheels were already spinning, hurtling me toward a hole where the deeper you dug, the more bodies you unearthed, every crack in the ice begetting another, every step one pace closer to rupture. Sink or swim.

The Safeway was jammed. I was a full hour late. Sam wouldn't be happy that I hadn't been there to set up, but at least I could arrive before our—*Mom's*—guests did. I'd have to put off the station until the following day.

I was already feeling crushed under the weight of that morning, but when I pulled up to our house and spotted Ray's pickup, whatever pep I had left vaporized. Had Mom and Ray come early? The green digits on my radio clock flashed zeros. It was two on the dot. With any luck, they'd just arrived.

I opened the door to find the kitchen counter carpeted: frozen spinach, Tater Tots, Eggo waffles, chicken thighs. Mom was emptying the freezer, rejiggering to make room, three stacked tubs of ice cream sweating near her wedges—*family-sized*. It was always like that whenever she came over. Not my house anymore but hers.

A fat bunch of bananas was heaped on the table, flanked by two cans of Reddi-wip. I set the hamburger buns down next to the tall jar of Maraschino cherries, destemmed clots a radioactive red.

"Banana splits." Mom crooked her neck toward me, beaming. "Ray's idea." She'd changed her hair again, two charred French braids, the black severe against her chalky complexion.

"What are you staring at?" Her tone veered, varnish already flaking.

"Nothing." I forced a smile. "I like your hair. What can I do to help?" I chirped, voice false as a plastic flower.

I was desperate to change—my shirt stank like hell—or to at least rinse my armpits, but I knew better than to sequester myself first thing. Mom's good mood never lasted. It wouldn't hurt to prop this one up awhile. She ran a hand over a braid, mollified.

"Boys are out back." She swung open the fridge, pushing two cans of Molson in my hand. "Here. Keep 'em happy."

I stepped outside. The table had already been moved from the porch to the yard and the spare camp chairs hauled up from the basement. The grill was unsheathed, with Ray hovering over it, scraping in full-bodied strokes. He'd stowed his T-shirt in the hammer loop on his jeans, and it rippled as his upper body lurched. Sam lumbered toward him, propane tank underarm.

"Hey, baby." I set the beers on the porch railing.

"Hey," he said, looking past me, voice flat. Mom and Ray must have been there awhile.

"Sorry I'm late." Sam crouched under the grill, switching out the tanks. "They were all out of buns. I had to go to the Superstore. You wouldn't believe the traffic."

Ray took a break from his work, hooking an arm under an elbow, joints cracking. "Shit, Sam, you ever clean this thing?" His eyes moved from the grill to me. "Look who's home." He smirked, stance wide, puffing up his hairless chest, ridiculous pinch of his nipples.

"What did you do, walk there, Jenny? Grind the wheat, bake the buns yourself?" He fished a cigarette from behind his ear. "Took you long enough."

I ignored him, reaching for Sam. "I brought you a beer."

"Thanks." He took it without looking at me. He was mad all right. What, had Mom and Ray shown up at noon?

"I'm going to hop in the shower," I eased off, backing toward the porch. No use crowding him.

"Need company?" Ray slapped Sam on the back and cackled. I'd have been miffed, too.

"I came home early," I heard Sam say. "Thought we'd get breakfast out." Blue flickered, then whooshed, licking up between the fingers of the grate. "You been shopping since eight A.M.?"

I froze, face burning, throat bunged up again.

"Jeez." Ray exhaled, breaking the silence. "Which Superstore you go to? Kamloops?"

I braced myself on the railing, light on my feet, as if they were plotting an escape from the rest of me. "Sam, I . . ."

"Go shower," he cut me off, face turned toward the grill again. "Your mom's friends will be here soon."

I locked the door to the washroom and peeled off my clothes, taking longer than I'd meant to in the shower, delaying the inevitable. Sam wasn't the type to make a scene—unlike Mom, who preferred an audience—but he wouldn't make it easy either. The monosyllabic answers, the downcast eyes. His wall was up. I was in for a long afternoon.

I stepped out of the tub, tripping over my laundry. The photo—I'd almost forgotten about it. I dug it out from my jeans' back pocket, ferrying it into the bedroom. Losing Rhoda's number had been bad enough. This was the key to everything. I studied it again, the Man with the Braid's sharp profile, his features slipping into someone familiar. André, but someone else, too. Who?

"Hey, Jenny, you got an extra cooler somewhere?" I heard Ray holler, the bang of the storage closet's door.

"Just a minute," I called back, slipping the photo between the pages of *Cannery Row* for safekeeping. The last place anybody would look.

By the time I'd toweled off, everyone had congregated out back, chairs splayed in a zigzagging half-moon around the grill, smoke drifting into afternoon blue. Two stockpots crammed with crushed ice and beer had been planted in the narrow shadow the table cast over the grass.

"We couldn't find that cooler," Mom said, crunching into a pickle. She'd reapplied her lipstick, peeled off her cropped jacket to unveil a lacy tank top, her padded and pushed-up tits.

The men had arrived. Five of Ray's old high school buddies and one I didn't recognize, a coworker from the mill. Square-jawed, his stubble pepper, the closest to Mom's age by far. Hank was the only one who introduced himself.

He was also the only one who'd brought a date. Marie, legs twisted, hugging herself, red curls haloed around her plump face. Her fingers twiddled the pendant that was clasped around her neck, one sawed-up half of a heart. *BFF.* She looked younger than I was and could have easily passed for Hank's daughter if it weren't for his meaty paw on her ass.

Marie was quiet, speaking only to Hank and, occasionally, to Mom and me. Complimenting the house, offering help the way women did. Men were oblivious to how food reached their plates. Mom ignored her, nudging potato salad off of a spoon with her thumb, slanting another paper plate. The girl wasn't pretty, but she was young. A worse offense.

"Can you believe she squeezed that fat ass into those shorts?" Mom fake-whispered, loud enough for Marie to hear. I laughed, cautious not to blight the mood. Sam had to run out, said Jim needed something. He'd dealt with them earlier. It was my turn now.

Clouds were starting to gather, the air turning cool. It looked like rain again. A part of me hoped it might push for an early end, but then Hank screwed open the bottle of Jim. If it rained, they'd just decamp, mud tracked in, the camp chairs pitched around the tube. I shook my head. Better to pray for the weather to hold, the mosquitoes to appear before the first stars—the stockpots left with only sitting water. My yard my own again.

The time for hope came and went.

The burgers were eaten, the cans of Reddi-wip detonated, the Hefty bag someone had strung around a tree branch misshapen with cans. The sun had been smothered, the bugs starting to bite. All that should have heralded the cookout's end. Instead, Mom snapped her fingers at me, a new command.

"Jenny, you haven't been drinking," she announced from Ray's lap, her wedges kicked off, one bare foot thumping grass. "You mind running to the store to restock?" She waved a wadded bill in my direction.

I didn't answer. Despite her posturing, she hadn't either. Mom only ever cracked the can, feigning sips to avoid suspicion. Beer poured down the toilet, watering houseplants. People didn't trust you if you didn't drink. Especially if you had a pair of breasts.

"Jenny." Mom straightened.

"I can go," Marie volunteered. Mom ignored her, eyes searing straight into my head.

"I'm the opener," I lied. I'd agreed to an afternoon, not an all-nighter. I might've not had the courage to kick them out, but I certainly wouldn't be the one filling those stockpots.

"Fi, don't bother," one of Ray's high school friends chimed in, de-escalating. "We'll make do." The swamp-colored swirled glass, meager thimble of green. He was the one in the drug rug. The bowl he produced wasn't surprising.

"No thanks." Hank held up a palm, his other hand draped around the back of Marie's chair. He lifted a cowboy boot and set it flat across his knee. I could see the neckline of his undershirt below his check-ered button-up. Of another generation than Ray and his friends, he'd lowered his hat when we'd shaken hands. Marie put her lips around the pipe, hacking.

Mom rose, going into the house for seconds. I don't even think she'd ever experimented. Her only vice the cigarettes.

André had been a user. Coke and speed, and meth, I later came to understand. The men she linked up with after André were dim, but none of them into anything hard like that. It was hard to believe that Ray could be a step up from anyone. Such was Mom's taste in men.

"Tim tell you about his night?" Another friend nudged Ray, fiddling with the brim of his John Deere hat. Mom hadn't disappeared but a minute before the conversation became one between men. "There's a new girl at the park. He says she really knows what she's doing."

"Christ," Ray muttered, scratching the welts on his forearms, smack-ing at a mosquito, his hand smeared red. "Fi's place is right by there. Lord lead me not into temptation." He shook his hands in mock prayer. All his buddies laughed. Hank stood, asking to use the washroom. Marie stared at her pale hands.

It was like we weren't listening, Marie and I, neither one of us avail-able or attached to any member in the band of friends. Like we weren't even there. They let it all fly, confirming what I'd only heard secondhand. There'd always been rumors, the boys in high school who'd saved up: ten for a handie, thirty for head. Men had needs. They couldn't help themselves. It was the women who were shameful. Dirty. Foul. Trash.

They hadn't always been there at the entrance of Fort George Park. It was sudden, their appearance, like when the last of the snow melts, the earth lively with crocuses, violet sash. Dark flowers popping up along the unlit road, painted faces ephemeral, discernable only with the hot sweep of light from a passing pickup. *Ladies of the night*, as Nana referred to them. *Powwow pussy*, one of Ray's friends was saying. The lump in my throat. Rhoda, Rachelle.

"You'd like her, Ray, she's older." Another friend, Tim, apparently, winked, wiping beer foam from around his mouth with the back of a rough hand. "Pretty sure she was wearing a wedding ring." He shook his head. "Shit."

Mom came back out balancing a tub of ice cream, the last of the bananas in her hands. The conversation fizzled.

"Hey, maybe it's your neighbor, Jenny." Ray poked my arm. "Finally found some work suited to her skill set." He laughed, his eyes squinty, pink, his hands reaching for the half-emptied bottle of Jim. He was hammered.

"What are you boys on about?" Mom asked, splitting a banana, steak knife running down its length.

"Nothing." Ray stood, staggering over, kissing her neck. "Baby, do you have another cigarette?" He slid his hands into her back pockets, kneading her ass.

I looked over at her yard, faintly lit by my porch lights. The rumors couldn't be true. She wasn't like that. Was she?

I glanced at Mom with her manufactured cleavage. Her jean skirt had been hiked up around her waist, and the way she was sitting, legs splayed on the grass, gave everyone a clear view of her underwear, like a little white surrender flag. She looked more like a whore than Rachelle. Or Rhoda, for that matter. Mom sucked at her Diet Coke, pushing the set of silver bangles down toward her elbow and then straightening her arm, bracelets rattling back.

How could I be sure? The ones I'd seen on *Cold Squad* had never been frumpy. Maybe I'd gotten their roles wrong. The sandals hers, designed to catch the light like a blinking neon *OPEN* sign. I remembered something. The scar down Rachelle's forearm. It could have been anything: a wily cat when she was small, a bicycle accident. But what if it wasn't? If I'd have looked closer, would I have seen them there? The same marks—*track marks*—notched upon Rachelle?

What if the Man in the Braid wasn't a boyfriend but a pimp? The thought refused to quiet, the episode blaring in my head. Rachelle drafted once Rhoda retired. If I looked around the perimeter of Fort George Park, was that where I'd find her? When the bottle of Jim was passed over, I drank as if dousing an inner fire.

"Who's got some starter?" I heard someone say. "I have some wood in my truck," another voice replied.

"The ban's still on," I interjected. It was the first I'd spoken to any of Ray's friends. "We're not getting charged with that ticket." I held steady.

If Sam had been there, they wouldn't even have suggested it. They would've already packed up their things and been on their way home. No one responded. Women had no authority. Ray was the next in command.

"We can keep the grill going." He struck a balance. "Jim'll keep us plenty warm, fellas."

I stood, setting toward the house with plans of locking myself in the washroom with Janet Evanovich and finishing my beer in the tub. It was Mom's party. I'd done my part.

"Jenny!" I heard Mom rasp after me. "You going to get those beers?"

"No." I turned around. I was at my limit. "I'm going to turn in."

"Fine," she snapped, bending over, angrily buckling her wedges. She'd reached hers, too. She started marching toward the house, shoes sinking into the still-damp grass.

"I'm working tomorrow," I called out after her, but she barreled past, the back door rattling off its hinges.

I found her by the kitchen counter, frown stitched across her face, hand jerking around in the depths of her purse, digging as if her life depended on it.

"It was fun," I lied, damage control. I just wanted my damn bath. "It's just getting late." She kept at her digging as if she hadn't heard me—as if I weren't there. "I have to be up."

With that, her puny frame went rigid. "And what?" She slammed down her purse, resting her arms across her chest. "We don't work?" She stared, slack-jawed, the creases between her eyebrows sharp as two skinning knives.

"What do you call what I've been doing all fucking day?" She was starting to shout. "God forbid we have a little fun." The men must have heard us. Soon the whole neighborhood would.

"That's not it," I whispered. Better one tiptoeing than two stomping around. "I'm just tired. It's getting late." I repeated those words like a prayer.

"Typical." She snatched her purse back up, car keys in hand. "You're a spoiled brat, you know that, Jenny? You never think about anyone but yourself."

Mom always knew just what to say. Get me kicking, fighting back. Damage control be damned.

"Don't act like this was for us." I was louder than she was, outrage circulating like oxygen through my lungs. "This was for you, and Ray, and his dipshit friends. You've never cared about me. You're the most selfish person I know."

"Selfish!" She huffed. And I'd always known just what to say back. "Selfish?" She was really going ballistic. "I've worked all my pitiful life to raise you. You think I had any help? A single mother. You think that was easy? You think it was fun?" Her breathing was shallow, her face twisted as twine.

"Didn't care about you? Tell me, Jenny, what'd you miss out on, huh?" She inched closer. "Christmas without presents? A birthday without cake?" I kept backing away, but soon her face was right up against mine.

"Some moms, they beat their kids. Don't give them no food, or clothes, or new fucking Rollerblades, or nothing. So don't you fucking tell me I didn't care." Spittle had gathered at the corners of her mouth, her face enflamed, red splotched down her chest. "Don't you fucking dare. All I did my whole life was care. Selfish." She wiped at her eyes, her voice a snapped branch. "I've given my whole life up for you." I wiped at mine.

No winning. Only pain. Why did I forget that? Every time.

There was a knock on the back door. Neither Mom nor I moved.

"Can I have a water?" Marie was asking, her voice even smaller than before.

Mom mowed past the girl, slamming the door. She'd left both her keys and her purse on the counter. I'd gotten what I'd wanted. Soon the party would be over. Except now it was my fault.

"Sure." I turned on the tap. Marie's legs were bitten to hell, pocked with old bites, the scabbed-over scars. "I got some calamine lotion in the washroom."

We sat like that for over an hour in the yellow light of my kitchen, Marie pressing polka dots across her thighs, her glass of water untouched. Peering out at the circle through my kitchen window until the dark became so final that all we could see was our own clouded reflections.

Sam wasn't back until well after the party was over, the creak of the door jolting me from what had already been a fitful start to the night. I was still jittery, the fight with Mom, the one looming on the horizon with Sam. I opened one eye, squinting at the alarm clock. It was near three A.M. I thought of Missy, Jim, out all night, the blackout curtains in their bedroom to blot the daylight. My new normal. The wife of an entry-level racketeer. Sam sunk into bed stinking of smoke. Jim was known to conduct business at the bar. Who was this man, I assessed, brow fitful even in sleep? The same one whose hands had trembled pinning my corsage? Who kissed Nana's unwashed, whiskered cheeks?

How could a face I knew so intimately suddenly feel so unknowable?

I slipped out from the covers, tiptoeing into the living room and curling up on the couch, not so much sleeping as letting my eyes rest.

It shouldn't have surprised me, the mess they'd left. I spent much of the next morning cleaning—the kitchen, the washroom—saving the yard for last. I'd seen it through the living room's windows; they hadn't even bothered to haul out their trash. *We didn't want to disturb you.* I didn't need to confront Mom to know what she'd say. *You were so-oo-oo tired.* The sarcasm. *Had to be up. Big important job at the mall.* I yanked the Hefty bag down from its branch, plastic splitting, entrails spewed across the grass. Cigarette butts had been secreted like Easter eggs, every third or fourth one I'd find blotched pink. Mom had left her mark. The shaggy row of lettuce flattened, the shape of her wedges. *That was the last time,* I told myself, hurling the bag in the garbage bin. It was always the last.

I was putting on a second pot of coffee when Sam came into the kitchen already dressed.

"Hey, baby," he said, pecking the top of my head. "Was thinking we could get breakfast out." He poured himself a cup, leaning against the counter, his demeanor easy, amiable even. Like yesterday had never happened. How many beers had he had?

"Sure," I chirped, amiable back.

I was expecting Denny's, but Sam was set on Grama's Kitchen, the diner off 97 better known for arson than omelets. In a little under five years, it'd burned down three times. No one I knew had actually ever eaten there—it was dinky, depressing, conjoined to a dung brick of a motel that had somehow always managed to elude the flames. I'd stopped there once, desperate for a coffee, the line up at the Timmy's a dozen vehicles long. You entered the restaurant through the motel's lobby, stepping through the sixties (drum lampshades, shag carpeting, infinite variations on the color brown) into the fifties, but budget: checkerboard painted right onto the linoleum, neon-trimmed jukebox a cardboard cutout. The diner changed hands after every fire.

Sam held the door open, the clink of the bell. I couldn't believe this was the same place. The diner was inviting, cozy even—everything homespun, cheery, bright. The curtains starched gingham, the tiles sparkling white, the jelly jars on each table with zinnias so perfect, I was sure the petals had to be plastic. The waitress was even calling one customer by name. I'd sent that family to Denny's, and here it was all along: the picture of the charming North. I wouldn't have been surprised to see a raspberry bush out back, the window steamed with cooling jam.

Sam ordered the hungry man's breakfast—two eggs, three strips of bacon, three sausages, and ham. I had the Belgian waffle with extra whipped.

"Eat your orange slices, kids, or you can't go out and play." The waitress lapped the room, her long bleached hair flapping behind her apron's straps. It was crowded, and she was out of breath, the laces on her chunky soled sneakers double-knotted, her frame cumbersome, the back of her T-shirt tinged with sweat. *Miss Betsy*, her name tag read.

Another woman with the same frilly apron stepped into the diner from the lobby.

"She arrives!" Miss Betsy was massaging a grandpa's shoulders while he was divvying up his eggs. "She's on Indian time," she announced to the room. "The other kind." The grandpa and the rest of his table laughed. The woman was Sikh, a gold hoop threaded through her nostril. Miss Betsy went over and ushered her to the back.

"Jim recommended this place," Sam was saying. I turned back to our table. *Jim?* I couldn't exactly picture him at the counter, tucking into a short stack.

"He invested," Sam continued. "After the fire." *Which one?* I took a big bite of waffle, mouth too full to speak. I didn't want to ruin it— whatever this was.

He didn't bring up what had happened yesterday, his mood light, sweet as the puddle of syrup on my plate. It made me uneasy. It wasn't like Sam. The man didn't bicker; he stewed. Usually it was days before he'd thaw. And there we were, the very next morning, out at breakfast.

"More coffee, hun?" I nodded my head. "Don't you two make a fine-looking couple," Miss Betsy cooed, patting Sam on the back. He laced his fingers through mine. It made me uneasy, but it was better than the alternative, I remember thinking, stepping right into the sprung-open trap.

Sam wanted to spend the day together. A walk along the Nechako, a movie at Famous Players—*Tomb Raider*, the first we'd seen in theaters together since forever. It was like we were dating again, Sam springing for popcorn, wrapping an arm around me. It hadn't always been like it'd become. Once there'd been butterflies, anticipation. Maybe this was an effort to rekindle that. I laid my head on his shoulder, sipping my Coke.

As the week wore on, it became clear: It wasn't an embrace. I was being restrained. I'd never seen that side of Sam before, jealous, scared, like if he let go, I might vanish completely, undoing everything—the two-bedroom, steak dinner, two and a half little bundles (fingers crossed)— that we were building together.

He'd assumed the worst of my absence that morning. That I'd been out all night, too, sneaking around. His mind must have reeled, etching in all the long weeks he'd been away, clichéd episode projected in his head.

He insisted on giving me a lift to and from work, topped off the tank while I did the week's shopping. He was there behind me every time I stood over the stove, vacuumed the carpet, folded his laundry.

Watching when I walked down our drive to the mailbox. There were worse reactions to his sort of suspicions. Still, it was suffocating, as if we were not two but one fused together. Or more like I'd been fused onto him. Eve glommed back onto Adam.

My only respite was at work or out in the yard, where Sam had a clear view of me from the windows. Pinning the washing, freeing the zucchinis from their vines. I'd already brought two Safeway bags into the store, dumping them onto the break room table, willing them to find a new home. Elyse had held one up, inspecting, as if it were the first zucchini she'd ever seen.

"What do you do with it?" She scrunched up her face. Apparently it was.

"It's a vegetable," I said. "You eat it. You can bake it into a cake." Her mouth gaped. "I'll bring some in."

She slipped one into her purse. "How about that."

I was just waiting for the wave to break, to lift my head up again. Every morning it beckoned, what I'd stashed between the pages of *Cannery Row*. The Man with the Braid probably halfway to Quebec.

I should just tell him, I reasoned Wednesday morning after another breakfast with Sam's fingers fastened to mine. Rachelle had been his neighbor, too. He must have noticed she'd been gone. Maybe it'd be a relief, an explanation for it all.

And maybe I'd win the Powerball.

The way he'd reacted that morning when she'd waved to me. *You hardly knew the woman*—Anne-Marie's advice. The truth was, another man would've been easier to account for. At least an affair would've made sense.

I was staring out at the rusted red truck when I realized—it wouldn't take much to pick up the phone. Sam started and ended his day with a shower. Mick had already filed the report. All he had to do was punch in the plate numbers. The Man probably already had a record. They could release a warrant. Save Rhoda. That was, if it wasn't already too late. Find out what happened to Rachelle. *You're talking like she's already dead.* I thought of Beth, gone nine, ten weeks. *We aren't giving up hope yet.*

The phone rang. Sam picked up. A minute later, he came padding into the kitchen.

"It was Jim. I got to head out for a minute." He paused. "You're staying here, right?" It was even better than a shower. I almost smiled, catching myself.

"Where else?" He chewed at his lip. It was wearing on him, too, the vigilance. It couldn't last forever, his wagon yoked so tautly to mine.

As soon as I heard his truck pull out, I flew into our bedroom, reaching for the book. I flipped through its pages. The photo was gone.

I squatted on the carpet, angling my face. Maybe it'd fallen, floated under the dresser. I shook the book out, gripping its spine. Checked the books underneath it. *Sanctuary. The Body Farm. One for the Money.* The photo fell to the floor.

Sam had gone through my things. My throat tightened. No wonder he thought I was cheating. He must have assumed the Man with the Braid was the other man. Why hadn't he just confronted me with it? What was he waiting for? To catch me red-handed?

I went into the living room, photo in hand, and picked up the phone. "I need to talk to Officer Mick. I have an update on a case."

"I'm sorry, who's speaking?" It was a different receptionist from the one I'd met, this one's speech tremulous, the drawl of the elderly.

"Jenny Hayes. I was in the other week. My neighbor went missing. Officer Mick filed the report." The receptionist was silent.

"I have a new lead."

"'A new lead,'" she repeated. "Can you spell your last name for me, dear?"

"Hayes," I enunciated. "*H-A-Y-E-S.*"

"*H-A-Y-A-S?*"

"No, *E.*"

"*H-E-Y-A-S?*"

"No," I said, patience wearing. It was like talking to Nana. "After the *Y. H-A-Y-E-S.*"

"Oh, H*a*yes." She went quiet again. "You know, dear, I'm just not seeing anything."

"Are you sure you're spelling it right?" How was that possible? "Maybe the report is under my neighbor's name? Murphy. Rachelle."

"Morping. That's *M-O-R-P—*"

"Is Officer Mick in?" I didn't want to go through a spelling bee again. "He has all the information. I was in the other week. If you'd just connect me to him . . ."

"Him who?" Sam was standing at the doorway. I hadn't heard him pull back in. *Fuck.* I slammed down the phone before realizing that was even more incriminating. *Double fuck.*

"I forgot something," Sam said, icy, striding toward the kitchen in his boots. This was it. The proof he'd been missing.

"Sam, wait." I trailed after him. "It's not what you think."

"You don't know what I think." He reached for his thermos, starting back toward the front door.

I couldn't keep it up. There was only one out.

"Rachelle's missing," I said, desperate, eyes misty, wide as a doe's.

"Who?" It took him a minute. "Al's wife?"

"It's been a couple weeks already." I held up the photo. "I found this on the road near her property. I was just calling the cops."

Without saying a word, he walked over toward me and lifted the receiver. Star sixty-nine. He waited, expressionless as a shovel. "Prince George, RCMP," I heard through the speaker. He hung up.

"So it was you poking around the station." He shook his head. "I told Jim he got it wrong."

"No." I blushed. I knew that other officer had been listening in. Jim's buddy. But what did he care what I did? "I went by once. On the way home from work." I backpedaled. "Figured there might be a connection. With Beth."

Sam had turned his face away from me again.

"I saw Al's old Fleetwood on the shoulder of 16. Maybe it's the same guy."

"Maybe." Sam zipped up his hoodie. "I'm late," he said, opening the door.

"You know"—he turned back—"you're not going to fix it. Whatever it is you think you're doing. I don't want you getting involved." He had the same look he got after we visited Nana. His lips pinched, his eyes heavy. "There are some messed-up people out there."

He wasn't angry anymore, I realized. He was worried. Sad.

He knew something, more than he was saying. I could see that, even then. Jim had a lot of associates. What if the Man with the Braid was one of them? I had a vague recollection of Sgt O'Flaherty's with Missy, Jim bumping his fist against a dark man's. I looked at the photo. Could it have been him?

Catch you later, he'd said, his hair black, trailing down. No, braided. The reason the Man looked so familiar. I'd seen him before. Jim's *buddy* in on it, whatever "business" they conducted. The report made to disappear. What Sam had said, as if he had firsthand knowledge. *There are some messed-up people out there.*

I looked up at him, but he'd already gone. Left alone for the first time that week, what should have been a breath of sweet relief curdled. The taste in my mouth nauseatingly sour.

seventeen

It was dizzying how quickly the dust settled, everything exactly as it was before. No more company in the kitchen, no rides to work, Sam starting early up in Mackenzie and ending late, another favor for Jim. In the days that followed, I interacted more with his laundry than him. I'd miscalculated. Crazy was better than adulterous. I was free again, the days long again, the TV always on again, laugh track the only intermission from the constant prattle in my head.

I dreamt of her for the first time the night of my revelation. Rachelle teetering on stilts in the misty-slick dark, other hands painting her lips clown-red. The sectioned-off ponytail morphing into a blade, a nunchuck, a slippery trout—the same hands force-feeding her, her gagging it down. There were rumors about Jim, what Missy's sisters-in-law spoke of when she was out of earshot. I'd watched enough *Cold Squad* to know they were linked: the drug trade and the trade that happened under night's cover at the entrance of the park. *He's a pimp*, one had said. Another correcting her: *He's the pimps' dealer. The candy man.*

I'd placed a few more calls to the station, a last-ditch effort, but Mick was always out. It was what stopped me from driving right over there, this new view of her. Well, coupled with the fact that I, too, was being watched.

What Ray's friend had said, the new girl, the wedding ring. One of the photos from the scant roll I'd had developed (a toilet seat, a pair of earrings, a girl's room, a bed—complete waste of 5.99). Those silvery shoes, sullied and stowed away under her bed. A dirty secret, a means of satisfying a habit, maybe even her idea of a good time. The track marks sure to be found on her arms. Maybe Rachelle hadn't disappeared. Maybe she *had* taken off. *She party?*

Sam wasn't wrong. Those men, they were dangerous. I'd been lucky so far. And even if I did solve whatever had happened, what did it matter?

Rachelle had chosen her path, forsaking her role, her two precious daughters. Maybe she'd simply gotten what was coming. You play with fire.

She appeared again in my dreams. My nightmares. Fishing lures dangling from her copper-dark nipples, the feathered creature she mounted, writhing upon. Obscene racket of moaning and screeching and screaming: my hands tied, unable to shield my eyes. "You should try it," she said, reaching to unsnap my bra. "She likes it," she breathed, words burning inside of me, the match that'd been struck. The warmth that rose like water in a basin, dripping out of my unwilling mouth.

I was through, I decided that next morning, knees in my garden, the sun harsh overhead. I looked out at her yard, silver flames licking up from the spokes of the warped kiddie bike. Quack grass was shooting through the maw of the toilet seat, the fruits on her blackberry bush all shrunken and shriveled like dead flies. The fireweed's flowers starting to wither, the pink brindled, ugly, dun brown. It was more than an eyesore—it cheapened our place. She'd been too lazy to haul all that crap to the dump. And now, there it was, left for someone else to clean up. *Typical.* The voice grew louder.

Anne-Marie was right. I hardly knew the woman. I brushed the soil from my hands.

She just happened to live across from me.

Mom called on Friday, the first we'd spoken since the party. Not to apologize or thank me but to do what she always did when she called. Ask for something. A last-minute sitter for the kids. Ray's band was playing, and she'd already missed last month's show. Well, not Ray's band per se—the band he played drums in. The Mike Owens Blues Band, a lineup that rotated as frequently as the doors at Value Village. Some shows the only recognizable face was Mike Owens's puckered one, his coarse gray braid whipping the fetid air at the Iron Horse while he shredded.

"Everyone else is busy. If you can't do it, I'll just have to bring them with."

I agreed for their sake, not hers. Sam was out again, anyway, helping his dad with the irrigation system. I cracked open a Coke, flipping past that used car commercial. It's not like I had any other big plans.

I arrived to find Mom in the same position I'd been, slurping a Coke—though hers was Diet—and working her way through a bag of Doritos, Cool Ranch. A cigarette, not a clicker, in her free hand.

"Ray's showering." She crunched between drags, not bothering to swivel her head. She'd been able to soft pedal over the phone, but seeing me there in the house where she'd raised me was, evidently, too much. She was pissed, forgetting that I was only there at her charge. It was almost laughable, Mom's non-logic. Almost.

"Hi, Jenny." Kyle waved. He lay sprawled on the couch, limp as a SpaghettiO, his eyes glued to an episode of *Cops*. They were answering a house call, the woman's robe slipping, her face punched into a wink. I remember the episode, the way one cop had looked conspiratorially into the camera. They couldn't help the woman because she couldn't sign the complaint form because the woman, middle-aged, couldn't read. I remember the episode because even in the grain of the night cam, her resemblance to Mom was uncanny.

"Should he be watching that?" I slipped off my Keds. Mom flapped a hand, back still turned, swatting away my question.

The door to the washroom swung open, Ray emerging from beneath a cloud of steam and AXE body spray. He was naked, in just a loosely slung towel, his hair slicked back like a boy's.

"Look, Jenny, just in time for the show." He grinned, alternating between flexing each pec.

"Funny." I took a seat next to Kyle, patting his shoulder. "Hey, bud."

"Ray, put some clothes on," Mom snapped, stubbing out her cigarette. "Dawn's asleep. Kyle's been fed. There's a pepperoni pizza in the freezer if you're hungry." She reapplied her lipstick in the reflection of the microwave, addressing me without so much as a glance in my direction. "Soon as Ray gets his ass in gear, we'll be out of your hair."

She smoothed the ruche along her dress. She was more Shania than Stevie now, in fake eyelashes and leopard print.

I stood, then squatted near the tower of VHS tapes. "Hey, Kyle, have you seen *E.T.* yet?"

"Ready." Ray came bounding from Mom's bedroom, tugging on his leather jacket. His black shirt was only buttoned after the fourth or fifth opportunity, a silver star cast around his neck. The star was inverted, its top points like two raised horns. A pentagram. The boys used to draw them on their binders in middle school, playing at something, like Ray was. I doubted he had any idea what it meant.

"Be back after last call." Ray latched an arm around Mom's waist. A wiser woman would have brought her pajamas.

I cranked on the oven, then retrieved the pizza from the freezer, leaving Kyle with a lisping Drew Barrymore and tiptoeing to check in on Dawn. She was zonked, dozing flat on her belly, one dimpled hand gripping a raggedy stuffed dog.

You like dogs? What Destiny had asked me. Little Beth was even younger than Dawn. Those poor girls. I wiped at my eyes. So small, so innocent—even if their mother wasn't. Asleep in strange rooms in strange beds in strange houses. Like Marie's BFF necklace, a heart cleaved apart.

That horrifying story that'd dominated the news. Her foster mother had sworn she was a violent sleeper, the toddler who'd been found *gasping and gurgling* (the phrase the reporters kept repeating, as if the other details weren't grisly enough), barely conscious. The harness was necessary to keep her from busting the crib; the bruises, well, she'd inflicted those upon herself.

The family had won awards for their care, the work no one else wanted to do. I remembered the discussion Mom had had with Sue in our kitchen over a decade back. Sue's cousin and her husband had taken one in, a boy, and one morning they'd woken to find all their valuables— the stereo, the TV, even the damn vacuum cleaner—had vanished. *He fled the scene in the Nikes they'd bought him. The thanks they got.* Sue had shaken her head. Some of them—most of them—were beyond help.

The reason for the toddler's death was undetermined. The coroner made no recommendations. It was a tragic story, but most people agreed. Accidents happen. The six other wards who were living with the family stayed put. Dawn's life wouldn't be easy, but it wouldn't be that. I reached a hand down to smooth back her hair, gilded ribbon curling at her ear.

I put Kyle to bed and ate my pizza on the couch, half watching *There's Something About Mary*, flipping the channel during the scene where she puts the spunk in her hair. Beth's *Crimestoppers* segment droned on, a bookend to the eleven o'clock news. I drifted off to the montage: Beth with her sister (or friend), the water of the lake behind them placid, unaware of the turbulence up ahead.

I dreamt this time of Beth, her freckled hands weaving a shield out of a mass of coarse hair. Something sharp in her hands—a needle, no, knife—Beth embroidering her work with a hot, looping red. "Do you want to know what happened to me?" Her sea-blue eyes met mine. "I can't tell you, but I can show you." She pressed herself against me, pushing me down—down, down, down, the hair rising like waves, like a mountain, sea blue supplanted by yellow, eyes shifty. Animal.

I woke gasping, heart furious, to the groan of the door. It was just Ray, fumbling with his boots and before shuffling into the kitchen, yanking open the freezer, and icing his cheek with a pack of skinless, boneless chicken breasts. His lip had been split open, his knuckles still raw, his right eyelid an indigo pincushion.

I could have seen it as a warning, the nightmare, the number someone had done to Ray. Violence was threatening, drawing near. Instead, I shrugged out from under it. Bunched it up like I had that red scarf. I wasn't sleeping well—all those nights Sam was on call. I was restless, my dreams hectic. Ray's face, though visceral, wasn't all that shocking. For some men it was how you ended your night. It was always something. A bad look, a blank stare. Sometimes it was nothing. *Some faces are for punching*, Jim liked to say. *Boys*, Missy would shrug, echoing Mom.

"Hi, sweetie," Mom said, plopping down next to me, picking the bobby pins out from her hair. Her face looked pale, her eyes rimmed with red. I checked the clock on the VCR. It was well past three A.M.

"Kids all right?" Mom croaked with a lopsided smile. She was too beat to remember that she was still angry. She even patted my arm when I left.

Ray had his claim staked on Mom's guest spot, so I'd parked my Buick along the perimeter of the park. It wasn't until I was out there, unlocking it, that I realized. The sign, illuminated by the flash of my headlights: *NO SOLICITING.*

They were bound to be out at the circular entrance of the park. It was just up around the corner, less than five hundred yards away. The women Ray's friends had talked about. *She party?*

I was about to find out.

There was a lineup of vehicles, long as a drive-through, the shadows pivoting from the driver's to the passenger's side. I was expecting something lurid, had braced myself for the sounds, but as it turned out, all was quiet and, for the most part, dark. Nobody's lights were on. I followed suit, not wanting to attract attention. The lit ends of cigarettes the sole guiding light.

The women weren't at all what I pictured. Huddled in circles or shivering alone, they looked bored or tired, killing time. Puffer coats unzipped, they wore dresses or jeans, one woman in sweatpants and shower sandals. A few faces, I noted to my mounting uneasiness, were round, flush with baby fat. I eased off the gas pedal, scanning for her. It was hard to differentiate in the dark.

There was someone up ahead, her neck long, her limbs lanky. The sheen of her heels—another flare in the night. I braked, eyes squinting. Her head was bowed, the flick of her lighter. One hand raking her long hair back. This was it. My breath quickened. I cranked my window down.

"Rachelle?" I managed to choke her name out. The shadow started toward me. Staggering. I hadn't wanted this hunch to be right.

"Hi, honey." The woman crouched near my window, flipping her hair. It was the same color as mine: mousy brown.

Her face was gaunt, the bridge of her nose pummeled, lipstick flaking from her parted mouth. If she was surprised to see me, another woman, in the driver's seat, she didn't let on.

"Sorry," I whispered. "I thought you were someone else."

"I can be whoever you want," she slurred, smiling. Her teeth were kernels, brown as bruised apples, her skin waxen. Bone white. I kept driving, and soon there was nothing but the night. She'd been the last in the lineup.

I always thought it was only them who did it. I wondered what had happened to bring that woman down so far. Despite the years of hard living, she still looked young. She couldn't have been much older than I was. Maybe if Mom had stayed with André, if drugs had been in the house. Maybe it would've been my forearm that was perforated, my tits in plain view as I crouched near, my body for purchase—well—rent.

I flicked on my blinker, turning back toward 97, passing under the billboard for Beth.

Or maybe everything would have turned out exactly the same. Our fates as fixed as the stars. Like Beth with her good family, her college degree. Ending up in the same place as Delphina, as Aurelie. As Rachelle.

I found myself turning onto her street and idled there in front of her drive. I heard something, a call—the bird cloaked behind birch leaves. Could almost see them, the owl's watchful yellow eyes. I was taken back to that day sitting at her kitchen table. The cup of coffee, how she'd welcomed me in.

What had I been thinking? The heels were probably from a wedding. *She party?* Sometimes a scar was just a scar. I'd let them get to me, Ray's friends. Sam's comment. What Anne-Marie had said. They didn't know her, hadn't seen her the way I had. Her sister, that was a different story. Rachelle might have been a number of things, but she definitely wasn't *that*.

I'd forgotten how tended to her front lawn was, the rosebushes in bloom, their soft heads just visible in the velvet dark. The grass had grown taller and would grow taller still, the dandelion, the nettle, the fireweed pushing up until the front began to mirror the back. In September, the mountain ash would lose all its berries. The crows a hellish clatter. All those hours she'd spent, pruners out, mower on, trying to do better, be better—balked.

She'd probably rebuked him, the Man with the Braid. Refused to give him what he took by force. It wasn't love, what had made Little Beth. *She likes it, huh, she likes it.* Rachelle was a victim of circumstances beyond her control. *Destiny.* Her little hands surfaced before me. I wiped the wet from my eyes.

I couldn't evade it. What was mine. We were knitted together, Rachelle and me. Our houses opposite each other. Hers full with two daughters—in need. Mine empty, a woman with nothing but time. It wasn't coincidence. It was fate. I gazed up at the twinkling sky.

I saw a light flip on, and I startled. It was just the neighbor, the widow next door. I'd seen her that morning, out on her porch, wearing the exact same bathrobe (a cornflower blue from Canadian Tire) that I was. I shifted gears, placing my foot back on the pedal.

I'm not sure now where exactly I thought my journey would take me. I've never come across a name for that direction. The one that drives you straight into yourself.

eighteen

I had yet another night of paltry sleep, too anxious to switch off my mind and rest. *I should have driven in that photo of the Man with the Braid days ago*, I remember thinking, regret mushrooming as it churned around. I was guilty of withholding crucial evidence, what might very well have solved the whole disappearance. By four A.M., the need to drive it in was acute, pelting down on me like hail.

I resolved to head to the station first thing that next morning, but I snored right through my alarm. My eyes met the clock. It was already nine. I was set to open the store in half an hour. It could've waited until after my shift, but by the afternoon, Mick would probably be out on patrol. I'd be useless at the store, I reasoned, tugging on my polo shirt and bringing along my toothbrush and a cup to spit in for the car. It'd be all I would think about. The cop shop wasn't exactly *on* the way, but it wasn't *out* of the way either. I'd just have to be quick about it.

On the drive over, I devised a plan, what I'd say to the receptionist, the room she'd prepare, a place to talk to Mick in private. I'd have to be firm, to hint that the station had been compromised. I wouldn't let myself be turned around. I pulled into the station, stashing the photo in my back pocket.

As it turned out, getting Mick alone required zero effort on my part. He was standing there in the station's parking lot, back against a squad car, when I arrived. I looked around. Wasn't another soul in sight. Not a bad start.

"Officer Mick." I waved. He squinted. He didn't seem to recognize me until I was about a foot in front of him.

"Jessie," he said, cigarette perched between his lips. He straightened himself, reaching out a hand. It was the right gesture, but the delivery was off. Mick shook at a ten, even with me. Most men dialed it down.

"It's Jenny," I corrected him, but he didn't acknowledge me. Instead, he lifted up a pack of Pall Malls, easing back against the car.

"You smoke?" he asked. I shook my head. He shrugged, grinning. "What brings you out?"

"I tried to call, but I couldn't get through. I wanted to show you this." I took the photo from my pocket. "It's Rachelle's sister's husband. The truck I told you about. It was him at her house, the day before she went missing." For the first time, my voice remained steady. Columbo would be proud. "I'm pretty sure her sister's gone, too."

Mick held up the photo, his eyes narrowing. "That's a truck all right." His gaze darted from the photo to me. He bit his lip, concentrating on something. This was it. I looked back at him, unflinching. He must have recognized the Man with the Braid. A fixture in *Crimestoppers,* no doubt.

Mick started to speak when the radio that was fastened to his hip crackled. "We need a ten sixty-two at the correctional center." He pressed a thumb against a button and spoke in a register that was low, authoritative, his eyes still hooked to mine.

"Roger," he said, opening the door, cigarette smoldering in his mouth. "Duty calls." He winked, starting to duck into his car.

"Wait." I stepped in to stop him. "Couldn't we look up the plates?" I didn't know how to phrase it. About the other officer. That whatever Mick found, the information was sensitive, had to be kept from prying eyes. It'd seem crazy if I just blurted it out. What I needed was more time.

"I have more to say, but"—I signaled toward the station with a jerk of my head—"I can't say it here. If you give me your number, I could call you directly. Or I could give you mine." I dug in my purse. "I have a pen somewhere."

Mick had stood upright again while I was speaking, and I realized, when I finished, we were no more than an inch or so apart. He dragged on his cigarette, and the smoke filled my nostrils. He'd left the car door flung wide.

"Jilly," he said. It was what Rhoda had called me. Jilly, Jessie, Jenny. *I can be whoever you want.*

"What are you really doing here?" He leaned in toward me, his hand on my arm, his breath hot against my ear. "Lonely? Husband's out late, don't look at you like he used to? I seen how many times you've called."

He frowned, pausing to knock the ash from his cigarette. "You don't have to be embarrassed. You ain't the first who's developed a little . . . crush." He savored that last word, hand squeezing my arm, my cheeks turning from pink to fire.

A *what*? I stepped back, wriggling from his grip, too stunned to respond.

"You're blushing," he said, his Cheshire cat smile, my silence as good a confirmation as any. He brushed his hair from his eyes like he had with the receptionist, a man accustomed to admirers. His tan was so deep, it looked painted on, his teeth as white as a bar of Dove. He was handsome, I guessed, but that didn't make him attractive. If only I'd had the gall to tell him that.

"You again." Before I could work out a response, another voice interjected. It was the officer with the cubicle next to Mick's. Jim's buddy. He was scarfing down a honey dip, a Timmy's cup in the other hand. You couldn't make this stuff up.

"Ready, partner?" He cocked his head at Mick, opening the squad car's passenger door.

Partner. The pavement seemed to buckle under me. Mick's continued disinterest. It was all coming together. They must have been in on it, the two of them. Whatever *it* was.

"Her necklace," I muttered, thinking aloud. "That's why she was never on the news." I looked over at Mick, half expecting him to peel off a mask, like at the end of an episode of *Scooby-Doo*. "You never filed the report, did you?" My voice reedy, all certitude washed. The tears weren't far.

Mick flicked his cigarette to the pavement, crushing it under a regulation boot. He adjusted his belt, straightening again. His smile evaporated.

"You good at math?" He stared at me. His face had hardened, his eyes like steel. "You know how many reports are filed each year? Five thousand. You don't have to be Einstein to get why there's not a press release for every single one." He shook his head, his tone indignant. "'Didn't file the report.' You know how many cases we're on?

"You work?" He didn't wait for me to respond. "Were you trained to do what you do? You ever have anyone come in, question you? Tell you how to do your job? Try to do it for you?"

Mick's attitude toward me had completely changed. Before, when he'd thought I was coming on to him, I was a flower. Delicate, defenseless. Now that I'd insulted him, I was just another thorn.

"Now I'm not sure where you found that picture, but you do realize breaking and entering is a crime, right? Punishable by up to ten years in prison?"

Prison? The tears arrived, more a deluge than a trickle. I wiped them away, but they kept barreling on.

"Come on, Mick," I heard the other officer say. "Go easy on her, man. We're on call."

Mick ignored him, digging in his pocket. For what? I stepped back, almost expecting him to write me a fine. He handed me something. A napkin from Timmy's, the paper rough as a file.

"It's clean," he said, indignation reeled in. "I hate to see a woman cry." I took it, its crinkly edges poking at my eyes.

"Now listen here, Missus. I'm sure your friend, she'll turn up. It's a scary world, I get it, but we're here to protect you. You let us take care of it. We're the professionals. No more playing detective, okay?" He was waiting until he caught my eyes. "Deal?" he asked. I flicked my eyes up at him, nodding.

"Deal." He spoke for me, patting my shoulder before ducking into the squad car, siren wailing like a newborn torn from the arms of her mother.

I was late for work, but I was having a hard time caring, my ass glued to the hot leather seat of my car. I sat there for a while in the station's parking lot, stupefied. How had that gone so wrong? It wasn't until the two were gone that I'd realized: the photo was missing. Mick must have pocketed it after I'd handed it over. Now he had everything. I was a dimwit, pinheaded, should have at least had the foresight to jot those plate numbers down.

I could have taken the plate numbers in to the station in Vanderhoof. *She party?* I remembered my phone call. He'd been absolutely unconcerned, that officer. Defensive even, thinking back. Whatever *it* was, could Vanderhoof have been implicated, too?

It snowballed, my guesswork, in the seat of my car, until the answer
to what was really happening on the highway became conspiratorial,
immeasurably dark, like an episode of *Dateline*.

What if Rhoda and Rachelle were two of many? Jim a minor player,
the Man with the Braid a patsy. That clearing in the bush far from
random, but a ritual site. I thought of Michelle, the subject of that psy-
chiatrist's book, *Michelle Remembers*, the horrors she'd described. I'd
never read it, but I'd seen the interview on *Oprah*. The unspeakable
things they did to women, to children. Satanists and their sacrificial
lambs. Who *they* were was never clear. *They* could be anyone—celebrities,
politicians. Policemen. That's what made it so chilling. Michelle was
Canadian, from Vancouver Island. Practically next door.

How else to explain it? How little they cared. All those women—little
girls even—a highway with a body count. Lost not by fluke but design.
With everyone looking, they still hadn't found Beth. What if *they* were
the ones to have made her vanish?

The thought, I knew, was crazy. But then I thought of those crosses,
little Aurelie Andrews, just nine years old. How crazy was it?

Sam had been right. I'd been naïve. Was no telling how deep this
all ran.

I was already parked in the mall's sprawling lot when I flipped open the
sun visor, coupon floating into my lap, miniature bottles of bleach suspended in nowhere.

4 Whenun Road. 10:00. The meeting the woman from the march
had told me about. With Sam at my back all week, I'd written it off as
an impossibility. She was my last recourse, that woman—truly the
deal of a lifetime. I started my car and exited the mall. It had to be
a sign.

It was well past nine thirty, closer to ten, but the truth was, the opener
only worked one extra half hour. Elyse was due in—there didn't need to
be two of us. I could say I had car trouble, an emergency. I'd speak my
piece and head straight back to the mall. I didn't know exactly where
Whenun Road was, but it was the Prince George reservation. It couldn't
be too far from town.

I dug out an atlas from my glove box, but I couldn't find Whenun anywhere. I drove to the nearest gas station and swung open the door to the convenience store, figuring the clerk might know better.

"'We-nun'?" he repeated. "No, never heard of it. Maybe try that?" He pointed to the rotating rack of maps.

"Are you looking for the rez?" A woman browsing the jerky bins craned her neck. Her blonde hair was cropped close to the back of her head, her bangs cascading to her pointed chin. "It's past the mill, off Northwood Pulp." Not exactly nearby. "Keep veering right. It's a left off the forest service road."

The rez. The woman didn't look Native. Maybe she knew where it was so she knew where to avoid. I looked down at her forearms. In summer, everybody wanted to be brown.

I didn't even check the clock before leaving. I was already late, already committed. Was bound, now more than ever, to find out what had happened to Rachelle.

I saw the smoke first, then the two gray cement towers, sprawling compound cropping up out of nowhere, what was otherwise just bush around. *PRIVATE*, a sign read. *CANFOR EMPLOYEES ONLY.* There was a shit-ton of money there—all that equipment, the lumber. The 500-pound bales of pulp. Train tracks fenced off the road from the mill. I'd always just figured it dead-ended there. I rode over them as the woman at the gas station had instructed, veering right.

Hues of rust, butter yellow, Yankee blue: the shipping containers were either halted along the tracks or parked against the wire fence, waiting to be weighted down. More windowless buildings, parking lot after parking lot. The mill seemed to go on forever. Then, just when I readied myself to turn and try the other direction, I saw trees again, a glimpse of water. The Fraser, snaking its way through. The mill had been built alongside its banks, waste churned directly out into the water. Washed away. Well—not *away* away. Further downstream. Someone else's problem.

The pavement soon gave way to gravel, a white road sign. *Beaver Forest SR.* Whenun would be coming up at any minute. I kept an eye to the left of me, pink bloom of the fireweed. Something lunging, suddenly, out from the pines. Coat black as oil, the dainty pouch of a tail. I slammed on my brakes. A black bear. Swallowed back into the bush, disappearing as suddenly as it'd materialized.

They were the reason we picked our berries as soon as they ripened, why we bolted our lids to our trash cans. In the city, they were a nuisance—holding up traffic, busting fences, mangling bird feeders and barbeques and hockey nets. Divested of what made them wild, what made us respect them, no longer a predator but a pest.

But out in the bush, they still inspired fear, the most gruesome stories legendary. Like Kellen Weaver, a boy from our graduating class. After a fight with his girlfriend he'd decided to forgo his camper, spending the night by the fire, bottle of Fireball in hand. His girlfriend woke to the rising sun and the singing birds and Kellen's severed arm in a pile of ash. The filling from his jacket a snowy path to a face that'd been mutilated beyond recognition.

That back road was bush enough for me. I'd never seen a bear so close before. I sat there for a moment, stunned. It felt meaningful, that encounter, like a sign, like a—what did they call them? *Spirit animal?* Each one imbued with meaning, capturing an essence, a quality. I thought of the bear that'd darted into the road. Big, burly, dark. Its mitts razor-sharp. Maybe it was more like a red flag.

nineteen

Another sign, just visible in the overgrowth, surfaced to the left of me. *Whenun*. I turned, Buick rattling, crater after crater, the road in much worse shape than Beaver Forest. Looked like the maintenance crews couldn't find it on the map either.

Up ahead on the shoulder, the first sign of human life since the mill. A stooped man, his wrists tangled around two sagging plastic bags, shuffling through the weeds. Something lancelike protruded from an armpit. A fishing rod. His skin, I saw, as I approached, was wrinkled, his hair a dusting, sparse white. He must have been over seventy. What was he doing on the shoulder like that?

"Hey." I waved, slowing down to a putter. But the man didn't hear me, or else he didn't want to be bothered. He kept walking past me, and so I drove on.

I passed a gas station with two standalone pumps, an outcropping of modest houses. I hadn't driven more than a click before the road dead-ended. Was that it? The rez?

The way people spoke, I was expecting hellfire, a scene worse than the trashiest trailer park. Where ankle bracelets weren't fashion accessories and so-called electric fires all too common. But the truth was, it looked like any other back road. Some houses more neglected than others, but nothing shocking. No yard nearly as derelict as Rachelle's.

The house of the driveway I'd turned around in was even scenic—and not just compared to the rest of the batch. A gable-front cottage with rocking chairs on its porch, its clapboards painted a faultless ivory. There were roses out front the color of Valentine hearts, the lawn freshly mowed, pink foxglove at attention. The garden was fabled, with corn bursting skyward, the beans trellised around the still-ripening squash. An automatic spindrift misted the lawn.

That sprinkler was the only action I'd spotted, the rest of the street dead, as if the sun had just crested, everyone still curled up in bed. *They're lazy is what.* Was it Sue, or Mom, or Missy, or Sam who'd said that? It was impossible to discern sometimes, whose voice was migrating through my head.

I was looking for 4, but there weren't any numbers on the mailboxes, and as far as I could tell, the gas station was the only nonresidential building there.

The store was corrugated aluminum, rectangular, and narrow—a shipping container in a past life. A woman stood behind the counter, turned away from the man at its other side. She was reaching for something.

"You got your status card?" She slid an envelope of tobacco toward the man. He nodded, holding up something that looked like a license, the first hint that I was really someplace else.

The Golden Ticket was what we called it. No tax on gas or tobacco or that shiny new four-runner. Education, healthcare—completely gratis. The man hoisted his JNCOs up around his waist. His hair was frosted at the tips, blondish.

I paced an aisle, starving, having forgone breakfast. There was everything you'd expect from any convenience store: the fridge of energy drinks, the aisle of potato chips, the double pots of coffee on their glowing warmers. And what you wouldn't: the single sticks of butter, the cans of beans, tomato paste, Tyson nuggets, Wonder Bread. In a basket at the end of one aisle, corn preshucked and shrink-wrapped. The nearest Safeway must have been at least twenty clicks out. The gas station was also the grocery store.

There were buns near the register, the same perfect white puffs from the woman at the march's dash. I picked up a package, still browsing.

In a display case at the end of the counter were six or so leather pouches. Mud-colored and implausibly small. I couldn't see how they were useful. Even a loonie, a one dollar coin, wouldn't have fit, let alone the inevitable pocketful of change.

In the bottom corner of the case, something else caught my eye. A pair of intricately beaded earrings the size, more or less, of my palm.

Shaped like birds. My heart pattered. Rachelle. They were just like the ones I'd found in her drawer. Was this where she'd bought them?

"Can I see those?"

The clerk removed them from the case, wordlessly passing them over. Hot in my palms, my imagination loped. How pretty they'd be, my hair a shade or two darker. I poked them through my ears, scouting for a mirror. The closest I could find was the reflection from the Pepsi fridge.

They were less showy than Rachelle's, the colors muted, the blues watery, cola browns, but still, hooked through my ears and flanking my wan, freckled face, they looked like a Halloween costume. I might as well have been toting a tomahawk.

I tugged them off. It was more than that. My calves were too sturdy, my hands too sure: meant to peel potatoes, scrub grout. Peasant stock. Rachelle's hands had been dainty, her neck slender and long like some rare-blooming hothouse flower. Some women just weren't meant for ornamentation. They were already neglected, the other earrings I'd found.

"Anything else?" The clerk stood with her arms crossed. She was as dark as Rhoda and just as mean-looking. Her tone flat as a pancake. I handed her the buns to prove I was buying.

"What are these?" I pointed to the pouches.

"Medicine bags." Her glasses were fitted with transitional lenses, and they kept shifting in the light. "You can stuff tobacco in 'em."

Her accent was strong, the *M*'s elongated, her mouth curling around the *O*'s, lips mimicking the shape of the letter. A lot of them spoke like that, as if they weren't from here—as if they'd only recently acquired the language and were still testing the way it felt coming out. The *rez accent*. Rhoda had one. So did her husband. Rachelle didn't, or else it had faded. All the years spent living with Al.

I realized then, what had set Rachelle apart. She really wasn't like the others. Rachelle was subtle, refined. Try as I might, I couldn't picture her there in that harshly lit aluminum box, piling her cart with dinged cans of kidney beans. Rachelle had shopped at Safeway like I did. I'd seen the bag lining the bin in her washroom.

"Just the buns." I dug out my wallet. There was a bulletin board nailed to the wall behind the counter, a xeroxed copy of a missing sign, the girl's name one I didn't recognize. I saw that it'd been tacked on top of another. "Hey." I suddenly remembered why I'd stopped there in the first place. "Do you know of a meeting happening? Supposed to be at number four?"

The clerk was quiet, punching at a calculator, digging in a plastic baggie for the change. "Four's the office." She kept her head down. "Just across the road."

I stepped outside. The squat brick building I'd mistaken for a house. The blinds were drawn, and there were only two vehicles parked in the driveway. Neither one of them a minivan. The woman was late. *Indian time*—she'd said it. I looked at either side of the empty road before bounding across it.

I knocked.

"You can just come on in," I heard someone call out, the quick footsteps toward the door. It was the woman from the march who opened it.

"Oh," she said, immediately reaching out a hand. "It's you. Glad you could make it." She guided me in.

Hardly any bigger than the gas station store, the office was just a single carpeted room, weakly lit and barely furnished. There was a makeshift buffet at one end of the room, three foam-topped card tables pushed together, blanketed with provisions. Some folding chairs were scattered around it, a cat-hair-caked couch deflating against a wall. The other end of the room looked slightly more official—the scratched wooden desk, the beige filing cabinet, the topographical map of BC.

"Something to drink?" the woman was asking, already handing me a cup from the stack. "We have Mountain Dew, Pepsi, Diet Pepsi, orange juice. Coffee, I forgot about the coffee." She shook her head. "Sorry, I've forgotten your name."

"Jenny," I said, pouring myself an orange juice. We hadn't introduced ourselves in her van.

"Jenny," she repeated. "Of course. Jenny." She spoke with such assurance, my name patent, self-evident, the two nothing syllables I'd responded to all my life. "We're just about to get started."

I glanced around. There were only three other people there, two of them senile, gnarled hands around Dixie cups, as moribund as the man I'd seen on the shoulder. The other was a woman who was either expecting or otherwise floundering along her weight-loss journey, her feet two flotation devices buoyed on the seat of a folding chair.

"Have you tried fry bread before?" The woman handed me what looked like a wrinkled pancake with a napkin. "Auntie Sylvie made these." She nodded at one of the crones.

"I brought these." I held out the buns. "Sorry, I didn't catch your name either."

"How thoughtful," the woman said, setting them on the table. How soon was too soon to tear into them? "Nevaeh." I took a bite of the fry bread.

I watched as she passed the basket around, her hands as freckled as her mottled face, the pure blue of eyes like bird's eggs or Crest. It's commonplace now, but that was the first time I'd heard the name. *Heaven* spelled backward, as every girl saddled with it would decode. Back then, I figured it had to be Native. I looked at Nevaeh again. In sensible jeans and Velcro-strapped hiking sandals, she could have been a second aunt, Erin's twin. She couldn't be Native. Could she?

The door swung open, and in hobbled a man in a threadbare denim jacket and a lopsided beret, one foot dragging behind him like a spare part.

"Wally." Nevaeh rushed over, helping the man as he tottered. "We're still waiting on Tina, and Eddie, and Bea."

"No problem." Wally supported himself against the table, his glasses fogged over with thumbprints. He was sweating, and it took some work for him to undo his jacket, his hands shaking as he draped it across the back of a chair.

"This is Jenny." Nevaeh handed him a cup. The tip of his right index finger was missing, I noticed, as he scratched at a cheek with a burnished nub. It didn't look like he'd had an easy go of it.

"Hi." I held out my hand.

"Wally Waters." He shook it, his hand as sheeny and soft as wax. "You métis?" He squinted.

"'Métis'?" I'd never heard that word before. Was that the name of his tribe? I thought the ones from PG were the Fort George Band.

Lheidli T'enneh—I'd learn that name later, after Fort George Park was renamed, when, every Thanksgiving, a newscaster would choke out the sounds.

"A half-breed, like me." Wally's grin was as lobed as an oak leaf. Nevaeh was at the door again, greeting a bottle blonde. "Maybe you just don't know it yet." He fiddled with the brim of his beret, the wool nubby, pilled to hell. Way too warm for the weather.

"Yeah, I was one of those taken kids. Didn't find out until I was thirty-eight. Was over in Yellowknife, working as a steamfitter in the diamond mines when I found her, my mom. The real one." His back was toward me as he talked, one hand stacking bread in the other's palm.

"I was one of the luckier ones," he continued. "My folks were fine. No funny business or nothing. I think Mom's parts were faulty. Plumbing wasn't quite right. They couldn't make one on their own, so they got one government-issued." He laughed, facing me again, his eyes just missing mine.

"One time, I was in Edmonton, must have been just fourteen, when this man, he comes over, and with one of those big rez accents, you know, he says, 'Hey, I know you. You're Lucinda's kid, Wally Waters. And I'm your uncle, Bobby Lewean.

"Now, mind you, I'd been living life as Mike Higgins, what my folks had named me. So I'm thinking, you know, he's had a few. So I shake his hand. 'Nice to meet you,' you know, 'See yous later,' and I don't think much of it. Just another drunk Indian." He grinned, shifting the bread from palm to palm.

I nodded, though the truth was he'd lost me. *Taken kids?* I thought of Melanie Fisher. Becca Girard, Joey White. Kidnapping was even bigger news than Beth, the headlines trickling all the way down to the States.

The way Wally told it, it sounded more like he'd been adopted. I thought of Sue's cousin, *the thanks they got.* Maybe it was just Wally's way to make sense of it. Mom and I butted heads, but at least she'd stuck around. Being given up—that wound must have cut to his core.

"Did I already tell you how I met her? My real mom? I have a brain injury, so sometimes I repeat myself." He passed the bread back around. He hadn't touched it. He'd barely stopped to take a breath.

I'd met people like him before, who told stories compulsively, almost mechanically, as if they were a whizzing toy that'd been wound. There was nothing to do but let them discharge. I'd learned growing up with Mom.

The one story she told, and told, and told again, an illustration of how hard life was as a single mother. Exhausted from the umpteenth sleepless night and the opener at the 7-Eleven, she'd stumbled down the stairwell in our building and tripped, knocking out three teeth and snapping an arm. It might as well have been a leg, too, for all it cost her. *I should start charging every time I smile.* She'd flash one for free.

I didn't remember it—I was only two at the time—but I could've recited the whole thing, including that stupid punch line.

When Mom did it, it was clear what she was doing. Trawling for sympathy, condolences, praise—as if the more people who felt bad for her, the bigger her badge. The more real her pain.

But with Wally it was different. More like he was trying to dull the edge, as if retreading would somehow soften the thistled ground.

"My girlfriend, Shelly, when she's with me, will do one of these." He thrust an elbow to the side. "She says, 'Wally, you're a hell of a deal. You talk so much, life feels twice as long with you.'" He laughed, sipping his Mountain Dew.

"I was married once, before her. Nadine. I was a lousy husband. For most of my life, I hated women, on account of me thinking my mom kicked me to the curb. Was a hard worker, though. Bought a million-dollar house in Edmonton. She's still living in it. I'm in a trailer now, but I tell you, I couldn't be happier. Wouldn't trade it for all the moniyaw money in the world."

"'Moniyaw'?" I'd never heard that word before either.

"'White man,'" he said. "You speak Cree?"

Cree?

Before I could answer, Nevaeh appeared. "I'm making a run to the station. Want to join?"

"Sure," I said. Wally lifted a piece of bread to his mouth.

"You girls go ahead." He spoke while chewing, tearing off another corner before he'd swallowed. "I'll hold down the fort."

Swinging open the door and stepping out into the sunshine, I almost felt like I was leaving a movie theater, that world as foreign as Lara Croft's. The feeble light of that room, the way Wally had spoken, quick as a flip-book, flitting from subject to subject, all those words—none I knew—the basket of fry bread, the bird earrings, the medicine pouches. I felt plugged in again, that same electric feeling, like when I'd first been invited over to Rachelle's.

It didn't even faze me when I was met with the oversized numbers of the store's digital wall clock. Eleven. I was officially an hour and a half late. There might've been a phone behind the counter, but the clerk must have been on a cigarette break. Just showing up would be more believable, I decided. If there'd really been an emergency, I would've been too preoccupied to call. I could rub my eyes red, feign exasperation. In the four years I'd been working there, I'd never been late.

"Need anything?" Nevaeh laid a bill on the counter, a bag of instant coffee and another jug of creamer in hand. No. I shook my head.

I could have asked her right then if she knew Rachelle, if anyone there knew the Blueclouds. But like I mentioned, being there, it was all so novel. I'd forgotten myself. I was Jilly, Jessie—a Jenny no one fully knew or could apprehend. It was exhilarating—that thought then.

Nevaeh had one more stop to make. Did I want to come? "For sure," I said. At that point, I would've followed her anywhere.

"Wally's sweet," she was saying as we turned down the road. "Will talk your ear off, but he's sweet. You must be ready to write his biography." She laughed.

"Yeah," I agreed, happy to be in on the joke. "He's got some story." She nodded.

"There was something he said that, I didn't quite understand. He said he was taken? Like, adopted?"

It was an innocent question. I hadn't meant any harm. But I'd clearly offended Nevaeh. The silence a snowdrift, socking us apart. I was transported back to Rachelle's kitchen table, that awkward moment after I'd brought up Beth.

"I mean, maybe I heard him wrong?" I tried to shovel myself out. "He was talking pretty fast."

"You didn't," Nevaeh said after more silence. "Wally escaped the residential schools, but he had it even worse. He's a survivor of the Sixties Scoop." She quickened her pace. "House is just up here."

The Sixties Scoop? I knew what those words meant individually but had no point of reference for them together. Was I supposed to?

And what did she mean by escaped? I thought of little Rhoda staring out from Rachelle's fridge. Residential was the word I'd been searching for. But the way I'd learned it, the schools were set up by the government to help, not harm. Started nearly at the beginning of our country, Native children were offered a fresh start: an education, free room and board—a chance at success.

Helmed by the church, the rumors weren't surprising. At least that's how Nana made sense of them. At any rate, at one point, our country decided that the schools' mission had failed, and by the midnineties, most had been razed to the ground.

Nana had taken me to the site of the one in Lejac years back, the pilgrimage she used to make every summer. The burial ground of Rose Prince, a woman the diocese was petitioning to have canonized, a former student whose biggest accomplishment was dying.

There was absolutely nothing special about her, Nana had said—and that was precisely the point. She had lived a humble life, staying on at the school after graduation, helping with the mending, the cleaning—her hands, when free, folded in prayer. She died at thirty-four of tuberculosis, a mark of the time, and was buried in the cemetery on the school's grounds.

At some point in the fifties, they decided to relocate the bodies. *All that cow shit was an embarrassment,* a visiting deacon had said. A father and son were tasked with the digging, and, for some reason—one the men themselves couldn't explain—they felt called to pry open each casket.

I could explain it, André had said to Mom, back when she used to accompany Nana.

The men were met with exactly what you'd expect: blackened bodies, the awful stench. The flesh we think of as invulnerable revealing itself. But when they got to Rose Prince, their hearts nearly stopped. Fresh as her namesake, her blouse crisp and white, her skin dewy, with *just a bit of a smile on her face*, she looked as if she were napping. *Even steak goes gray after a day out of the fridge.* It was the priest who led the pilgrimage's favorite analogy. *The sign of incorruption. Acts 13:35.* I couldn't look at a hamburger for a year after that.

We stopped in front of that white gabled house, Nevaeh digging in her pocket for something. Keys. So it was hers, that perfect house. Well— perfect excluding its surroundings. She was almost like an inverse Rachelle.

"Just a sec." Nevaeh left me in the entryway, disappearing around a corner, then drifting to a room at the back. Still, I overheard her when she spoke, melodious cadence of an alien language. *Cree*, it must've been; what Wally had mentioned. So she was Native. At least in part.

"I'll come later," a voice answered in English. A teenage girl's whine. There were no shoes in that entryway.

Instead, everything was beautifully ordered, the walls enlivened by a series of paintings, thick brushstrokes in red, white, yellow, blue, black A wolf, a whale, an eagle with its wings spread, a hummingbird flitting near a flower. There was a scrubbed entry table, a speckled vase brimming with fireweed, as if it were not a nuisance but a flower. Laid at its base was a flaxen braid—but not one of human hair. I picked it up. It looked like hay but smelled sweet, like vanilla. Someone had burnt it at one end.

"It's important, Jess." I heard Nevaeh's steps and immediately put the braid down. She appeared before me, holding up an electric kettle and smiling, all the friction from before vaporizing. "Coffee's on," she sang.

She was peppy again on our walk back to the office, chattering away. Her daughter was starting high school that fall. They used to be inseparable, and now Nevaeh's questions were met with monosyllabic answers. "They sure grow up fast, don't they?" she said, and I nodded, as if I had any clue.

"Herman!" Nevaeh raised a hand.

It was the same man I'd seen on the shoulder, lumbering at the same leaden pace. He was working on dislodging one of the plastic bags. He thrust it toward her.

"No, no." Nevaeh shook her head. He croaked out a few words in what must have been Cree, and Nevaeh relented, finally taking the bag. It was dripping.

"Herman fishes in the river," she said as we worked our way up the drive to the office. "You'd be surprised at what he finds. Covered in sores, fish twice the size they should be. Once he even caught one with two heads. You mind getting the door?

"Even if they look okay, they're still contaminated. All the runoff from the mill." She placed the kettle down on the makeshift banquet, emptying a Pepsi bottle refilled with water into the tank. "Herman doesn't care. He cooks up the normal ones, if you can believe it. He says the experience of the fish is ours, too. No disconnection."

"These"—she held up the bag—"will go in my compost." She lifted a paper plate from a stack and slid it under the bag, a drip tray for the leaking river water. "From fish to flowers. Can't get better than that."

Nevaeh excused herself, welcoming another woman who must have arrived while we were out. *Mutant fish?* The novelty of this new world was starting to wear. I looked around. Wally was gone. When was this meeting going to start anyway? It felt at once like I'd been there for hours and no time at all—but it must have been noon at least.

Sam wasn't due home until night, but what if he was early again? Standing there alone beside the shrieking kettle, I had the sudden, sinking feeling I'd miscalculated. Carole, the manager, was working that afternoon. My home number was printed in the break room. Elyse might've called. And if she hadn't, Carole would've. Sam answering, the dust hardly settled from my last lie. If I sped, I might make it in time.

"I have to run." I tapped Nevaeh on the shoulder, half hoping she might stop me.

"No problem." She smiled.

It would've been too sudden, I told myself, *bringing up Rachelle like that*. Sam was headed back up to Tumbler Ridge on Monday. I could meet Nevaeh for coffee then. I asked for her number for next time.

I was distracted on my way out, studying her business card. *Nevaeh Bennet, Artist.* The paintings in the entryway must have been hers. I didn't know you could make a living doing something like that. I knocked into someone on his way in.

"Sorry," I muttered, stopping dead when I saw it. Trailing down his back, the long, coarse braid. Bitumen black. I felt faint. What were the chances?

The bottle-blonde in the tube top came bounding toward the man, wrapping her arms around his neck. This man was young, I realized on second glance. No older than sixteen, gangly, still growing into himself. The resemblance was striking, nonetheless. The Man with the Braid, thirty years back.

The boy lifted the girl up, fingers gripping her ass.

"Stop it, Ricky." She laughed, her back arching, her feet kicking at air.

Holy shit. I went weak again—the two of them were a reenactment of Mom's wedding photo. That was it, why the Man felt so familiar. Rhoda's husband was the spitting image of my dad.

In an instant, everything clicked into place. Why no one ever talked about him. Why Mom resented me. Why I was so hard to love. *That was a mistake, end of story.* I was like him. *Métis,* Wally had said. I thought of the man flashing his status card, Nevaeh's hair, a shade lighter than mine. The woman from the day care, how she'd mistaken me. Was that why I'd been so drawn to Rachelle?

It was as if other hands were at the wheel, carrying me down that forest service road. Twenty-four years' worth of experience recast, the sky shattering open, all that startling light. My entire life as I knew it had been built around him leaving when the truth was, he'd been forced out. That was why he'd never tried to get in touch. I hadn't been abandoned. He'd been exiled. But if he hadn't been, would anyone else have stuck around?

Would Missy have befriended me? Would Sam have proposed? I thought of Nevaeh, her fair skin not enough to keep her off the rez. *I was young and stupid,* Mom would say, when I pestered her. *I didn't know any better.* I never understood what she meant. But I did now.

Native. I gnawed at my thumbnail. *Some squaw bitch,* the words like a boot to the head. Was that why it'd happened? What was too shameful to speak? *She likes it, huh, she likes it.* I was the only one, out of all my friends. Out of anyone I had ever met.

I didn't have to fake what came as I pushed open the doors to the mall. The tears a torrent, the valve stuck. *My mom*, I blubbered. *Ray's kids.* Carole didn't ask for specifics. *These things happen*, she assured me, a hand patting my back. It made me cry harder, being so easily forgiven. If she knew what I was, it would've gone different.

If she knew what I was, she wouldn't have hired me in the first place.

twenty

Sam arrived just as I was straining the pasta, cloud of steam blotting my view. Meatballs were browning in the oven, and the heady aroma of sautéed onions in butter still peppered the air. With an apron around my waist, I was the picture of a perfect wife. Barren, and with an even darker secret, but at least there was spaghetti when my man came home. I struggled to keep my eyes dry.

"My favorite," he said, wrapping his arms around me as I jiggled the colander, sunny, and genuinely so—nothing forced, like the days prior.

He had something for me, a surprise. "Close your eyes," he instructed, pulling his hands behind his back. I forced a smile.

"Pick a hand." I pointed to the left, and he spread an empty, calloused palm. In his right fist were two paper stubs. "Puddle of Mudd, tomorrow night. Floor seats." He grinned. "Jim hooked us up."

Jim. I clenched, trying to mirror his excitement, the knot in my stomach tightening.

"We can get dinner before the concert," he was saying. Anyplace I liked. The Keg Steakhouse, Mr. Jake's. Jim had given him an advance.

"Wherever," I squeaked. I knew how it went. The more Sam accepted, the more he'd owe. The harder it'd be to ever be free. "You pick." I pecked him on the cheek, cautious not to seem ungrateful. I just wanted to go straight to bed.

"Things are going to be different." Sam looked at me adoringly. Duped by omission.

I thought of his reaction to Rachelle. *Come by, again?* The radish seeds were probably still on her counter, fated to lie dormant, paper envelope as close to the earth as they'd ever get.

Seed packets, the general manager had included on his list on the tour of the pulp mill we'd taken in seventh grade. *Almost every paper product you can think of starts here.* The box of tissues, the stack of bills, the dog-eared Sears catalogue. Masking tape, Molson labels, wallpaper, toilet roll. They piled the pulp into hide-colored hills. They'd looked to me like burial mounds.

"Sure are," I said, wringing my hands. More than he could ever guess.

Would I have done anything differently? Sometimes, when I find my head craning toward the window, I bat that question around. *Everything* is the answer some days. *I did what I could* is my conclusion on others. But the concert—even now, it twists me up inside. Even then, I think I knew. It wasn't teeth that I would've found if I'd pried that horse's mouth wide.

The phone rang just as I was stepping out of the shower the next evening. Its trill made me jump, and I nearly ate it on the tile. It was Missy on the other end, calling to invite us over for beers before the concert.

I looked over at Sam, his feet propped up on the recliner. *Floor seats, huh?* He hadn't mentioned they came in pairs.

"A beer sounds good," he said, eyes trained on the game. It wasn't up for discussion. Jim didn't suggest; he prescribed. "We can just go to dinner a little earlier." He switched off the tube, standing.

"Earlier." I nodded, my hair sopping wet. It was half past five. The concert started at eight. He meant now.

I'd ironed a dress, had been planning on putting on a little makeup, giving those gold earrings another try. Instead, I tugged my hair into a braid and buttoned up an old pair of Wranglers. I'd look ridiculous all done up with a wet head.

We were led to a booth in the back room by the hostess, her ponytail swishing in time to the music, an old Kenny Rogers song. The red pleather was damp, the smell acrid. The booth must have just been wiped down. It was just before six, and Mr. Jake's was empty. We were even ahead of the early birds, the only other customer the lone day drinker propping himself up at the bar.

"This Kiss" came on next.

When Faith Hill screamed the chorus, I could barely hear Sam. The music was always too loud at the steak house, conversation a fruitless endeavor. I supposed that was the point.

There was one other couple I hadn't noticed before, skin ruched and liver-spotted, in the booth directly across from us, chewing in silence. The woman was staring a hole into her baked potato, the man's eyelids struggling to stay open. 50 Happy Years, I imagined the banner at their anniversary. A thumbprint of butter was glommed to the woman's chin. Like a mirror image, we were seated on the same side.

The waitress came over. Sam ordered a steak, medium rare. I asked for a bowl of the French onion soup.

"That's it?" Sam reached his hand toward mine from across the table.

I wasn't sure if I could even stomach that much. I'd felt nauseous since stepping into the truck. I ordered a side salad. Sam added on a plate of cheese fries.

He knew I wouldn't like it, was why he hadn't told me. Seeing Missy and Jim during the day was one thing, but spending an entire evening with them, late into the night, was another. After a certain hour, they moved on from alcohol, Missy with a finger at her gums, the coffee table flecked white. After a certain hour, you could switch yourself out with a sack of potatoes, wouldn't give them much pause. TV blaring, Missy babbling quick as a boiling pot, Jim in a corner, twirling a butterfly knife.

They'd probably be blasted by the time we arrived. Probably just needed someone sober to drive. But when Missy opened the door, she was surprisingly lucid, neon straw floating up from her can of Diet Coke to keep her lip gloss from rubbing.

"No shoes, remember?" She reached an arm around my back, slurping at the can. It was probably spiked with something.

She looked stunning, like a slutty angel, in a skintight black minidress that laced up the sides, her blonde hair braided around her head. From her ears hung a pair of ladle-sized hoops, her forearms banded with a pair of cuffs that were marabou feathered. I looked down at my T-shirt, three sizes too large, the white sleeves pooling at my elbows. The ketchup bottle had exploded when I'd squeezed, splattering my striped T-shirt as if I'd not only butchered Sam's steak but had slaughtered the whole damn cow. He always kept a fresh Hanes in his glove compartment. I undid my braid, combing through the crimps with my fingers. At least my hair had dried.

Missy pulled me into the kitchen. "What are you drinking?" She swung open the fridge.

"I'll take a Coke."

"All out." She handed me a Mike's Hard Lemonade, poking her tongue ring at me.

Jim was at the table with a milk glass in front of him, the liquid unctuous, saddle brown. He nodded as we entered, holding up a fist for Sam to pound. "Hey, man."

Whether it was his first drink or fifth was hard to tell. I'd never seen Jim buzzed—only shit-faced. He wasn't there yet. Missy started to pour Sam a matching glass.

The doorbell rang. Another surprise? I looked over at Sam, who just shrugged, his mouth forming a line.

"Party's here." My heart did a nosedive.

It was Alistair, the man from the bush party, in the same DayGlo shorts and a Limp Bizkit T-shirt, pumping a twelve-pack of Molson over his head. *You've got to be kidding me.* I looked back at Sam, his face eclipsed behind the upturned glass.

"Did I show you this yet?" Missy turned, nudging me to lift the gauze that was taped below her shoulder. It was a Japanese symbol hemmed in by rogue petals—the tattoo wet-looking, as if it were marker. "It means 'happiness.' An early birthday present from my hubby."

"Nice," I said. The skin surrounding the symbol was swollen, isles of distended red. "Looks like it hurt."

"She likes it rough," Alistair interjected, grinning. He was squatting near the dogs, Misty scuttling around his flapping hand. Misty growled, baring her teeth and yipping as she launched at his fingers, spittle foaming at the corners of her maw. Alistair laughed, yanking the dog up by her collar and pretending to bite back.

"Remind me how you tell these two apart again?" He looked at Jim.

"You're coming to the concert?" I asked, my voice preternaturally high.

"If that's all right by you." His attention moved from Misty to me. "I hate to be the fifth wheel, but my girlfriend, she couldn't make it. I got a nine-inch boa constrictor at home. She was up all night." His eyes were on mine, waiting for a reaction. "Come on over sometime, I'll introduce you." He broke out into that hissing laugh. I should have kept my mouth shut. Simply greeting a man like him marked you: fair game.

"At least the music will be loud," Sam leaned over and whispered. I laughed.

"What's that, Samuel?" Alistair's tone hardened. "Care to share with the class?"

"Leave it, Al," Jim commanded. Like a third Pomeranian, Alistair shrunk right back down. Sam coughed, tugging at the knees of his jeans.

"Fuck it," Alistair said, stabbing a key into the side of a beer can and draining it in seconds flat. "Let's get blasted."

On Jim's orders, we all piled into Missy's minivan. She hadn't been drinking, and the road would be lousy with cops, he said, always was when there was a big act at the multiplex. I'd had three drinks myself—a coping strategy—and I couldn't argue against his logic, even if it meant our wagon was hitched to theirs for the night.

Two car seats were blocking the second row, and we were already running late. "Just leave them," Missy said. "There's plenty of room in the back."

Alistair insisted on riding in the trunk, refusing to sit in the same row as Sam, even with me in between. It was like they were brothers, *Jim's boys*, set against each other, each vying for Daddy's affection.

The stadium was packed, and Missy had to circle the lot three times before finally finding a spot. When we left the van, Sam pulled me aside. "See, we can have our own fun." He laced his fingers through mine. The sheer energy of the place helped convince me (well, that and those three hard lemonades). I nodded, smiling. Sam was right. Even the nausea was starting to settle. Why shouldn't we have a good time?

We stopped at the bar for more beers, and a rum and Coke for Missy. Jim footed the bill, flipping through his rubber-banded wad and doling out our drinks one by one.

I saw Ray first—that familiar wine-hued hide. For a moment, I wasn't sure it was Mom's, the ass his hand was resting on. She'd dyed her hair again, Stevie blonde, but styled more like Rachel from *Friends*. Ray's head was swiveling, the redhead in Lucite platforms at the bar. "Baby." I saw Mom's manicure clawing through his hair. She didn't see me. I turned my head, following the others as we made our way to the floor.

The band opened with their hit, the only song any of us actually knew. I belted along, Sam knotting his arms around me as we swayed, our faces drenched in the shifting light. I leaned my head back onto his chest, sipping my beer. I felt happy—free, my mind like a basin, housing only soft texture, color, sound. Sam's mouth met mine, and I kissed him back readily. Maybe things really would be different. Jim side-stepped back into our row, his arms crowded with more beers. He wasn't so bad once you got to know him. I drained mine, reaching for another. Sometimes talk was just talk. I gave him a high five.

I felt a tug at my hand. "Washroom," Missy mouthed, dragging me from our row. I gripped on to the railing, staggering up the stairs. I was well past tipsy, drunker than I'd realized. I really should have eaten more than soup.

Missy planted herself on the counter, touching up her mascara in the mirror, twisting open her lip gloss, lacquering her parted lips peachy wet. She caught my eyes in the reflection.

"Here," she said, commanding my shoulders. "Let me fix you up. Open." I lowered my jaw.

I angled my head past her, catching the mirror. *Vixen*, the sticker on the bottom of her lip gloss read. It was alluring on Missy, even under the ruthlessness of the fluorescents. I looked more like the old woman at the steak house, hands too unsteady to wipe the butter from my mouth.

"I'm not finished yet." Missy yanked my face back toward her, cracking open the blush.

I never felt at ease there, in the world of girls like Missy. I came from a line of sensible women. Erin's beauty routine consisted of SPF 30 and an elastic band for her ponytail, and Nana used lard as a moisturizer. Mom was the only outlier. Not that she ever offered any guidance.

Anything that had to do with me becoming a woman was unspeakable: bras, deodorant, menstruation. I was left to figure it all out for myself. The first time I shaved, I pushed down so hard that I sliced into my shin as if I were peeling a carrot, blood pooling brightly around my teetering foot, receding down the drain. I skipped the other leg. Missy demonstrated the next time she came over, lathering her pits with Mom's raspberry-scented foam. She'd always been two steps ahead.

"It's a good thing Jim's doing for Sam," she was saying, dabbing my eyelids with a brush. "He's going to set you up. You'll see. Bigger place, new car. A whole new life." She gulped her drink. "Maybe Sam'll even finally knock you up." She burped.

"I shouldn't say it yet, but just between us girls"—her voice lowered to a whisper—"there's no rum in this Coke." She grinned, one hand patting her belly.

The nausea was back. It felt like I'd been force-fed a plateful of nettles, my insides stinging, hot. Missy had just had Brielle six months ago. She'd smoked through all two of her pregnancies. The two she'd kept. With Kayden she'd insisted that one drink was fine. She'd never made a single meal from scratch. Was it even safe to get a tattoo while carrying? I hadn't seen her drink any water all night.

"There," she said, twisting me toward the mirror. "Look at you."

In my T-shirt and jeans, I looked more like a stay-at-home mom than she did. I had to hold back the tears. It wasn't fair. She was on number three. I had never even had a false start. I was cursed with a broken body. A spiteful womb. Missy already had beauty. What did she need to be a baby-making machine for, too?

"Go on without me," I told her as we left. "I'm going to grab my sweater from the van."

I stepped out into the night, gulping for air. I parked on the curb and let my face fall into my hands. What if I really was cursed? A twenty-four-year-old secret. I thought of my dad. *Métis.* Maybe if I told Sam, the curse would lift. Maybe if I told him, he'd leave. I was trapped in a doorless room, any out an illusion—shadow dancing upon wall.

I raised my head. My hands were shimmering, had sponged up the colors—petal pink and baby blue—that Missy had masked on me. I should have scrubbed my face clean after she left. Who was I kidding? I was hardly a woman. My cycle hadn't lasted two full days that month.

I couldn't blame him, the father I'd never known. Native women popped out babies.

The curse must have come from the other side. I thought of my great-grandmother, Nana her miracle, no one else to work the farm. Maybe it skipped a generation. Maybe it descended from two, to one, to none. I stood, using the underside of my shirt to wipe my face. Sam would be wondering where I went.

I clicked the button on the key fob, red glow of the rear lights guiding me to the van. I had one hand on the handle when I heard someone come up behind me. In an instant, I was wedged against the door.

I opened my mouth to scream, but nothing came out, the stranger's palm clamping down like a muzzle. I tried to break free, but the man's weight was leveraged against mine. I was bound in place.

"Practically the only woman up here," he was muttering, that horrible thing pushing into my back. "It's different after, not as tight."

I heard him unzipping his fly. The tears came, but that didn't deter him. He wrested open the front of my jeans, dislodging a button in his hurry. It clinked to the floor. Someone had to have heard it. I started to pray, searching the glass for something, car light, sneaker, anything other than my own unblinking eyes—pupils beetle black and just as easily pulverized.

I shut them, conjuring other scenes. *Sunlight scattering the clouds. The sweet smell of pine. The moment your feet hit the trail.*

"Forgot what it feels like." He flicked the flimsy cotton of my underwear aside, fingers darting up inside of me, cold as death, my body jostling up and down. It was no longer mine. A puppet, a joystick—I was a thing that action happened to. A nail.

A lake so clear, you can see right to the bottom. The new greens of spring, the plush greens of summer. Birdsong in the air.

The double beep of a vehicle that was being unlocked. *Please*, I pleaded, *please be near.* I opened my eyes, seeing red. The rear lights one vehicle over.

"Shit." The man retracted his hand. His weight lifting off me, his footsteps farther and farther away. He was gone just as quickly as he'd appeared.

I crouched to the ground, fastening my jeans, my hands shaking as I pawed at the pavement for the missing button. I opened the van's door. Why had I come out here again? My sweater. I reached for the green heap, burying my face in its folds.

"Everything okay?" a woman's voice was asking.

"I think your friend went back inside," a man was saying. Friend. *Forgot what it feels like.* I would have recognized that wooden affect anywhere. I think I knew even before he spoke, his boots pounding upon the pavement like he had a score to settle with the ground. Jim.

I couldn't stop it. My mouth opened, and it all came pouring out, chunk-strewn puddle fencing the couple off from me.

"She's just drunk," I heard the man whisper. "Honey, let's let her be."

"Sorry." I managed to say, managed to wipe the vomit from my chin before being bowled over and retching again.

I rinsed my mouth out in the washroom, scrubbed my face with a sopping paper towel, pump after pump of that disturbingly pink soap. I combed through my hair with my fingers, smoothing it back in attempts of appearing presentable, of erasing his influence, the awful thing he'd done.

I stared in the mirror. All the color had been siphoned from my face, but somehow my cheeks still glistened. The roll-on stick of body glitter, the only part of Missy's makeover that had endured. I smiled, practicing. *Some concert.* What I really wanted to do was to lock myself in a stall and howl.

I don't know why I didn't. Sam was stuck in the winding line at the concession stand, Missy explained when I found his seat empty. He hadn't even noticed I'd gone.

We left before the encore. *Avoid the swarming masses.* I couldn't bring myself to look at Jim when he spoke. I stood behind Sam like a shadow, keeping my head down in order to keep my eyes dry, willing the night to just end. My only relief was that at least Alistair had gone. He'd met someone at the bar who was giving him a ride. "And a lift home, too." He'd wagged his tongue.

"Jenny." Someone grabbed at my shoulder. It was Mom, her blue eyes like searchlights. In one hand her keys, a cigarette, her lighter, an ice-cubed cup darkened with squirts of Diet Coke, brown sloshing and splattering onto the floor. It was like she could smell it on me—or so I imagined. "What's wrong?" she said. Or maybe "What's up?"

"Hi, Fi!" Missy crooked an elbow around hers.

"Miss Missy." I heard Mom's voice go high, felt her touch evaporate.

"We're going," someone's man directed.

Mom's mouth must have opened. "Jenny," she must have said. But my head didn't turn. My legs walked toward the exit. My self, it had scattered, like dimethyl sulfide, methyl mercaptan—clusters of invisible, insignificant particles, suspended somewhere far above.

"You okay?" Sam was asking, my hands jumpy as I tugged at the seat belt. He had to help buckle me in.

Early morning, after snow, before any tire parted perfect white. A hot, soapy shower. Vanilla Bean.

"Just tired," I heard myself squeak.

Jim had bought a CD, and the song the band had opened with blared through the speakers. The smoke from his cigarette kept missing the cracked window, blowing right back, into my nostrils. *Cinnamon Apple. Cinnabon. A hot cup of coffee with creamer.*

"One for the road?" We stood in their driveway, Jim's eyes locked on to Sam's. Missy's silver heels clacked in her hands as she treaded up the front steps. She turned, grimacing.

"Baby, I'm beat."

Jim ignored her, the invitation still open. *One, two, three, four.* I kept my eyes on the lawn, counting each blade of grass, trying to remember to breathe. There was no point in protesting. This was their discussion, between men, not even the province of Jim's pregnant wife.

"Sorry, man," Sam said, walking toward him. "My last shift starts tomorrow. I was supposed to leave tonight. I got to be up by four." They bumped fists. "That was fun." Fun. *A big, fluffy blanket. Twinkling lights.* "Thanks again." Jim nodded.

"Drive safe," Missy called out after us. My body rocked as the wheels turned under me.

She stayed under the porch lights as we drove away, barefoot and pregnant, her face distorted by the glare. One hand overhead, waving frantically, as if signaling for rescue. Or shooing it away.

twenty-one

"That was fun," Sam said again, shifting gears.

He fiddled with the radio. He'd bought a CD, too, but his truck only had a tape deck. "We guarantee the work for ten months or five thousand miles, whichever comes first," the advertiser droned. Sam lowered the volume.

I didn't answer. I couldn't.

Seeding cabbage in the garden. The first strawberries from the vine. Pink dahlias, wild roses. Dandelion fluff ferried by the wind.

"I know you don't like the guy, but you got to admit, it was nice." *Fireweed lurching against the fence. The flames licking up. Smoke blotting air.*

"He's actually pretty decent." *My head in the dirt. His hand on my mouth. Dead needles stitched through my hair.* It cracked, what I'd epoxied together. The tears, the words, it all roiled to the surface.

"He followed me to the van."

"What?" Sam didn't turn, his eyes steady on the barren road.

"While you were in line, I was getting my sweater. It was like out of nowhere. He held me down; I couldn't move." Color started creeping up Sam's neck, the same shade as the traffic light above us.

"What are you saying?" He still hadn't looked at me. "What did you do?"

"He . . ." I couldn't say it. *Fingered.* I'd never liked the word. It was too dirty. What they used when they found their guy. *We've fingered the perp.* The other expression even worse. I fingerbanged her, what Robbie Taylor had said in eighth grade about one of the Leclerc sisters. *Banged.* Like on every man's hand was a collapsible bludgeon.

"He went in my pants." My face was burning. "Tried to. A couple came just in time."

Sam was quiet. The *click, click, click* of the blinker weighted, like a bomb. He turned onto our street, putting his truck in park and just sitting there in the driver's seat.

His head was still bowed when he finally spoke, one hand running back and forth through his hair. "Just . . . how could you let him?" *Let him?* I was speechless, my whole body heaving, the tears in double time. We sat in silence, facing front, away from each other, as if we were still in motion. At some point, the automatic light in the garage switched itself off, and Sam got out, leaving me alone, pitched further into the dark. I stayed a bit longer, debating whether to go for a drive. Ultimately, I decided against it. There was no place to go, I realized. I was already home.

Sam had brought a pillow to the couch and was either asleep or pretending to be by the time I came in. I took as hot and as long of a shower as I could stand, holding the bottle of body wash upside down. *Freesia.* I squeezed and squeezed and squeezed. There was no getting clean enough.

I lay in bed awake, shoveling what was piling higher, merciless thoughts as oppressive as the dank on a humid day. I shouldn't have told him. What had I expected? That he'd turn the car around, teach Jim a lesson: *Don't you touch my wife ever again.*

He might've gotten in a few good licks. Maybe he'd have even knocked Jim's ass to the ground. And then what? One black eye wouldn't be the end of it.

Jim doesn't get mad; he gets even. I remembered what Missy had said at the barbeque at their place on Canada Day, the man who'd arrived with both arms in plaster. He'd been caught stealing. She'd shrugged, crushing her cigarette against the side of the table. What was Jim supposed to do? Send him to a time-out?

It was business, she had justified, was always justifying. The missing nails on her manicure, the bruises on her wrists, her forearms, choked around her neck.

The truth was, I didn't want anything from Jim. Didn't want anything to do with Jim. Didn't want to see his face or hear his voice or step foot in his house ever again.

The truth was, I wanted Sam.

I wanted Sam to say, *How could he? That piece of shit. I'll kill him, that asshole, that motherfucking asshole. Motherfucker, he's done for, dead. We're through.* To break that stupid CD into a hundred pieces, ram his fist against the horn.

Wanted Sam to start his truck and drive us far. Far out of range of PG and its dim, deserted parking lots, and its bush parties, and its nameless dirt roads and dead ends. Far from the shadow cast by the mountain, the Highway marred with little white crosses, the Highway that swallowed girls as young as nine years old whole. Far from the Officer Micks and their doughnut-eating partners, from the men under Jim's influence. And the women. Far from the drugs, the painted faces in Fort George Park, the snaking line up of idling trucks—far from the women's customer base. The mills, the mines, the oil camps, the service roads, the men paid for the muscle, their ability to haul and hurl and thrust and pound and saw and drill and thwack, and bang.

Far from the forests gashed open for lumber, from the two poisoned rivers and the fish with two heads. Far from the flyers with faces tacked over faces, and the half of me that was like them. And the other half.

I wanted Sam to say nothing, to handle me tenderly as a carton of eggs, to take my face in his hands, wipe my eyes, stroke my hair.

I wanted Sam to know without a shadow of a doubt that I hadn't *let* Jim do anything. That he did what he wanted, took what he wanted, his hand zippering my mouth. To know without a shadow of a doubt that it wasn't my fault.

It wasn't my fault, I repeated to myself. *It wasn't my fault, it wasn't my fault.* As if saying the words would convince me, as if saying the words would somehow snuff the other argument. I was the only one this kept happening to. The mark couldn't be seen, but was sensed.

Day broke like it always did, the light wedging itself through the slats of my blinds, cheery yellow somehow an offense.

I couldn't sleep. I didn't know what to do with myself. I was exhausted, but at the same time, electric, as if I'd been plugged into a sparking socket, Jim's socket. His breath on my neck, wash of red. I kept turning and expecting to find him there, padding up behind me in his steel-toed boots, pinning my body against the TV console, the washroom sink, the wall. I practically jumped when the mail truck grated to a halt, glass of orange juice shattering across the linoleum.

Fresh air should help, I remember thinking, swinging open the door and pacing the backyard, looking for a chance to change my mind. The lawn was mowed, the washing folded and put away. I'd harvested the last of the zucchinis on Friday and had already weeded the rest. The cucumbers were finished, the green beans, too. The first tomatoes had swelled from the size of a thimble to a fist. It happened every year— summer ending, just like that.

I looked out at Rachelle's yard. How many hours had it been now? The seasons would change, and change again. She'd still be gone. Her house swept of her belongings, the rusting red truck lugged to the dump. *Good riddance.* I could already hear the chatter.

Everyone in the neighborhood had gotten it wrong. Rachelle was a good person: a loving mother, a loyal wife. Friendly, forgiving. Beautiful. I thought of Nevaeh, in a nicer house than any on our block. An artist. Successful, self-assured. I'd gotten it wrong, too.

What I'd assumed was a defect was, on occasion, a boon. Maybe it wasn't that side that was the problem. The ugly duckling all those years, I'd been paddling in the wrong pond. Had Rachelle been able to tell?

I stepped on something, soft clump sticking to the bottom of my bare foot. Fur. I held it up to the light. It felt synthetic, too uniformly blonde to be from a dog or a fox. Someone had given Barbie a haircut. Destiny. I eyed the kiddie pool, the broken swing, the ribbon-wrapped Hula-Hoops like tide pools in the overgrown grass. The hair must have blown over in the wind. The girls. My focus shifted, my own problems insignificant, a mote when held against their asteroid. Victims. No one even looking for their mother. As long as she stayed lost, they did, too.

I started toward the house, galvanized. I knew what I had to do. I picked up the phone, punching in the numbers.

"Jenny," Nevaeh answered, the warmth in her voice a welcome respite from the thoughts doing doughnuts in my head. "It's good to hear from you."

The way she said it, I could tell she meant it. I thought of something, what she'd told me about the meeting. *You know our relationship to the clock.* Our. Had she known, too?

"What's going on?" I didn't know where to start.

"There's something I meant to tell you at the meeting," I said, my voice shakier than I'd anticipated. She was the first person I'd talked to all morning, the first other voice since the ride home with Sam.

"Is everything okay?" I took a deep breath. *Focus, Jen.*

"It's my neighbor. Rachelle Murphy. She's one of the women. Taken on 16."

"When?" I heard a drawer open. She was finding a pen.

"Three weeks ago. A Wednesday, I think." Or was it Thursday? I tried to remember. Nana used to say it was easier before the microwave, the washing machine. Mondays were for milking, Tuesdays for churning, Wednesdays for baking the bread. A housewife in the nineties was spoiled with time. Subtract kids from the equation, and, well.

"Did you call anyone?"

"The cops when it first happened, but it was like they didn't believe me. There's this officer. He's friends with this—this man." The tears came. "I don't think we can trust them. I'm pretty sure they never even filed the report." My voice was breaking again.

"What about her family?" Nevaeh asked, rerouting. This was urgent; she understood. She needed to get all the facts. "Did you call any of her friends?"

"Her sister, but I think she might be gone now, too. It was her husband's truck at Rachelle's the night before she went missing. He had this energy like my mom's ex. The violent type, I'm sure of it. You could just tell."

The line went quiet.

"Hm," she said after a considerable pause. "So there's no other family? Anyone else in the neighborhood who knew her well?"

"No." I hesitated. "I mean, as far as I can tell. Her husband died a year ago. I never saw any visitors. The neighbors don't—" I paused, rephrasing. "I'm the only one looking. There's nobody else." The line was quiet again. Maybe the connection was bad? "Hello?"

"I'm here," she said, her voice different, smaller somehow.

"Her sister's last name is Bluecloud. Rhoda. I don't know her husband's first name, but he's tall, over six feet at least, with a long black braid. Maybe someone knows him, you know, from the rez?"

"Maybe." The less responsive she was, the more pressing it seemed to dispatch all the information.

"They live in Vanderhoof. I think the Man with the Braid is connected to that other man I mentioned." I couldn't even choke out his name. "The one who's friends with all the cops.

"There are drugs involved. Lots of money. There was this clearing right above where I found Rachelle's car. All the trees were marked with the same symbol. Have you read *Michelle Remembers*? It almost looked like some sort of ritual site.

"I found her necklace in campfire ash. I took it in, but like I told you, the cops can't be trusted. They're in on it with J-that, that man."

The more I talked about it, the more I believed it. *They* no longer guesswork but fact. We all knew how the drugs made their way up from Mexico. I'd seen it, I realized, on Alistair's arm. A horned skull, poorly rendered, fringed by a pinion—the Hells Angels mascot. The Harleys, the posse, the rubber-banded rolls of hundreds. Jim, I'd convinced myself, had to be at the snake's head.

"Maybe that's where he takes all the women." I thought of all the names on the signs. Aurelie, and countless others. Never mind the timeline. I was thinking out loud when I said it. "Maybe that's what happened to Beth."

Nevaeh was quiet a long while.

"Hello?" I asked again.

I heard her clear her throat. "Maybe" was all she said.

What happened to the opened drawer, the piece of paper, the pen? I could see how it might've sounded far-fetched, but no more so than a highway with a victim count in the dozens. There had to be an answer. I was on the verge of solving it. PG's darkest secret. Didn't she get that?

"I'll put word out," she was saying, rerouting again. Her questions, it dawned on me, weren't to cover the bases, but to poke holes instead. "I can try to find her family. I'm sure she has people, other people in her life. I'm sure they're looking, too." It was my turn to be quiet then.

"You there?" she asked.

"Yes," I said. She was no different from anybody else.

"Look, I know you're trying to be helpful, but I don't know your relationship, how close you two were. It's all a little . . ." She stopped herself, sighing. *"Michelle Remembers* was a fabrication. A horror story. Some people find them exciting. Do you see where I'm going with this, Jenny?"

No, I thought, wiping away the tears that were streaming down to my neck. Everyone was against me. Against Rachelle.

"You don't know what you don't know until you know," she said, but I couldn't understand that—not then.

"I have to go pick up my daughter. We'll talk more later, okay?"

"Okay," I managed to say, managed to stand, managed to place the phone in its cradle. She didn't believe me. No one ever did. That call confirmed it, what I'd known all along. I really was alone.

I sat on the kitchen floor in a heap for a while, staring out into nothing. The phone rang. I let the answering machine deal with it, my voice sunny, five years younger, the recording from when we first moved in. "You've reached the Hayes." A unit. I remembered how I'd beamed. "We'll get back to you as soon as we can." *We*—the power of those two humble letters, the burden of being one lifted. Until it wasn't. I always listened to that damn machine by myself.

It was Mom. Did I want to come over? Ray had off. It was such a perfect day. *Could you watch the kids?* The question implicit—so routine, she didn't even vocalize. *Jenny's free.* I could hear the subtext beneath her yammering. *Jenny never has anything else to do.* I didn't budge.

It rang again. Mom was nothing if not persistent. I thought about getting up, taking scissors to the cord, but it was as if someone had packed earth around me, my whole body inert.

It was Anne-Marie. Jesse had off, too. There'd been an accident at the mill, right after opening. They'd shut down for the day.

That never happened as far as I knew. Men lost fingers and toes all the time, sustained puncture wounds, strains, sprains, burns, fractures—the logs kept being shuttled down the line. The pulp hooks, the pickaroons, the slippery metal floor, the chipper, the splitter, the acid steam at the digester. I'd seen a chart somewhere, the rate of injuries in the pulp and paper industry compared to all other manufacturing. One line hovering high above the other.

Something big must have happened for them to lose a whole day.

If it'd been Missy, she would've opened with the spatter, but Anne-Marie didn't say exactly. She was never one for gore. She and Jesse were taking Tanner to Eskers. Did I want to tag along? *Tag along.* Like a stray dog, a leaf stuck to a boot. On the wrong side of *we*—I was *you.* An option, dispensable. *We'd love it if you came.* A life so empty, it needed filling. *It'll give you something to do.* A woman alone was in waiting—for something to do or to be done to her. A woman alone needed to be put to use.

My stomach was howling. I hadn't eaten since I'd spewed dinner. I reached my arms toward the table and hoisted myself up, opening the fridge and scanning, before settling on a pudding cup.

I stood, scooping chocolate with an index finger, alternating with sips of milk from the carton, when the tree floated up from the clutter, the postcard Erin had sent me years ago, the Hollow Tree in Stanley Park, the tallest western red cedar of them all. The woman underneath it made miniature, her long, ironed hair more like a wingspan. I slipped it out from underneath the magnet, flipping it around. *Vancouver.* It wasn't just a postcard. That tree existed.

> *I can't wait to take you here.*
> *All my love,*
> *Aunt Erin*

Erin. I marched straight to my bedroom and unzipped my suit-case, packing handfuls of T-shirts, enough underwear for a week. I took the floral blue dress off its hanger, balled up my raincoat, a fleece in case the temperature dropped.

I filled a mug with cold coffee, the last of Sam's pot. I was too tired to talk. I could call Erin from the road after I'd logged a few hours. I didn't need to leave a note. Sam would be away two whole weeks. He'd never even notice I was gone. No one would.

I took the postcard off the fridge and tucked it into my back pocket, leaving the empty mug on the counter, the way Sam always would. Some-one else's problem.

twenty-two

As soon as I turned out of our neighborhood, I could breathe again, the belt that'd been cinched around my lungs loosening with every click south, every click farther from PG.

The route to Vancouver was idiotproof. 97-S sailed straight down to the midpoint between the two cities—Cache Creek. From there it was either a right or a left, winding through the mountains on 99 or horseshoeing around them on 1. No map necessary. I'd barely need to keep my eyes on the road.

It was like that, I realized, consulting my atlas that morning, any big leap across the province, all the highways like arrows, direct and unbending, only two options: this way or that. It was the local roads where it all went muddy. The malposed street signs, the sudden dead ends.

I tore open a Snickers with my teeth. Before leaving, I'd counted out the roll I kept tucked in the toe of a hiking boot. My savings account, the one Sam didn't know about, what Nana called *wife insurance*. What every woman should have in case things took a turn. Roughly six hundred dollars. More cash than I'd ever had on me. Five years of stashing away. Mom kept hers in an oven mitt. André had taught her to get creative.

I'd see what the damage was from the drive there—make sure to set enough aside for the way back. Even if I stayed the whole two weeks in Vancouver, was no way I'd go through it all. It made me anxious, thinking about that boot empty, but that's what it was there for. In case things took a turn. I cranked down my windows, finally free from the dank, the constant stream of warm air rinsing everything other than its whoosh away.

A cattle ranch cropped up to my left, the air permeated with that acrid smell. I rolled the windows back up, flicking the radio on. The stations had changed, and what was soft rock in PG was Christian country now. The signs had changed, too, I realized, after Quesnel. I'd never been that far south before. I was still on 97-S, but what we called *Hart Highway* was *Caribou* now. *16-W* was *Yellowhead* all the miles to Rupert. Or the *Highway of Tears*, depending on who you asked. I wondered whether 97 had any other names. If there'd ever been a march along its shoulder or names written in red.

"Problem is, it's too much of an intersection," a man being interviewed on the six o'clock news had said, his thumbs hooked under the straps of his overalls.

"We've got trucks coming in from all four directions. The territories, Alberta. The US. PG's a hub for all sorts of activity. You've got an individual. Maybe things get out of hand. Wouldn't be hard to hide a body." He was talking about Beth. "Tell the truth"—he scratched his temple—"it'd be harder to be found out."

I pushed the door lock down. The road in front of me (and behind me) was empty. Endless bush, there wasn't so much as a phone booth around. PG was a hub, but what did that matter? A tire gone flat, a tank edging near empty. *You've got an individual. Maybe things get out of hand.*

I took a deep breath. My tank was plenty full. I knew how to change a tire, I reminded myself, and even had a spare in the back. The sun was out; Trisha Yearwood was playing. I turned the radio up, my shoulders easing back down.

My stomach rumbled. I'd just passed 150 Mile House. 100 Mile would be next. We'd learned about those names in school, 97 once host not to big rigs and Buicks but covered wagons, pioneers on the quest for gold. Before the road, it'd been a mule path. Now there was an Esso, a red-roofed shopping center with an index of its offerings stacked on a pole. *150 Mile Realty. Valley Video. Restaurant*, no other qualifiers. I didn't see any house.

It wasn't long before I realized I should have stopped at *Restaurant*. *Lac La Hache*, the next sign read. *50 miles.* I popped open the center console. Toonies, loonies, a bent-up straw. Not even a stray stick of gum.

Just as I'd resigned myself to waiting, as if by magic, a third sign appeared. *THE ALAMO: Restaurant, Motel, RV.* I turned in.

A torn sheet of paper had been tacked up against a window. *NO CASH LEFT ON PREMISES.* I swung open the door.

Each padded booth was empty, every swivel stool still. Another sheet of paper was propped against the register: *4 service, ring bell.*

Ding. The waitress punched through the dinged saloon doors.

"Kitchen's closed, but I can make you a sandwich," she spoke as she walked, panting after each word. "Ham and cheese, or ham, or cheese." She must have been close to Nana's age, a woman of generous proportions. Speaking seemed to require the same effort as hacking into a log.

"Ham and cheese," I said. "And a coffee. To go." She was already retrieving a Styrofoam cup from a stack, pink polyester rustling as she huffed. She was wearing one of those old-fashioned diner uniforms with the little white collar and the puffed-up sleeves. It felt a bit silly, considering her age, the support stockings she surely had on underneath.

The coffee was weak and lukewarm, but the sandwich wasn't half bad. "Plenty of mustard and mayo could make gravel appetizing," Nana used to say. I crumpled the tinfoil, taking the last bite. Yellow droppings spotted the thighs of my jeans. I rubbed at them with a napkin, one eye still on the road. *You're just setting the stain.* I could hear Mom's reproach. Even two hundred clicks away, there they were, strapped in beside me, whether I wanted them or not.

There was no escaping it, where you came from. I didn't have a single lived memory of my dad, yet there he was, too, his hands on the wheel, steering me toward him, toward the truth. It was him who'd drawn me toward Rachelle, the reason I'd felt something kindred. It wasn't just a metaphor. We were sisters. Maybe even from the same tribe.

The thought almost worked to quiet the other one. *I was the only one this kept happening to.* Phantom fingers jabbed inside. I dug my nails into the wheel, steadying myself. I turned the radio loud. The vocals of a grown man rhyming *nookie* with *cookie.* Limp Bizkit. I thought of Alistair's shirt. I switched the station. I never liked that stupid song.

I glanced at the clock. Three thirty. I'd been driving for nearly four hours. If I kept the same pace, I'd be in Vancouver by nine. Erin had always been a night owl, the teetering pile of books she'd dig into, mug of Earl Grey ringing whatever spot she'd absently set it upon. Nine wasn't too late, but I needed to get to a phone. I didn't know why I hadn't tried her sooner.

I pulled over in Clinton, another town bisected by the highway, its outcropping of clapboard buildings weathered, as if held together with some glue and a prayer. As if the whole place had been lifted from the set of a Western. There was even a dinky-looking saloon.

I counted a total of five antique stores, two of which faced each other directly. There was a rack on the sidewalk in front of one of them—Carhartts, flannels, a pair of suspendered ski pants. One of those old tin wash buckets, a set of Pyrex pans. A crackling pair of children's red cowboy boots. I thought of the mall, the mirror image of soap stores. *Body care*, my manager, Carole, would correct me. Words were funny like that. Slap a sign over a drawer of rusty silverware and it became something of value. *Antique*. Soap wasn't just soap; it was an experience. *Care*. The same hunk of ash and fat. I'd need to call her, too, but that could wait. I wasn't on the schedule for a couple days yet.

I spotted a pay phone at the Esso up ahead. My legs were road numbed, and my knee buckled as I walked. *Of course Erin would be welcoming*, I kept telling myself. *Come visit!* she'd practically plead. *You're welcome anytime.*

I stepped into the booth and punched in her number. Despite how infrequently I used it, it was one of the ones I still knew by heart. The phone rang until the machine picked up, that familiar automated voice. She'd never personalized it. "Please leave a message after the beep."

Beep. It was a weekday, I remembered. She was probably still at work. I paused before setting down the receiver. It wasn't like she could call me back. I still had another four hours. I'd try again later, after six. She was sure to pick up then.

Across the road was a white brick building, its window draped with a floral bedsheet, crimson motif sun-faded. There was a basket on a table near its front door, tomatoes in nearly every hue: pink, red, yellow, orange. Even purple and green. *Heirlooms*, someone had scrawled in blue marker. The perfect gift for Erin. There was no sign, but the door was open.

"Hello?" I called out, purple tomatoes in hand.

No one answered. The space was divided, and the half to my left looked more like a living room than a store—the two couches reupholstered with musty-looking, fringed blankets, a pair of knitting needles on one of the arms, a half-finished baby sock. I couldn't even see the coffee table. Upon it was an empty tray of seedlings, a crushed Oreo box, jelly jars filled with what was either anemic coffee or chamomile that'd steeped too long. *TRANSITIONS INTERNATIONAL*, read a hand-painted sign on the other. *HERE 4 U + EACH OTHER.*

To the right was a table covered with another dusty blanket, a kitchen scale, a calculator, and a hand drum, along with several Gerber jars. Two shelves stretched along the opposite wall, lined with canning jars and big white tubs and brown paper bags neatly stapled at the top. *Lavender, Motherwort, Colt's Foot, Hops*, the jars were labeled. *St. John's Wort*, one brown bag read, a Post-It stuck to its side: *FOR WILLIE.*

On the far end of the shelves was a stout glass bowl housing what appeared to be dirt. *Kinnikinnick* in the same blue marker. *Smoking tobacco for ceremony. 3-.*

"Hello?" I tried again. Behind the blanketed table was a hallway, the door at the back of the building ajar. I thought I saw someone there, out in the light, but it was just the washing flapping in the wind.

I picked one up one of the jars, the original label scrubbed off, the inside caulked with something close to wax. *Fireweed Salve*, someone had written. *Anti-inflammatory and antibacterial. Wound healer.* The difference between a plant and a weed all depends on your perspective. I checked for a price tag, but there wasn't one. I hadn't seen a register or a cashbox either. I set the jar back down.

I had a toonie in my pocket. Two tomatoes couldn't cost more than that, even if they were purple. I left it on the blue table, next to the hand drum, and started back toward the door. There was a piece of paper propped against a music stand near the entrance. I'd missed it before.

Affirmation, it read in wavy type.

*Am I seeking . . . a **something**?*

*Were this **something** for You to involve permanent culture gardening, some experimental solar and wind energy projects, venturing into the mountains, attending music festivals, engaging in a faire trade economy to create a subsistent living, whilst not paying rent?*

Then we at Transitions have a potential home for You!

You was capitalized as if it were a name. Like *Joe*, or *Sally*, or *God*. There was a phone number at the bottom, a cartoon stick figure with squiggles for hair dancing and playing a flute.

"Hey," a voice called out. I startled. "Shit." A woman was standing behind the table. "Didn't mean to scare ya."

I looked at her, but her neck was bowed, her fingers combing through a sheet of muddy blonde. She flipped back upright, tugging the sheet into a high pony. I did a double take. She could have been Beth's twin.

"Let me know if you have any questions," she said, the same line I'd recited about a hundred times. Retail was retail, even at Transitions.

"Thanks." I stepped toward her. It really was uncanny. *Lost on the highway.* It took on a whole other meaning. What happened to them, the girls who ran away. Some found in a duffel bag, others spotted in the city, adrift on the sidewalk in the swell of chanting, orange-robed, bald-headed men. Stepping into death. Stepping into an entirely new life. There wasn't much difference between the two, was there?

Gone is gone.

I looked around. There was no TV or radio. It didn't seem like the kind of place to get the paper. Maybe they hadn't found her because she hadn't wanted to be found. Maybe my first hunch had been right after all.

"Beth?" I asked, my voice louder than I'd intended.

"What?" The woman's voice was hoarse, verging on snappy. She was biting what little nail remained on her thumb. I realized her cheeks were marked with acne, not freckles, her nose rounder, more bulb than button. Her whole countenance rougher upon closer inspection: Beth—assembled from closeout parts.

"You buying something, or . . ." She was fully snappy now, her mouth hanging open, the jagged pileup of bottom teeth. She'd never had braces. Her mother, like my own, had never worn pearls. I doubted anyone cared what she wanted to be when she grew up. Wherever she was from—PG or Williams Lake or another Northern town—I doubted anyone cared that she'd gone.

"Just these." I held up the tomatoes. "I already left a toonie." I picked up the Gerber jar. "How much for this?"

"Another toonie and we're square." I handed her a coin, turning back toward the door.

"Hey," she said, smile sliding across her face, her mood brightening considerably, the universal power of a sale. "You should take some tobacco. Josiah grew it out back."

"I don't smoke."

"It's for ceremony." She walked over to the bowl, scooping it out with a hand. She'd taken a pair of scissors to the bottom of her T-shirt, and her navel—as well as the long pink scar that arced below it—was in plain view. Her skin like poured milk, even paler than mine.

"Here." She handed me a plastic baggie, what looked like a spade's worth of freshly turned soil. "Namaste!" She stood at the door.

She was still standing there when I drove away, her slight frame wavering in the doorway—another version of Beth, an alternate end. The farther I drove, the less visible her bare legs, the dark growth at the top of her head. She could have been anyone—Missy, Anne-Marie. Rachelle. It was that flimsy, what we thought was bedrock. All you had to do was call a number. Step out of one *something* and into *something* new.

Change your hair, change your life. Mom's favorite saying popped into my head as the landscape faded further still. Cache Creek was up next. I was entering the great Canadian desert, *what made BC so beautiful*, Mom's voice giving way to Erin's. We were home to every type of landscape. Sagebrush shielded the cracking earth, its antiseptic sweetness blowing through the air.

The road was quiet. A freight train, brown as a snake, was winding through the hills, brown as the freighter, in the opposite direction of my LeSabre. I glanced at my clock. It was five thirty on the dot, the light thin, the land tinged the color of straw. It made the occasional swatch of green that much more disorienting, acid fields of sugar beets and corn as out of place as a nipple cropping up on a knee.

HUNGRY? The question hung in the air. Below it was another sign, shaped like an arrow and pointing toward a crowded lot. *HERBIE'S DRIVE-THRU.*

I ate dinner over the steering wheel, rogue tomato landing on my crotch. The two picnic tables to the left of the take-out window were occupied, and a busboy was mopping up a milkshake inside. The mix of industrial cleaner and malt made me gag, my nose sensitive, probably from stewing in my own air all day. I could've counted off every soiled diaper in the place. I leaned back in my seat, rolling my windows down. "Cut it out," I heard the waitress say, laughing despite her directive. Two boys in checkered shirts were sitting at one of the picnic tables, their hair buzzed, their necks red, cowboy boots jutting up to the mid-calves of their jeans. As she bent to serve the other table, one of the boys had placed his hand on her back, lowering it farther and farther down while his friend laughed. When she bent again, he grabbed a handful of ass.

"I said, quit it!" She swiped his hand away, her tone still playful, though her smile had dimmed. What else could she do? She didn't want to be a bitch, or worse. A prude.

Boys will be boys. Like Missy, and Mom, and every other woman I'd ever known would say. When Tanner took ahold of Kayden's ear and twisted like he was wringing out a rag. Starting as early as they could pinch or slap or grab.

It wasn't my fault. The voice was small and easily drowned out.

The sun had crouched down below the horizon, the sandy, cow-spotted hills going green again. I'd left the desert as quickly as I'd entered it, the Fraser reappearing, its waters wet concrete under the sapped light. I hadn't considered that the sun would set earlier down there. *Blink and you'll miss it.* Nana was right.

I'd parted ways with the river up near Williams Lake, even though we were both rushing in the same direction. The Fraser cut through the mountains, what no one bothered to pave, and I didn't catch up to it again until Lytton and all those oddly named places. Spuzzum, Squeah, Hells Gate, Hope. Nothing places, as far as I could tell, with little more to offer than gas.

Erin had sent me a postcard from Hells Gate during her PhD. The zigzagging froth of the river the centerfold, suspension bridge dainty in comparison, a misty apple red. It sounded mythical, that name, like out of a fairy tale or the Book of Genesis. Something someone made up. But I guessed all names were like that. Things people made up. Well, not people. Men.

In Hells Gate's case, that man was Simon Fraser, the fur trader who'd mapped out much of the great Canadian West. And named it, too—mostly after himself. The river, the lake, the towns, the valley. Many of the streets and roads. In PG alone there was Simon Fraser Avenue, and Fraser Road, and Fraser Way. The bridge my grandpa's Chevy flew from. In Vancouver, Erin would take the Fraser Highway to school.

They weren't just places on the map, she'd explained once on one of our walks. Every scientific law and theory, mathematical equations, the Latin names of plants. Ray was a junior; Sam was a junior's junior. Nana even had a bingo friend named Frankette.

It was the construction of the Canadian Northern Railway in 1914 that caused it, the rockslide that suddenly cinched the river as if someone were wielding a lasso, yanking hard. *Before, Hells Gate was one of the most important fishing sites in the lower mainland*, I remembered Erin explaining.

The rockslide had obstructed the path the salmon took to spawn, and year after year, their numbers dwindled—not only in Hells Gate, but the Fraser as a whole. It was one of the first fishways they built in the forties, after decades of watching the once steady population nosedive. *Problems like that are never localized*, Erin had written. *At least not for long. They kept blaming the tribes for the longest time. Overfishing. It only took them thirty years to realize it was the train.*

The same one slithering through the hills alongside me—abridged rainbow of freight cars. What was stationary in PG put to motion, lumber on its way to the States. The spruce and pine Ray and Jesse sawed down. The spruce and pine the tree planters replanted. Another cycle, another loop, with no beginning or end.

It was half past seven when I drove into Hope, the biggest town of the lot. *Erin has to be home by now*, I thought, pulling into an Esso. The cable in the phone booth had been cut. I eyed the Shell across the street. The *H* had crapped out, neon spelling something else entirely. It didn't seem to have one. I stepped into the convenience store.

An elderly Chinese man was fixed behind the counter, his hands resting upon his paunch as if he were pregnant. His face was turned upward, the TV nailed in the corner, *Wheel of Fortune* coming through in splashy grain. A tanned brunette was spinning the wheel, her pony-tail bobbing as she gave it all she had.

"Give me a *T*." Vanna White's sequins shimmered as she turned the letters, her hands lifting in applause. A red Mustang convertible rotated in the background like a chicken on a spit. The *tick-tick-tick* of the wheel. "*N*."

"There are two *N*s."

I asked if I could use the phone. "It's local." The man's eyes fluttered from the screen to me and back again as he lifted the cordless receiver. Still no answer. The wheel spun again. Had she changed her number? My heart started to patter. Suddenly I couldn't remember the last time we'd talked. Last Christmas, I'd missed her—she'd gone straight to voicemail. My birthday last year? *No*, I remembered. Like every year, she'd been out of town.

It was August, it dawned on me. Academics didn't have the same schedule as the rest of us. Erin and Michael were off the whole summer. They were probably moored on that little island she always wrote about—Savary—where Michael's family had a house. Too small for its own postcards, Erin would send ones she'd pick up on the way. *Greetings from the Sunshine Coast.* I handed back the phone, my stomach a pretzel, flutes starting to flare, boom of the announcer.

FORTUNE FAVORS THE BOLD, the board read, the prize an all-expenses-paid trip to the Sheraton Conquistador Golf and Tennis Resort in Tucson, Arizona. The stubby arms of cacti set against a bleeding sunset.

I'd never seen Vancouver, I lamented, opening my car door. I was so close. It seemed a shame to just turn back. I started my engine, gear still in park. But what would I do there? And where would I stay? With big-city prices, I might as well chuck my roll of cash in the trash.

I only got a few clicks north before I spun the wheel, aiming my Buick back in the opposite direction. There was a sign for a motel farther down the road. *TV, AIR CON, LOW WEEKLY RATES.* 19.99 a night. I'd give myself the chance to sleep on it. It was better to navigate in daylight.

Besides, I could barely see my surroundings. The dark so encompassing and the highway unlit, reliant on the negligible range of my headlights or those of an oncoming car. It was hard to say which was better. To be alone or to feel the sweep of the unknown passersby.

The Coquihalla Motel was L-shaped and pavement-colored, blending into its parking lot. The highway standard: a spot in front of each scuffed door. You could just about step out of your vehicle and land on your bed in one unhurried breath.

I'd only stayed in a motel once before, with Mom, after a woman in our building started a fire in her unit. She was so relaxed from her soak, she said, that she'd forgotten all about them, the colony of candles she'd left burning in her bathroom. Only waking when she heard the sirens, the ones that came at two A.M.

Relaxed all right, Mom had muttered, yanking my arm and wresting me from the crowd that'd gathered on the grass. No longer just neighbors but spectators, eyes upturned like on Canada Day, smoke like a parted curtain overhead.

I remembered watching the woman who'd lit the offending candles, sitting with her bare legs stretched out in front of her, cigarette smoldering at her lips. Her toes wiggled as she leaned back on her elbows, took another drag. She looked more like she was sitting at a bonfire as opposed to watching her belongings turn to ash. Like if it were happening to somebody else, a channel she'd switched to—she could always switch back.

Don't sit there. Mom had shooed me off the bedspread. *For Christ's sake, Jenny, it's probably covered in jizz.* She'd ducked into the bathroom, the frantic spin of the toilet paper roll. I'd stood there, six years old, in flip-flops on the carpet, half asleep with less than half a notion of what *jizz* was. *Here.* She flung back the bedspread with a toilet-roll-wrapped hand.

The room was dark, even with the overhead light on, and seemed typical, at least in my limited experience. Beige, beige, and more beige: the carpet, the laminated wood, the floral polyester. I peeled the sheets back, slipping off my Keds and stretching out on the bed. *Don't touch anything*, Mom had warned. *The sheets are all they clean.*

I picked up the remote, already forgetting.

"Life and death on Mount Baker. Help arrives, but it's too late for one hiker. A deadly crash. Police pursuit ends with an innocent bystander killed. Blame Canada. The soft-wood lumber war from both sides of the border."

The news always opened with bloodshed. I watched the whole hour, but there was no mention of the accident at the mill. I wondered whether it had even made the local stations. Something big must have happened. Someone must have died. Ain't news. Occupational hazard, I guessed.

I changed the channel. *Cold Squad* was on, a woman who was believed to have been murdered reappearing fifteen years later, taken in for shoplifting during a routine traffic stop. She kept claiming she was someone else, but her fingerprints matched those of another woman, a prostitute who'd supposedly been burned to death. There was a flash of something: Rachelle's necklace in the ashes. My insides twisted up again. I turned off the tube and stood, double bolting the door.

I fell asleep in my clothes, waking early with the sun. The curtains were about an inch too short and thin, made of material that looked like it could easily be hosed down. It'd been a restless night, every sound rumble of an engine, creak of an opening door, slam of one shutting—a potential threat.

It sobered me, that night away. *It'd be worse in Vancouver*, I realized, splashing water on my face. I met myself in the mirror. The unwashed hair, the puffiness, the circles dark as bruises under my eyes. The perfect victim, someone no one would miss. If I had been smart, I'd have turned right back at the Esso.

There was a complimentary breakfast in the reception at seven. Green bunch of bananas, a pitcher of orange juice, a soup bowl of jam. There were no chairs or any other tables beside the one with the scant spread. I reached for a cup and poured myself a coffee.

A man in a windbreaker shuffled in, the squeak of his loafers, which he wore sockless. "Morning," his voice boomed. A woman at least half his age lagged behind him, her bleached hair matted into several tiny nests.

"Shit," the man said, sidling up beside me. "Look, Missy, we must've woken her." The woman fiddled with her belly button ring, shifting in her salt-chewed Uggs, ignoring him.

"Excuse me." I felt a hand flat against my back. *Missy.* The man leaned in close, his arm reaching over me, the stink of beer on his breath. *It's different after, not as tight.* The red flash. I felt it again, the weight of him on me. Negating the weight of me. My coffee tumbled to the carpet.

"Damn," I heard the man start to say, but I didn't catch the rest. I'd already turned, swinging open the door. Strapping myself into my car and revving my engine. The waitress back in Cache Creek, she'd called those boys by name. She'd known them, their bleary eyes trained to her breasts.

Within minutes, that town became a blip. Its cacti and its horny teenage cowboys specks, no bigger than fruit flies. Just like PG's pines and its horny backwoods drug dealers. Unable to touch me as I soared along the road.

Affirmation. Was I seeking a something? I wasn't sure anymore, but sometimes escape could lead you down the same path.

twenty-three

The lanes on 1 mushroomed the closer I got to the city, along with the gas stations, and the big box stores, and the strip malls, and the houses, and the apartment buildings, and the traffic lights, and the traffic. It was bumper-to-bumper. For the first time since PG, I used my rearview mirror for something other than paranoia. I turned into a Timmy's, joining the drive-through's winding line.

I passed a sign for Chilliwack and felt a jolt of recognition. Where did I know that name from again? I couldn't remember. Maybe it'd been one of the towns mentioned the night before, on the news. After all those miles, all those names on the signs became meaningless. Except the one.

Erin's descriptions hadn't done the city justice, I remember thinking, biting into a glazed sour cream. It wasn't just that it was bigger, or older, or richer; it was in a completely different category. When I crossed that bridge into Vancouver, it was as if I were crossing into a whole other world. One with signs in Chinese and buildings a hundred stories tall, with sidewalks teeming with people and air that smelled of fried meat and diesel and then something else, something fresh. The Pacific. I'd left the dank far behind.

I hadn't started my car that morning with any specific place in mind, but I soon realized that I was driving west, roughly toward the address I'd looked up when I first left, the one Erin scribbled in all the corners of her letters. I was heading to 12 Langara Avenue, right near the ocean, *where you can taste the salt.* I sniffed again, the brine affecting. I was close. My heart pounded, my head pervaded with all the fears I'd been keeping at bay. Chances were, Erin wouldn't even be home. But what if she was? What if she really had changed her number and hadn't bothered to tell me? What if, somehow, she'd been screening my calls?

She hadn't visited in over half a decade. She'd never flown me out. When was it exactly, the last time we spoke? For years, it'd been voicemails, all those piddling postcards. I felt my cheeks burning, the belt yanked tight.

Outside was the opposite, clenched fist of the city unfurling, concrete swapped for jewel greens. Every leaf-dappled house swelling in size, along with the spaces between them. Each lawn impeccably manicured, with box hedges, tall cypress, red-barked manzanitas. There were daylilies and blazing stars, trellised passionflower, hydrangeas that looked like they belonged on wedding cakes. Bright rushes of zinnias lined meandering walkways, paths leading to gurgling fountains. At one house there was even a footbridge spanning the berth of a man-made stream and pond.

32 Langara Avenue. I knew Michael was rich, but I'd only seen PG money. I thrummed on my steering wheel, taking a breath. The salt was stronger, the air scrubbed clean. 26, 24, 22. *Beach is just around the corner*, Erin had written. *Come anytime*. How she'd always sign off. *I'd been calling from pay phones*, I reminded myself. There was no way she was avoiding me. All those voicemails she left every Christmas. It was me who never called back. I relaxed, anxiety easing. It was Erin. Of course she'd be glad. That is, if she was home in the first place.

12. I pushed on the brake.

The house was more charming than I could've ever imagined. Sunshiny yellow and a sprawling two stories, it, too, looked like it belonged on a cake. A painted staircase with a number of bright potted plants led to the front porch, which wrapped around the side of the house. Jute furniture, a bench swing. Geraniums at windowsills. There was even a white picket fence. I pulled into a spot nearby.

There was a light on in the kitchen. I stepped onto the staircase, all the fear flooding back. It was all too perfect; part of me wanted to turn right around. *Come on, Jenny.* I trudged forward. *You've made it this far.* I lifted the heavy, gilded knocker. It looked like it cost more than my car.

A squat woman answered, pink kerchief knotted around her dark head. I'd forgotten one last possibility. That Erin hadn't just changed her number but moved.

"Sorry," I blurted, nearly bursting into tears. The woman looked up at me, perplexed. I realized she was wearing a pair of those yellow gloves that came up to the elbow. "Owner not here." She wagged a sheathed finger. There was a coatrack tacked to the wall behind her. From the doorway I spotted Erin's old gardening hat. I exhaled. "Do you know when she'll be back?" "No English." The woman shook her head. "Sorry." I heard her bolt the door.

I stood there for a minute, debating whether I should knock again. I could have left a note, but what good would that have done? It wasn't like I had an address there or a number. I opened my car door. I could have waited a few days, found a cheap place to stay. I thought of the motel, wincing. Or someplace nicer. I opened the glove compartment, eying my wad. Forget about the gas money for the drive back—I'd sooner run out of cash to feed myself.

I felt like a jackass, a grade A dolt. Some master plan. To think my dad was guiding me. *You don't know what you don't know until you know.* I thought of the conversation with Nevaeh. *Rachelle,* I remembered. Another failure. Nothing ever worked out.

You're so goddamn dramatic. Mom's voice swelled in my head. My eyes the same color as dirt, as him. Her fault.

Just then, a woman walked by toting an outsized straw bag. I could still hear the slap of her flip-flops as she disappeared from view. *Beach is just around the corner.* I'd only seen the ocean once, in Prince Rupert, but it was a shipping port. That couldn't count. *Fuck it.* I pocketed my keys. I'd already come all that way. The least I could do was wiggle my toes in the sand.

I toddled up to the shoreline, froth drenching my Keds. I kicked them off. The horizon would've gone on forever if the mountains hadn't cut in, that cloudy blue, saw-toothed crown.

The beach was packed, with circles of teenagers sprawled across blankets, young families slathering sunscreen on shoulders and backs. Girls my age in itty bikinis, turning over to even out their tans. Wasn't it a weekday? I supposed the workweek mattered less, the girls probably university students living off Daddy's money, unbound to the daily grind.

If there were a beach in PG, I'd have been about the only one on it on a random Tuesday morning. Maybe the St. Vinnie's crowd.

There was a stand selling ice cream on the other side of the sand. The day was an oven, growing hotter. What was another toonie anyway? I stood in line.

There was shade by the showers, and I scarfed my cone there, burying my feet in the sand. Pistachio. Nana's and my favorite. Sam liked vanilla, the family-sized tubs we'd dig out of the freezer. He hadn't taken me out for a cone since prom.

"I'm not *not* into him," I overheard one of two bikinied girls saying. "He just tries too hard." She wielded an aerosol can of sunscreen over her arms. "You know?"

The other girl nodded, leafing through a magazine. A quiz on one page: *Are You Good Girl Hot or Bad Girl Hot?*

I finished my ice cream and leaned back in the sand. I was exhausted, the sand yielding, adjusting to my shape, bending to all my sharp edges. Held like that, I fell right asleep, hands pressed beneath my cheek as if in prayer.

When I woke, the light was scarce. The beach quiet: not a soul in the water, all the circles broken, the towels shaken out. I didn't need my watch to tell me that the day was ending. I stretched my arms up over my head. I'd slept deeper than I had in weeks. A dreamless sleep, a sleep so refreshing, it felt like a gift, like my batteries had been swapped out. I could splurge on one night in a decent hotel. Start early. I'd be home in time to fix dinner. Or I could stay a second night. Spend another day by the ocean. I'd brought my bathing suit. I loved to swim. Or at least I used to.

I passed by Erin's on my way to my car. The light was still on. How long did it take to clean that house?

Someone moved, the shadow willowy behind the gauze of the curtain. Erin. My heart hammered. I started up the driveway and lifted the knocker.

"Jenny, I can't believe it."

I'd be lying if I said I instantly recognized her. She was different, glossier—her hair blonder, her skin freckled, her whole person smiled down upon by the sun. I almost felt embarrassed, pasty in comparison, ten pounds heavier than when she had last saw me at my wedding. She wrapped her arms around me for a second time, pulling me closer and squeezing me tight. There she was, my aunt Erin. Everything other than that feeling melted. I was home.

"Is anyone else with you?" Erin peeked her head around the door-frame. "Fi? Sam?" Her voice grew hushed, sober. "Is everything okay?"

"I'm fine." I nodded. "It's just me. I tried to call. I had your address. I thought maybe your number had changed."

"Same number." She cocked her head. The way she was standing, it was almost as if she were blocking the door. "You've got some timing. We just got back in town, like, three hours ago. Michael had a reading in Toronto." I forced a smile.

It wasn't just the bleach job. Erin was stiffer, an approximation of herself. City Erin. In place of her usual cargo pants was a white linen dress, shapeless as a pillowcase and yet somehow still flattering. She'd lost what I'd gained—ten, maybe even fifteen pounds. A pair of hammered silver earrings glimmered as she talked, a matching pendant dangling from her neck. I'd never seen her in jewelry excluding her loupe and, after Michael, her wedding band. She used to dress more like the woman scientist in *Jurassic Park*. Now all they had in common was their hair color.

She put her hands back on my shoulders, excusing herself. "You must be exhausted, and look at me, just standing here. Come in," she said. "Come in."

I'd never been inside a house like that before. It even smelled expensive, like lilacs or leather or freshly hewn wood. There sure was a lot of it in the house. The exposed beams on the ceiling, the wide planks on the floor, all the bookshelves built right into the walls. The windows were wide, and a few of them were open, casting the leather sectional in wan ocean light.

A sheepskin was draped across the back of a chair that looked more like a concept than a place to rest. There weren't many other personal touches. A ceramic vase housing two lonesome gladioli was placed on the dining-room table, spray of sparse, withdrawn white. The sole object leaned against the fireplace mantle was a frame of not a photo or painting but a tiny beige square imprinted with a geometric pattern. It was a mirrored image, I realized upon closer inspection, like those snowflakes grade-school children cut out.

"It's a birchbark biting." Erin stepped toward me. "If you can believe it, an Indigenous woman did that with her teeth. They're humming-birds." I squinted. "Messengers of joy."

We went upstairs, where she showed me the guest room, then back downstairs to the linen closet, where she placed a set of towels in my hands. Then to the kitchen, where she started a kettle, wondering if I needed any help with my bags. When I explained that I hadn't brought much, she led me to the laundry room and demonstrated how to turn on the machine, which detergent to use for delicates, colors, whites.

The linen closet, the laundry room, an entire bedroom just for guests. How impressive it was, even if, technically, Sam and I had those things, too. What we had was shabby. *I guess that'll do.* An inflatable mattress wedged between my sewing table and the bench press that Sam hardly ever used. Wrinkled piles of whatever sheets and towels I'd found on sale, the colors clashing: mustard yellows, Heinz reds.

Hers were all a uniform shade of ivory, the sheets crisply ironed, the towels fluffed. The laundry room tiled with hand-painted squares from Italy, machines discreetly tucked beneath a gleaming granite slab. Missy would've had to pick her jaw up off the floor. Mop up her drool while she was at it. PG fancy was nothing in comparison. I finally understood what was meant by *McMansion.*

Erin adjusted the temperature on the oven, arranged a tray of tea, nuts, and chocolate, and carried it into the living room.

She was the perfect hostess, warm and curious, asking me about work, about Sam, about Mom, about how my friends were, about what I'd planted that year. Still, something felt off—formal, perfunctory, the new Erin hollow as her surroundings. I kept clinging to what I'd felt after we'd hugged that second time. *It's been six years,* I reminded myself, lifting an impossibly small cup of steaming tea. *They're Japanese,* she'd explained, my fingers burning.

We set the table at seven, Erin adjusting the oven, twisting open a bottle of red wine and pouring it into a convoluted-looking vessel. A house where wine was *decanted,* where tea was served by the thimbleful, where chocolate was bitter and pitch-black. The cheese in her fridge was wrapped in stamped paper, the jars containing olives that'd been weighed by the pound, the jam homemade somewhere in France. The milk was stored in an unlabeled glass jar, as if it'd been delivered by a man in a jaunty white cap. The eggs she kept on the counter (*like in Europe*), the candle she lit that was honey-scented (*beeswax*), the price tag I glimpsed on the back of the wine bottle (*sixty-five*), all serving to push me further from the Erin I knew, as we sat in the kitchen waiting for her husband.

"He usually calls," Erin said, standing. "Something must have come up." She brought out some butter, sawed into a loaf of unsliced bread.

Michael didn't arrive until ten. No apology. He came home the same way Sam did, stepping out of his shoes and heading straight to the kitchen, ready to tuck into his plate.

"Jenny?" He tried to hide his astonishment with an exaggerated smile, vigorously shaking my hand.

"Good to see you. What brings you out here?" He didn't wait for an answer. He walked past me, planting his lips onto Erin's. "What a surprise, dear."

His hair had gone snowy, and his considerable paunch protruded from the band of his slacks. Standing there in his dress socks, the contrast was stark. Their fourteen-year age gap glaring, depressing. He looked paternal, pulling her aside like that.

"I already told you, I didn't know she was coming," I could hear Erin whisper from the hall. "I tried your office. Twice. You must have stepped out." Michael whinnied. In all my daydreaming about what it'd be like to be there, I realized I'd often omitted him altogether.

He came back into the dining room and took a seat at the head of the table, rolling up his shirt's sleeves, smile still pasted on. Erin followed, standing over the table dutifully, portioning out the contents of a wide enamel pan: slow-roasted tomatoes and zucchinis and eggplants, the sweet stink of garlic, woody clippings of thyme.

"Ratatouille." Michael looked over at me, lisping. "Provençal."

"We went vegetarian," Erin elaborated. "Michael's heart." She'd forgotten to take her apron off. She looked like June Cleaver, wooden spoon still in hand.

The old Erin had never been much of a cook. *Food is fuel*, she liked to say, *eating an equation*. The right ratio of proteins, fats, and carbs. Bologna sandwiches, apples and peanut butter, hard-boiled eggs and a pot of Rice-A-Roni. Mashed carrots were about as gourmet as she got. I lifted a forkful of vegetable mush to my mouth, gulping at my wine.

Michael zeroed his attention in on me, asking all the same questions Erin had posed. Polite ones, without teeth: more about other people than myself. He was dancing around it, what he really wanted to know.

"Such a pleasant surprise. Erin always talks about how much she misses you." He said her name like an accusation.

Michael had turned his body toward me, away from Erin, his elbows angled on the table to further fence her off. I realized that during the course of our dinner, he hadn't once addressed her directly. I'd never seen that tactic before.

The bruises from men like André, how Sam went stony, cold. These were straightforward—obvious. What Michael was doing was worse, I thought as he refilled my wine glass. He was using me as a means of punishing her. The two of us were having a perfectly good time. I drained my glass, trying to catch Erin's eyes.

"I must admit, I'm curious." Michael readjusted his napkin. "What prompted such a . . . spontaneous, let's say, visit?" Even Erin hadn't asked that yet.

"It's Sam's last two weeks on," I answered, chewing a thumbnail, as if that explained it. "Work's been slow." He was silent.

"The weather's been nice?" I heard my voice lift. "I've always been meaning to get down here." What else could I say? That my best friend's husband had treated me like a sock puppet? That when I told my own husband, he left me sobbing in our garage? That my neighbor went missing and no one gave a damn?

That I could go missing and no one would give a damn?

"I tried to call." I could feel the crest of emotion. "I guess I didn't really think it through." Erin reached over the table, gripping my hand.

"It's been, what, six years since your wedding? About time you came down here." Then, more quietly, "You're family."

"She could have left a message." Erin was steering in another direction, but Michael wasn't about to let go of the wheel. It was clear he was talking to her, his eyes still on me. "No matter." He lifted his wineglass. "Santé. Welcome."

I thought that meal might never end. After the vegetable mush, there was cheese. And after cheese, there was more of that repellent chocolate. I'd loaded all the dishes into the washer while Michael sipped his espresso, but when Erin came into the kitchen, she pulled them out one by one. They were ceramic, she said, made with a special clay, and needed to be washed by hand.

She walked up to the guest room with me. She'd opened the windows earlier to air it out, and the whole room smelled fresh, perfumed a sharp green: *Pine Breeze*, or at least what it wished it was. "The wainscoting is all local pine." Erin smiled, positioning a jar of black-eyed Susans she'd snipped from the garden in a vase on the nightstand. The plants were a comfort. A wispy fern along one windowsill; in the corner, a waxy snake plant. The heart-shaped tendrils of devil's ivy floating down the edge of the dresser. The guest room felt more like her, the Erin I'd known, green blotting out every window in her cramped apartment, vines tacked to the ceiling, her massive aloe plant. The one in Mom's bathroom was an offshoot from Erin's. Fifteen years old, it had moved with Erin to every apartment. I hadn't seen it or any of her old plants.

"You comfortable?" She perched herself at the end of the bed, smoothing back the fuzz on a knit blanket. "Need anything else?"

Do you? I wanted to ask, wrest out what she was tamping down.

She'd stiffened again during dinner, her smile fraught, one false move and everything unlatching. I knew that smile well. I'd seen it on Missy, on Mom, felt it, pinned to my own face. I would have never thought I'd see it on Erin. But I guess I would have never bet on her bending over an oven, or ironing her sheets, or hand-washing her dinner plates right beside a dishwasher either.

Instead, I said, "No, nothing at all," and we hugged before saying good night.

twenty-four

Michael left early for the university the next morning. When I woke, the house was ours again. I found Erin in the kitchen, peeling off a pair of dirt-caked gloves, the woven basket of tomatoes still warm from the sun. The purple ones in my car. I rushed to find them. The fireweed salve had gone AWOL.

"Look at these," Erin cooed, as if her basket wasn't flush. "Anything special you want to see today?" she asked, ripping into a croissant. She'd gone to the bakery early, the grease-mottled paper bag packed to its brim. I'd never had one before, and haven't had many since. I took another bite. Like eating flaky butter. I could have eaten ten.

"No." I remembered the postcard. "Is Stanley Park nearby?"

It didn't take long to find. Taller than I could have ever imagined and wide as a logging truck, the tree was like a bridge to infinity—as near to heaven as an earthly thing could get. No photo could capture it, the magic of being made so small. I stood with my head back in awe.

"It's a monument tree." Erin tilted her head back, too. "The whole park was made up of them before the loggers. The monuments were the ones that were too big to fell. This one is estimated to be near a thousand years old." I grinned. There she was, the old Erin. We could have been back in PG, ambling along the Fraser's bends. She hooked her arm through mine.

It was hard to believe we were still in the city. Sure, there was a paved road cluttered with station wagons and motorcyclists and mountain bikers, but as soon as you set down one of the trails, it felt like you were out in the bush, swaddled in green.

"You must come here every day," I said. She smiled.

"Not quite." She tucked her hands under the sleeves of her sweater, pausing in front of a spindly tree and plucking off a few berries. "Here."

She handed me one, small and bright as candy. Floor polish. I spat it out.

"Pacific dogwood. Takes some getting used to," she said, laughing, popping one into her mouth. "When I came here for undergrad, I told myself I'd eat one wild thing a day. I got used to bitter."

She wasn't working at the moment. She was waiting. There weren't any openings in her department, but one would come with time. Last fall, she'd received an offer from a university in Nova Scotia, but Michael had just been made chair. It wouldn't have made sense for them to upheave their lives.

"I stay busy." The Japanese classes, the position she'd created for herself at a local middle school, teaching an introduction to botany. With Michael's position, they hosted dinners at least once, sometimes three times, a week. Not to mention the house, her sprawling vegetable garden.

I was no stranger to it, the shape her life had taken—a housewife without any diapers to change or mouths to wipe. Another woman lousy with time. Erin cursed with the same affliction as me.

She always used to talk about adoption as an option. I'd only brought it up the one time. The way Sam had looked at me, as if I'd just suggested we barbeque his childhood collie. Men didn't trust adoption. Not even men like Michael, all those showy letters after his name. *Why would we raise something that's not ours?* Sam had asked. *Something.* Not even a person, a thing. I always felt like I could grow to love any baby, but who knew? Get applesauce flung in your sleep-impoverished face enough and you might start wondering whether you could take that *something* back. Maybe it wasn't as simple as a mothering instinct. Maybe what it required was plain stupidity, an idiot's faith that it would all work out. But I guess that was true for any parent, bound by paper or blood.

We ate lunch in a restaurant no bigger than my garage, sitting Indian-style on two under-stuffed cushions that'd been set atop a woven mat. Japanese food. Plate after plate of what was stranger and stranger: vegetables fried in airy batter, squashed green bean, tiny bowl of salty brown soup. Raw fish was the main course, and it arrived in slices, limply balanced against a clump of rice or wrapped into cylinders in a sort of stiff little jacket. *Sushi*, the word wispy as a wave. It sounded like Nevaeh's language. I picked one up and dunked it into the dish of inky sauce before noticing Erin's chopsticks. Smooth metal, they were tucked into the cloth napkin beside my plate.

"It takes some practice." Erin laughed, demonstrating, dabbing at the paste, bright green and coiled, and stirring it into her sauce. I made the mistake of imitating her. Raw fish was one thing, but what the hell was *that*? It felt like my sinuses had been singed off.

The plates kept arriving. More sushi, a seaweed salad, two slices of something called yuzu cheesecake. "Japan's next on my list," Erin was saying between bites. "Everything there, it's an art form."

I nodded, half listening, tallying the bill in my head. It was all so dainty. It had to be expensive. If she ate like that every day, my roll of cash wouldn't see me through the workweek. Meanwhile Erin was dreaming about Japan.

That was the difference, I realized, what her degrees had earned her. Or maybe, more what Michael's money had facilitated. The world was open to Erin in a way it would never be for me. Even this trip to Vancouver felt like a stretch.

"We have to try the mochi," she said, and I blanched. There was always the credit card.

Reserved for emergencies, I almost never used it. I didn't like the idea of spending cash I didn't have. Missy charged everything, even a coffee at Timmy's. Sam and I used to joke about it. That was before. I looked down and realized my hands were twisting my napkin. The card was in his name, and he kept track of it. How would I explain a charge in Vancouver at a fancy restaurant?

If I just keep on driving, I won't have to, a small voice inside of me said. My heart thumped, the surge of adrenaline. I hadn't considered it, not going back. Driving farther, to the States. Washington, or North Dakota, or Montana. Was that where this was leading? That empty feeling. The missing piece. The truth about where I came from. Who I really was. My dad.

Erin had to have known. Why hadn't she told me? The light seemed to shift, her features made harsh. Had they all made some type of a pact?

The check came, and she reached straight for it, slipping her credit card between the folds of the leather envelope without even glancing at the damage. She grinned, her face softening again. Mom had probably kept it hidden. Erin wasn't the type to pry. Despite how close Erin and I once were, I'd never worked up the courage to ask.

Maybe that's why she'd always brought up the Native population in her ecological rants. She was hinting at it, what Mom had sworn her to keep mum. Maybe she'd been waiting for me to bring him up.

"It's nothing," Erin assured me when I started to thank her. It was such a nice moment, the subject too touchy. I didn't want to ruin our day. *The right time would appear,* I remember thinking, popping the ball, rubbery as the raw fish, into my mouth and swallowing.

We walked from the restaurant to the center of the city. It was mesmerizing, the endless procession of things to look at, to eat, to drink, to buy, or to want to buy. Erin swung open the door to a clothing store.

"This one's a favorite."

I immediately saw where she'd found her new color palette. Everything in there was the same subdued hue—silt, sand, ash, clay, as if dyed with pigment from the beach. As soon as I stepped in, I felt raggedy, a country mouse, in my outfit of hand-me-downs. Anne-Marie's old jean cutoffs that were belted to fit, a pilled T-shirt from Value Village, the collar warped to hell. My Keds were the only things I'd bought new. That and my underwear. I avoided the floor-length mirrors.

Sweaters were folded on a raised wooden platform, each achingly soft and featherlight. I picked one up, the brightest thing in there, the color of new growth on a spruce.

"Try it on." I hadn't seen that Erin was behind me. My face flushed, out of my depths. I hadn't checked, but the price had to be in the triple digits. The store was practically empty, with about a forearm's length between each hanging item, the message clear: we don't need to sell much.

"My treat," Erin was saying. I shook my head. She'd already bought me lunch. "Really," she insisted. "An early birthday present." She pushed me toward the fitting room, and I slipped the sweater over my head.

I didn't pay much attention to the mirror, but just the feeling of it on was bliss. I wanted to live in that fabric, drape it over my entire body, my bed, my couch, my whole house. The saleswoman at the register held the sweater gingerly, as if it were breathing, swaddling it in thick tissue paper. I winced when I saw the price flash on the register. It was more than our monthly mortgage.

"You'll have it forever," Erin whispered, leaning over, handing her credit card to the saleswoman without pause.

Erin needed to stop by a spice shop for dinner. She was planning on curry, if that was okay. *Buttered bread would have been okay*, I could have said. *Dry bread—stale bread, crumbs even.* Instead, I just nodded, following along. The shop was east of where we were. There was no better way to see the city than to walk it.

"It's actually quite small, relatively speaking," she said as we marched from block to block, an hour from where we'd first started. How adaptable we are. I wondered how long it'd take me to think of an hour's walk as short, of a two-hundred-and-some-dollar sweater as an *investment*. The old Erin used to wait for the sales days at Value Village. The new one had her sights set on Kyoto.

Heading east, the city was reshaped, and then reshaped again. The buildings inflating, then shrinking again, throngs of people appearing only to vanish—to morph into other, slicker selves. Business suits traded in for Nikes and jeans. Double after double of women like Erin, in pillowcase dresses and flat, woven sandals, tucking loose strands of sunkissed hair behind ears. We passed coffee shops and more clothing stores, a window display of wooden sculptures, a silver soup ladle embossed with an eagle. *NATIVE ART*, the sign read. A geometric square just like the one on Erin's fireplace. I glanced at the price tag, which was displayed below. *400—.* I nearly choked on the breath mint Erin had given me.

At some point the sidewalks narrowed with bursting market bins—fruits studded with spikes, the skins tough as leather, fish floating pale bellies up in dark brine. Chicken feet were strung above them like twinkling Christmas lights, the branches of scrubbed ginger as big as a man's outspread hand.

"We're in Chinatown." Erin ushered me along. "Almost there." We made a left on a street called Hastings. A name I'll never forget. It looked no different from any other, except for the swarms of people—destitute, raging, zonked out. Tarps were spread across the concrete like picnic blankets, some people squatting, some sleeping, others pacing, muttering, sometimes shouting to no one in particular. One man was missing an entire arm. The sidewalk couldn't contain them all, and a woman stumbled into the street—cars honking, another woman yelling, removing her flip-flop, and launching it skyward. It felt like a scene from a parking lot after last call, except it was day, not even four P.M.

"Is there something going on?" I asked, my voice hushed. Erin shook her head, quickening her pace.

Almost every single person on that street was Native. Like the corner of St. Vinnie's multiplied. There was a man on crutches missing his shirt, his chest carved into, wood chip mess of dark scars. Another in a windbreaker, one white sleeve muddied, hitched around a woman stroking the patchy fur of a dog. The stench was unmistakable—days, if not weeks, of piss-soaked pants. There were sleeping bags, a few shopping carts, one tent fashioned out of Hefty bags.

We passed an official-looking building that seemed to be the nexus of much of the activity, its stairs planted with more street dwellers, its doors swinging open as if counting time. The two stone columns, the capped dome. I'd seen it before, I realized, on TV. In the backdrop, when they'd showed all the drumming. *Find Our Stolen Sisters*, the signs had read. *I WANT TO LIVE*. Erin linked an arm around mine.

"It's an old public library." She tugged us both forward. "They made it a community center for"—she paused—"the people here."

We passed a woman on the sidewalk, leaning against the side of the building's iron fence, my age, if not younger, retying the straps of her neon-green halter. She caught me looking and leered. Her skin was white, like mine. *Métis*. My cheeks burned, the word a hot coal. Her arms and thighs were mottled like they'd been taken to with a skewer. Seeing them in broad daylight, they looked nothing like Rhoda's. Actual track marks. What else had I gotten wrong?

"Can I get a dollar?" Another woman's opened hand. I reached into my purse, placing a coin in her palm. It slid, clattering to the ground.

"Thanks." The woman crouched down, fingers grazing the cement. She wasn't blind, I didn't think—she just didn't seem to be in control of her hands.

I knew I was staring, but I couldn't help myself. There was something achingly familiar about the woman. She tilted upright, falling back onto her tailbone, deciding to stay there. Her small, withered face, the sheet of black hair. She raked it back with a stiffened hand.

"God bless," she said, crumpled cigarette igniting. *Rachelle*, I thought, her smoke swimming into my mouth. I saw then how easily it could happen. I thought of Transitions and fake Beth. Death not the only way to vanish.

I hadn't mentioned her once, the motive for my trip. *FIND BETH*, the bumper stickers had guided me all the way here. If I forgot Rachelle, what would be left of her? I handed the woman another loonie, and this time her fingers closed over her palm.

We crossed over onto the next block, and all went calm, the only movement the shade from a few staggered young maples, the sidewalk empty, swept. From hell and back, one block to the next.

"Heroin's the real issue," Erin was saying, her face shadowed with the shifting leaves. "The cycle of addiction is so real." She was speaking at her normal volume again. "They want to open methadone clinics, like what they have in Europe. At least it'd be regulated. Sometimes it goes so far; they're beyond help." Her gait had slowed. "Are you okay? Did something happen?" My face had cracked open without my consent, my eyes red, shining wet.

"I'm sorry," Erin said, squeezing my hand. "I didn't mean for you to see all that."

"I'm fine," I insisted, wiping my tears. "Just tired," I croaked. She nodded her head.

"It's hard," she said, her face as earnest as ever. "It makes you feel powerless. So much desperation." She wrapped an arm around me, guiding me forward. "We just have to keep doing what we can."

Yes, I agreed, keeping pace, though, to be honest, I hadn't the slightest idea what she meant.

Michael had a dinner—it would just be us girls, Erin informed me that evening, stirring garlic around another mammoth enamel pan. She was nervous, or maybe more like unnerved, babbling about her garden, reminding herself to make me an envelope of kabocha seeds to take home, what she was sawing into, the blaze-orange fleshed squash from Japan. Too polite to prod, I could see she was waiting for me to bring it up. Whatever it was that had happened earlier, whatever it was that had brought me there.

While the curry simmered inside, we went out, drinking more tea and eating more nuts under a latticed arch of grapevines. *Pergola*, another new word. *Decanter, wasabi, Provençal*. It was like the rich spoke another language entirely.

"So," Erin said, clearing her throat. "How's everything with Fi?" Dipping a toe in, testing the water. That was as direct as she got. "How's Sam?"

"He's fine. Everyone's fine."

Her voice lifted like it always did whenever she'd mention him, as if his whole person was up for debate. It wasn't that she didn't like him. She was disappointed; the finger pointed at me. What she'd said when I first called her to tell her about our engagement. *You're sure you don't want to wait?*

When I made that call at eighteen, it'd been four years since I'd seen her. Despite all her promises, she'd left, and she'd never come back. Part of me enjoyed it, showing her how far I'd strayed. I wasn't going to college like we'd planned. I'd be married in September and pregnant by October. Maybe things would have been different if she had stuck around.

Even then I realized it wasn't anything to be proud of. Following in Mom's footsteps, not hers. I couldn't have known that my body was faulty, that my choice would be emptier than I could have ever imagined. That the days would drag on like a silted-up river, that I'd spend twenty-one nights out of thirty on my own.

That the boy I'd dove in with would swim farther and farther, until I was left treading all that sunless, leaden water, utterly alone.

It probably wouldn't surprise her, any of it. Especially not what Sam had become. Or, maybe, always was.

"It's not him." I didn't want to get into it. I really couldn't stand the way she said his name.

"I came for my neighbor," I said, and in that moment, I believed it. "She's missing. I thought maybe you could help."

"Oh my God, Jenny." Erin straightened herself, her eyes recast. "What happened?"

I started from the beginning, adept, finally, at recounting what had transpired. At that point, it was practiced. The appearance of the pickup, the sudden disappearance of Rachelle. Her Fleetwood on the shoulder of 16, spotlessly clean and empty.

"Wait," Erin interrupted before I could even mention the Man with the Braid. "When was this?" I hadn't done the math before she'd asked.

A month, I counted back, *more than that. The first twenty-four hours are the most important.*

"Sunday," I lied. It had to seem urgent. Otherwise it wouldn't make any sense—any of it.

"Christ," Erin said. "First Beth and now this." She paused, her face flooding with color, the adrenaline of what this meant. "It means he's still out there, targeting women. It wasn't an isolated event." She shook her head. "This should be all over the news. You called the RCMP already, right? Has there been any follow-up? There's really been no sign of her since?"

I didn't know how to answer. She was the first person I'd told who was ready to help, and I'd fudged the timeline, more concerned with shielding myself. How would I explain everything else?

"I meant a month ago. A Sunday." Erin squinted. "Sorry, I think I'm still wore out from the drive."

"'A month ago,'" she repeated, shoulders dropping as she eased against the back of her chair, resolve melting to detachment, swift as butter in a smoking pan.

Erin was a scientist, fluent in probabilities. A month meant Rachelle was already long gone, decomposing in a ditch, zipped up in a duffel bag. Even someone who'd never watched a single episode of *Cold Squad* could tell you that.

"Why didn't it make the news?" she said softly. The only outlier—it didn't make sense. *Rachelle.* I could see her trying to place the name. Erin had never seen our place, but I was sure Mom had filled her in like she had everyone else.

"The one across from you?" I nodded. "Oh." She finally got it.

"She's got two kids, little girls," I urged, playing to her sympathy. "The RCMP up there, they couldn't care less. She needs us. The youngest is still a baby."

Erin sat up straight again, nodding—a mission.

"We can talk to the RCMP here, but they should have already been notified. There's a lot of movement between here and PG. There was a story a couple years ago. Twenty prostitutes who their families claim vanished. But the mayor dismissed it. There was no evidence. If there's no evidence, there's not much they can do." She chewed on a thumbnail, an old habit that had persisted despite the coat of nude polish that had been, by the looks of it, professionally applied.

"Michael has a friend in the First Nations Studies Department. Maybe he'll have some ideas." She was staring into her teacup, as if willing the dregs to give her the answer. "I don't know. There are so many stories like that.

"We'll see what we can do," she was saying. I nodded, my eyes wet again. Her delivery was different, but the sentiment was the same. *We'll see.* Or in other words: *Don't hold your breath.*

Women go missing every day. Whatever had happened to Rachelle wasn't special. Even Erin hadn't been surprised. *I'm sure your friend will be back.* The casualness in the first RCMP officer's voice. Or she won't. Some women just mattered less. Were damaged, marked. *Practically the only woman up here.* Like I was.

Erin changed the subject. Something about the bamboo her neighbor had planted without realizing it was an invasive, the willowy reeds seeding themselves on the wrong side of the fence. *An invasive.* I nodded, half listening, lifting the cup of tea I'd forgotten about. Lapsang souchong. It smelled and tasted like fire. Dead needles in my hair, the acid rising. I bolted up, but I didn't make it, my knees hitting the grass, spraying the hydrangeas with the day's lunch.

I spent an hour in the bathroom with my arms around the can. *The sushi hadn't agreed with me*, I reasoned, muffling the other voice in my head. Erin brought a cold washcloth for my forehead and a glass of water with a bobbing lemon wedge.

"I guess curry's out," she said, sitting on the bed. I smiled. "You sure everything's okay?" She was smoothing my hair back the way she used to when I was little. When she was my everything, the one person I could trust completely. When she was my best friend.

She never felt adult in the same way that Mom did, Mom with her drawer full of lacy thongs and her miniskirts, lassoed in one man's arms or the next. Erin had always felt closer to my age, less a woman, more a girl—sexless and innocent. Untainted. Pure.

I nodded, shrugging off her hand. It was why I'd never told her about what had happened. Why I couldn't tell her that it had happened again.

Her kiss on my forehead felt forced, babyish. I wasn't a little girl anymore, and neither was she, with her blonde hair and her apron and her string of pearls knitted, like fingers, around her neck.

twenty-five

Michael stood by the counter the way Sam often would, draining a glass of orange juice with his briefcase in hand, Erin washing up at the sink beside him. They had a dinner that evening, just some colleagues from the department. Nothing exciting. I wouldn't mind if he stole his wife back, would I?

"Or, if you'd like, you could come with?" Erin turned her head. Michael's back was still toward her. She couldn't see how his smile collapsed.

"I'll be fine on my own," I said. "I should call Sam, check in on Nana. Really," I insisted. Erin nodded.

"If you're sure." As if either of us had any say in the matter.

As soon as the door shut, the clouds lifted. It was sunny and perfect, and we had the whole day together. Erin packed sandwiches, stopping at a fruit stand on our drive toward campus and loading up her backpack.

We weren't hiking, but the descent (or, more rightly, the eventual ascent) to get to Wreck Beach would be vigorous. *The crown jewel of the university's campus,* she'd described it before, a central figure in the stories of her undergrad years. The never-ending staircase that wound its way down through the cedars to what was, in her opinion, heaven.

In mine, too, I decided when we finally reached the bottom. No ice-cream truck, or public shower, or smell of dirty hot-dog water. Only mountain, lapping wave, downy white sand. It was like arriving on an island. There was even drumming, native sound.

The circle of people, mostly old, mostly men, banged on the drums they'd wedged between their legs, one lone woman's tits swinging as she jerked a tambourine around. I did a double take. Everyone in the circle was buck naked. I'd forgotten Erin's warning. The beach clothing

optional. Another old man strutted by wearing only a pair of hiking sandals and a fanny pack. I kept my eyes on the sand.

"So," Erin said as we spread our blanket down shore from the drum-
mers. "What do you think?" She unpacked the contents of her backpack,
passing me a foil-wrapped sandwich. Tuna fish. The smell so strong, I
couldn't even manage one polite bite.

"It's beautiful here." I revisited the carton of sour cherries we'd
dipped into during the drive. Fruit was the only thing I could seem to
stomach. "I see why you love it."

"You know, applications open soon. I could talk to my colleagues,
I'm sure you could audit a class. You could test it out, see if you like it.
You could stay with us, to start."

To start. I nodded. *Meaning my old life finished.* I thought of the soap
store, the Safeway, Sam's laundry pile. Would that really be such an
awful thing? But what would I even study? I slipped my ring from my
left hand to my right, testing it out.

I always thought I'd make a good teacher. I was patient, good with
kids—at least, Ray's loved me. *You just focus on having your own.* I could
already hear what Sam would say. The sour cherries had calmed it, but
it was always there—the nausea. I put the ring back on my left finger.

"Once you're settled, he could join you," I heard Erin say. She must
have realized how she sounded.

"Yeah." I smiled, setting down the carton. "Hey, do you want to go
in?" I didn't want to think about it. I took Erin's hand, and we charged
into the water, my first time in the ocean. Waves washing over me, the
salt that both stings and heals wounds.

Erin looked gorgeous as she floated down the staircase, her dress floor-
length and slinky, like a sophisticated version of junior prom. She stood
in her kitten heels, heating up a veggie patty in the microwave, insisting
on sitting with me while I picked at it. We were an odd pair, me in her
old UBC sweatshirt over my bikini top, her after a good two hours of
grooming.

"I feel just terrible leaving you here," she kept saying. "At the very
least you don't have to eat alone."

Would be no different than any other random Wednesday, I thought
but didn't say. Erin was a lot more sensitive than before, her eyes glassy,
the tears always close. I didn't want her mascara to smear.
Michael was upstairs in the shower. I'd been in the guest room when
he'd come home. I hadn't heard anything, but when I stepped into the
kitchen, the air was electric. An argument, or one primed, waiting for a
lit match.

I banged against the base of the ketchup bottle, and what had been
stuck came spurting out, splattering across my chest. Twice in one week.
Just my dumb luck.

"Be right back," I excused myself. It was Erin's sweatshirt, and I didn't
want the stain to set. I hurried into the bathroom, peeling it off and
working the soap into a lather. I rinsed it out, turned off the faucet.
Michael's booming voice echoed into the bathroom.

"So she hasn't brought it up yet?" I went rigid.

"I already told you, no."

"Have you?"

"I—no. There hasn't been a good time."

"You've had all day together, Erin. You've had nothing but time."

He hadn't raised his voice once, but his anger was palpable anyway.
His tone more like a drill sergeant's or an embittered employer's, Erin
his inferior, the way I'd heard Missy's dad speak to his sons.

"Something happened to her neighbor. She's preoccupied.
It's her father, Michael. She never knew him. Can you imagine how
that'd feel?"

My dad. My heart stopped. This was it, what I'd been waiting for. I
hadn't even had to bring it up. They both went quiet. Had they moved
into another room? I pulled a different sweatshirt over my head and took
a deep breath. It was now or never. I opened the door.

They were there in the kitchen; they'd just fallen silent. Michael
leaned up against the sink, Erin at the table with her face in her hands.
Her back was toward him.

"I'm sorry, I . . ." I opened my mouth, but it had gone completely dry.
"What about my dad?"

Michael scoffed, his prim little bow tie wobbling in time with his
big, pompous head.

"Told you," he said, his eyes on Erin. "You overestimate your sister." She didn't respond.

"Ten minutes," he threated. "Ten and I'm leaving." The heels on his dress shoes clacked as he turned into the hallway. "I'll be in my study, and then I'm getting in the car."

"Erin?" I asked. She'd lifted her head, but she still hadn't spoken. It was like she'd gone mute. "What's he talking about?" My voice was shaking. Somewhere, deep down, I already knew.

"Your dad," she began, wiping at the dark that was leaking from her eyes. "He, um. He passed away."

Everything stilled. I felt my mouth open, but it was like someone else was speaking, the words creaking out. "When?"

"About two weeks ago. I'm sorry, Jenny. I thought Fi told you. I—we thought you knew. We thought maybe that's what this trip was about."

"I already told you what this trip was about." I tugged at the sleeve of my sweatshirt, mopping up the tears. Just another dead Indian. Beyond help. Of course she'd known. And me, I was half of whomever he'd been. Is that why she'd never flown me out?

"What happened? An overdose?" Maybe he'd never really gone back to the States. Maybe he'd been down here—on Hastings Street all along.

"What?" She shook her head. "No. A car accident. I'm really sorry, Jenny. You shouldn't have had to find out like this." She reached out to take my hand, but I pulled away. I caught her sneaking a glance at the microwave's clock.

"Is it because he's Native?" The voice was loud now, furious. "Is that why no one ever talked about him? Why I was never allowed to meet him?" They'd taken everything from me—her and Mom. They didn't let me have a father, but worse than that. They'd axed my connection to who I really was: my people, my tribe. Mom I expected, but Erin? Erin, who said, *Indigenous*, not *Indian*. Erin was an ugly surprise.

"Did he live here? Would you see him?"

"See him? Jenny, this is the first I'd heard of him since he and Fi split. God, I don't know, twenty-two years ago?" She was looking straight at me now, her eyes earnest, wide. "He lived in the States. California, I think. At least, that's where he died."

"What tribe was he?"

"Tribe?" It was like she didn't recognize the word.

"Cree? Fort George?" They were the only two I knew. So much had been taken from me. Stolen.

"Jenny," Erin said, finally managing to place a hand on mine. "I don't know who told you what, but your dad is American. His family was Irish, like ours. His last name was Miller. Robert Miller."

My breath went thin. I'd been waiting my whole life to learn that name. Now it was here. Now it was too late.

"He . . ." Erin paused. "Had issues. He was abusive to your mom. From the beginning, but it only got worse. We tried to talk to her, but you know your mom. She's stubborn. Thought he might change.

"He went to prison when you were two, was extradited back to the States. Fi was in the hospital for a week. She was lucky she survived. Nana was supposed to babysit. She got there just in time."

When I was two. So it hadn't been a stairwell. It'd been him. The room went dark.

"They never legalized their divorce. That's why she got the call. Next of kin." Erin stood, opening a drawer and handing me a cloth napkin, too pretty to cover in snot. I used it anyway. Not only was I not Native but I was the daughter of a wifebeater. A murderer, had Nana been running behind. I felt Erin's hand on my back.

"They still talked during his sentence. He made a lot of promises. I don't know what happened exactly, but as soon as he was released, he left. Fi tried, I think for a couple years actually, but she couldn't find him. She didn't know where he was until, well, this.

"I'm sorry, Jenny." She bit at her lip. "We didn't want to hurt you. For you to think less of yourself because of him. He wasn't a very nice person. At least, not back then. Maybe he changed. I don't know. I don't know what's right."

"Erin." Michael was standing in the archway of the kitchen. He must have been listening, waiting for the right moment to chime in. Erin ignored him.

"I'm not leaving," she said, not to him but to me. She wrapped an arm around me. "I'm staying right here."

"No." I slipped out from under her. "It's better if you go." There was nothing left to say. Besides, her ten minutes were up.

Erin started to cry—sob, actually. Face ruined, her cheeks bruised with the ink of her mascara. I couldn't feel for her. I couldn't feel anything. A cord had been cut, what had bound my heart to the rest of me, organ untethered, emptied of everything.

"She's a grown woman, Erin." Michael lectured from the archway. "You'll have all day tomorrow."

Erin nodded, wiping her face with the heels of her hands.

As soon as they left, I was alone and joined by hordes, the thoughts swarming around the inside of my head. I ran the tap and flushed my face with cold water, trying to sift through.

In an instant, I was fatherless. Had been, for two weeks. I was livid. When exactly was Mom planning on telling me? She'd told Erin. Nana probably knew. Did they all think I would never find out?

The porch lights switched on, cued by the dark. I dried my face, met with my reflection. His eyes stared back at me. Brown as shit. *She was lucky she survived.*

Their "farmhouse" kitchen suddenly enraged me. The stupid tea towels embroidered with haystacks, the ceramic rooster preening atop a shelf. I'd never been so pissed off by gingham, and it was taking everything in me not to smash that smug little rooster to the floor. A country kitchen. Erin could've stayed in PG for that. I needed to get out of that house fast.

My feet carried me, though it wasn't clear where. I was too busy sopping up the tears. The truth was, I'd been fatherless nearly all my life. It wasn't the man I was mourning, but the decades of hope. Who he might've been. Who I might've been. I looked up and found myself at the shore.

The beach was deserted. The laughter and the smoke both faint, coming from behind the shuttered snack bar, out of view. All else was quiet. Even the seagulls had cleared out. I slipped off my shoes.

It wasn't a conscious decision. I was like a fish caught on a lure. After the first startling steps, the cold ceased to be cold. I dunked my head and paddled, useless against the pull.

"Hey!" I heard someone call out. I turned onto my back, letting the water carry me. There wasn't a star in the moonless sky. Erin's telescope must be gathering dust somewhere. I remembered the way her index finger used to trace the shapes in the shifting night sky. She'd moved to a place where she couldn't see them, their twinkle overtaken by other, brighter lights. The red flicker in the distance: a satellite, a plane. An approximation of a star.

"Hey!" The voice was louder. *Stars were just approximations anyway,* she'd once told me. *Light from hunks of plasma and gas, already dead.* My body kept sinking. I puffed my chest, flapping my arms. It was so much work, staying afloat.

"Hello?" There was one last weak attempt.

"It's probably nothing," I heard another voice say. They sounded young, teenagers, probably. Sharing a joint, they didn't want to get caught.

"Let's go," another said.

My head dipped below the water's surface, the frothy brine seeping into my mouth. My arms were getting tired. I kicked my legs. *Sink or swim,* the voice echoed out. Flung into chlorinated blue by a pair of burly arms. It must have been one of my first memories. Who'd said that? And who'd done the flinging? There had been gravel in that voice. Was it his?

Robert Miller. Bob. He sounded like any other dope at the bar.

Except he hadn't been. He'd almost killed her—his wife. The mother of his toddler. Maybe he'd wanted to. I'd fantasized about the very same thing in the thick of a shouting match. An anvil like in *Looney Tunes,* a piano from the sky: something, anything to shut her lousy mouth for good. I always felt like garbage afterward. Fucked-up, beyond repair. Here was an explanation. My father's daughter, the seed he'd planted. I was marked, all right.

All I had to do to escape it was nothing, but nothing took effort. I shot back up, gasping. The lungs want air. The body life. Never mind about the mind.

Stones. I needed something to tip the scales. I swam back to shore, shivering as I paced, my eyes glued to the sand. There were shells, a few pebbles, nothing any bigger than a loonie. *Figures.* I sat, staring off into the vastness. I laid back, fingers laced behind my wet head. I hit something hard. A plastic mold in the shape of an owl. A sand toy someone had left behind.

Snowy, horned, barn, striped. *Rachelle.* A light inside of me flicked back on. What about Destiny, Little Beth? Beth had never known her father. Now she'd barely remember her mom. It was a sign—it had to be.

I didn't have to be like him. I could be good. I could have purpose. I could save Rachelle.

There weren't any open spots nearby. I had to cruise around awhile. The street was just as crowded as it'd been during the day, or louder at least— or maybe just scarier, even less predictable, all those voices in the dark. I marched up the steps and swung open the building's cracked glass door.

The glare of the fluorescents was blinding and, at the same time, comforting somehow. There was a pay phone with a hunched man attached to its receiver, a steaming Styrofoam cup in his free hand. Two dark-haired women stood behind him waiting, glimpses of red everywhere. I felt dizzy, the tile cold against my bare feet. I'd forgotten I'd never found my Keds.

OFFICE, a sign read, the arrow pointing down a hallway. The room was windowless and cramped, with only one person at one of the two desks. In contrast, nearly every folding chair was occupied, some people talking, one woman attempting to smoke, others with their necks bending, eyes closed, dreaming while still upright.

I marched to the desk, and it all just came out, my foot off the pedal, as if it wasn't even there. Rachelle, the girls, Rhoda, Jim. I couldn't even focus on the person I was talking to, less a woman, more amorphous beige shape.

"Are you fucking kidding me?" Another shape sprung up from her chair. "Wait your turn, you cunt," the woman barked, snapping me from my daze.

"Sorry, I didn't know." I looked down and, for a moment, thought I'd pissed myself. My clothes were still pretty damp, and I realized then that I was dripping, a tiny puddle forming below me.

"Are you okay?" The woman at the desk started coming into focus. "If you need a shower or a change of clothes, I can try to check you in

somewhere for the night. You know the women's center? On Columbia?"
She leafed through a stack of papers.
"So the moniyaw gets priority?" The barking woman spat. "Good
to know."
"Oh, shut your trap," another voice chimed in. "Look at her, she's
soaking wet."
"There's coffee in the cafeteria." The woman at the desk handed me a
form. "Get this filled out and then come back here. We'll get you situated."
"You're confused," I said, handing the form back to her. "I'm not one
of them. I'm just trying to find my friend." The woman nodded.
"Fill this out and we'll get to you." She handed the form back. The
puddle and the bare feet didn't help. There was no use arguing. I tucked
it underneath an arm, turning to leave. She couldn't have known that I
had a steady job, a mortgage, a husband, a Buick.
"Hey, wait," I heard someone call out. A man in a netted Canfor hat
limped behind me. He was small, barely reaching my shoulders, and
scrawny, with a face as worn as a coffee filter post-pot.
"I think I seen your friend on the street. She's working for a Quebe-
cois. Always talking about them two little girls. Long hair?"
"Rachelle?" I couldn't believe it.
Maybe nothing was random. Finding out about my father had led
me to the beach, to the owl, to standing in front of this man. Even what
had happened at the concert—it had brought me there, to this moment.
The one where I found Rachelle.
"Working where?"
"On the block." My stomach dropped. *She party?*
"Can you take me to her?" The man went quiet, as if he didn't understand the question. "Do you know where she is? Rachelle?" He rubbed
at a bloodshot eye.
"Yeah, Raquel, that's it. She likes licorice, right?" I just stood there,
quiet. She might've. "Horseback rider. Feeds the stray cats. Always singing Willie Nelson." My stomach was twisting. "Came from a big family
with all them girls?" I could only confirm the one sister.
"Michelle, yeah, yeah, that was it. From the prairies." The man
scratched at a cheek. "Big girl, real sweetheart. Johnny Abenaki said he
knew her. Your friend. Maquel."

The man was on something, I realized, *or at least had been on something for so long that the altered state had become the norm.* Most people there were like that. Deluded, talking nonsense. And there I was, fitting right in.

Searching for a person who probably didn't even exist anymore. A person who, I was realizing, I didn't know the first thing about. *You don't know what you don't know until you know.* That woman hadn't been wrong in handing me that form. I thanked the man, opening the door.

"Hey," he said, his smile broad. "Hope they give you your shoes back, honey!" His voice drifted up and dissolved into the cool night air, into nothing, like everything else.

twenty-six

I didn't know where else to go. I figured it was as good a place as any. *Better than pulling off on the shoulder*, I remember thinking, jerking my seat back. At least I knew the neighborhood was safe.

I'd wake with the sun, would start driving first thing. Sam wouldn't be home for another week. I'd have plenty of time to straighten up. Get the groceries—steak, like he liked. It all seemed so silly then. The woman on the postcard, the owl. *Signs.* I shook my head. The only ones of any importance were on 1, 97, 16, 99. I thought of the bumper sticker, the Ford Explorer I'd followed from Surrey to Coquitlam: *LIFE SUCKS AND THEN YOU DIE.* I didn't have a blanket, but I did have one of those foil accordions Nana had given me to keep my leather seats from broiling. I laid it over my knees and drifted off.

In the end, it wasn't the sun that woke me. It was sirens, a *tap-tap-tap* at my window. A man's face pressed in close, his mouth moving without sound. I rubbed my eyes, cranking my window down.

Erin stood behind the man, the beading on her dress tinted scarlet. She'd come home early from her dinner, had called the RCMP as soon as she'd realized I wasn't there. They were able to find my plates in the system, had issued a special alert. A squad had been sent to search the surroundings. It was Michael's suggestion that had led them to the beach and the mostly empty parking lot there.

"I thought maybe she'd met some students. They tend to congregate here at night." He was gesturing to the officer. "My wife, you can imagine her alarm. What with what's happened to that young lady, Beth."

"You gave your aunt and uncle a real scare," the officer was saying. "A young woman like yourself, you shouldn't be out here alone at night.

Next time you're locked out, come to the station. We'll make sure you get home safe and sound."

Erin was at the bathroom door again for the fifth time since I'd turned on the shower.

"Everything okay?" she asked. I hadn't even started to shampoo my hair.

"Everything's fine," I called back, singsong.

She was scared. They both were. "We thought something terrible had happened," she'd told me on the drive back. "You can't imagine the things that run through your head." She'd insisted on driving me back in my Buick. I'd checked the clock—it was just past two A.M. Even if they'd gotten home at nine, I couldn't have been gone for more than four hours before they'd sounded the alarm. The cavalry arriving at lightning speed: about seven, maybe eight squealing cars.

"Your mom's been calling," Erin said, setting a glass on the nightstand. Warm milk with honey, what even Mom would make me, a cure from Nana for any sleepless night.

"She didn't even know you were down here." She looked at me, her eyes searching. I looked down.

"I get that you're mad at her." Erin still hadn't changed out of her dress, but her updo was undone, her hair shooting out from her head. "I probably would be, too. Fi's a lot of things, but she does love you. She wanted to protect you, Jenny. We all did."

The phone rang. She'd brought the receiver upstairs, slim hunk of plastic bleating between the folds of the comforter. I didn't move.

"It doesn't have to be a whole conversation. She just wants to know you're okay."

It rang again. Erin's eyes were going from shining to wet. I'd have to talk to Mom eventually. *Might as well just get it over with*, I reasoned, picking up. Erin left me to it.

"Hello? Jenny?" It didn't sound like her, the voice on the other line small and panicked.

"Hi, Mom," I said.

"Jesus H. Christ, Jenny, what the fuck was you thinking?" She'd regained her footing. "Taking off like that."

She was waiting for an answer, but I stayed quiet. I didn't need to duke it out. I wasn't under her roof or even in our hometown. If I felt like it, all I had to do was slam the receiver down.

"I was worried sick, ringing Erin's phone off the goddamn hook. I talked to her while you were showering. She said you got locked out of the house. I didn't even know you went down there." She paused, testing something. "Miss Big City Girl didn't think to give you a key?" She snorted. I stayed silent.

"She was saying you might apply for the school down there." Her voice had changed, drained of the sarcasm. "You know, it ain't such a bad idea. You and Sam don't have any kids yet. Nothing's keeping you here.

"Besides, I'll come down and visit. Escape the snow. Anywhere's better than here, you know that. Ain't shit to do." I heard the flick of her lighter, her words muffled, cigarette clenched in mouth. "I mean, look at me. My best years down the shitter. You still got time.

"I always said you were too smart for this town. Way smarter than your old mom ever was." She sighed.

She'd never said any of that—not to me, at least. It was as heartfelt as I'd ever heard her. I didn't know how to respond.

It'd always been there, buried underfoot. Now the path was in plain sight. A fresh start in a beautiful room, in a beautiful house, steps away from the shore. I could swim every morning if I wanted. Every evening, too. Hang my degrees in my own beautiful house. Find someone new. Start a family, a baby at my hip as I bobbed between the western reds. A baby. I gnawed on my thumbnail, abyss in my stomach dilating.

Jim would become nothing more than a distant bad dream. And Missy and Anne-Marie. And Sam. Sacrifice was a given. You had to hack down the pine to keep the rain from coming in. Burn it to ash to keep warm. Rip potato from the earth, slit hen's throat, eviscerate the sow. Some blood was always spilled to keep yours pumping. That's life.

My eyes were wet. But that wasn't like any of those things. I couldn't even say the word. Not even to myself.

"I love you, Jenny," Mom was saying. "I just want what's best for you. You know that."

No matter who you were, you couldn't escape it. The weight of being a mother, the constant sense of fear, alarm. That weight was multiplied, depending. If your child was born with a clubbed foot, some rare, incurable disease. A girl.

"You, too." I wiped the tears from my eyes. I didn't even know for sure. We'd been trying for years.

"If you need cash or something . . ." She trailed off. "Just give us a shout."

"I will," I said. I went quiet. So did she. She hadn't brought him up, and neither had I. Whatever mistakes Mom had made, even then I could see that protecting me from my dad hadn't been one of them.

There was a picture that I hadn't noticed before on the bureau. Mom and Erin, adolescent, arms tangled around each other, the kind of light where it's impossible to tell whether the day's beginning or ending. Mom couldn't have been much older than twelve, but there was that expression already. Smile masked onto her face, Erin beaming, pure innocence, all the more jarring comparatively. *Your mom's had it rough*, what Erin once told me, Mom's pigtails almost a playact. It came to me, the way she'd looked at me at the concert. Her horror more like recognition.

Womanhood isn't always something you grow into. Sometimes it's something that happens *to* you instead.

We stayed on the line a little longer, until one of us, I can't remember who, placed the phone back in its cradle.

Epilogue 2011

I was seven weeks already when that fateful second line appeared. While I was driving north, shepherding, unbeknown to me, a miracle the approximate size of a sweet pea, on her way to an ash berry, a radish, a waterlogged zucchini, the wildfires raged to the south, and the bodies—those twenty vanished women Erin had mentioned, tally snowballing that spring every time you switched on the news—were still buried, were still waiting to be discovered, at Pickton's farm, to the west.

Sam never ended up working for Jim. He got another offer; Jim was better off finding someone else. It stunk like horseshit, his excuse, but Jim took it in stride. It wasn't like him. He didn't let things, or people, go so easily.

Sam must have had something good on him, Missy had said one icy-dark morning at Denny's, twisting over her plate of waffles to wipe jam from Brielle's pout. Annie had gone to the washroom, the twins at her mother's for a rare semi-day off, and Missy stood, waddling over to the play section to peel Kayden off Tanner, velour sweatshirt riding up her waxing moon of a belly, my hands resting on my own. I was just starting to feel the first kicks.

Missy slid back into the booth, dumping a pack of Splenda into her decaf. "Or someone who did must've cut in."

Jesse was the one who tipped Sam off on the opening. It wasn't ideal, but Vanderhoof was a lot closer than Tumbler Ridge. He was home in time for dinner. We managed.

The years moved at double time after Faith was born. Those first few months, the fact that I'd ever had hours to burn was a marvel.

Faith turned two, and Mom and Ray imploded. He got back together with his ex and, six months later, became a dad again. "Says there was no overlap," Mom had scoffed. "Like I can't do the math."

Mom was single for about a week. She bumped into him at a 7-Eleven, Mike Owens, the front man of the blues band. When Faith turned three, she scattered rose petals at their wedding. He wasn't perfect, but he was nothing like his stage persona—surprisingly timid, a grandfather himself, in the program for the past twenty-five years. Ray didn't drum for them anymore.

When Faith turned five, Missy filed for bankruptcy and, shortly after, divorce. I'd managed to avoid him, even the mention of him, always meeting out, at Timmy's, my place, or Anne-Marie's new home. Farther east along the highway, at the start of ranching country, a fixer-upper, but with ample advantages. Not too far from town but still far enough—air fresh, free from the dank, surrounding hills specked with flowers in springtime and, in the summer, cow-studded. There were apple trees in the front and a creek in the back. Plenty of space for the boys to muck around.

Missy had to move back in with her folks and choke down a whopping slice of humble pie. She found Jesus and, shortly after, Joe, an electrical engineer with an honest paycheck and a full head of hair. They eloped the year Faith turned seven.

Around Faith's first birthday, the neighbors moved in, and the rusting truck was towed away. The washer, the lawn chairs, the broken baby swing—all hurled into a dumpster by a pair of shirtless, sunburnt men until there was zero trace of her left. The yard staked in June with cautionary orange. Sprayed by professionals. No dandelion yellow or nettle green. No giddy pink, what had always poked past the fence. I never did find that jar of salve I'd bought for Erin. Sometimes that whole summer felt like invention.

Faith celebrated her ninth birthday three months ago, in March. I'm hanging the washing on the line when she comes bounding toward me. She's been playing across the yard with Wayne and Faye's boys, trapping ladybugs in a jar. I finish the pinning, set the pork out to defrost, go out into the garden, and give water to the new starts. Sam comes home around six, and we all eat together, him at his end of the table and me at mine, with Faith sandwiched in between. Spaghetti and meatballs. Our family's favorite. *Ours.* I read Faith a story and tuck her into bed, kissing her forehead before flicking off the lights.

I click on the news.

It's her again. Juliette Rogers, yellow hair peeking out from a camouflage baseball hat. *If anyone has any information.* Nineteen years old, a local girl from Fort St. James. Vanished along the highway—nearly ten years to the day. There's a billboard for Juliette a few clicks after Beth's. Every time I drive past her tattered face, I wonder why they didn't just replace it. Or if they'll ever take it down. Sometimes you'll still catch sight of one of them, those bumper stickers whose letters have faded: *FIND BETH.*

I finish the last of the dishes, pitch the sandals Faith has left by the door into the pile. Cap Magic Markers, nestle crayons into their box, follow the trail of Barbie's scattered accessories and toss them into Faith's toy chest, giving Sam a peck as I pass his recliner. I slip out of my jeans and into my nightshirt, dabbing cream around my eyes and catching them in my reflection. Cinnamon, milky coffee, maple syrup, toffee: the same brown as my daughter's. I run a brush through my scant hair. There were pains postpartum but gifts, too. Pregnancy healed my eczema, the skin around my neck mended, itch-free.

I write myself a Post-It and stick it onto the mirror. *ORANGE SLICES.* I'm on snack duty for soccer practice.

I curl into bed, one last task before rest. What I've done every night since I first saw that blue cross. What I imagine every mother does—no matter how dubious of who, if anyone, is listening.

I pray. I always pray for Faith first. To protect her from the evils of the world, to keep her happy, healthy, *safe.* That her name is never known—not like that. That her face never finds itself smiling from any billboard.

I pray for Sam next, then Mom, then Erin. Nana, who passed on when Faith was seven. Missy and her three girls. Anne-Marie and her boys. With boys, I notice, the prayers take on a different shape. The neighbor boys wield eyeglasses over an anthill while Faith plucks grass for a jar. With boys, you worry more about them ending up in a cell, not a duffel bag. A dusty white cross, pinprick on the highway. Or worse, no ending at all: not bow or even knot. Just dangling threads.

Sometimes at the Esso, a curtain of long black hair. I used to reach out, heart thumping. But that was years ago. That morning, a Fleetwood stopped in front of me at the light. I didn't notice any bumper sticker, was distracted by the family (mom, dad, boy, dog, baby) decaled on the back. My pulse didn't quicken; my breath remained steady. Faith asked me to put on *Bella Donna*. I didn't even think about it. My neighbor, her story. Until the car was gone.

Rachelle, I whisper, her name gummy, still hot, even a decade later. Her daughters teenagers now, I realize. Strangers, if I were to see them. And maybe I have. The possibility its own type of salve. Last summer, or the one before, at the fair, the two sisters in line for the swing ride. Smiling, arms entangled, hair streaming like wings as their feet lifted from the ground. The ends of a silken scarf flapping behind them, red ribboned through the air. I rarely think of her sister or the Man with the Braid. Motherhood comes with its own buffers. I linger there, in kaleidoscope shadow of the carousel. Shielded, against the true dark.

I pray for Juliette, conjuring her smile. I even pray for Beth sometimes. *The other girls*, the thought slips in, *all those names on the signs*. The women who were, and then suddenly weren't. The women those girls never had the chance to be. I grope my way back toward the light.

The image burnished, a worry stone, all those lost reanimated, swaying along the shoulders of the highway. Lupin, prairie smoke, pink flame of the fireweed.

Those poor women. I sigh. *Those poor girls.*

Father. I tap my forehead, my chest, eastern shoulder, then west. *I pray that you're listening.*

I can feel my heart beating as my eyes shut.

Author's Note

On June 21, 2002 Nicole Hoar, a white middle-class woman, went missing on Highway 16 right outside Prince George, British Columbia. She wasn't the first woman to disappear along the route but she was the first to receive national attention, the search for her urgent, a Canadian effort.

Monica Ignas, Alberta Williams, cousins Cecilia and Delphine Nikal, Ramona Wilson, Roxanne Thiara, Alisha Germaine, Lana Derrick. The disappearances, according to reports, date back to 1969.

Margaret Nooski, Mary George, Tamara Chipman, Aielah Saric-Auger, Beverly Warbrick, Bonnie Joseph, Emmalee Mclean, Madison Scott, Jane Doe, Anita Thorne, Roberta Sims, Frances Brown, Chantelle Simpson, Jessica Patrick, Cynthia Martin, Laureen Fabian, Crystal Chambers, Chelsey Quaw.

Eighteen women, twenty-seven women, more than forty women. The numbers jump depending on the source. The majority of Highway 16's—or what locals call the Highway of Tears—victims were Indigenous, a minority of them not yet women but girls.

I first heard of the Highway while studying herbalism in Vancouver, BC, and although I can't remember the exact context of this encounter, I can still feel the emotions it whipped up. Those emotions intensified upon uncovering each disturbing detail.

I was indignant when I learned of the failings of the Royal Canadian Mounted Police. Aghast at the prejudice baked into the communities in the North. Another feeling surfacing: my own virtue affirmed. How could *they* let this happen?

The injustice of it all was *heart-wrenching*.

It's this response that *Fireweed* aims to explore. I found myself drawn to the Highway like a fish to a lure, a sense of urgency thrumming through me, the adrenaline the consumption of true crime can inject. But my response to the Highway wasn't as simple as this, a voyeur's thrill at someone else's gruesome end; the more I dug, the more I was faced with the misshapen truth of my interest in the Highway, the double-edged nature of my concern.

What is it I'm hoping to find when I seek out stories based on lived violence and oppression? If my interest stems from a concern for others, a desire to "do good," in what ways is this concern clouded by self-preoccupation, a desire to prove my own blamelessness?

In 2016, after fifteen years' worth of efforts by the Native Women's Association of Canada, the government launched its National Inquiry into Missing and Murdered Indigenous Women and Girls, its mission to reveal the root cause behind the staggering rates of violence.

Through the testimonies of families and survivors, a portrait of colonialism as not a historic term but a persistent lived experience was portrayed, its violence enforced by the following four pathways: historical, multigenerational, and intergenerational trauma. Social and economic marginalization. Maintaining the status quo and institutional lack of will. Ignoring the agency and expertise of Indigenous women and girls.

It is this bleak reality that I chose to illustrate in *Fireweed*. By narrating the story in a voice like Jenny's, I sought to lift a mirror to both our fascination with missing women and girls and the ways in which we can (often unwittingly) use the injustices faced by marginalized communities to confirm our own goodness; how by ignoring the agency of these communities, we end up centering ourselves. Jam, marinara sauce, ketchup, blood droplets: throughout the narrative, Jenny's hands are stained red. By narrating the story in a voice like hers I sought to reveal how our failings can be yoked to our good intentions.

When I started writing the novel I hadn't yet visited the city where it's set, but as a Detroiter, Prince George felt familiar. Home, at a time, to the most pulp and paper mills in the world and located in the northern reaches of BC, PG is a contradiction of wilderness and industry, a place versed in dualities. Each time I went up there, the "truth" bifurcated. I was asked to hold how one can be both the perpetrator of violence and the victim of it, afforded privileges based on the color of one's skin and marginalized based on one's gender and class. How there is nothing more useless than "thoughts and prayers" and also—somehow—nothing more powerful. On my first visit to PG I met Nicole Fox, who would come to serve as my unofficial guide to the place. Randy Dakota, Angelique Merasty, Shirley Babcock, Norman Retasket: *Fireweed*, in many ways, was born out of the relationships I formed there. In this I include my relationship with the plants—particularly fireweed. Shooting up along the roadsides, in the charred remains of forests razed by wildfires, fireweed is what we call a *vulnerary* in herbalism. A wound healer. *Fireweed* is a novel that exposes our wounds, but it's also intended to function as a salve: self-awareness as the first step toward effective action. Loosening the strings of the mask of concern we all might find ourselves wearing.

Acknowledgments

Fireweed wouldn't exist without the generosity of spirit of the people I met in PG. Thank you to Nicole Fox, my unofficial guide to the city, Terry Fox, Angelique Merasty, Shirley Babcock, Randy Dakota, Norman Retasket, and the waitresses at Grama's Kitchen, among others. Thanks again to Nicole and to Terry Fox for being early readers. PG forever. Thanks to my parents, Janet and Daniel Haddad, for your unwavering love and support. Thank you to Special Agent Zoe Howard, who understood the vision from day one. Thanks to Rola Harb, whose insights were invaluable. Thanks to Emily Bell, Rachael Small, Tiffany Gonzalez, and the whole team at Astra House for the tender care. Thanks to Frankie DiGiovanni for the cover of my dreams.

Special thanks to Sara Davis, without whom this novel would've stayed in a drawer. Thanks to Sandra Bialystock, Leigh N. Gallagher, and Diane Cook. Thank you to the NAIRS Foundation and to Sibylle Carloni and Gian-Andri Töndury. Thank you to my sister Katarzyna Stodulkiewicz, who drove nine hours north with me during my first round of research and always brings a sense of possibility and adventure.

Thank you to Lucas Olivet, for all of our collective dreaming and our collective hearts, Rosalind and Lisette.

Photo by Lucas Olivet

About the Author

Lauren Haddad is a writer, herbalist, and mother. Born in metro Detroit, she currently lives in a small village in Switzerland with her family. Her writing on Prince George has appeared in *Medicine Tree*, and her first novel, *Fireweed*, was born out of years of relationship to that place, owing itself to the people there.